The Radical Novel Reconsidered

A series of paperback reissues of mid-twentieth-century U.S. left-wing fiction, with new biographical and critical introductions by contemporary scholars.

Series Editor
Alan Wald, University of Michigan

Books in the Series

To Make My Bread
Grace Lumpkin

Moscow Yankee
Myra Page

The People from Heaven
John Sanford

Salome of the Tenements
Anzia Yezierska

To Make My Bread

To Make My Bread

Grace Lumpkin

Introduction by Suzanne Sowinska

University of Illinois Press
Urbana and Chicago

Frontispiece appears courtesy of the South Caroliniana Library.

Manufactured in the United States of America
P 5 4 3 2 1

This book is printed on acid-free paper.

Digitally reprinted from the fourth paperback printing

UNIVERSITY OF ILLINOIS PRESS
1325 SOUTH OAK STREET
CHAMPAIGN, ILLINOIS 61820-6903
WWW.PRESS.UILLINOIS.EDU

Library of Congress Cataloging-in-Publication Data

Lumpkin, Grace, 1892?–1980.
To make my bread / Grace Lumpkin ; introduction by Suzanne Sowinska.
p. cm. — (The radical novel reconsidered)
Includes bibliographical references.
ISBN 0-252-06501-8 (alk. paper)
1. Textile Workers' Strike, Gastonia, N.C., 1929—Fiction. I. Title. II. Series.
PS3523.U54T6 1995
813'.52—dc20 95-3561
CIP

INTRODUCTION

Suzanne Sowinska

Where do prize-winning novelist Grace Lumpkin and her acclaimed novel *To Make My Bread* (1932) fit in the annals of literary history? If one were to look in the *Columbia Literary History of the United States* (1988), the *Dictionary of Literary Biography* (1978–88), or any of a number of the standard reference texts that trace the history of American literature, one would find no mention of Lumpkin, a writer whose work one 1935 reviewer for the *New York Daily Mirror* opined "should rate high on the Pulitzer Prize list of selections."[1] Hers was the fate of many radical writers of the 1930s who, in response to the economic and social crisis brought about by the Great Depression and by cataclysmic changes in world politics, embraced social realism as the literary form they felt would best portray the problems America faced and provide new forms of artistic intervention. Their contributions to American literature have been largely lost to history, an ironic situation for many radicals and writers, like Lumpkin, who felt so adamantly in the 1930s that history was on their side. As it happened, the decade of the 1930s faded into the 1940s and eventually (tragically, for depression era social realist writers) the 1950s. Narratives of radical social change were eclipsed in our cultural memory by narratives of the dangers of radicals. Little wonder that as McCarthyite witchunts, fueled by the perceived threat of Communist infiltrators at the highest levels of government and other cold war agendas, took hold of the collective American consciousness, radical writers from the 1930s began to avalanche down the slippery slope of literary acceptance. Except for brief bursts of appreciation for their work, they remain forgotten, waiting to be recovered.

Yet there is more to Grace Lumpkin's story than just right-wing erasure. Many members of the literary left would also like to see her work remain buried. Perhaps no woman novelist fits better into a discussion of the certainties and contradictions for writers who came of age as radicals in the 1930s and lived through what Lillian Hellman so appropriately described as the "scoundrel time" of the 1950s. Lumpkin's life and writing was dramatically influenced by cultural radicalism, with its links to U.S. Communism in the 1930s, and the ferreting out of Communists and Communist sympathizers in the 1950s. She was both a revolutionary and a scoundrel. Lumpkin was actively, adamantly, passionately, and politically Communist during the 1920s and 1930s, yet in 1953, before a Senate subcommittee convened by Senator Joseph McCarthy, she carefully spelled out her former associates' names, letter by letter, for an insistent Roy Cohn, definitively proclaiming that "this country needs to have [Communism] cleaned out, here and abroad."[2] How could the writer of *To Make My Bread*—which Robert Cantwell, a reviewer for *The Nation,* described with such certainty as "effective propaganda"[3]—have become so aggressively reactionary twenty years later? What caused the winner of the 1932 Maxim Gorky Award for the best labor novel to give up radicalism and turn instead to religion? The resolution of these contradictions lies partly in Lumpkin's southern agrarian and Christian roots and partly in her experiences of radicalism in the 1930s, especially in relation to the personal, political, and literary associations and alliances she made around the time she was working on her first novel.

Revolutionary, Scoundrel, or Witness?

Grace Lumpkin was born close to the turn of the century, probably in 1892, in Milledgeville, Georgia. She was the ninth of eleven children born to Annette Caroline Morris and William Wallace Lumpkin. Hers was a prominent but economically unstable aristocratic Georgian family.[4] Hoping to rebuild the family fortune lost during Reconstruction, her father moved the family to Columbia, South Carolina, around 1900, where they suffered briefly from the pains of relocation. The Lumpkin family name, much respected in Georgia, where there was both a town and a county named for them, was not as quickly recognized by those in their new surroundings. However, as Grace's sister Katherine Du Pre Lumpkin, later a respected sociologist, reformer, and educator, described in her autobiography *The Making of a Southerner* (1947), three essential southern institutions helped the family adjust: genealogy, ties to the Confederacy, and religion.

The Lumpkins were from what their new South Carolinian neighbors considered to be "good family." William was also a Civil War veteran who, along with many southern men of his generation, was devoted to the memory of the Confederacy. He encouraged his children to participate in Confederate reunions and other celebrations that revolved around the romantic yet failed majesty of the Lost Cause. The image of a young girl's fiery rendition of Confederate poetry in front of Grandpap Kirkland and an appreciative crowd of Confederate veterans that opens chapter 28 of *To Make My Bread* is drawn from one of Grace's childhood memories: on "Memorial Day, dressed in white with a red ribbon sash about my middle, I would stand beside the iron fence that surrounds the grave of General Wade Hampton in Trinity Churchyard and with Daughters of the Confederacy and others looking on, recite 'Furl That Banner,' written by Father Ryan, poet-priest of the Confederacy."[5] The fact that the Lumpkins were Episcopalian and had immediately established a connection with the socially elite Trinity Church also helped them gain social acceptance after leaving their native Georgia. Trinity Church would later become the setting for Grace's novel *The Wedding* (1939) and would play an important role in her last novel, *Full Circle* (1962). And it was to these Episcopalian roots that she eventually retreated when she decided to break with Communism and "return to God."

Around 1910, William moved the family one final time, to a farm in Richland County, South Carolina. There, Grace and Katherine had their first close associations with black and white sharecroppers. Fieldwork on the Lumpkin family farm was performed by black laborers, and the Lumpkin children attended school with white children from the "poorest classes." Katherine describes the family sojourn in Richland County: "for the first time in my experience I had been set down to live day after day in close companionship with deep poverty suffered by whites, a poverty to which I had not hitherto been imperceptibly hardened."[6] Just three months after the family began to farm, however, William died. Their financial health suffered and for a while the Lumpkins attempted to make a living off the farm. Katherine tried to help by picking cotton herself. So that she could also help support the family, Grace borrowed money from an older brother and crammed into one year a two-year teacher's training program at Brenau College in Gainesville, Georgia.[7]

In the next few years, Grace worked at a variety of jobs that provided her with background material for her novels and helped shape her early political consciousness. She taught school near the place where she lived in the country, organized an adult night school for farmers and their wives, and had a position with the government as a home demonstration agent. During most summers she lived out in the mountains of North Carolina and at different times stayed with people who worked in the cotton mills. She spent a year in France, where she worked as a recreation director for French Girls in Industry (an organization for French working girls) and as a YWCA director. She also worked as an industrial secretary for the YWCA in South Carolina for two years but became "convinced" that "the workers could only better their lives by means of unions."[8] Through her YWCA work, Grace was exposed to the interracial commissions and summer conferences sponsored by the YWCA and YMCA. These organizations offered some of the most progressive views about race relations then available to a southern woman of her class, race, and generation.

Grace had been publishing stories in college and other school magazines since 1908, but it was not until her mother's death in 1925 that she decided to take seriously her career as a writer. Her mother's reading of *Pilgrim's Progress, Nicholas Nickleby,* and other books to her as a child first made Grace want to write: "she used to say writers were the greatest people in the world, and would tell me with awe in her voice about the many books in the Congressional Library in Washington."[9] Katherine remembered Grace as not fully able to concentrate her energies in any one direction until she began to write: "writing and New York City consciously became her goal. Any Southern woman interested in becoming a writer went to New York."[10] Using YWCA connections, Grace landed a job in the fall of 1925 as a member of the office staff at *The World Tomorrow,* a monthly Quaker publication aimed at promoting peace, conscientious objection to war, and "social order based on the principles of Jesus."[11] She moved into a boardinghouse near Columbia University and enrolled in some creative writing and journalism courses offered in the evening.

The office of *The World Tomorrow* was a base for a great deal of pacifist and mildly socialist radicalism. It was run according to interracial and progressive principles and had a staff of African-American, Jewish, and other immigrant and ethnic workers. The publishers, editors, office staff, and contributors attended demonstrations, joined picket lines, spoke at conferences and meetings, and generally supported pacifist, socialist, and radical causes.[12] Contributors to *The World Tomorrow* included social reformers, suffrage leaders, black intellectuals, labor activists, and a range of other progressives. In the year and a half that Lumpkin was employed by *The World Tomorrow,* articles appeared by Jane Adams, Carrie Chapman Cott, Babette Deutsch, Alain Locke, A. J. Muste, Reinhold Niebuhr, William Pickens, Upton Sinclair, Olive Schreiner, Vida Scudder, and Wallace Thurman. The staff of *The World Tomorrow* was especially concerned with what was widely referred to among white radicals on the Left during this period as the "Negro Question."[13] Three separate special issues on race—"Some Aspects of Race Betterment," "The White Peril," and "Social Equality—The Crux of Negro-White Relations"—were released during Lumpkin's tenure. Her first published article, "The Artist in a Hostile Environment," appeared in one of these issues. The essay, coauthored with Esther Shemitz, then advertising manager for the magazine, calls for the black artist "to replace for us with interesting human beings the current minstrel, mammy and uncle types" and describes the "tortured person" embodied in every black artist who tries to use their art to represent experiences of racism for reserved and unappreciative white audiences.[14] The biographical sketch of Lumpkin prepared for *The World Tomorrow* describes her as "a student of interracial problems both in the North and the South."[15]

In Esther Shemitz, Lumpkin found a kindred spirit, soul mate, companion, fellow artist, and political ally. They were about the same age and shared an enthusiasm to become active participants in what they saw as a rapidly transforming American society. While Lumpkin studied writing and journalism, Shemitz studied at the Art Students League and the Leonardo da Vinci Art School, where students paid very little money for instruction with some of the finest Italian sculptors and painters in New York City. In an unpublished short story based, like much of her later fiction, on a mixture of thinly veiled autobiography and carefully constructed anti-Communist polemic, Lumpkin described their relationship to politics and culture: "with the encouragement of our leaders, we had taken part in demonstrations for peace and in strikes, though ART with capitals still came first. We spent money on books, attended all the shows on 57th Street and as many concerts at Carnegie Hall as we could afford."[16] In 1926, Shemitz and Lumpkin moved into a small house on East 11th Street.[17] They also began to move farther to the left. They had been sent by *The World Tomorrow* to cover the long, momentous, and recurrently violent textile strike in Passaic, New Jersey, the first mass walkout in the United States to be led by the Communist party (CP). Shemitz later remembered being "beaten up during an ensuing riot."[18] Having experienced firsthand the revolutionary fervor of the Passaic workers and their leaders, the women returned to New York with a new dedication to the principles and goals of the Communist party, its commitment to the worker, its promise for the artist, and its vision of the future.

As their engagement with and dedication to the CP increased, the women grew impatient with the mild-mannered pacifism of their Quaker employers. Lumpkin later explained: "to us religion [became] an outmoded custom that the higher civilization which Communism would bring in would finally eliminate."[19] Shemitz quit the magazine, got a job working with the Soviet government–affiliated Amtorg Trading Company, and joined a branch of the Communist-affiliated John Reed Club, an organization for writers. A few months later Lumpkin followed Shemitz to Amtorg, where she worked on and off for the next five years. She also joined the John Reed Club; her first published sketch, "White Man—A Story," appeared in the proletarian monthly *The New Masses.* Although Lumpkin never officially joined the CP, she became a dedicated fellow traveler. In 1927 she was arrested with other Communists at a picket sponsored by the Sacco and Vanzetti Defense Committee; in 1928 she joined the staff of *The New Masses;* in 1929 she was sent south by the CP to organize among black sharecroppers and to observe and participate in the Communist-led Gastonia textile strikes.[20] This trip provided Lumpkin with much of the material for her first novel. In writing about Gastonia, she saw a way to connect her nascent awareness of a radical political agenda and her prerogative to create art that would serve the proletariat with the landscape of her youth.

Back in New York in the house on 11th Street, Lumpkin began to write *To Make My Bread.* The house became an informal gathering place for a small group of Communists: "they made our house a meeting place where we talked, played records of Bach, Brahams, Beethoven, . . . and planned the perfect world we were going to make."[21] Among those who dropped in were Michael Intrator and Whittaker Chambers, two younger men Lumpkin and Shemitz met first at the Passaic strike and later in the bookshop at the New York City headquarters of the CP. Intrator was a fur worker who had grown up on the Lower East Side and had gained some prominence in the Communist-backed unions of the needle trades. Chambers had joined the CP in 1925 and was slowly working his way onto the staff of the *Daily Worker,* the official newspaper of the Communist Party of the United States of America (CPUSA). Intrator and Chambers eventually became coeditors of *The Textile Worker,* a newspaper aimed at the burgeoning CP-sponsored trade union movement and widely circulated among the Gastonia and Marion textile workers. Other soon-to-be prominent Communists who visited the house on 11th Street were Grace Hutchins and Anna Rochester, a wealthy, older, lesbian couple who were both writers on labor, women, and children's issues and were patrons of proletarian art. Hutchins and Rochester were editors at *The World Tomorrow* while Lumpkin and Shemitz were employed there. They had also moved away from Quakerism toward the CP.[22] Lumpkin quit her job at Amtorg and, "thinking it would give me more time for writing, became a chambermaid," but with "50 beds to make and rooms and bathrooms to clean," she found herself too exhausted to write.[23] She borrowed money from Hutchins and Rochester so she could work on her novel,[24] but when she ran out of money again, she returned briefly to office work. By the spring of 1931, half of *To Make My Bread* was completed. Shemitz convinced Lumpkin to take what she had finished to Macauley. Four days later Lumpkin signed a contract that included an advance so that she was able to drop her office work and finish the novel. *To Make My Bread* was completed within a year and was released in the fall of 1932.

To radicals, 1932 was a watershed year. The Depression had reached its pinnacle; millions were unemployed and standing in breadlines. National hunger marches held in December 1931 and again in 1932 brought thousands of unemployed citizens to Washington to petition Congress for help. Local unemployment councils in almost every state organized hunger and jobless marches. A Bonus Army of World War I veterans demanding payment of long-promised government compensation for military service was forcefully ejected from Washington by federal troops. The year 1932 was also when F.D.R. first used the term "New Deal" to cement his successful bid for the presidency. Long-cherished institutions and authorities appeared to be crumbling and the moment seemed ripe for radical social change. The 1931 publications of *The Good Earth,* by Pearl S. Buck, *Living My Life,* by Emma Goldman, and *Autobiography,* by Lincoln Steffens were joined on radical reading lists in 1932 by *Nineteen Nineteen,* by John Dos Passos, *Tobacco Road,* by Erskine Caldwell, *Young Lonigan,* by James T. Farrell, *The Thin Man,* by Dashiel Hammet, and *Brave New World,* by the British writer Aldous Huxley. In addition to Lumpkin's novel, three others that used the Gastonia strike as a setting appeared in 1932: *Beyond Desire,* by Sherwood Anderson, *Call Home the Heart,* by Fielding Burke, and *Gathering Storm,* by Myra Page.[25]

For Lumpkin, the next few years were a whirlwind of activity. The publication of *To Make My Bread* launched her career as a writer and gave her a new prominence on the literary left. Among her many friends and acquaintances, she counted Sherwood Anderson, John Dos Passos, Max Eastman, Joseph Freeman, Michael Gold, William Gropper, Josephine Herbst, Granville Hicks, Joshua Kunitz, Lewis Mumford, Scott Nearing, Joseph North, Myra Page, Herbert Solow, Isidor Schneider, Genevieve Taggard, Mary Heaton Vorse, and Edmund Wilson. She was asked to contribute a short story to the first issue of the new radical literary journal *The Partisan Review* (1934); she completed another story for the more writerly *Virginia Quarterly Review* (1935); and she went to work on her second novel, *A Sign for Cain* (1935). In the meantime, a new edition of *To Make My Bread* (1933) was issued in London by Gollancz, and excerpts from the novel appeared in the January 30, 1934, issue of *Working Woman,* the CP magazine aimed at women readers, in the landmark anthology *Proletarian Literature in the United States* (1935), and in the influential social science collection *The Family, Past and Present* (1938). In 1936 a play by Albert Bein, based on the latter half of *To Make My Bread,* opened to critical acclaim at the Broadhurst Theatre in New York City. Unusual in its interracial casting of actors to play the roles of striking workers, the play ran for the better part of a year. A review of the play in the *Daily Worker* applauded its depiction of "a youthful and gigantic proletariat testing its strength" and of "the unity of black and white workers being welded over prejudice and lies by a common interest."[26] Eleanor Roosevelt was among those in attendance; her presence was a sign of the extent to which a radical agenda had made its way into the mainstream political focus.

Lumpkin's involvement and influence in Communist party circles also increased. She contributed articles to the *Daily Worker* and became, as one wry observer later noted, "a hot shot Commie," giving talks at CP and other gatherings, traveling to rallies and demonstrations, and altering her writing to more directly address the literary agenda of the CP.[27] Lumpkin frequently spoke for the CP about race relations and the need for unity among black and white workers. As a member of the National Committee for the Defense of Political Prisoners she was sent to the South to investigate lynching, and she wrote about the highly publicized Scottsboro case that helped crystallize African-American support for the CP.[28]

Although Lumpkin's literary record from the early and mid-1930s is easy to trace, events in her personal and political life are much less clear. This is the most difficult period of her life to describe with accuracy, for she herself later reconstructed it in several different ways. She initially tailored her recollections to protect her friends during the Chambers-Hiss espionage and perjury trials, later to vindicate herself during the McCarthy hearings, and finally to suit her agenda as a Christian "witness" of the evils of Communism. From these various reconstructions, from the recollections and research of others, and from a general discussion of her associations during this period, a picture of the ambiguities and complexities of Lumpkin's experiences as a radical and, later, as a reactionary can be compiled.

Lumpkin was adamantly pro-Communist in the late 1920s when she first met Michael Intrator. They eventually became lovers and may have married.[29] Intrator was everything Lumpkin was not. He was irreverent toward the CP, which she worshiped. He was brash, independent, and confident, whereas she, although spirited, constantly needed support and collective affirmation. Intrator was also, as Chambers describes him, "a child of the slums, almost wholly self-taught," a vibrant example of an organic intellectual, a type both valued and romanticized in leftist fiction of the period.[30] In contrast, Lumpkin was downwardly mobile, descending from a cultured southern aristocracy to join the ranks of the proletariat. In their remembrances of Intrator, both Chambers and Lumpkin good-humoredly emphasize the pun in his name (In-traitor).[31] His experiences in New York's fur markets, where he watched fierce and violent battles among Communist factions, caused him to support the right wing of the CP that had made considerable inroads in the fur and needle trades. For this support he was expelled from the Party as a Lovestoneite in 1929.[32] By all accounts, however, Lumpkin remained in the good graces of the CP until she voluntarily left it around 1939.

Sometime in 1930, Intrator's good friend Whittaker Chambers, also guilty of Lovestoneite tendencies, began to court Esther Shemitz. Chambers too had been ostracized from CP circles, but unlike Intrator, his vilification was relatively brief. He was able to restore his reputation by writing four proletarian short stories for *The New Masses* in 1931, the most popular of which, "Can You Make Out Their Voices," was reprinted and distributed by the CPUSA in pamphlet form and eventually drew the attention of a leading Soviet critic, who proclaimed that it was the first story in American literature to raise "the image of the Bolshevik."[33] Based on his literary achievements and his new international notoriety, Chambers became an editor of *The New Masses.* After he and Shemitz married in 1931, they lived with Lumpkin and Intrator, sharing close quarters in the 11th Street house and attracting criticism from friends. Many who knew the two men suspected that they had been sexually involved with one another before they paired up with Lumpkin and Shemitz. Even though Intrator and Chambers maintained heterosexual relationships with Lumpkin and Shemitz, their openly living together was considered scandalous.[34] During this time, Chambers, a flamboyant and secretive person one former friend described as a "writer who preferred to live his novels rather than to write them," became increasingly attracted to the Communist party underground.[35] In 1932 he left his high-profile job as an openly Communist editor and assumed a new identity and new responsibilities as an underground Communist courier. He and Shemitz left New York and for the next six years, while maintaining ties to Intrator and Lumpkin, lived the furtive lives of secret CP functionaries, assuming a variety of pseudonyms and moving from place to place.[36]

Lumpkin and Intrator remained in New York, but the house on 11th Street was not the same. Lumpkin's good friend, comrade, fellow artist, and literary adviser Shemitz was gone, and because of Intrator's CP expulsion, her friends in the Party stayed away. Myra Page, who was in Lumpkin's writing group, recalled that she was invited to the 11th Street house by Lumpkin but, "influenced by the general attitude" toward Intrator, refused to go. Lumpkin argued with Page: "This is a big mistake. It's like the Baptists and the Methodists: both are Christians. You and I both believe in socialism and the working class. We might not agree on everything but we are all working for the same thing." Page, however, still refused to visit Lumpkin, insisting that Intrator "was not working for the same thing as we were and I just didn't want to be around him."[37] Grace Hutchins and Anna Rochester had also withdrawn their friendship, although they continued to lend financial support.

Just as Lumpkin's writing career was taking off, she had become embroiled in Communist party factionalism. Attempting to walk a fine line between the left wing of the Party, which was supporting her literary endeavors, and the right wing, where her ever fewer personal alliances remained, she found her balance increasingly shaken. She had been an idealistic believer in the revolutionary mission of the CP but, coached by Intrator and Chambers, was beginning to have strong doubts about the methods certain factions of the Party were willing to use to achieve their political goals.[38] She was also becoming increasingly concerned about CP discipline. In her 1953 testimony before the Senate Sub-Committee on Government Operations, she complained that in 1934, fearing her alliance with Intrator, Joshua Kunitz, then editor of *The New Masses,* threatened to break her career as a writer if her new novel, *A Sign for Cain,* had anything against the Party line in it.[39]

Yet the deepest crisis that Lumpkin experienced in the mid- to late 1930s was a personal one. She became pregnant with Intrator's child and decided to have an abortion. Friends speculated that Intrator "had something to do with the decision because they lacked the economic basis to raise a family" and that Lumpkin later regretted having aborted her child.[40] Soon after, their relationship ended. Both the abortion and the separation from Intrator were very painful for Lumpkin. She had been present at the births of Esther and Whittaker Chambers's two children and saw how delighted Esther was to be a mother. She stayed alone in the house on 11th Street, "distressed because the fountain of inspiration remained dry as a desert."[41] Lumpkin's third novel, *The Wedding* (1939), avoided CP politics altogether, focusing instead on a domestic drama. By the time of its publication, Stalin had signed a nonaggression pact with Hitler and radicals began to leave the Communist party in droves

Lumpkin not only shunned Party functions, she became actively anti-Communist. She joined the Moral Re-Armament movement (MRA), a popular, activist religious movement that emphasized spiritual and moral renewal as a basis for social, racial, and economic justice. MRA's national headquarters was at the Calvery Church in New York City where the "Four Absolutes" of the MRA, and the practices of "Sharing" and "Guidance," were promoted by Reverend Samuel Shoemaker, a prominent Episcopalian minister.[42] Politically, the MRA was adamantly anti-Communist; ironically, however, its basic structure strongly resembled that of the CP. Individual MRA followers formed small groups, or cells, with a leader who brought messages and directives from MRA headquarters. Large MRA world assemblies and training meetings were held, attended by hand-chosen delegates who shared the evangelism and political ideology of the MRA. This must have all seemed very familiar to Lumpkin, a recognizable and comfortable terrain. The main difference, however, was that instead of providing a cure for social problems, Communism was seen as an obstacle, a pernicious evil, a demonic force that hindered all social progress.

From the MRA religious practice of "Sharing as Witness," where those who had recently converted gave semipublic testimony of private and public sins, Lumpkin found validation for the importance of confessing and repudiating what she later described as her "inner unhappiness and disillusionment" and "a mind that had become . . . raddled with Communist/socialist thinking."[43] She also learned convincing strategies for representing her Communist past in relation to her newfound Christian beliefs that would later serve her well. In 1941, Shoemaker became involved in a dispute with other MRA leaders that resulted in the MRA's expulsion from Calvery Church. Siding with Shoemaker, who advocated a return to more orthodox religious practices, Lumpkin left the MRA and rejoined the Episcopal church. Shemitz had once filled the role of literary adviser, and Intrator and Chambers had been her political advisers; in her new life, Lumpkin's spiritual adviser was Shoemaker. Lumpkin eventually moved into the Calvery Parish House where, amid Shoemaker's quasi-spiritual McCarthyism, she lived a relatively peaceful existence until late in 1948, when she was asked to provide information for the defense in the Alger Hiss perjury case.[44]

Nine years before, Whittaker Chambers had resurfaced in New York, where he had taken a job at *Time*.[45] Fearing for his life during a purge of right-wing elements in the CPUSA, Chambers had abandoned his role as a spy, become virulently anti-Communist, and began to write articles attacking both Communist and New Deal liberals. In exchange for immunity from prosecution, he also began to give testimony to various U.S. government agencies detailing his activities while both an open and a secret member of the CP. At the time, his statements were largely ignored. However, as the cold war began and politicians became obsessed with charges of espionage carried on by clandestine Communists, Chambers's declarations were unearthed. In 1948 he was called before the House Committee on Un-American Activities (HUAC), where he testified that, among others, he had worked with Alger Hiss as part of a secret underground CP apparatus while Hiss had been an official of the State Department. Hiss originally denied the allegations, but in 1949 he was indicted by a grand jury for perjury. When a private investigator hired by Hiss's defense attorney visited Lumpkin, he was hoping that she would provide information about Chambers's "deviant behavior" that would help destroy his credibility on the witness stand.[46] Instead, he found one of Chambers's staunchest allies. Lumpkin had "complete faith" in Chambers and "an understanding of what he was trying to do" with his insistence that Hiss was a spy.[47] She provided no evidence against Chambers, and the investigator left empty-handed.[48] Later that year the F.B.I. also visited Lumpkin to inquire about Chambers's character. Once again she had only positive things to say about him, his family, and her relations with them.[49]

As the Hiss case erupted into the American consciousness, Lumpkin began her last phase of political activism, an activism that, as she indicated in the title of her final novel, had moved her "full circle" back to her childhood championing of conservative causes from within the relative sanctity and safety of the Episcopalian ministry. Chambers now became her poet-priest, and Lumpkin, inspired by his example, took on the stridency and responsibility of becoming an anti-Communist witness.[50] Late in 1949, she wrote a letter to Eleanor Roosevelt requesting that she support Chambers's accusations against Hiss. She was angered when Roosevelt's "My Day" column devoted to the Chambers-Hiss affair solidly supported Hiss's innocence. For the next four years Lumpkin spoke at churches throughout New England about the dangers of Communism. In 1953 she was pleased to be called before the Senate Sub-Committee on Government Operations where she got her long-awaited chance to vindicate herself against her former associates and also the opportunity to witness against the excesses of Communism. She met with investigators in both private and open committee sessions.[51] Lumpkin got what she wanted from the subcommittee, and the subcommittee got all that it wanted from Lumpkin. Many of her former friends were appalled at her actions. Attempting to understand Lumpkin's political about-face, one former friend and fellow writer remarked: "I wouldn't have [appeared before the subcommittee] if they'd drawn and quartered me. You know, to be a fanatical Communist requires the same mental situation as to be a violent anti-Communist, there's a certain fanaticism."[52] Lumpkin maintained that it was good for her to appear before the subcommittee to finally rid herself of the underlying subconscious corruptions of the Party and of what she described as the "inner consent to murder" that adherence to Communism promoted.[53]

Soon after her testimony Lumpkin left New York City for good and returned to the South. She spent several years in Virginia before finally moving back to Columbia, South Carolina. In the years following her testimony, lectures and writing became her final acts of witnessing. She was a frequent speaker in church circles and joined the Christian Freedom Foundation, an interfaith council of anti-Communist Christians. All of her later writing was devoted to exposing the evils of Communism; her last published novel, an unfinished novel, a play, several short stories, and several occasional pieces explored Communist-to-Christian conversion experiences.[54]

Lumpkin told several variants of her own conversion story. The most frequent was one that linked her to Whittaker Chambers, who she had come to view as an important historical personage. To Lumpkin, Chambers's book *Witness* was "one of the great books of the 20th Century." She felt that her own writing—separated into two distinct literary periods, "the Communist phase" and the "return to God phase"—was inextricably connected to Chambers. In this version of her conversion story, she quit Communism in 1938 after Chambers came to her "again and again" to urge her to reexamine her prejudice against religion.[55] In another, more secular version of her redemption, Lumpkin explained that on one of her trips with the CP to organize black sharecroppers in the South, she had visited the graveyard where several generations of her family were buried and the courthouse where they had registered their last wills. Her understanding of how much her Communist lifestyle betrayed the traditional American values that her ancestors had believed in marked the beginning of her conversion.[56] Whatever prompted her religious conversion, her feelings about her Communist period remained adamantly negative. Once Lumpkin had completed the "long, slow, painful journey toward willingness to stand up and be counted on the side of eternal laws," she never again spoke positively about her first novel, *To Make My Bread,* or of the radical culture out of which it was born.[57] She continued writing, lecturing, and attending church functions until her death in 1980.

The Literary Reception of *To Make My Bread*

Grace Lumpkin's unpretentious first novel, *To Make My Bread,* was everything the literary left of 1932 and its radical readership was looking for. Her salient description of the struggle of poor Appalachian farmers, forced by economic hardship to leave their traditional mountain homes to find work in the exploitative Piedmont textile mills, was hailed as one of the first great contributions to the American proletarian novel. Ever since Mike Gold's infamous call in 1929 for socially conscious young writers to "Go Left,"[58] radicals were on the lookout for new forms of revolutionary writing—the kind of writing that, as V. J. Jerome, the Communist party's chief cultural authority, argued in his review of Lumpkin's novel, would become a "weapon with which the working-class" could wield "decisive blows at the literary arsenal of the enemy." In Jerome's view, the Depression was fueling a class war waged by American workers, a war requiring "stimulating revolutionary literary forms" that could record "the great heroic struggles, the deeds, the martyrdom's, the victories, the losses and the advances of the American proletariat." Yet Jerome also conveyed his misgivings that, as proletarian literature, Lumpkin's novel was not fully formed. Against the richly detailed mountain landscapes and domestic dramas of the McClure family, he felt that the scenes of industrial class conflict were too slightly rendered. Her idyllic, pastoral settings ran the danger of a "certain fetishism of local color." They could be incorrectly interpreted, he thought, as a nostalgia or homesickness for the mountains instead of as "the mighty reverberations of a proletariat in birth."[59] Reviewing the novel for *The New Masses,* A. B. Magil agreed. In his view Lumpkin's narrative displayed "the defects of a young, groping, inexperienced proletarian literature that will stumble and fall a great many times before it learns to walk."[60] Although these reviewers offered correctives and advice for improvement, their criticisms were not meant to be seen as condemnations of the novel. Even to their programmatic way of thinking, Lumpkin's narrative, although flawed, had a concrete ideological purpose in an era of few solutions, the descriptive force to give voice to the silenced masses, and the beginnings of a new aesthetic that could challenge prevailing modes of literary representation.

Other reviewers on the literary left were kinder. Robert Cantwell disagreed with Jerome and Magil, asserting in *The Nation* that *To Make My Bread* was one of the "few concrete examples" of proletarian literature,[61] while a reviewer for *The New Republic* applauded the novel's groundbreaking depiction of a "hitherto almost unknown social group" and felt that it was the best of all the books to appear on the Gastonia strike.[62] More mainstream reviewers agreed. A *New York Times* writer declared Lumpkin's book to be "one more milestone on the road to the return of social consciousness in American Literature."[63] A. Soskin, writing in the *New York Evening Post,* found the book's ending to be a bit didactic but recognized and appreciated Lumpkin's novel for its realistic representations of religion and poverty in southern milltowns.[64] All reviewers admired the quality of the writing in Lumpkin's novel and were unanimous in their opinion that it was a carefully structured, well-written first novel.[65] Many years after its publication, *To Make My Bread* was remembered by participants in the Gastonia strike and the trials that followed as the only novel written about Gastonia to really capture the complexities and contradictions of the first generation of poor white mountain folk to immigrate to the milltowns for employment. Lois McDonald, a southern labor organizer who spent several weeks in Gastonia as an observer during the trials, remarked that the portion of the novel describing the exodus of the southern poor from mountain to mill was "the best thing I've ever read." Similarly, Olive Stone, who was also involved in organizing poor white and black workers into unions in the South during the 1930s, praised *To Make My Bread* for its excellence in depicting poor southern workers and their resistances to their plight.[66]

As McDonald's and Stone's memories confirm, although out of print for sixty years, Lumpkin's novel and its impact have never been completely forgotten. Since mid-century, when an interest in "lost novels" from the 1930s first surfaced, both the novel and its author have been included in a number of scholarly articles and books that survey the period.[67] Interest in Lumpkin's novel has also emerged in historical scholarship on the Gastonia strike and the trials that followed. Indeed, Lumpkin's is the third of the Gastonia novels written by women to be brought back into print in the last decade, in part because of the evocative combination of historical, feminist, and literary interest these novels provide.

Recent literary scholarship on Lumpkin has classified her writing as part of a southern agrarian tradition, has focused on feminist readings of her novels within this tradition, and has discussed her participation in promoting progressive representations of race relations as part of her literary agenda. Much of this criticism has directly descended from Sylvia J. Cook's excellent study of "Poor Whites, Feminists, and Marxists," in which she discusses Lumpkin's first two novels in relation to the "proletarian possibilities" provided for radical writers by the Gastonia strike. In Cook's view, Lumpkin is writing out of both a "factual and fictional history of the poor white in the 1930s" and is "interested in the plight of poor white women,"[68] though she avoids the subject of birth control or of any new radical role for women that the other more consciously feminist Gastonia writers take up. Similarly, James Mellard sees Lumpkin's writing as part of a tradition of women writers, working within a feminist context, who refocus southern agrarian themes to include a specifically Marxist revolutionary social vision.[69] Paula Rabinowitz and Barbara Foley consider both Lumpkin and her novels in their feminist readings of women's experience of leftist cultural radicalism in the 1930s, while my own work examines Lumpkin's attempt to consciously incorporate answers to the "Negro Question" in her representations of labor organizing among poor white and black southern workers.[70]

Contemporary Contexts for Reading *To Make My Bread*

To Make My Bread describes the trials and tribulations of three generations of the McClure family as they face the rapid changes to Appalachian identity that come as a result of industrialization. The novel symbolically opens with a birth. John McClure, one of the novel's protagonists, arrives in the world in a single-room mountain cabin during an unseasonable spring storm in the first year of the twentieth century. The scene foreshadows the themes that Lumpkin takes up in her historical drama of Appalachian displacement: the feelings of exposure and vulnerability experienced by John's mother, Emma, during his difficult birth; her sense of self reduced to that of a beast; her laboring body weakened and worn down; the hungry bodies of her young children; and the shame she feels as they witness what she views as a humiliating event. Lumpkin's mountaineers do not have easy lives nor lives that, for all their attunement to the natural world, are easily romanticized. The McClure family has been stripped of its livelihood; there is no work in the mountains except for the occasional deliveries of bootleg liquor that get Grandpap Kirkland sent to jail. The family almost starves to death during one brutal winter; they lack proper clothing; the other members of their small mountain community are equally dispossessed and unable to help. The McClures do not recognize how they are caught up in the machine of capitalism, a perhaps more significant deprivation in Lumpkin's view. Grandpap fails to understand that when he sells the family land to a lumber company, the family will eventually be evicted from their cabin. Eager to believe the promises ("lifetime jobs," schools for the children, and a "house with a kitchen stove and electric lights") proffered by a representative for the mills sent to recruit unsuspecting laborers, he and Emma naïvely decide to leave the mountains for the "bright, shining dollars" that will "pour in" from the mills. In spite of, or perhaps because of, their fierce independence, the McClures have been living outside history. In the context of industrialization, self-reliance is anachronistic. Though weakened by an almost endless succession of ordeals and hardships, Lumpkin's characters eventually learn to discover ways of resisting their prescribed roles within the framework of American capitalism rather than remaining victims of it.

The principal harbingers of the change from working-class passivity to collective agency in the novel are Emma's youngest children, twins Bonnie and John. As Foley has suggested, Lumpkin utilizes the paradigm of the proletarian bildungsroman to construct their parallel political development and to contrast their nascent awareness of class consciousness and collective values with their older brother Basil's pursuit of status quo respectability and a loveless marriage to the wealthy daughter of one of the town's leading citizens.[71] From their first childhood experiences together, Bonnie emerges as the stronger of the two. When, early in the novel, John encounters and then does not realize the danger of a rattlesnake that has intruded on his Edenic search with his sister for blackberries, Bonnie pulls John safely away. This pattern of Bonnie's leadership and quick intuition about the best way to act in the face of adversity continues throughout the narrative as both brother and sister confront the more pernicious evil of the mills and millowners: exploitative paternalism. Like the other women writers of novels about Gastonia, all of whom place strong female protagonists at the center of their texts, Lumpkin hopes to recreate the actual history of the strike that included a large number of women and girls. Bonnie's character is not only generically representative of these women millhands, the most ardent and forceful supporters of the strike, but she is based on the historical figure of Ella May Wiggins, a mother of nine children and the only striker killed at Gastonia. Wiggins was shot by company thugs before fifty witnesses, yet the five Loray Mill employees indicted for her murder were never convicted.

Bonnie's coming of age as a radical in the novel is as much influenced by an awareness and confrontation of gender troubles as it is by her burgeoning class consciousness. Many of the instances of exploitation and abuse that oppress her (and out of which she eventually develops resistances) are the result of the inequities of gender. For Lumpkin, Bonnie's character represents the plight of working-class women and the ideological links between women's oppression and the exploitation of the working class. Like generations of women in her family, Bonnie suffers from lack of education, overwork, continual pregnancy, child-rearing, and the double burden of work outside and inside the home. She is forced to leave grade school to provide childcare, is sexually abused by a male cousin with whom she is forced to share sleeping quarters, and when her mother falls ill must find work in the mills even though she is still a child. Although it begins well, her eventual marriage to Jim Calhoun dwindles into failure when an accident in the mill leaves him unable to work and he abandons her and their children. Yet for all the pain she has endured, Bonnie is an early organizer and enthusiastic supporter of the walkouts and eventual strike of the mill. The devastating physical and psychological effects of her oppression as both a woman and a laborer have led her to understand the historical necessity for workers' unity and working-class resistance. Lumpkin hopes her readers will see how Bonnie's newfound consciousness so dramatically liberates her from bondage to oppressive gender and class ideologies that she becomes creative for the first time in her life. In a flash of inspiration, Bonnie begins to write ballads about women workers. Her songs not only describe and validate the lives of the women millhands she has known, they also play a central role in helping to keep workers calm and focused during various marches and pickets.

Like Bonnie, John McClure also arrives at a level of consciousness by the end of the novel that leaves him fully ready to adopt the politics of collective rebellion. Generations of shame and a lack of entitlement that John has witnessed—Grandpap Kirkland's deferential behavior with authority figures and erratic employment, his brother Kirk's manly yet disastrous passions, and his brother Basil's flawed attempts to pull himself up by his bootstraps—prepare John for his proletarian journey. Just as Bonnie's recognition of her place within a history of collective action is fueled by changes in both the personal and public sphere, John's transformation occurs along similar lines. He confronts moral issues of sexuality, religion, and manhood, as well as his rise to a position of respect and promise as a supervisor of other workers in the mill. His character development is not complete until he rejects the sexual solicitations of Minnie Hawkins, a former mountaineer-turned-prostitute who has successfully seduced both of his brothers, and the manipulations of Ruth Gordon, a well-intentioned social worker with allegiances to the millowners who offers him money to spy and report on the union-building activities of other workers. Lumpkin also uses John's character to discuss the threat to progressive action posed by the mountaineers' adherence to outmoded religious doctrines that work to maintain the paternalistic relationship between the laborers and the millowners. The hypocrisy and confusion John experiences in his encounters with Mr. Warmsley, the town preacher, lead him to suspect and eventually reject religion. He refuses to participate in the religious revival that Bonnie and many of the other millhands feel obliged to attend.

Finally, as pressures on John to take a position as the male head of the family increase, he must successfully interrupt violent impulses, born out of desperation, that make him want to escape. Although he feels "strained and impotent," he resists the urge to pick up a gun and kill all of his weakened family and then himself. His instincts for a better life are eventually rewarded when, after a speed-up is introduced by the millowners, he seeks out the advice of John Stevens, an older mentor figure he has worked with in the mills. Stevens, slowly and carefully over a four-year period, explains the principles of Communism to John. He tells John about the martyrdom of the anarchists Sacco and Vanzetti, talks him through Soviet socialism using examples from the Bible, and helps him discriminate between company and Communist unions—all without ever directly using any words or phrases like "Communist," "anarchist," or "red." The implicit meaning of Steven's unnamed paradigm is clear, however, to John and to the readers. His conversion to Communism in the last pages of the novel, symbolized by the red armband he wears, is complete. It is Lumpkin's hope that, after having identified with Bonnie's and John's experiences and transformations, the reader is now also ready to undergo a similar conversion.

While the transformations that Bonnie and John experience are the main focus of Lumpkin's construction of the personal and political processes that the mountaineers must complete to develop a conscious sense of agency, the characters in Lumpkin's novel collectively defy many other myths of the poor white. These include myths of the mountaineers' resistance to change, their passivity, their proclivities for violent acts, their adherence to reductionistic religious beliefs, and their reliance on traditional sex role stereotypes. Lumpkin's most persistent confrontation, however, is with the notion that poor whites are believers in the fiercest of racial stereotypes and are full of ingrained racist behaviors that are impossible to alter. Every member of the McClure family learns to resist the narratives of race domination that permeate many of the interactions they have with other whites. Grandpap Kirkland, the family patriarch who advises other members of the family early in the novel that whites and blacks should not mix, later is forced to reexamine his opinions when he learns from his black neighbor how to plant cotton. John witnesses the brutal beating of a black man on a chain gang, and Bonnie, Ora, and Zinie sort out their feelings about race after reactionary elements in the milltown try their hands at strikebreaking by circulating a racist handbill. Lumpkin is particularly interested in representing the need for alliances between white and black women workers. She depicts this shared dependence in the friendship that develops between Bonnie and a black co-worker, Mary Allen, who sweeps the floor around Bonnie's loom. Circumstance creates a cross-race class bond between these two women who share their resources. Later, their friendship becomes essential in the successful building of a union as Bonnie uses her connection with Mary to set up a meeting of blacks in Stumptown and persuades the black workers not to scab. But the alliance between whites and blacks, engineered by Bonnie, comes at a high cost. Bonnie, like Gastonia's Ella Wiggins, is murdered for her part in organizing among the black workers. The novel ends with her funeral procession. Mary Allen symbolically walks at a prominent place in the procession, just behind Bonnie's aunt Ora.

Because of its status as a relatively rare chronicle of poor white migration from rural mountain farms to industrial towns, an investigation of the cultural, religious, social, and political heritage of southern millworkers, and a history of the tensions behind the Gastonia textile strike, *To Make My Bread* will always be remembered as a significant contribution to American social realism. Yet Lumpkin's novel is valuable to contemporary students of the agrarian tradition, the literature of social commitment, women's revolutionary fiction, radical literary culture, and other literary disciplines for more than its qualification as a historical document. Questions raised by Lumpkin's Gastonia novel that remain at the center of both current theoretical debate and discussions about literary practice include: What is the proper relationship between ideology and fiction? What is the relation between politics and aesthetics? How does race, class, and gender oppression intersect in personal experience and literary practice? What is the best way for white writers to represent progressive cross-class and/or cross-race alliances?

Lumpkin was particularly invested in responding to these questions, and she hoped to infuse *To Make My Bread* with her knowledge of the struggles of the poor white in the South, her experiences of racism, and her intellectual understanding of radical strategies for social change. Thus, toward the end of her novel, she establishes the importance of necessary alliances between white and black women workers, based on mutual understanding and need, that cement her belief that solidarity across racial lines is essential to the survival of both groups. This conclusion alone marks Lumpkin as a valuable precursor for feminist and cultural historians who have yet to fully examine the work of prior generations of women radicals committed to addressing the difficult nexus of class and race. If the observation made by one of Lumpkin's first critics—who argued that the constraints experienced by elite white women living within a gendered double standard created a sensitivity among them to the situation of black and white workers—is true, then there are many rich possibilities to explore in Lumpkin's understanding of this class of progressive and radical white women.[72] Above all else, there remains one final reason for reexamining Lumpkin's novel of the 1930s. In no other American era did women radicals try so consistently in their fiction to focus their attention on the process by which external forces shape a literary work or by which a radical agenda could be incorporated into fiction. There are many experiences of disparity and injustice in American society represented in novels like Lumpkin's, along with potential visions of progressive social change. This dialectic is an essential part of an American literary heritage that needs further excavations to enrich our understanding of literary culture in the early part of this century.

A Guide for Researchers

In 1971, Grace Lumpkin established a collection of her papers for the South Caroliniana Library at the University of South Carolina in Columbia. Among this collection is the final typescript of *To Make My Bread,* several unpublished short story manuscripts, an unpublished play, the correspondence she carefully selected for inclusion, and her autographed and heavily annotated copies of Whittaker Chambers's *Witness* and *Cold Friday.* In addition to these papers there is a Grace Lumpkin file that is part of Katherine Lumpkin's collected papers in the Southern Historical Collection at the University of North Carolina at Chapel Hill. A final source for information on Lumpkin is the files that were collected on her by the Federal Bureau of Investigation. She was investigated because of her own activities, during background checks on Whittaker Chambers and Alger Hiss, and because her brother, Joseph Lumpkin, was a U.S. senator from South Carolina.

NOTES

Research for this essay was supported in part by the National Endowment for the Humanities Summer Institute on the 1930s, during the summer of 1993. A special thanks to Roseanne Vaile Camacho for her lucid conversation, comraderie, and willingness to share her research with me while we were both using the Southern Historical Collection. Thanks also to Allen Stokes, librarian at the South Caroliniana Library, for permission to quote from Lumpkin's papers, to Barbara Foley and Alan Wald for reading early drafts of this essay, and to Sandra Adickes and Christina Baker for sharing interviews from their personal collections.

The following abbreviations are used in the notes:

GL File	Grace Lumpkin File, Katherine Lumpkin Papers, Southern Historical Collection, University of North Carolina, Chapel Hill.
GL Papers	Grace Lumpkin Papers, The South Caroliniana Library, University of South Carolina, Columbia.
GL Testimony	Grace Lumpkin Testimony, April 2, 1953, in "Hearing before the Permanent Sub-Committee on Investigations of the Committee on Government Operations, United States Senate," part 2 (Washington, D.C.: United States Government Printing Office, 1953).
SOHP	The Southern Oral History Program, Southern Historical Collection, University of North Carolina, Chapel Hill.

1. Charles Wagner, "Books," *New York Daily Mirror* (Oct. 15, 1935). Brief sketches of Lumpkin do appear in: *20th Century Authors,* ed. Stanley J. Kunitz (New York: W. W. Wilson, 1942); *20th Century Authors: First Supplement,* ed. Stanley J. Kunitz (New York: W. W. Wilson, 1955); *Southern Writers: A Biographical Dictionary,* ed. Joseph M. Flora and Louis D. Rubin Jr. (Baton Rouge: Louisiana State University Press, 1979); Mary Jo Buhle, *Women and the American Left: A Guide to Sources* (Boston: G. K. Hall, 1983); and *American Women Writers,* ed. Lina Mainero and Langdon Faust (New York: Frederick Ungar, 1988).

2. GL Testimony, 159.

3. Robert Cantwell, "Effective Propaganda," *Nation* (Oct. 19, 1932): 372.

4. There is some dispute about Lumpkin's actual birthdate. She frequently gave 1900 or 1901 as the year she was born, but according to a family genealogy compiled by her brother Bryan in 1936, she was born before 1893. Katherine Du Pre Lumpkin, her younger sister, born in 1897, indicated in a letter to Lillian Gilkes, who wrote the Afterword to the 1976 edition of Lumpkin's third novel, *The Wedding,* that Grace was eighty-eight when she died in 1980. Four of Annette Morris Lumpkin's children died in infancy. See GL File.

5. See "Memorial Day—1961," GL File.

6. Katharine Du Pre Lumpkin, *The Making of a Southerner* (1946; Athens: University of Georgia Press, 1991): 182.

7. Like her sister Grace, Katherine was profoundly affected by her experiences of white southern racism and devoted much of her life's work as a sociologist to penetrating the myths and contradictions of race relations. Katherine's strategies in confronting racism were academic while Grace's were literary and activist. The third book of Katherine's autobiography, "A Child Inherits a Lost Cause," is an in-depth view of the Lumpkin family during the period they lived in South Carolina.

8. *20th Century Authors,* s.v. "Grace Lumpkin," 860.

9. Grace Lumpkin, "Annette Caroline Morris," in family genealogy compiled in 1936 by Bryan H. Lumpkin, Katherine Lumpkin Papers, Southern Historical Collection, University of North Carolina, Chapel Hill.

10. Katherine Du Pre Lumpkin, interview with Christina L. Baker, 22 Mar. 1987 (private collection).

11. Quotation from the masthead of *The World Tomorrow* (Apr. 1926).

12. According to Lumpkin, the Quakers "were quite radical and encouraged the girls in the office to go on demonstrations and picket lines in strikes. They had, as a matter of principle, all sorts of girls of various nationalities and political views working in that outer office. There were two Negro Girls, two Spanish Anarchists, a Communist, a Jewish socialist, and a 'peacenik' who was myself. I had just come up from the South and all that happened was continually edifying me and astonishing me. I became enthusiastic about going on picket lines etc. and about the Communist 'fractions' that led the demonstrations and picketing. They had the answer to Everything: When the Communists have changed the world we will have no more wars, no more poverty, no more racial hatred etc." (Grace Lumpkin to Kenneth Toombs, June 22, 1971, GL Papers). Toombs was an archivist for the South Caroliniana Library with whom Lumpkin corresponded about the materials she deposited there.

13. On the "Negro Question" see Mark Naison, *Communists in Harlem during the Depression* (Urbana: University of Illinois Press, 1983); Robin Kelley, *Hammer and Hoe: Alabama Communists during the Great Depression* (Chapel Hill: University of North Carolina Press, 1990); Suzanne Sowinska, "American Women Writers and the Radical Agenda, 1929–1940" (Ph.D. diss., University of Washington, 1992); and Barbara Foley, *Radical Representations: Politics and Form in U.S. Proletarian Fiction, 1929–1941* (Durham: Duke University Press, 1993).

14. Grace Lumpkin and Esther Shemitz, "The Artist in a Hostile Environment," *World Tomorrow* (Apr. 1926): 108–10.

15. "Who's Who in This Issue," *World Tomorrow* (Apr. 1926): 106.

16. See "Kok-I House," GL Papers.

17. Whittaker Chambers describes Shemitz, Lumpkin, and the house on 11th Street in some detail: "Grace Lumpkin and Esther Shemitz had been friends for years. They were widely known in the Communist movement for their inviolable 'prudery,' which was, in fact, chiefly their way of living uncontaminated by that steaming emotional jungle in which the party had raised promiscuity to a Marxist principle. They had taken a little house together in New York's East Side, on 11th Street. . . . It was one of those brick houses that stand at the back of a courtyard behind the cold-water tenements, which towered over it and cut off most of the light. Hence the popular name for such rear houses:

tuberculosis traps. The girls were clever with their hands and had remodeled the interior of the little house so that, when the fire was burning in the living-room fireplace, it was like a cozy farmhouse in the heart of the slum. . . . They had almost no money. But by eating as seldom as possible, and editing other irrelevancies out of their lives, they were able to dedicate themselves rather relentlessly to Art" (*Witness* [New York: Random House, 1952]: 266).

18. Quoted in Allen Weinstein, *Perjury: The Hiss-Chambers Case* (New York: Alfred A. Knopf, 1978): 109. Chambers recreates this scene quite dramatically in *Witness:* "The strikers were in one of the strike halls. The doors were shut and the police were massed in force to keep them shut and to keep the strikers from marching. Inside, the strikers were evidently buzzing like swarming bees. Now and again, the doors would be thrown partly open. The police would close in and slam them shut again. At last the doors were forced wide open, apparently by the weight of massed men and women strikers behind them.

"A slender girl in a brown beret rushed out before the police could stop her. The demonstration surged after her. 'Get that bitch in the brown beret,' an officer shouted. Without flinching, she walked forward as the police closed in, swinging their clubs. But the demonstration poured over them and swept them back. 'There,' I thought, 'is a Communist' " (231).

19. Grace Lumpkin, "The Law and the Spirit," *National Review* (May 25, 1957): 498.

20. The Loray Mill Strike in Gastonia, North Carolina, in the spring and summer of 1929, was of great historical significance to the movement for industrial unionization and to the development of social realist writing during the depression. While Gastonia erupted into violent conflict between pro-union southern textile millworkers and the reactionary forces at work within their communities, it also provided radical writers with an opportunity to witness and chronicle the revolutionary changes they hoped for in both society and literature. For histories of the strike and the trials that followed, see Fred Beal, *Proletarian Journey* (New York: Hillman-Curl, 1937); Liston Pope, *Millhands and Preachers: A Study of Gastonia* (New Haven: Yale University Press, 1942); Theodore Draper, "Gastonia Revisited," *Social Research* 38 (1971): 3–29; John M. Reilly, "Images of Gastonia: A Revolutionary Chapter in American Social Fiction," *Georgia Review* 28 (1972): 516; Dan McCurry and Carolyn Ashbaugh, "Gastonia, 1929: Strike at the Loray Mill," *Southern Exposure* (Winter 1973–74): 185–203; John R. Earle, Dean D. Knudsen, and Donald W. Shriver Jr., *Spindles and Spires: A Restudy of Religion and Social Change in Gastonia* (Atlanta: John Knox Press, 1976); Vera Buch Weisbord, *A Radical Life* (Bloomington: Indiana University Press, 1977); and Jacquelyn Dowd Hall et al., *Like a Family: The Making of a Southern Cotton Mill World* (Chapel Hill:

University of North Carolina Press, 1987). See also James A. Hodges, "Challenge to the New South: The Great Textile Strike in Elizabethton, Tennessee, 1929," *Tennessee Historical Quarterly* 23 (Dec. 1964): 343–57; Bert Cochran, *Labor and Communism: The Conflict That Shaped American Unions* (Princeton: Princeton University Press, 1977); Ron Eller, *Miners, Millhands, and Mountaineers: Industrialization of the Appalachian South, 1880–1930* (Knoxville: University of Tennessee Press, 1982); Sylvia J. Cook, "Critical Afterword," in Fielding Burke's *Call Home the Heart* (Old Westbury, N.Y.: Feminist Press, 1983): 447–62; and Jacquelyn Dowd Hall, "Disorderly Women: Gender and Labor Militancy in the Appalachian South," in *Gender and American History since 1890,* ed. Barbara Melosh (New York: Routledge, 1993): 240–81.

21. Grace Lumpkin to Kenneth Toombs, June 22, 1971, GL Papers.

22. Hutchins and Rochester both joined the CPUSA in 1927. Hutchins's landmark study, *Women Who Work* (New York: International, 1934), criticizes feminism for placing its emphasis on property rights and professional opportunity for middle- and upper-class white women instead of on the "double burden" as household and wage workers faced by black and white working-class women.

23. *20th Century Authors,* s.v. "Grace Lumpkin," 860.

24. Ibid. Hutchins and Rochester also loaned Shemitz money so she could paint and were witnesses at her marriage to Whittaker Chambers (see Chambers, *Witness,* 265–68).

25. Fielding Burke is a pseudonym for Olive Tilford Dargan, who wrote two novels about textile workers in the Piedmont district: *Call Home the Heart* (1932; Old Westbury, N.Y.: Feminist Press, 1983), and *A Stone Came Rolling* (New York: Longmans, Green & Co., 1935). Myra Page is a pseudonym for Dorothy Markey, who also wrote under the names Dorothy Page Gary and Dorothy Myra Page. Her Gastonia novel is *Gathering Storm: A Story of the Black Belt* (New York: International, 1932). Other novels about the Gastonia strike include Mary Heaton Vorse, *Strike!* (1930; Urbana: University of Illinois Press, 1991); Sherwood Anderson, *Beyond Desire* (New York: Horace Liveright, 1932); and William Rollins, *The Shadow Before* (New York: Robert McBride & Co. 1934).

26. Don West, *Daily Worker* (Nov. 18, 1935). See Grace Lumpkin, "John Stevens," in *Proletarian Literature in the United States,* ed. Granville Hicks (New York: International, 1935); Grace Lumpkin, "From Farm to Mill," in *The Family, Past and Present,* ed. Bernhard J. Stern (New York: D. Appleton-Century, 1938). Movie rights to the play were later acquired by MGM Studios.

27. Lois MacDonald, interview with Marion Roydhouse, June 24, 1975, SOHP; GL Testimony, 157; and Grace Lumpkin, "Why I as a White Southern Woman Will Vote Communist," *Daily Worker* (Aug. 12, 1932): 4.

28. The Scottsboro case erupted in Alabama in 1931 and soon became a clarion call for the Communist party, which used it to fuel a national debate about race relations. The Communists won the right to defend the Scottsboro Boys from the NAACP and insisted that the case was not simply an isolated incident of injustice but represented a common manifestation of racism and class rule in the South. Accused of raping two white women on a freight train, nine young black men were arrested on March 25, 1932, tried without adequate counsel, and hastily convicted on the basis of shallow evidence. One of the women later repudiated her testimony.

Written partly in response to the Scottsboro case, Lumpkin's second novel, *A Sign for Cain,* examines race relations in the South, taking up volatile questions of interracial rape, white lynch mobs, and white racism in a small southern community. Interestingly enough, two main characters in Lumpkin's last published novel, *Full Circle,* which is adamantly anti-Communist, are based on two Scottsboro figures, Mrs. Craik Speed and her daughter Jane, who were much celebrated by the Communists for their role in helping them during the Scottsboro case. Although members of a distinguished and much-revered white Alabama aristocratic family, both mother and daughter were forced into exile because of their support of the Scottsboro Boys. Lumpkin's fictionalized versions of the Speeds eventually repudiate Communism and return to their southern roots. See Dan T. Carter, *Scottsboro: A Tragedy of the American South* (Baton Rouge: Louisiana State University Press, 1984): 260–61; and Grace Lumpkin, "Southern Woman Bares Tricks of Higher-Ups to Shunt Lynch Mob Blame" *Daily Worker* (Nov. 27, 1933): 3.

Lumpkin's last contribution to social realism, written around 1939, was "The Treasure," an O'Henry prize story of 1940 that originally appeared in the *Southern Review.*

29. Lumpkin frequently stated that she and Intrator were married in 1931 (Chambers confirms this in *Witness,* 265). It was not uncommon, however, for radicals of this period to, in the words of Elizabeth Bently, another ex-Communist witness, reject marriage as a "bourgeois constraint" (*Out of Bondage* [New York: Devin-Adair, 1951]). In response to a request for information about her marriage from Lillian Gilkes, Lumpkin said that she seemed to have misplaced her marriage certificate and asked Gilkes to make no mention of a divorce in her Afterword (correspondence between Grace Lumpkin and Lillian Gilkes, GL File). Myra Page, a fellow writer and good friend of Lumpkin's during the early 1930s, said about Intrator: "I don't think he ever married her, so that depressed her" (Christina Baker, *In a Generous Spirit: The Life of Myra Page* [under contract with the University of Illinois Press]). Among other reasons, Lumpkin would have wanted to conceal the fact that she was never married from her future employers at the Calvery Church in

New York City and to avoid slurs (like those Bently received) when questioned by the F.B.I. during the Chambers-Hiss case and during her appearances before the Senate subcommittee.

30. Whittaker Chambers to William F. Buckley Jr., May 19, 1957, quoted in William F. Buckley Jr., *Odyssey of a Friend* (New York: G. P. Putnam's Sons, 1970): 180.

31. See Chambers, *Witness,* 229; and Grace Lumpkin to Kenneth Toombs, June 22, 1971, GL Papers.

32. Named after Jay Lovestone, the voice of the "Right Opposition" in the CPUSA. The Lovestoneites were very influential in the needle trades. During the late 1920s, they took a middle position between Trotskyists and Communist regulars and sought to support positive developments in the Soviet Union while maintaining a criticism of its bureaucracy. Lovestone and his followers were expelled from the CP in 1929. See Paul Buhle, "Lovestoneites," in *Encyclopedia of the American Left,* ed. Mari Jo Buhle, Paul Buhle, and Dan Georgakas (1990; Urbana: University of Illinois Press, 1992): 435–47; and Robert Alexander, *The Right Opposition* (Westport, Conn.: Greenwood Press, 1981). See also Philip S. Foner, *The Fur and Leather Workers Union: A Story of Dramatic Struggles and Achievements* (Newark, N.J.: Nordan Press, 1950).

33. See Chambers, *Witness,* 263; and Weinstein, *Perjury,* 108. All four stories are reprinted in Terry Teachout, *Ghosts on the Roof: Selected Journalism of Whittaker Chambers, 1931–1959* (Washington, D.C.: Regnery Gateway, 1989).

34. Chambers's homosexuality is well documented. Lumpkin and Intrator, however, both claimed they knew nothing about it when questioned by F.B.I. investigators during the Hiss trials. Jacob Burck, a close friend of the foursome during the 1930s, recounted to Allen Weinstein that he disapproved of the Chambers-Intrator-Lumpkin-Shemitz living arrangements. "You are all living in a sea of shit," he told Chambers at the time. Sender Garlin, who at one time worked for *The Daily Worker,* also claimed he thought that the relationship between Intrator and Chambers was homosexual. See Weinstein, *Perjury,* 110, 382.

35. Jacob Burck, interview with Allen Weinstein, Dec. 30, 1974, quoted in Weinstein, *Perjury,* 113.

36. Lumpkin occasionally lent the Chamberses money when they needed it. See Chambers, *Witness,* 61.

37. See Baker, *In a Generous Spirit.*

38. Chambers describes this relationship in one of his letters to Buckley: "I can recall one occasion, when Mike and I were out of the CP, and Grace and Esther were rapidly being drawn in. It was the time when Stalin took over, and the girls were arguing fiercely that the party is democratic. Mike and I were pointing out that a dictatorship cannot, by definition, be democratic. For several days thereafter, the ladies would not speak to us" (*Odyssey of a Friend,* 182).

39. GL Testimony, 157.

40. See Baker, *In a Generous Spirit.* Myra Page also remembered that Intrator "was having affairs for a long time even before he left her, but [Grace] had put up with that" (Myra Page, interview with Sandra Adickes, August 1984 and February 1986 [private collection]). In 1933 and 1936, Lumpkin played a significant role in the birth of Esther Chambers's two children, commenting in the margins of her copy of *Witness* where Chambers describes the birth of his daughter: "Whit forgot that he had spent most that night tramping up and down our living room," and "I was at the hospital that morning the baby was beautiful—not red at all—and with big brown eyes and long lashes" (Lumpkin's personal copy of *Witness,* GL Papers).

41. After Intrator left, Lumpkin rarely directly mentioned her relationship with him. See Grace Lumpkin, Postscript to *The Wedding* (1939; Carbondale: Southern Illinois University Press, 1976).

42. Followers of the MRA were also called "Buchmanites," after the American clergyman Frank Nathan Daniel Buchman, whose Oxford Group, founded in England in 1920, later became known as Moral Re-Armament. The international popularity and appeal of the MRA, as well as its political clout, should not be underestimated. Buchman had influence with at least four U.S. presidents, with many international leaders, and, although he never won it, was twice nominated for the Nobel Prize. In the religious practice of the MRA, the Four Absolutes, each suggesting a separate aspect of MRA doctrine, are Absolute Honesty, Absolute Purity, Absolute Unselfishness, and Absolute Love. "Sharing" is the confession of sins, either privately to another MRA member or clergyman or, in the practice of "Sharing as Witness," semipublicly in a group meeting or house party. "Guidance" refers both to guidance from God and from MRA leaders. See Frank N. D. Buchman, *Remaking the World* (New York: Robert M. McBride, 1949); and Tom Driberg, *The Mystery of Moral Re-Armament* (London: Secker & Warburg, 1964).

43. Grace Lumpkin, "How I Returned to the Christian Faith," *Christian Economics* (June 23, 1964): 1.

44. As a thirty-five-year-old freshman congressman in 1948, Richard Nixon's reputation and his political career were made by the Hiss case. Nixon writes in *Six Crises* (New York: Simon & Schuster, 1990) that, had it not been for the Hiss case, he would never have made it to the White House. In addition to those studies already mentioned, see Alger Hiss, *In the Court of Public Opinion* (New York: Knopf, 1957); Fred J. Cook, *The Unfinished Story of Alger Hiss* (New York: Morrow, 1958); Bert Andrews, *A Tragedy of History* (Washington, D.C.: Luce, 1962); Herbert Packer, *Ex-Communist Witnesses* (Stanford: Stanford University Press, 1962); Meyer Zeligs, *Friendship and Fratricide* (New York: Viking Press, 1967); John Cabot Smith, *Alger Hiss: The True Story* (New York: Holt, Rinehart, Winston, 1976); Alger Hiss, *Recollections of a Life*

(New York: Seaver Books/Holt, 1988). See also Ethan Klingsberg, "Case Closed on Alger Hiss?" *Nation* (Nov. 8, 1993): 528–32.

45. Esther Chambers and the children remained in hiding at the family farm outside Baltimore. Lumpkin visited them quite often. See GL Papers.

46. One of the possible tactics discussed by the Hiss defense was to try to slur Chambers by intimating that he was a homosexual and/or mentally ill.

47. Lumpkin, "The Law and the Spirit," 498.

48. Lumpkin was first visited by Horace Schmahl, an investigator hired by Edward C. McLean, Hiss's chief attorney, in New York City in late December 1948. She did not talk to Schmahl immediately but arranged to meet him a week later. This allowed her plenty of time to meet with Chambers first. Soon after Schmahl met with Lumpkin, Chambers prepared a statement for the F.B.I. detailing his homosexual activities, information he had previously withheld. Lumpkin was most likely one of Chambers's sources for knowing what questions the Hiss defense was asking potential witnesses. Lumpkin frequently exaggerated the importance of her role in the Hiss case. She claimed she convinced both Schmahl and McLean that Hiss was guilty. (She never actually met McLean). She also claimed that the Hiss defense bribed her to testify against Chambers and that she lost her job at Calvery Church because Hiss's lawyers harassed Shoemaker's wife. See Lumpkin, "The Law and the Spirit," 499; and a draft letter from Lumpkin to Lillian Gilkes, 30 Dec. 1974, GL File.

49. The F.B.I. interviewed Lumpkin on April 6, 1949, mainly to question her about her knowledge of Chambers's personal life. She denied any knowledge of his homosexuality.

50. Even a cursory examination of Lumpkin's papers substantiates this claim about her fixation with Chambers. She requested that the curator of her papers set up a special Chambers collection within her papers to contain not only her letters from Esther and Whittaker Chambers but the scores of articles about Chambers that she had clipped and annotated over the years. A heavily annotated autographed copy of *Witness,* replete with Lumpkin's commentary, is part of the collection. After the publication of *Witness,* Lumpkin altered any statements she made about her past to conform to Chambers's account. She carried a copy of *Witness* with her to all her speaking engagements and frequently read aloud from it. Even in her 1974 SOHP interview, more than twenty years after Chambers's death, she felt compelled to read sections of *Witness* aloud to her interviewer.

51. Ostensibly, Lumpkin was called before the Sub-Committee on Government Operations to discuss why excerpts of her novel *To Make My Bread* and the complete text of *A Sign for Cain* (both were Com-

munist propaganda according to the committee) had been included in a State Department–sponsored international library program. Among those called before the open subcommittee sessions were Herbert Aptheker, Earl Browder, Philip Foner, William Groper, Dashiell Hammett, Langston Hughes, Eslanda Robeson, and Bernard Stern, editor of the controversial text *The Family, Past and Present,* in which an excerpt from *To Make My Bread* appears.

52. Interview with Lois MacDonald, June 24, 1975, SOHP. McDonald's novel is *Swing Shift* (New York: Citadel Press, 1951). In understanding Lumpkin's new activism and McDonald's reaction to it, one is reminded of Louis Fischer's definition of the "anti-Communist 'Communist' " as an ex-Communist who, upon finding a new totalitarianism, "fights Communism with Communist-like violence and intolerance" (223–24 of Fischer's untitled essay in part 2: "Worshipers from Afar" of *The God That Failed,* ed. Richard Crossman [New York: Harper & Bros., 1949]: 196–228).

53. GL Testimony, 158.

54. See Grace Lumpkin, *Full Circle* (Boston: Western Islands, 1962). For unpublished materials, see GL Papers.

55. See Lumpkin, "The Law and the Spirit," 498; and Lumpkin to Toombs, June 22, 1971, GL Papers. Chambers disagreed with Lumpkin's depiction of him in her article for the *National Review:* "Lumpinova's tale . . . has most surprised me. . . . The picture of me as a Billy Graham of the Left, slipping in and out of the 11th Street house to save Grace's soul, well . . ." (final ellipses in original; Chambers, *Odyssey of a Friend,* 180).

56. Fictionalized versions of this account occur in *Full Circle* and in the unpublished story "Laughter in Heaven," GL Papers.

57. Lumpkin, "Kok-I House," 11, GL Papers.

58. See Michael Gold, "Go Left, Young Writers," *New Masses* (Jan. 1929): 3–4. Several recent studies have pointed out the sexism of Gold's manifesto and have described the literary left of the 1930s as a radical cultural milieu that was at times almost stultifyingly masculinist. See Alice Kessler-Harris and Paul Lauter, "Introduction," in Myra Page's *Daughter of the Hills* (1950; New York: Feminist Press, 1983): vii–xvii; Deborah Rosenfelt, "From the Thirties: Tillie Olsen and the Radical Tradition," in *Feminist Criticism and Social Change,* ed. Judith Newton and Deborah Rosenfelt (New York: Methuen Press, 1985): 216–48; Constance Coiner, "Literature of Resistance: The Intersection of Feminism and the Communist Left in Meridel Le Sueur and Tillie Olsen," in *Left Politics and the Literary Profession,* ed. Lennard J. Davis and M. Bella Mirabella (New York: Columbia University Press, 1990): 176–83; Paula Rabinowitz, *Labor and Desire: Women's Revolutionary Fiction in Depression America* (Chapel Hill: University of North Carolina Press,

1991); and Nora Ruth Roberts, "Radical Women Writers of the Thirties and the New Feminist Response," *Left Curve* 17 (1993): 85–93.

59. V. J. Jerome, "A Contribution to the American Proletarian Novel," *Daily Worker* (Jan. 3, 1933): 4.

60. A. B. Magil, review of Lumpkin's *To Make My Bread,* in *New Masses* 8–9 (Feb. 1933): 19–20.

61. Cantwell, "Effective Propaganda."

62. Anonymous, "Grind My Bones," *New Republic* (Dec. 7, 1932).

63. Anonymous, "A Novel of the Southern Mills," *New York Times Book Review* (Sept. 25, 1932): 7.

64. A. Soskin, *New York Evening Post* (Oct. 2, 1932). See also Cyrilly Abels, review of Lumpkin's *To Make My Bread,* in *Bookman* (Nov. 1932): 739–40; Harlan Hatcher, *Creating the Modern American Novel* (New York: Farrar & Rinehart, 1935).

65. In fact, Lumpkin is the only contemporary woman novelist to be honored by being included in Bernard B. Zakheim's "Library," one of the famous frescoes decorating the walls of Coit Tower, a San Francisco landmark. Commissioned by the U.S. government in 1933–34 as a Public Works of Art project, the mural depicts a worker in a library filled with revolutionary texts reaching for a copy of Karl Marx's *Das Kapital.* An untitled book with Lumpkin's name on the spine is in the same bookcase, on a shelf just below Marx's book.

66. Interview with McDonald, SOHP; interview with Olive Stone, Aug. 13, 1975, by Sherna Gluck, SOHP.

67. See, for example, Robert Cantwell, "No Landmarks," in *Literary Opinion in America,* ed. Morton Dauwen Zabel (New York: Harper, 1937): 530–40; Walter B. Rideout, *The Radical Novel in the United States, 1900–1954* (Cambridge: Harvard University Press, 1956); Daniel Aaron, *Writers on the Left* (1961; New York: Columbia University Press, 1992); Leo Gurko, "John Dos Passos' U.S.A.: A 1930s Spectacular," in *Proletarian Writers of the Thirties,* ed. David Madden (Carbondale: Southern Illinois University Press, 1968): 46–63; James Burkhart Gilbert, *Writers and Partisans: A History of Literary Radicalism in America* (New York: John Wiley and Sons, 1968); Fay M. Blake, *The Strike in the American Novel* (Metuchen, N.J.: Scarecrow Press, 1972); and Linda Wagner-Martin, *The Modern American Novel, 1914–1945: A Critical History* (Boston: Twayne, 1990).

68. Sylvia J. Cook, *From Tobacco Road to Route 66* (Chapel Hill: University of North Carolina Press, 1976): 85–124.

69. James Mellard, "The Fiction of Social Commitment," in *The History of Southern Literature,* ed. Louis D. Rubin Jr. (Baton Rouge: Louisiana State University Press, 1985): 351–62.

70. See Rabinowitz, *Labor and Desire*; Foley, *Radical Representations*; Barbara Foley, "Women and the Left in the 1930s," *American*

Literary History 2 (Spring 1990): 150–69; and Suzanne Sowinska, "Writing across the Color Line: White Women Writers and the 'Negro Question' in the Gastonia Novels," in *Radical Revisions: Rereading 1930s Culture,* ed. Bill Mullen and Sherry Lee Linkon (Urbana: University of Illinois Press, forthcoming). Other feminist readings of Lumpkin's novels include Joseph R. Urgo, "Proletarian Literature and Feminism: The Gastonia Novels and Feminist Protest," *Minnesota Review* 24 (Spring 1985): 64–84; Candida Ann Lacey, "Engendering Conflict: American Women and the Making of a Proletarian Fiction" (Ph.D. diss., University of Sussex, 1985); and Jessica Kimball Printz, "Tracing the Fault Lines of the Radical Female Subject: Grace Lumpkin's *The Wedding,*" in *Radical Revisions,* ed. Mullen and Linkon.

71. See Foley, *Radical Representations,* 321–61.

72. See E. A. Schachner, "Revolutionary Literature in the United States Today," *Windsor Quarterly* 2 (Spring 1934): 27–64.

BIBLIOGRAPHY

Selected Works by Grace Lumpkin

"The Artist in a Hostile Environment" (with Esther Shemitz). *World Tomorrow,* Apr. 1926: 108–10.

"The Bridesmaids Carried Lilies." *North American Review* 243:2 (Summer 1937): 4.

Full Circle. Boston: Western Islands, 1962.

"How I Returned to the Christian Faith." *Christian Economics,* 23 June 1964: 4.

"The Law and the Spirit." *National Review,* 25 May 1957: 498–99.

To Make My Bread. New York: Macauley, 1932; London: Gollanz, 1933.

"A Miserable Offender." *Virginia Quarterly Review* 11:2 (Apr. 1935): 281–88.

A Sign for Cain. New York: Lee Furman, 1935.

"Southern Woman Bares Tricks of Higher Ups to Shunt Lynch Mob Blame." *Daily Worker,* 27 Nov. 1933: 3.

"The Treasure." In *O. Henry Memorial Award Prize Stories of 1940.* Ed. Harry Hansen. New York: Doubleday, Doran & Co., 1940.

"Two Sketches." *Partisan Review* 1:1 (1934): 3–11.

The Wedding. New York: Lee Furman, 1939; Carbondale: Southern Illinois University Press, 1976; London: Feffer & Simons, 1976.

"White Man—A Story." *New Masses,* Sept. 1927: 7–8.

"Why I as a White Southern Woman Will Vote Communist." *Daily Worker,* 12 Aug. 1932: 4.

Reviews of *To Make My Bread*

Abels, Cyrilly. Review of *To Make My Bread. Bookman,* Nov. 1932: 739–40.

Anonymous. "Grind My Bones." *New Republic,* 7 Dec. 1932.

Anonymous. "A Novel of the Southern Mills." *New York Times Book Review,* 25 Sept. 1932: 7.

Cantwell, Robert. "Effective Propaganda." *Nation,* 19 Oct. 1932: 372.

Jerome, V. J. "A Contribution to the American Proletarian Novel." *Daily Worker,* 3 Jan. 1933: 4.

Magil, A. B. Review of *To Make My Bread. New Masses,* Feb. 1933: 19–20.

Soskin, A. Review of *To Make My Bread. New York Evening Post,* 2 Oct. 1932.

Other Sources

Coiner, Constance. "Literature of Resistance: The Intersection of Feminism and the Communist Left in Meridel Le Sueur and Tillie Olsen." In *Left Politics and the Literary Profession.* Ed. Lennard J. Davis and M. Bella Mirabella. New York: Columbia University Press, 1990.

Cook, Sylvia J. *From Tobacco Road to Route 66.* Chapel Hill: University of North Carolina Press, 1976.

Foley, Barbara. *Radical Representations: Politics and Form in U.S. Proletarian Fiction, 1929–1941.* Durham: Duke University Press, 1993.

Hatcher, Harlan. *Creating the Modern American Novel.* New York: Farrar & Rinehart, 1935.

Lumpkin, Katharine Du Pre. *The Making of a Southerner.* 1946; Athens: University of Georgia Press, 1991.

Mellard, James. "The Fiction of Social Commitment." In *The History of Southern Literature.* Ed. Louis D. Rubin Jr. Baton Rouge: Louisiana State University Press, 1985.

Rabinowitz, Paula. *Labor and Desire: Women's Revolutionary Fiction in Depression America.* Chapel Hill: University of North Carolina Press, 1991.

Rosenfelt, Deborah. "From the Thirties: Tillie Olsen and the Radical Tradition." In *Feminist Criticism and Social Change.* Ed. Judith Newton and Deborah Rosenfelt. New York: Methuen Press, 1985.

Schachner, E. A. "Revolutionary Literature in the United States Today." *Windsor Quarterly* 2 (Spring 1934): 27–64.

Sowinska, Suzanne. "Writing across the Color Line: White Women Writers and the 'Negro Question' in the Gastonia Novels." In *Radical Revisions: Rereading 1930s Culture.* Ed. Bill Mullen and Sherry Lee Linkon. Urbana: University of Illinois Press, forthcoming.

Urgo, Joseph R. "Proletarian Literature and Feminism: The Gastonia Novels and Feminist Protest." *Minnesota Review* 24 (Spring 1985): 64–84.

To Make My Bread

1

BEGINNING this side of South Range and thirty miles as the crow flies to North Range, the life of the mountain people centers around Swain's Crossing. At one place the road to the outside crosses the trail from South Range and Thunderhead. Here is Swain's store and post office. Beyond the store and the road, Laurel Creek runs in long, uneven curves. Seen from the side of Choah Mountain it is like a huge snake, the largest part just below, its head crawling past Swain's, and the tail somewhere out of sight toward North Range.

On April the nineteenth, 1900, two men left their steers, hitched to sledges, in front of the store and joined another man around the stove inside. A light snow had begun to fall and the warmth of the stove was very welcome. Presently another man came in. He was Sam Wesley, whose cabin was in Possum Hollow, on the South Range trail.

Sam took out his pipe and sat down on one of the unoccupied boxes at the stove.

"A sack of meal," he said to Hal Swain. Hal went to the back of the store and lifted a sack to the counter behind Sam, who reached in his pocket and laid the change on the counter beside the sack.

"Still snowing?" Fraser McDonald asked Sam.

"Yes," Sam answered, and being reminded of the snow, felt his shoulders to see if the wet had come through.

"Think it'll come up hard?" Jim Hawkins asked the company. No one answered. But presently Fraser McDonald said, "No danger of it coming up hard."

"If it was winter," Jim Hawkins said, "and it a-snowing, I'd be making tracks for my cabin."

The men sat bent over, close to the stove. They puffed at their pipes and occasionally one of them spoke.

Young Sam McEachern, whose steer was hitched outside the store, had been at Siler's Cove earlier in the day. He had business there with old man Kirkland who had come to live with his daughter, Emma McClure. John Kirkland was from the South Mountains and the two older McEachern brothers still lived there. They had sent word to Sam that he must find old man Kirkland and get his help in the business they carried on.

"See Emma?" Sam Wesley asked McEachern. He had been a friend of Jim McClure's before Jim's death.

"Yes," Sam answered and looked at Wesley as if he expected another question and was making up some particular answer. The question did not come, though Sam Wesley wished to ask if Emma's child had been born. His woman would wish to know. But the McEacherns could make a fool out of a man sometimes, with their smart answers, and unless a man was ready for a fight it was best not to give one of them a chance to get ugly.

With winter over, the afternoons were already getting longer. It was still almost two hours before dark and the men were in no hurry to leave the fire. The air near the stove had been quite warm. Gradually it became colder. Hal Swain moved uncomfortably on his box, then got up and filled the stove with short green hickory logs. Jim Hawkins, who was sitting behind the stove, quivered with a sudden chill. The pipe he held loosely between his teeth fell to the floor.

Sam McEachern, on a box next to Jim, looked out of the corners of his small, cunning eyes at his neighbor. "A rabbit run over your grave?" he asked.

"No," Jim leaned over to pick up the pipe. "But a blast of air cold as the tomb came up through that hole." He pointed with the stem of his pipe to a large crack in the floor. He was ashamed of that sudden chill; and to keep his eyes from meeting those of his neighbors he began to fill the bowl of his pipe.

From outside the store came a deep, melancholy bellow.

"That your steer?" Fraser asked Sam McEachern.

"It ain't my cow," Sam answered quickly.

"I reckon mine's a-ra'ring to get home," Fraser said calmly. But he did not move to go. He was comfortable by the stove, and his cabin was a two-mile drive over a rough road. A steer does not cover two miles in a hurry.

The steer's bellowing roused Sam Wesley from his comfort. He remembered that his woman must have the meal for supper. There was none left in the cabin. He raised himself from the box, and taking up the sack, limped between the counters to the door.

Steers hitched to the two sledges outside were standing with their thick necks bent down. The necks were not relaxed. They were taut as if the animals were preparing for an enemy. As Sam looked one of them raised its head a little, opened its mouth and gave a bellow. The other moved restlessly and planted its forefeet further apart in the mud. A cold northwest wind had come up as if a storm was getting ready to break. Yet there was so little snow in the air the mountains across Laurel Creek could be seen very clearly. Sam looked at them, then let the sack slide off his shoulders and spoke to the others.

"Something's a-happening up yonder," he said.

He spoke quietly. But the others sensed an unusual inflection in his voice. There was excitement in it, and some apprehension. They came and stood about him.

The long summits of Choah and Little Snowbird were completely hidden by a snowstorm. Lower down the trees and bushes were visible. On top the sheets of snow curled and bellied like clothes hung out on a line in a high wind.

Fraser sniffed at the air. He gave another look at the storm raging on top of the mountains. Then he buttoned his short coat to the neck.

"I'd best be getting across that ford," he said. "Something's about to break loose."

His anxiety was felt by the other men. They left Hal Swain alone in the store and went out to the sledges. Jim Hawkins climbed up with Sam McEachern, for his cabin was on the same side of the creek as Sam's. Fraser drove away behind them. The sledges with their wooden runners bumped uncomfortably over the rocks in the deep ruts. Sam Wesley slung the sack of meal across his shoulder and limped behind them until he turned to the left toward Possum Hollow.

Half an hour later dark came suddenly over the whole region. Thick whirlwinds of snow filled the coves and valleys so that each isolated cabin was cut off more than ever from the world around it. The wind howled through the trees like a pack of hounds let loose.

Doors were shut against the storm except in places where the men were out hunting for the precious animals they had neglected to shelter. At these cabins there was much activity. Women stood outside the doors with the snow stinging their faces like wasps and called to their men, or crawled to meet them, trying to make their shrill voices heard above the wind. The excited cries went on until the absent ones staggered in.

The same thing was repeated in Siler's Cove, where the McClure cabin sat far down between mountains. In fair weather it was like a tiny boat in the trough of huge waves. Since the blizzard began the cabin was obliterated. It had become a part of the blank whiteness from which nothing stood out.

Granpap Kirkland and Emma McClure's two sons had ventured out to find the steer and cow. When they did not return Emma stood outside the door and screamed to them. She could not stand long against the strong wind. It blew her against the wall of the cabin with the force of a strong man's fist. Leaning over she held to the woodblock that served as a step and kept up intermittent screams until the others returned. They came crawling on hands and knees, and she did not see them until they were right on her, and Granpap called into her ear that they were safe.

She did not learn until later that the steer and cow were lost, for as soon as her anxiety for Granpap and the boys was over, Emma felt a first sharp pain and knew that her time had come. Inside the cabin with the door shut she crouched over the fire trying to get some of the warmth of it into her body. The icy wind had reached the very marrow of her bones.

The hickory log fire shone on her twisted face, and on the form that protruded from her belly in an oval shape. It seemed as if the child in her womb had already been born and was lying wrapped up in her lap asleep.

On the floor at Emma's right eight-year-old Kirk lay and stared into the fire, and between them in a poplar log cradle Bonnie, the youngest, whimpered in her sleep. On the other side of the fire, Basil, who was a year older than Kirk, sat against the chimney, his legs spread out before him on the floor.

The wind sniffed at the doors and blew gusts of icy breath

through the cracks of the log cabin. Clothes hanging to pegs on the walls flapped out into the room, making strange balancing movements. If the wind died down for a moment they suddenly collapsed against the wall as a man does who gives up the struggle to keep on his drunken legs.

In the half darkness of the small space between the circle of firelight and the end wall of the cabin, John Kirkland walked the floor. His boots stamped on the split-log flooring regularly, hesitating when he turned at the wall and again when he turned just behind Emma's chair.

Granpap Kirkland's life had been full of varied experiences. A fight with a she bear had left three long scars across his right cheek, and there was a scar on his side from a wound received in battle. He was not a fearful man by nature. But he had known fear and dread in the last few moments since he knew that some time in the night he must deliver Emma of her child.

Emma instructed Granpap. She took his thumb for a measure. The cord must be cut so far from the child. Neither of them had much fear for Emma. She was a strong woman. A few months before, just after Jim McClure died of fever and before Granpap had come to stay with her, Emma, then five months gone with child, had carried the best part of a thirty-pound shoat the twelve miles over steep mountain trails to Swain's Crossing. Nevertheless her children always came hard, and Emma knew there would be plenty of pain even before the child made its final struggle.

Bonnie cried out loud. Emma walked to the wall where the clothes hung and took down a pair of old jeans. She tucked them into the cradle around the child. Back in the chair with her foot against the cradle she set it rocking slowly, and the child quieted for a moment.

The old man came and stood behind Emma. His shoulders were bowed a little, but he was very tall, and stood high above her.

"Do you think it'll be soon, Emma?" he asked. His voice was anxious and querulous.

Emma did not answer. She knew he wanted it over and done with. But so did she. There was no way to hurry the child.

"Are you going to bed?" he asked. She straightened up.

"When hit's time, Pap. Hit's s' cold there."

The wind slapped against the cabin and snarled down the chimney. Snow blew in under the north door and spread over the floor in a hurry and flurry like an unwelcome guest who is trying to make himself at home.

During one of the quiet times between the pains Emma took the coffee pot from the fire and poured out a drink for each one in the tin cups. Above the kerosene lamp on the table strings of dried apples hanging from the rafters stirred and as the lamp flame gutted and flared up the apple strings made long crooked shadows across the bed in the corner.

"Hit'll warm up our backs," Emma said and handed the cups. She walked over and picked up the water bucket that was in a dark corner behind Kirk.

"Here, Kirk," she said. "Hold the pan."

The water was frozen. Emma broke through the ice with her fist. When she poured it out of the bucket it clinked against the bottom of the tin basin. She set the basin down in the ashes against the live embers.

"You'll need the hot water," she said to Granpap. As she gulped down the warm coffee she wished in herself there was a woman who would know what to do without telling. And she wished the men were where they belonged when a woman was in travail—somewhere out on the mountains or at a neighbor's. There was a shame in having her sons near, and Granpap must see her as he had not seen her since she was a naked baby in her mother's arms. Soon, maybe, it would be over. The pains had begun to get worse, as if it was the end.

In the bed away from the others, Emma let go. She was shaking with cold yet the quilts and her cotton flannel skirt were too much and she pushed them off. Sitting up in bed she pressed down slowly with her hands over the great lump stirring inside. Others had done this for her before to help the child come. She found that she could not do it for herself. The hot pulling cramp forced her to lie back and scream again. A bear was gnawing at her belly, pulling at the muscles with its strong teeth. She felt its fur on her face and beat at the fur with her arms.

It was Granpap's beard. He was trying to tell her to keep covered as long as she could. She pushed him off. It was not possible to bear the agony of one hair touching her. There was no Granpap and no children now. Nothing mattered but herself and the pain.

Bonnie kept up a fretful wail, and Granpap walked up and down the room. Outside the storm brushed against the cabin as if all the trees on the mountains had been uprooted and their dry branches were scraping over the roof and against the outside walls.

Kirk was quiet. Now he stood with his back to the chimney, watching the corner with frightened eyes. Suddenly Emma cried out sharply to Granpap. He stooped over the bed and peered down.

"Bring the lamp, Kirk," he ordered. "And you, Basil, put that pan of water and bucket on the table."

He rolled up his sleeves and walking quickly to the fire leaned far over to rub his cold hands in the flames.

Kirk held the lamp over the bed and kept his eyes on Granpap. On the bed was a woman he did not recognize as his mother. She was a stranger, a sort of beast. Granpap stood between him and the new thing, and he kept his eyes on the wide back where Granpap's old shirt and patched jeans were familiar and safe. Kirk saw the old man bending over working with his hands at Emma's body and he smelled blood. It made a familiar shudder run over him. Granpap bending over the bed was like a man bending over at a slaughtering and Emma's last cries were the same as those of a pig with a knife at its throat.

For a while Kirk had not heard the storm because Emma's cries were closer than the sounds outside. But when they stopped there was the storm again, wheezing around the cabin and pushing at the door. When Granpap at last stood up he held in his hands something that looked to be a mass of blood and matter. But it was really a living thing. For as Granpap shook it the mass made a wailing sound—a sort of echo of the storm outside.

There was washing to be done, and Kirk stood and held the lamp until the old man finished. At last Granpap covered Emma where she lay exhausted on the dry side of the cold bed. Then he put the washed baby in the cradle with Bonnie to keep it warm until Emma would come to and let it suck.

2

THROUGH the summer of 1906 Granpap made mysterious journeys across the mountains. He was absent for days at a time. With the bags of corn the McEacherns had sprouted on his back, the old man climbed South Range and down again into another state. On the other side at a certain place the corn was ground and Granpap walked back again with the sweet meal. Here the mash was made into ferment and distilled.

The revenue men were thick through the mountains. If Granpap was caught with the sprouted corn he would be arrested. And he got very little money for the risk. The McEacherns took most of the money because they owned the still and peddled the liquor. That, of course, was most dangerous, for it meant going down into the outside. They had tried to persuade Granpap to peddle. But they had offered him little more money than he got for carrying the sprouted corn and mash. He had insisted that if he took the greatest risk he must get at least half the money. And they had refused. Only they promised him half a jug of liquor. This was not to be sneezed at, for the McEachern liquor was the best made in that part of the country. But Granpap enjoyed walking over the hills, though sometimes it meant climbing in the night across South Range. And he hated going to the outside, into the towns. If he did that part he must be properly paid for the risk and discomfort.

Emma knew the risks Granpap was running and each time he left the cabin for his journey she became weary and cross. For the smallest reason she threatened John with a hickory. Or she said to Bonnie, "I'll slap ye over." She never carried out her threats, but they made the cabin an uncomfortable place.

Hoeing time was over and it was not yet the season for shucking corn and getting the potatoes in. John and Bonnie played in the cove. They used moss and rocks for a house. Under a large walnut tree they outlined a room with rocks, and left an open space for a door through which they carefully walked each time they wished to go in or out. There was a bed made of moss. Later John added another room. Granpap was planning to add a room to their own cabin in the fall. He had promised that John might help to get the logs down from the mountain. And when the room was finished, instead of sleeping in the bed with the women while Granpap slept on the floor with Kirk and Basil, John was to sleep in the new room in one of the two homemade beds with Granpap. Emma was already preparing the tops for some new quilts from pieces she had accumulated in the old trunk. The money Granpap was earning would buy cotton for the inside of the coverings.

Whenever John thought of the two new experiences ahead of him a feeling of excitement ran through him. In anticipation of the events he outlined the other room under the tree with rocks and made a large bed of moss for himself. While he was building he spat frequently, like a man.

Something happened about this time that made the two children keep close to the cabin. They had lost interest in the play cabin and went further away from the clearing. Emma had warned them about rattlers, and both knew the sound of a diamond back. A skin hung on the wall of the cabin beside Granpap's fiddle. There was a long finger's length of rattles. If the skin was shaken hard enough the queer shaped little compartments made their peculiar sound.

Stories of people getting snake-bit were swapped across the hearth when Ora and Frank McClure were at the cabin, or Jennie Martin and her husband. There were discussions about the best cure. Ora said rattle-snake plant would cure, if the juice was put on with the right words. Strong whisky applied inside and out was good. Granpap had known people in Georgy to use equal parts of tobacco, onion and salt made into a poultice. The best thing to do was to cut the bite criss-cross with a jack-knife and suck the poison out—that is, if the person who sucked had no sore in his mouth. And he must be sure to make the cross straight over the wound, just as a person, when he forgets something and returns to the cabin for it, must make a cross with his heel and spit straight into the middle. Granpap knew about this cure for a snake-bite from experience. For he had made a cut on Fraser McDonald and sucked the poison out. The skin on the wall of the cabin was the skin of the snake that had bitten Fraser.

In spite of Emma's warnings the children often forgot to think of snakes, especially when the blackberries were getting ripe. There was a large patch of these up the side of the mountain on a rocky bald spot. John and Bonnie were making for that patch one morning. Below the berry patch some large gray bowlders pointed out over the hill and flattened along the side of the slope. John walked ahead of Bonnie. He was anxious to reach the berries first. Up above the rocks the light green leaves of the berry patch shone in the sun, and between the leaves he could already see the red berries hanging.

He was concentrated on the berries, and his mouth was already watering for a taste when the ugly rattle sounded in front. The snake must have been lying out beside the rocks sunning itself. It was just above him on the slope, hardly a man's length away. Bonnie saw it, and stepped back. John did not move. Bonnie wanted to run, but John seemed not to realize danger. He simply stood with his back to her, facing the snake. She could not see his face, but she could see the snake that was curled in rings, ready to strike. Its scales gleamed in the sun. The clumsy, rounded head on the neck that was raised from the coiled part swayed toward the boy. The head was almost as high as his own head, for he was on a lower slope. The little eyes of the rattler watched him closely. The tongue stuck straight out from the open mouth and quivered. The evil little eyes and the tongue menaced and fascinated the boy. He could do nothing. And Bonnie saw that he could do nothing. In another second, she knew, the snake would strike. She caught the back of John's jeans and clumsily jerked him against her. The impact of his body on hers brought them down on the slope together, and they rolled downhill until a rock stopped them.

When they had untangled themselves and stood up the snake was not in sight. They did not stay long to look, for Bonnie had a bad bruise over her right eye where she had struck a sharp edge of the rock. A large drop of blood was oozing out of the puffed-up place. And on the way to the cabin it began to turn blue and yellow. It was very curious to see Bonnie's flesh turn the different colors. It was curious to John. Bonnie was only interested in the fact that the bruise hurt. And under their interest in the bruise they were both badly shaken by the experience.

But they kept it to themselves. Emma took it for granted that Bonnie had fallen down and hurt herself on a rock, and they let this part truth rest in her mind. For some days after the experience they stayed close to the cabin. And because Granpap, who was the most important person in his world, was away, John missed him and wondered about the places outside.

In the cove as far as he could see on every side there were mountains. If he climbed Thunderhead with Emma and Bonnie and looked far away there were still mountains upon mountains. At times they looked so vast and heavy he would turn away from them and put his head to the ground to smell the black earth. If he turned clear around on his heel down in the clearing that was what he saw—hills reaching into the sky.

One day he stood outside the cabin in the hot sunshine. The sky was an even blue. It was a quilt with a yellow calico sun. On rainy days John and Bonnie sometimes played a silly game that Bonnie had made up. They sat on the bed across from each other and made a sort of cabin by holding a quilt over their heads. When their arms were tired they let the quilt come down and sat in the darkness, pretending great fear.

John felt that the sky was a quilt and the mountains piled up on each other were big children sitting close together, bent over, holding up the quilt with their shoulders. He wondered what would happen if the big children got tired and let the quilt loose from their shoulders, so it came down on the cove and covered the cabin and clearing. It would be dark. The dark would come suddenly as Emma had told him it came the afternoon before he was born. He thought, if the dark came down like that in summer, he would run into the cabin. Granpap would be there and could play the fiddle as he did on long winter evenings.

Granpap came back from his last trip that summer with money in his pocket. He gave most of it to Emma who put the nickels and quarters away in the gourd on the chimney shelf. John liked to stand on a chair and shake the gourd to hear the money clink. As he was feeling around on the shelf he found Granpap's rosin and put it to his nose. It smelled dusty and stale, not like new rosin just out of a pine. But he sniffed at it again.

"If I had the fiddle," he told Bonnie, "I could play 'Big-Eyed Rabbit.' "

Bonnie looked at the fiddle hanging on the south wall and then at John. She did not believe he would dare to touch it.

"You wouldn't," she said, and sucked in her cheeks making a rabbit mouth at him. Her proud wriggling nose angered John. He had not yet learned to make a rabbit mouth, and Bonnie knew she was superior to him. He felt that he must show her there were things he could do that she would never dare attempt.

He lifted a chair over to the wall under the fiddle. The rabbit mouth left Bonnie's face and she watched him with her mouth wide open. He saw her wonder and admiration and felt that everything was right again.

Down in the chair he laid the fiddle across his knees, and rubbed the rosin up and down the bow. The tow hair hanging across his forehead swung back and forth as he moved his arm. Then he took up the instrument and the bow, but found that he could not manage both. So he began tuning as he would a banjo. First he twanged a string timidly and turned a peg. The string whined at them. The first trial was so successful, the little whine that came from the string was so queer, he tried again. This time he was not so timid; and the second and third times the string hummed quite loud.

"Do it again," Bonnie said. "Do it again." She shut her mouth tight and made a sound through her nose like the fiddle. John curved his finger hard and brought it across the string. This was too much. With a snap the gut broke across and the ends curled back with tiny protesting whines.

"Now!" Bonnie said. She looked up at the door. Granpap was standing there. He had heard the sound of the fiddle out in the clearing. His anger was terrible. Bonnie held to the chair John was sitting on. She was afraid to move, though she would have liked to run away.

"For that," Granpap said to John. "You can stay down and pull fodder when we go up for the logs." He was really distressed, for a new string cost money and must be ordered by Hal Swain from the outside. In his distress and anger Granpap had hurt John in a most vulnerable place. The boy had looked forward so long to helping with the new room.

During the next day John sulked by himself. While Emma and

Bonnie were grabbling potatoes, he sat on a corn row down in the patch. The stalks of corn hid him from his mother and sister. Each time he heard the ax bite into the wood up on the side of the mountain he felt grieved again. The sound came down clear into the cove. It came down one blow immediately after another, for Granpap had borrowed a second ax. The ax sounds came flat and mournful. They seemed to come flat across John's belly and make it ache. He sat hunched over and felt very melancholy and sorry for himself as he looked up at the side of the mountain where Basil and Kirk were working with Granpap. A tree cracked up there and began to fall. He saw its top move among the other trees. There was no breeze and all the other trees were still. Only this one swayed a little, then sank down gently with a sound like water falling over a rock cliff.

All morning John hid himself in the cove. When dinner was ready inside Emma called and sent Bonnie to look through the corn patch. John was not there. He had gone to hide out like a dog when it is sick.

Early next morning the little boy was in front of the cabin, lolling carelessly on the woodblock. He pretended that he was indifferent to everything and everybody. But underneath was the hope that if Granpap saw him he would say, "Come, John." Granpap did see him. But he and the boys went by without a word. Even Kirk who usually had some word for John was silent. He was at the moment wearing the red bird feather John had found in the woods and given him for the band of his old felt hat. But he did not say to Granpap, "Take John." He walked past without looking.

The evening before John had seen Granpap eying the corn patch that he had not touched. If it was necessary to work the corn patch he would do it. Then they might give him some notice, when they found he could work like any of them.

So he worked all day at the fodder. And when he saw the strips tied to the corn stalks that evening and knew that his arms and hands had done the work, he felt proud.

"What are you scared of?" he asked himself when he thought of begging Granpap to take him up next day. "He can't kill ye."

The next morning he walked up to Granpap. To his own surprise instead of begging he lifted up his face that did not reach to the old man's belly and said, "I'm a-going with you to-day, Granpap." His mouth was stretched in a wide grin, but there was no real laughter in him. He was really afraid.

Granpap turned away to eat his breakfast. And John felt the same weight on himself that he had felt on the first day. He had tied the fodder. His arms ached from stretching up to the corn stalks. And it was no good.

Granpap finished his coffee and got his ax from the corner of the cabin. John watched him. He was going away without a word, like the day before. Of course John had not finished all the corn, but half of it. At the door Granpap turned his head and said, "Come along, Son," to John. It was as if he had been holding the ax over John's neck to chop it off, and had suddenly lifted it away. John rushed after the others and followed them up the mountain in the fresh morning air.

For several days after this they chopped down the trees and lopped off their branches, making them into good, even logs. While Granpap and the boys took turns in whacking at a tree John played in the woods with the two dogs. He was hunting bears, and each time the dogs caught a scent, or pretended to, John followed them, and joined in their excited search. Sometimes the dogs lost the scent or simply got tired of playing, or John felt they were going too far from the sound of the axes. Then he would call the dogs and go back to Granpap, for he must be there to watch each tree when it fell. He liked the moment when Granpap and Kirk or Basil, whichever one was helping, stood away from the tree. There would be a still second. Then the crack of the wood breaking in half came. John was never tired of hearing that sound and feeling the excitement that came when the great tree fell straight down the slope. It swished against the air and its branches brushed against the branches of the other trees that were still intact. Down the broken tree came and slid away from the trunk before it came to rest on its under branches a little distance above the ground.

When there were enough logs cut they began hauling them down with a steer hired from Swain. The boys chopped out a runway in the bushes where the trees were thinnest. The steer was hitched to one end of the log by chains. With a long branch of sweet gum tree for a whip, John walked just behind the ox and yelled, "Get up, there," in his deepest voice. The chains clanked as the brown and white beast stooped and strained to pull the log that bumped over the uneven ground. When it caught on a bush or stob Granpap and the boys lifted and heaved it over. At the runway John came back and helped the others push the log around into place for going down hill.

Here the whip was of no use. Kirk got hold of the halter and held back to keep the ox from going on its head. Granpap and Basil took the rope tied to the other end of the log.

"Get behind," Granpap said to John. "And when I say pull—pull the rope like all hell was after ye."

Looking down between Granpap's legs along the log John saw the ox plant its feet in the soft earth of the mountain; and each time its feet braced, the hindquarters came up slowly. At a slippery wet place Granpap called, "Pull!" and the boy braced his feet deep down against a stob of laurel bush, and as he bent over, like the ox his hindquarters came slowly up. He watched Basil and Granpap, and just as they did, he let the rope go from his hands gradually, so the log would not slide down on to the backside of the steer.

Toward midday they had several logs alongside each other on the trail. The steer, freed from the chains and watered at the stream below, bent its forelegs and lay down with a long grunt.

Granpap was satisfied with the morning's work. He lit his pipe and gave Basil and Kirk a share of tobacco. He hoped in another year they would have a steer of their own. Somehow money went fast and it was hard to save up for a beast, when there was so little to begin with. And Granpap liked folderols. He liked to bring candy from Swain's on Saturday nights for the young ones. Once he bought a ball for John, and Emma scolded—when they needed meal, she said, and coffee.

But they had a cabin and the land around it. Nothing could take that from them. Granpap looked down the trail to the cabin. The lower props were already up for the new room and this was something to have pride in.

He remembered when he had lost his own cabin and land and how he had felt of no account.

"You're free men," he said to the boys, "so long as you've got your own potato patch and house and a gun. The house might not be fine. When I was down in Georgy I saw some fine places with windows you could see through, and the houses painted. But I wouldn't swap them for what we've got if I didn't own."

At fourteen Granpap ran away from his stepfather. He went over South Range to the outside and joined up to fight in the war that was going on out there. He was big for his age and the Confederates were glad to get him.

"I wouldn't change with anybody," he repeated. "Long as I'd got my piece of land and a roof."

Basil was sixteen, almost grown, and he understood about Granpap. The old man had let someone cheat him out of the Kirkland land so that in the end he had nothing. And Basil thought, "Granpap couldn't keep what he had. And this isn't his. It's McClure land."

Basil did not know that at the time he was cheated Granpap had oiled his shot gun, ready for Tate, the man who cheated him. Then word had come that Jim McClure was dead and Emma wished for him to come. Perhaps because he was getting older and perhaps because of Emma, Granpap changed the form of his revenge. He loaded a gun with small shot and when the occasion rose, as it did while Tate was climbing a trail to the big still on the mountains, Granpap, hidden behind some bushes, filled Tate's backside with shot.

He could still enjoy a secretive chuckle when he thought of that time. For Tate had been obliged to lie in bed face down on his fat belly. And when he got up, for many days he was forced to stand at the table to eat. And while others were sitting comfortably in chairs by the fire, he whose comfort had always come first must stand up and nurse his sore backside.

3

By November the new room was finished. Frank McClure and Jim Martin came over to help with splitting the logs and laying them. There was a passageway between the two rooms with a split-log flooring. Inside the small place were two beds in opposite corners. Emma's bed in the other room had a head board and foot. It had belonged to the Kirklands. These were built in. Granpap had nailed two posts to the floor the right distance from the wall and enclosed them with split logs on three sides. Underneath small saplings nailed close together made the bottoms.

"If the dogs don't get too many fleas in them, you'll sleep sound," Emma said to Granpap. They were looking at the beds, and watching while John and Bonnie brought in dried grass for mattresses. The boys had gone to Swain's for cotton to fill the new quilts.

John leaned against the bed nearest the door and spat on the floor. He was close to being a man.

"Bring in some more straw," Granpap said to him. "Hit's got to be high as your belly and higher."

"I wish," he told Emma, "we could have a window in the other room with glass."

John, just going out the door, stopped to listen.

"Pap," Emma said sharply. She had seen that wishing look in Granpap's face before and when he had too much to drink there was no telling what he might do. "We've got doors," she said.

"There was one in a book at Swain's," Granpap went on. "Hit costs s' little."

Emma caught her breath. Granpap could not understand how they needed money for food. A man did not watch the meal get lower in the bag and wonder where money for the next lot would come. He didn't see the slab of fatback get smaller until there was just a greasy end left for boiling with cabbage. And then no more.

"Four panes of glass," Granpap said.

"Pap, you ain't done it!"

"No," Granpap said. "I ain't. But I wanted to."

It made him angry that he wanted to and could not. He had to think of Emma just when he was about to order the window from Swain.

"Ain't ye gone yet?" he rasped at John. "Go get your hay. Look at Bonnie. There's a woman for ye."

Bonnie was in the door with both hands stretched over a heap of grass in her skirt. She looked as if she was holding in a big belly that was about to burst.

"Put it down," Emma said to Bonnie, "and come help me with the quilts."

"Windows!" Emma said to Bonnie when they were settled in the other room. "Windows, when we've spent most of the change for cotton and backing for the quilts. And we need a cow and a steer."

She held up a quilt top with a Bear Paw design made of pieces kept carefully for years in the trunk, and looked at one corner.

"Your stitches," she said to Bonnie, "are like chicken tracks. I'm most ashamed to let Ora and Jennie see them."

The boys had carried word to Ora and Jennie that Emma would be glad to have them next day for quilting.

"You're both boy-girls." Emma folded the quilt top and took out the Lone Star she had made the winter before John was born and never got the cotton nor backing for. "Always wanting to run around like boys instead of helping your Mas."

"Is Ora's Sally coming over?" Bonnie asked.

"No," Emma said shortly. "Sally's got to stay home."

"To work for her Ma," Bonnie added. She looked at Emma and Emma looked at her.

"Some day you'll get too big for your breeches," Emma said. "Thinking you're smarter than your Ma. Take that end and stand away from me and be quiet."

The next day Ora McClure came and Jennie Martin walked from Possum Hollow. The McClures had in a way of speaking swapped forces, for Granpap and the boys were over helping Frank put up a new shed. John was left at home. It was not often that Granpap and the boys included him in their excursions, for they still felt that he belonged with the women. He stood by the fire while the women sat at the hickory frame set up in the middle of the room out of the way of cold air blowing between the doors, but close enough for light. On the fire a pot of cabbage boiled, and John had put a jug of cider that Jennie brought down in the spring.

Bonnie pressed up against the frame to watch. When it was time she handed the thread. Emma sat at the head, high above the frame, but not so high as Ora, for Ora was a tall rawboned woman. Her face was rectangular and the features were big, as if they had been carved out of a rock on the side of a mountain. With a face like that she should have been enough to frighten anyone. But there was a kindness in her big mouth and when she was not talking her whole face showed a Rock of Ages, cleft for me, let me hide myself in thee feeling. She had great hands that surprised because they were so skillful with the needle. Jennie Martin looked so small beside the two others. Her tiny pinched face did not come far above the frame and she had to get out of the chair when the stitches took her across to the center of the quilt.

"When we were young ones," Emma said with her head bent over the frame, "they had regular parties for quilting."

"Yes." Ora snapped a piece of thread between her teeth. "We lived close together there. Hit was a big settlement."

"But never any dancing, like here," Emma said. "We had quiltings and maybe played Weavily Wheat or some other game, but no dancing. They thought Pap was a sinner for playing dance tunes."

They were really talking to Jennie Martin. She and Jim had recently moved to Possum Hollow from over North Range. Jim was kin of the McClures.

"Everybody," Ora said, "took to religion like boys take after a gal."

"But the religion didn't keep them from drinking," Emma added. "Boys and men, they drank same as here."

"Recollect that still above the church?"

"Near the haunted thicket. I reckon I do."

"The men used to go up and come back refreshed as with the water of life," Ora chuckled.

"And sometimes they would tell about the ghost."

"I saw it once," Ora said.

Jennie Martin looked up. "Was hit real?"

John sat down and leaned against the chimney. The women bent over the frame. It was late fall and the sun got down behind the west mountains early. There were already dark corners in the room where the light from the doors and the fire did not reach. Bonnie, feeling lonesome, went over and sat near John by the fire.

"I saw something," Ora said. "Something white way back in the laurel thicket. And hit moved."

"Tell about it," Emma urged.

"Late one evening," Ora said, talking mostly to Jennie, "Frank McClure and Jim McClure dared Emma and me to go up and see the ghost. It was just before church one evening. And we went."

Emma interrupted. "But when we got just below I was too scared to go any further."

Ora went right on. "The still was above the thicket in a little cove. The thicket was alongside a trail high up on the mountain. Hit was a dark thicket. The leaves were high on top and under were black limbs. Up above, the leaves rustled in the wind, but under where the dark limbs were hit was all quiet like church at night when the preacher is about to make a prayer.

"We got there and stood just outside the thicket with me standing between the two boys shivering and hoping I wouldn't see what I had come to see. And while we watched something white rose up and moved around between the black limbs of laurel, something long and white."

Jennie Martin looked over her shoulder into the dark corner of the room. "Oh," she gasped.

"There's a lot of shadows in thickets," Emma said.

"I may be wrong," Ora was not one to press too far. "I said so then, and I'll say it now. But I wouldn't go there by myself. It was a Tate still," she explained to Jennie, "and old man Tate was killed up there by the Law. People said hit was his ghost."

"Do you believe the dead come back?" Jennie asked.

Ora answered, "I've heard of visitations."

"I've got a husband and three young ones in the burying ground," Emma said. "And they've never come back."

"Sometimes they have to walk where they're laid," Ora told her.

"I declare," Jennie sighed. "I'm glad Jim's a-coming for me to-night. I'd be plumb scared to go home by myself."

"Well," Emma wanted to comfort Jennie. "I've never seen anything. Hit may be that ghosts walk. But maybe they don't. Maybe what Ora saw was a shadow, or one of Tate's sheep."

"How's Granma Wesley?" Ora asked Jennie.

"She's still in the bed with her rheumatic fever," Jennie answered. The Wesleys were her near neighbors in Possum Hollow. "She says hit's a sure sign of a hard winter, her getting the fever so soon."

"She'll never live to finish that coverlet," Ora said.

Over at the Wesleys, under a shed joined to the cabin, there was a frame for weaving. The treadles were worn, for the frame had belonged to the first Wesleys who had settled in the mountains no one knew how many years before. In the cabin by the fireplace was a spinning wheel. Granma Wesley owned two sheep and she planned to finish a coverlet from their wool before she died. Each year she sheared the animals herself, combed the wool and spun it into thread for the loom. In the summer on a clear day anyone passing through Possum Hollow near enough to the cabin could hear the loom. Everyone knew about Granma Wesley's sheep and her great wish to finish the coverlet before she died.

"Pore old woman," Emma said. "I hope she'll finish. She'll never rest quiet in her grave unless she does."

"Every year she gets the fever sooner than the year before," Ora said. "Hit looks bad."

Jennie went back to something she had said before. "She says hit's a sign of a hard winter—that she's laid up so early."

"We've had mighty light weather so far," Ora said. "But maybe she's right. You never can tell what the Lord will send."

4

GRANMA WESLEY's prophecy came true. That winter was the worst in years. And the cold was harder to bear because the fall had been so balmy and spring-like. Heavy snows kept the ground covered. Food became scarce. To make matters worse, the Swains came down on credit at the store. Hal would possibly have helped his neighbors, but Sally, his wife, would not allow it. She said they could not support the whole community. If they gave credit, the money would never be paid back. What she said was true. Yet there was a hushed up resentment felt at her and at Hal. Everyone knew they and their children had enough, while others were close to starvation.

For some time the McClures had potatoes, and as long as the shot lasted there was an occasional rabbit. Then the shot gave out, and one day Emma had to tell the others that the last potato had been eaten. It had been hard for her to believe this. She had got down into the trench and felt in every corner, hoping she might find some small ones hidden in the straw. There was not a single potato left.

Now there was only one hope for food. Granpap and the boys dragged themselves out of the cabin each day and waded through the snow looking for rabbit tracks. There was no ammunition for the guns, and the dogs were too weak from hunger to be of any use. One day they did track a rabbit. Kirk went ahead of the others. He had a piece of knotted pine wood in his hand. Kirk was swifter than Granpap and Basil though they tried to keep up. When they had their usual strength either Kirk or Basil could have run a rabbit down in the snow and killed it with a stick. But it was different now. Kirk felt ashamed and angry that he could not outrun the little animal that was handicapped by the deep snow into which its hind legs sunk each time it leaped. The little cotton tail flying up and down before him seemed to mock at his weakness. Too exhausted to follow any further he flung the stick after the little animal. The stick fell far away from the rabbit, and with a final leap the animal disappeared in the woods. Kirk stood in the snow and called out every vile name he knew after the rabbit. And when he turned around and saw Granpap and Basil behind him watching, he cursed them. Granpap took up a double handful of snow and threw it deliberately into Kirk's face. In an instant Kirk was on the old man like a wildcat and they wallowed together in the snow. It did not take long for this sudden spurt of nervous energy to wear itself out. When Basil had got them apart they lay in the snow side by side without moving. Only they breathed with heavy nervous breaths, like sobs.

They walked back to the cabin slowly. It was an effort for Granpap and Kirk to lift their feet. Basil, who had a little energy left, walked ahead. Kirk was glad for him to be the first to show Emma and the children their empty hands. For the past few days he had wanted never to return to the cabin, because there he must see Emma's eyes dart to his hands.

At the cabin Emma watched the young ones grow thinner. She saw John's brows knit as they had done since he was a baby when he was in pain. For the first time John knew what it meant to have pains in his belly because it was empty. He had been hungry before for a day perhaps, but Granpap had always managed to provide something. Now his belly had been empty for three days. The pains were grasshoppers jumping from one blade of grass to another. They hopped from one place to another in his belly and each time they lit a sharp pain struck him. Bonnie felt the pains. She sat in a corner with her arms pressed tightly over her belly. She was trying to hold the grasshoppers from jumping. Emma watched them. There was nothing for her to do but watch. Her eyes were bright like small kerosene lamps with reflectors behind them. And the lamps gleamed out at the children and at Granpap and the boys when they came from the woods. She was ready and waiting to get up and cook whatever they brought in. But they brought nothing.

They could not go to Ora's for help, for the other McClures were cleaned out and there they had more mouths to feed. During this time neighbors kept away from neighbors as if they were afraid or ashamed to show each other their misery.

Only in Possum Hollow there was food for a little while. For Sam Wesley killed Granma Wesley's precious sheep. They were old and tough, but the meat, boiled for a day in the wash pot, saved the family. The Martins got a share, and other neighbors who were closer than the McClures, who were divided from the people around Swain's Crossing by the snow-covered summit of Thunderhead. Granma Wesley, lying in bed, knew nothing of the slaughter of the sheep. If she lasted out the winter Sam would tell her when it was necessary. They fed her soup from the meat, and Sam told Jim Martin he had lied until his God could never forgive him about the source of the juice Granma had swallowed.

One morning Emma opened the door and found instead of the dark made by clouds the bright light of the sun. Her weak eyes closed to shut out the glare of the sun on snow, and she went inside the cabin. It was good to have the sun, but at present she was not able to bear the sudden change. By nightfall much of the snow had melted. And it seemed that the sun brought good luck. For the next morning Frank McClure walked over in the slush to pass word that Swain was giving credit. One slab of fatback, a half sack of meal, and a round of shot to every family.

The question was, who would go for the food. Frank McClure was already exhausted with his four-mile walk across the mountains. He brought good news. Yet those who received it sat without a word at first. They sat as they had been sitting for the past two days, listlessly around the fire, except when one of them had dragged out for wood.

"Well," Emma said at last. "It looks as if we can't meet our good fortune."

"Hit's late coming," Granpap told her.

Kirk got up slowly. He took his old felt hat down from the wall and buttoned his shirt at the neck. They watched him go. They were still listless. The hope had not got into them, really.

Later Frank recovered a little and got up to go. Granpap and Basil went with him. They met Kirk just on the other side of Thunderhead. He had stopped on the trail, and was very sick from some crackers he had eaten at the store. Beside him was the food for the two families. And inside the meal sacks were two big soupbones. Swain had slaughtered a steer. There was very little meat on the bones, but at least the marrow would make enough flavor for soup. Frank left them at the fork of his trail and walked down carrying his part of the raw food.

Hearing that Kirk had been sick from the crackers, Emma

made them all wait for soup. Her eyes glistened as she looked at the food. Before they had shone with a cold hard spark. Now they glistened warmly. She looked at the children warmly. For the last two days she had almost hated them, because she could do nothing to help them in their misery.

Long before all the power had been cooked from the bone she served the soup. She was forced to do this. For as soon as the soup began to send out an odor of cooked meat the faces in the cabin drew closer to the pot and hung over it. She was dizzy with hunger, and she saw the faces in a sort of daze as they moved closer to the pot. When the last drop of soup had been gulped down, Granpap took the bone from the pot. He laid it on the table and taking his ax from the corner tried to crush the bone. He was too weak to raise the ax very high, and it bounded off. The slippery bone fell to the floor. Everyone was watching Granpap. Their hunger was still very strong. And the dogs were watching. They pounced on the bone and would have taken it, but Kirk and Basil kicked them off. Granpap motioned the two boys away and raised his ax over the bone that lay on the floor. This time he smashed the bone in pieces, and there was enough for all of them. For some time after there was the sound of people sucking at bones, and when they were finished the dogs took what was left. They crunched with their sharper teeth and in their turn sucked at the edges.

Emma cooked the fatback and made corn pones. Then Granpap and the boys were strong enough to use the shot Kirk had brought from Swain's. As long as that lasted they would have meat.

5

THE dogs, lean from the winter, dug into mole hills and ate scraps from the rabbits, so they grew a shade less scrawny. Plott, Granpap's bitch, was big with puppies. One day before light she woke them up with her howling and before John and Bonnie could reach her four puppies were born. Three were dead. The fourth John and Bonnie took for their own. They named it Georgy after the place outside where Granpap had fought when he was a boy.

John and Bonnie nursed the little furry pup as they sat around the fire at night. Though the spring was balmy as the fall had been, the nights were still frosty. Now they were all able to look back on the hard days and talk about them. The cold winter reminded Granpap and Emma of the great blizzard. John envied Kirk and Basil, for they remembered seeing the frozen cattle. The night of that storm some twenty frightened cattle, blinded by the snow, rushed across Swain's meadow until the rocky cliff of Barren She Mountain stopped them.

Jim Hawkins, who lived on the meadow side of Laurel Creek, had left Swain's store just in time, for as he reached his cabin the terrible blizzard began. He heard the animals scream. Two days later when people could travel through the snow, word went around that there was a sight to be seen in Swain's meadow. Granpap and the boys went with Frank McClure. They saw the frozen animals piled up against the cliff, like a monument carved out of the rock. Below was a mass of twisted legs, curved backs and upturned bellies frozen stiff together. On this mass were two yearlings. One of them had bitten into the neck of its brother. The bitten head leaned against the rock cliff, and its frozen eyes stared wide open at a laurel bush growing out of a crack in the rock just above. The mouth of the yearling, Granpap said, was wide open and the teeth showed. It seemed to be laughing at the others below.

The carefree days and evenings did not last very long. The

shot gave out and about the same time Emma reached the bottom of the meal bag. There were other things needed at this time —seed and a steer for plowing. Granpap appealed to Swain. What he got was two pounds of meal—a back-door gift—but no credit. Granpap took the meal gratefully, but halfway back to the cabin he began to get angry at himself and at Swain. He was willing to pay debts. Hal knew he would pay what he owed. There and then he made up his mind that he would get some money and pay Hal for the little two pounds of meal, the back-door gift.

He carried the meal to Emma, and without waiting for a taste of corn pone, started away again. Emma wanted to know where he was going. Granpap did not answer. It was not necessary for Emma to know he was going to the McEacherns.

He was away three days. It took him this long to drive a load of wood far down the mountains to the outside. Under the wood there were some jugs and he carried them to a certain place, the back door of a cheap restaurant in Leesville. There he unloaded the wagon after dark and received some money, of which Bud and Sam gave him a small part. He took what the McEacherns offered to give, and it was not much. They were true to the promise they had made before, and added a bottle of drink to the money.

The old man stopped by Swain's and bought the necessary supplies. There were shot in his jeans and he could feel their weight. It made him proud and confident to have the shot there, though some of his pride and confidence came from the drink out of Sam's bottle. When Granpap left the store a steer hired from Swain plodded along behind him. Along the way he found it necessary to drink often. By the time he reached the cabin the bottle was empty. No one was waiting in front of the cabin. Granpap left the steer hitched outside and lifted the supplies into the room. Emma came in the back door and watched the old man trying to place them on the table.

"So ye're back," she said. Granpap let the bundles slide to the floor. He looked around for the others. It was important for them all to know what he had done.

"They are over to Ora's," Emma said, answering his look.

"I made money, Emma," Granpap said. "And I paid Hal Swain for his back-door meal. And I bought more and have got money left." He took five nickels from his pocket and shook them in his hand. They clinked together and made a sound of big money. It sounded as if there was a fortune done up in his big fist. He walked unsteadily to the fireplace and held the money over the gourd. He tried to make the gesture big and strong, but it ended up wavering and uncertain. The coins he dropped from his hand fell to the floor and rolled away. They struck the floor with flat sounds as if they were of no account.

"Sit down, Pap. Do sit down," Emma said.

"Ain't ye glad, Emma?"

"Yes, I'm glad. I'm proud we've got so much." Emma looked up from the floor where she was searching for the lost pieces of change. "Yes, I'm glad," she repeated. "But I wish you would sit down."

Granpap walked to Emma and stood above her. He balanced backward and forward on his toes first, and then on his heels. She thought for a moment that he was going to fall on her, and drew back, sitting on her heels.

"Hal Swain didn't want to take the money for the meal," Granpap said. "He said no, and just then Sally came in, and I said, 'Sally, here's some money I owe you,' and she took it. So he's paid. Even to the uttermost farthing," Granpap roared out as the preacher sometimes did in church.

Emma left her search for the precious money. She took Granpap's arm and led him resolutely to the bed. In a few moments he was asleep, and she was able to find the fifth nickel that had rolled under the water bucket where it stood over a crack.

The next afternoon Granpap was out with Basil plowing up the ground. Emma had Bonnie and John in front of the cabin, helping to plant gourd seed. Granpap had slept off his drinks. He walked with plenty of assurance as he came around the cabin with Basil. It was almost time for supper.

"Kirk back yet?" Granpap asked. No one answered. It was clear that Kirk was not there. He had walked to the blacksmith's to get a metal ring put on a whittled sapling end for a bull tongue to be used in planting.

"Sure enough, then," Granpap said, and he looked slyly at Emma. "He's gone to get a look at Minnie."

"Maybe," Emma said. And suddenly she left the gourd place and spoke sharply to Bonnie. "Now, Bonnie, you come on in. It's about time we made supper."

As Granpap expected, Kirk came back by the short trail. Along with the bull tongue he brought three horseshoes and an iron rod beaten into a point at one end.

"Did ye see Minnie?" Granpap asked Kirk. John was sitting on the log step of the cabin. He saw that in answer to Granpap's baiting Kirk only brought the ax down harder on the iron stob he was knocking into the hard ground.

Basil spoke up. "Did ye see Minnie?" he asked Kirk.

"If I did it's none of your worry," Kirk grunted.

"If you did it was on the sly," Basil said. Which was probably true. Even John knew that Minnie Hawkins' pap kept all the boys off his sixteen-year-old daughter. He would not let them come within rocking distance of the cabin.

"You're a liar," Kirk said. John saw Kirk's fists clench and the anger in his brother's voice made the blood run up in his head. It made him want to get up and fight.

Kirk edged up to Basil. Both the boys had their fists ready. They swayed toward each other like two saplings in a high wind.

"Kirk," Granpap said. At the sound in Granpap's voice Kirk turned as if a wildcat had jumped on him from behind.

Granpap was looking toward Thunderhead. Below the high mountain on the second hill a man's figure stumped down the open trail. Very quietly Granpap sat down on the woodblock and the boys leaned against the cabin. There was a stillness, a quick hush. Even the mountains seemed to be holding back. The dogs lay on the ground inert in the late afternoon sunshine. They had not yet scented the stranger.

John was still like the others; and like them his muscles were tense. He knew, as they knew, this was no kin or person known coming down to them. Yet Granpap on his woodblock and the boys leaning against the cabin looked quiet and gentle, as if the stranger from the trail had sent down a spell that put them all to sleep.

The man disappeared behind a hill. As he came over the last rise and down the last slope the low sun shone on him slantwise from the west and made him black against the tree trunks and the hillside. There was no face to be seen, only on the back a large burden that made the legs stump down slowly and carefully along the trail.

The dogs ran ahead and met the stranger at the spring. Their barking broke the spell. Granpap moved.

"Call the dogs, Kirk," he said. And Kirk went forward. Before he reached the spring, the stranger had let the pack slide from his back. He held it in front of him on the ground. Looking up through the hair that dangled in front of his eyes, John saw that the man was afraid of the dogs. And he smiled in himself. Then he looked again straight at the man. For there was something unusual about him, something astonishing. His shoulders had grown all awry. They were not the naturally bowed shoulders of people like Granpap and Emma who have leaned over a plow and hoe or a fireplace all their lives. There was a hump on the left side, like another head covered over with the shirt.

"It's Small Hardy, a peddler," Kirk said, coming back with the dogs in front and the stranger not far behind.

Small Hardy set his pack on the ground and said Howdy to Granpap.

"Sit ye down," Granpap told him and the man sat on the ground.

There was a silence.

"Come from far?" Granpap asked.

"From the towns," Hardy said. He wiped his face with a red handkerchief. When he took off his soft hat a wide forehead showed with hair growing far back. The head looked like a hill, bald on one side with trees growing halfway down on the other.

"Going far?" Granpap asked.

"I'm aiming for Georgy," the hump-back said. "They tell me you know the best trails."

Granpap looked at the peddler suspiciously. The little man looked back. He seemed to be holding in words, as if he liked to talk, but held back because of the company he was in.

"You want steep trails or easy ones?" Granpap asked and he watched Hardy.

"Give me the easy ones," Hardy said. Granpap seemed to be satisfied.

"Stay the night," he told the peddler.

"If it won't put you out," Small Hardy said.

"Emma," Granpap called. Emma and Bonnie were already standing in the door. Emma answered.

"The stranger's staying," Granpap said.

"He's welcome," Emma spoke up, "to what we have."

John wished to feel the pack on the ground by Small Hardy. It had the most curious shapes. And Small Hardy with the hump and his bulging pockets was like another pack himself, full of mysterious and unknown things. John edged closer to them. Perhaps he could reach out and touch.

Just then Georgy, the puppy he and Bonnie loved, came trotting into the front yard.

"Yours?" Hardy turned around and asked John. The question was so unexpected John drew back from the little man, who was only trying to make himself pleasant.

"Yes," John said, looking at Hardy from under his lids.

"Want to sell?"

"Sell?"

"I could use the skin," Hardy said, smiling.

Without answering John picked up the puppy and carried him into the house. He hated the little man, who showed up evil wanting to skin his dog. Yet John was still curious about the packs and hung around the door watching. But he held the dog in his arms. Presently the men came in from the yard and gathered around the fire.

When supper was over Emma cleared away the dishes. Granpap and the stranger sat in chairs near the fire, the others on the floor. Emma, who had waited as usual, sat at the table having her own supper.

"Got something in the pack?" Granpap asked.

Small Hardy had been waiting for this. He pushed back his chair and pulled the pack along the floor. Emma, seeing what was going on, left her corn bread and lit the lamp. There was a little oil left in the bottom.

The hump-back drew his pack to the place where the dim light shone on the floor. He leaned over untying various strings and as he leaned his hump stood up from his back like a mountain peak from a ridge. Emma stooped over him. The others stayed back in the shadows. Only John edged closer along the floor, always keeping the pack between him and the man who had wanted to skin Georgy. Bonnie, the sleepy head, was dozing in a corner by the fire.

There was some red calico in the pack. It was a different pattern from that at Swain's. Small Hardy held a red silk waist with glass buttons against his chest to show its beauty. It looked queer against his small face, but in his enthusiasm for the goods he seemed to forget himself. From different pockets of the pack he took many things—a Bible, some cotton thread; gold-eyed needles, and pins with colored tops. With a great flourish he showed them a fine looking knitted thing, a fascinator, he called it.

"This is what you should wear," he said to Emma.

It was bright red, with a border knitted from silver thread. The silver shimmered in the light as Small Hardy let the scarf trail over his hands. Suddenly he gathered it into a ball with his long fingers, and held it between his two palms.

"Oh," Emma said. She thought he had ruined the pretty thing. But when he let go it sprang from his hands as if it was alive and fell over them again in soft folds.

"How pretty," Emma said, and bent her neck over it.

"Fine ladies wear them like this," Small Hardy told her. He reached up and put the fascinator over Emma's hair, crossed the end pieces under her chin and let them fall across her shoulders, down her back. He dug in one of his pockets, brought out a mirror, and held it up close to the lamp so Emma could see. She looked so fine with some of her brown curls coming out in front against her face. Kirk and Basil stared at her, and she felt their eyes were admiring. Her face became softer, and her lips curved up at the corners. Her eyes turned toward the money gourd on the shelf.

"It's sure pretty," she said to Small Hardy. But she did not ask how much. She lifted the red, soft thing from her head and folded it up, letting it rest at each fold in her two hands.

"It's sure pretty," she said again and gave it back to Hardy.

He laid it away carefully and brought from the same pocket two strings of beads, red, one longer than the other. Emma held them up to the light. They hung from her fingers. The light pierced into them and came away in little red rays.

"Are they jewels?" Emma asked, her voice soft with admiring them. She had heard Sally Swain talk about the jewels rich women on the outside wore.

"No," Small Hardy said. "If they were real they'd be worth more than a hundred dollars."

"I've heard," Granpap spoke out of the dark, "they find real stones somewhere up in the hills. I remember there was gold down in Georgy, mixed right in the sand."

"I did see some real stones in Leesville. They'd found them somewhere in the mountains. Sapphires large as the end of your finger. If you found one of them you would have something to live on."

"It would be nice," Emma said. "Just to go out, pick up a stone like you'd pick up a mouth rock and be rich."

"Well," Small Hardy sat back on his haunches. "They say poor folks are going to get rich now."

He let them taste this news. Bonnie, trying to get to bed, stumbled over Plott, who gave a sleepy grunt. All the others were looking at Small Hardy. Even the eyes back in the shadows, Kirk's eyes and Basil's, were looking at him. Only Bonnie, done up with sleep, lay on the bed.

"Down in Leesville," Hardy went on, "a Mr. Wentworth, a rich man, has a mill for making cloth like this." He pointed to the calico. "And they say whoever goes down to work there is going to be rich like him—for he started out as poor as the next one. They say out there the rivers flow with milk and honey and money grows on trees."

"Do," Emma said. "And have you seen?"

"Well," Small Hardy put his head on one side considering. His big head leaned against the hump and he moved his right shoulder that sloped so far down as if he was not quite comfortable. His bright black eyes looked up at Emma. "You see, I haven't been there much. But they said I was to spread the news. It's the poor folks' time if they'll pick up and go."

"It's a long way," Emma said.

"Forty miles from here as the crow flies," Small Hardy told her.

"There's a store," he went on. "Where they sell beads and other things cheap. And you get a house with windows and cook on a real stove,—no more bending over a chimney."

"I'll lay the house ain't your own," Granpap said. "Nor the land."

Small Hardy had been talking to Emma. He shrank back when Granpap's voice came out of the shadows. "Maybe so," he said when he recovered. "But the money's yours. Real money. Lots of it."

"I like to have my own land," Granpap answered. He got up to knock the ashes from his pipe. He stood there, and Hardy knew the evening was finished. He returned the goods to their pockets, folded the pack, and set it in the corner by the chimney. Emma held the light for them to cross the passageway, then blew it out. John, who would sleep with her that night, sat on the floor trying to keep his eyes open.

"They was pretty things," Emma whispered. She sighed. "Come on, John. Get to sleep," she said and leaned over the bed to shake Bonnie and turn down the covers.

6

THE next morning, after all Emma's holding back, before Small Hardy left she bought a piece of red calico for Bonnie. As a result on Sunday, the first Sunday of the year when they had meeting, there was no change for collection. Emma could shake the money gourd all she wanted, pretending that she had expected to find something. The gourd was empty.

"The preacher'll have to do with our company," she said half to herself, half to Bonnie and John who were waiting to start out.

John was very impatient. Granpap and the boys had gone long ago. They would be halfway to church. Emma still wanted to treat him as a baby and make him go with her. And the worst of it was the boys would not have him. He looked at Bonnie and saw her pulling at the narrow skirt of her new dress, trying to make it full and handsome.

"Look at Bonnie a-strutting," he said.

"Let her strut," Emma scolded. "She's a need to with her first new dress."

"Some day," she told John, "you'll have new jeans, not patched ones that come from the boys."

She pulled her knitted black shawl over her head and followed the children up the trail. Bonnie ran on, stepping proudly along the path in her bare feet. The red calico dress with its long tight little waist and narrow gathered skirt looked nice and new.

They walked single file along the trail. Over one hill and down another side—over another higher one and along the ridge leading to Thunderhead. They could see Frank McClure's place down in the valley. Not a sound there. It was a good three miles away from that point but sound travels a long distance on a clear day. They knew the McClures had gone.

Close to Thunderhead they got into the shade of the early spring leaves. The trail sloped up to the divide over Thunderhead. On the other side of the mountain the narrow sledge road took them zigzag across the steep face of the mountain. All that side of Thunderhead was quilted zigzag by the trail and at the bottom the trail went down between the sides of other mountains like a loose thread a woman has left hanging off the side of a quilt.

All the way down the shut-in they walked by a stream that grew wider toward the bottom. Emma took off her shoes and waded over the stream when the trail crossed, but the children splashed through. Bonnie held her dress so high to protect it from the water, Emma had to call out and make her let it down, for there was nothing underneath. Just below the Martins' house they crossed the footway, across the branch, and after that it was only a little distance to the road.

The church, a small log building, was up a short trail at the left. Across the road, on a slope, was the burying ground. Emma's husband and the three children who had come between Kirk and Bonnie were laid away there. There were no flowers in the burying ground. The graves lay flat and plain on the slope. The dead were dead and there was enough to do caring for the living. There was not a woman around that country who did not have one child or more in the ground. When a woman was ripe she gave birth, and if the child died, it did not help much, after the first days of sorrow, to weep. What was done was done.

Sunday School did not last very long. When it was over the women stayed on the benches inside and talked. Bonnie hung around Minnie Hawkins and Sally McClure and some of the older girls. They were near the window and outside stood Kirk and Basil and Jesse McDonald. The boys pretended that they were interested in talk, but the girls knew well enough why they were there.

Bonnie moved up close to Minnie, who was talking to the others in a low voice so the women wouldn't hear. Ora was eying the girls. She was not sure she wanted her Sally talking so intimately with Minnie Hawkins, though she had nothing against Minnie, not anything she could show. Minnie had a beautiful white complexion. Her blue eyes and black hair made her the prettiest girl around the valley. She was plump where the others were rather skinny. Boys and men eyed her whenever she came into any gathering. And this perhaps was the reason the women did not trust her very much. Then they remembered her mother.

But the very fact that the boys and men were interested in Minnie made her more interesting to the younger girls. Ora's Sally would have followed her anywhere.

Minnie felt Bonnie's face nosing at her shoulder. She lifted her hand, laid it on Bonnie's cheek, and not ungently pushed her away.

"This talk ain't for young ones," she said. The other girls laughed. Even Sally, who was Bonnie's own kin, laughed. The little girl went back to Emma feeling left out and disgraced.

The men stood outside in the cleared place in front of the church. John had slipped away from Emma and hung behind Granpap away from the boys, though they probably would not have noticed him since they had plenty to hold their attention. There was a song they had sung after the preacher in church that said:

"I am so glad that Jesus loves me,
Jesus loves me, Jesus loves me,
I am so glad that Jesus loves me,
Jesus loves even me."

It was an easy song to remember and half under his breath but loud enough for the girls to hear, Kirk with his hat pushed on one side, perky and insolent, sang softly into the window, which had no panes, but was an opening for light to come in:

"I am so glad that Minnie loves me,
Minnie loves me, Minnie loves me,
I am so glad that Minnie loves me,
Minnie loves even me."

Halfway through, Jesse McDonald joined in, singing low like Kirk. Even Basil joined in on the last line. But he kept one eye on Jim Hawkins, who was standing around in front with the other men.

John was giving most of his attention to the boys and he hadn't heard the men talking. Just then Granpap, who was sitting on a log behind John, spoke out so loud even the boys hushed and listened.

"David danced before the Lord," Granpap said.

The preacher hadn't yet come for midday meeting. Hal Swain, because he could read, carried on Sunday School.

"I'm not saying it's wrong—nor right," Hal Swain shook his

head. "But the preacher'll be telling us it's wrong before the day's out."

"Like he told us last year and the year before that," Granpap added.

"And next winter, if it's a good winter, we'll be at it same as ever." Fraser McDonald spoke up from the steps where he was whittling a green Judas tree stick.

"If I thought it was wrong," Jim Martin, who was twice as tall as his little wife, Jennie, boomed down from where he was standing by the church, "I'd quit. But I haven't ever seen the wrong. We danced in my cabin last week, and I'm not afraid to say so. My God is a just God and he won't punish me or my young ones for sashayin' around some to the music of Granpap's fiddle and Sam Wesley's banjo."

"To my mind," Jim Hawkins spoke very carefully, "hit's plumb wrong and lascivious. My gal's going to stay home with her daddy till her man comes along and takes her in marriage. If she can't get a man without sashaying around for it, then unmarried she stays."

There was a silence after Jim Hawkins had spoken. Each man was digging down into himself, holding himself back. Jim Hawkins looked at them defiantly. He knew what was in their minds about his wife. He had found her in the back shed with a fellow who lived under South Range and he had turned the woman out and done nothing to the man. Only he kept Minnie at home, never leaving her at night except for Saturday evenings when he went to the store. And his neighbors went down in their minds remembering all this. But they kept silent.

Granpap broke up the silence. "David danced before the Lord," he repeated. "And I ain't ashamed to play before the Lord. He can look and see there's no sin in my heart."

"Yes," Fraser McDonald insisted. "Hit's what's in your heart that counts. Some of the round dances I've heard tell of are wrong. That's what you might call lascivious, Jim Hawkins, a-hugging up a woman for a whole dance. But young ones or old ones a prancing around doing a Ladies' Chain or Do Si Do can't be harm."

"There's the preacher," Hal Swain said. Preacher Warren hitched his horse to a tree down the slope. He reached in his saddle bags, got out what he wanted, and came along to the door of the church. The men followed him in silently. They sat on the homemade benches on one side and the women and children on the other. Up front there was a table with a pitcher of water and a glass that Sally Swain had brought from the store. Sally took up almost the whole of the front bench, for she weighed over two hundred pounds. Behind the pitcher the preacher laid the big Bible he carried around with him in the saddle bag.

He was a small man from one of the settlements near a church school on the other side of North Range. During May he would come every Sunday and after that only once a month until summer was over. Standing behind the table, he gave out the words of the hymn. For such a little man he had a strong voice and led the singing. First he cleared his throat and hummed down in it to get the key.

"We'll sing to-day, 'Come ye sinners,'" he said and cleared his throat again. Line after line they sang with him.

"Come, ye sinners poor and needy,
Weak and wounded, sick and sore,
Jesus ready stands to save you
Full of pity, love and power.

"Now, ye needy—come, and welcome.
God's free bounty glorify,
True belief and true repentance,
Every grace that brings you nigh.

"Come ye weary, heavy laden,
Bruised and mangled by the fall.
If you tarry till you're better
You will never come at all."

Bonnie, who was good at remembering words, did not need the preacher to lay the lines out for her. She could have sung right on, having learned this one the summer before. She had a good voice. John, sitting on the other side of Emma, heard her letting it out. She lifted up her nose and sang right through it. The prayer was a long one, and John was very tired before it was over. He tried to get Bonnie's attention, but Bonnie held her eyes straight in front. She liked to listen to the sing-song of the words. John was simply not interested in them. There was another song and then the sermon.

The preacher looked down at the Bible, turned the pages over to a place at the front, cleared his throat and with head bent looked impressively from under his eyebrows. He eyed them all, men, women and children, threateningly. It was what he had seen other preachers do down in the towns. And he thought it the right manner to use with a wayward flock.

The text was, "And Abraham said, 'Here am I, Lord.'" He read from the Bible about Abraham being ready to sacrifice Isaac in the land of Moriah on top of a mountain. "And Abraham said, 'Here am I, Lord,' when the Lord called him. And the Lord said Abraham must take his only son, even the son he loved, and sacrifice him to the Lord. So Abraham rose up early in the morning and cut wood and took some fire and went to the place he could see afar off, the place the Lord had told him. And up on the mountain he bound his son on the wood of an altar and took up a knife to slay him. But just in time the Lord showed Abraham a ram in a thicket so that Abraham could offer up the ram instead of his son. So the Lord blessed Abraham because he was willing to sacrifice his son that he loved."

The preacher closed the book with a snap. "How many of you," he asked, "can say with a clean heart, 'Here am I, Lord'? How many, while you're working in your corn patch or sitting by your fire, or while you're dancing your Chains and Under the Garden Gates can say, 'Here am I, Lord,' and feel that for the Lord you would sacrifice anything or anybody, your son or your dancing or your playing?

"There's one amongst you," he went on—and waited a moment, looking around at them all. "There's one amongst you that calls figures and plays the music. He leads the young ones into sin. He's old, nearing his grave, and ought to know better. Instead of playing for dancing he'd do better making his peace with the Lord."

Suddenly preacher Warren pointed straight at Granpap. "What will you say, John Kirkland?" He called out in a high voice.

Emma gasped. All heads turned and all eyes stared at Granpap. The old man sat up straight and looked neither to the right nor to the left. He sat there like a rock with his blue eyes narrowed. He looked between the slits at the preacher.

"What will you say," the preacher repeated, "when the Lord calls you, John Kirkland, John Kirkland?"

Granpap stood up. "I'll say this" he answered, and John felt the bench under him shake with the sound of Granpap's big voice. "I'll say David danced before the Lord and he played on the cymbal and the lute—and if King David could then John Kirkland can. And that's between him and his Lord. Now," Granpap said, "John Kirkland's not a-going to stay and be rebuked before his brethren."

The preacher's hand fell to his side. Granpap edged his way past Fraser McDonald and Jim Martin into the aisle and walked to the door. What a meaning there was in the sound of his boots on the floor! How they said to the preacher at every step. "You can't dictate to John Kirkland—and you can't disgrace him before his kin and neighbors."

Everyone was looking at the place where Granpap had gone out of the door. Their heads were turned one way—away from the preacher. Then the heads came slowly around and neighbor was looking into neighbor's eyes. Emma was not looking at anyone. She wanted to follow Granpap. Must she get up and go with everyone watching? She clasped her hands together and unclasped them, twisting the shawl in her fingers. Her indecision lasted only a second. Almost as soon as Granpap was out of the door she was on her feet.

"Come on, John," she whispered and taking Bonnie and John by the hands, she led them out of the door.

And a queer thing happened that people talked about long afterward. Kirk McClure got up from the men's side and followed Emma. The preacher trying not to notice began, "We must be willing to sacrifice like Abraham was willing to sacrifice. . . ."

Not waiting to hear the rest, Ora McClure got up. Frank McClure met her in the aisle and they walked to the door. Behind them came their six children, for Ora had the seventh in her arms. Fraser McDonald came next and his wife. Like cattle going down to the stream to drink, all the others went until only Jim Hawkins and Basil and Minnie were left.

Talking about it afterward, Ora and Emma agreed that this could never have happened at their old settlement where few people danced, and where the preacher was better liked. And the resentment did not last long.

The next Sunday all the folks were back again just as if nothing happened. Basil was there, but the rest of Emma's family stayed at home.

7

EMMA would have gone if Granpap had not been obstinate.

"Hit's s' little," she said to him. "Other folks have been rebuked."

Granpap would not listen. "Hit don't take a big seed to hurt a sore tooth," he said. "The preacher hinted at me last year and the year before and I stood it. But last Sunday was the end. I'm not a-going back till they change the preacher. Sam Wesley plays the banjo and because he's not at church he don't get a word. I'm not a-going."

Kirk walked over toward South Ridge with his gun. John and Bonnie, remembering the story from the Bible, played Abraham and the Lord. Near the spring Bonnie sat under an apple tree. John climbed out on a limb above her and made his voice as big as possible. He called out, "Abraham, Abraham." And Bonnie, sitting below, answered, "Here am I, Lord." And the Lord gave Abraham instructions, sometimes being corrected by Abraham who had a better memory.

Then Bonnie would say, "Now, Isaac, we must go up the mountain for a sacrifice. Come along, Isaac, or I'll slap ye over." Isaac was Georgy the puppy, and he was not meek and lowly, but would run away when Abraham tried to pick him up to carry him up the trail. Each time Bonnie came back, and the Lord still resting on the branch called down to her "Abraham, Abraham." And the play began again until they were tired.

And the Lord came down from the tree.

"We ought really to sacrifice something, not play," Bonnie said. Her eyes stretched out wide, and they looked solemn and earnest.

"What?" John asked.

"A young one."

John looked at Bonnie. Women got big with child. But Bonnie was little and slim, seven and a half years old, not yet a woman.

"We haven't got a young one," he said.

"Then somebody we love, like . . . like . . . Georgy." Bonnie's voice was solemn and it became troubled and hesitant when she looked at Georgy and spoke his name. The puppy ran about at their feet in the grass. Simply the fact that he stayed close to them meant that he had confidence in their power to protect him. And they must betray his confidence.

John turned away his head. He could not bear it. He looked at Bonnie. She meant every word she had said.

"We got to sacrifice," she insisted. "To show we love the Lord. Granpap's made the Lord mad. We got to sacrifice."

John would not say yes. He could do the thing but he would not talk about it. He caught Georgy and held him in his arms. Bonnie could see that he was ready to go. She got the knife from the table in the cabin and lit a large piece of lightwood at the chimney.

"What are you young ones up to?" Emma asked her while she was getting the fire.

"Nothing," Bonnie said. She was sunk down in her own life and hardly understood that Emma had spoken.

Outside John looked up toward Thunderhead. "Hit's a long way," he said. He would not have thought it a long way at another time or for another reason, for on the south side the trail to the divide over Thunderhead was not steep or long. With Georgy inside his shirt, John walked ahead of Bonnie up the trail. He carried splinters from the woodpile. Bonnie had the fire and the knife. On the turn of the trail just under Thunderhead Bonnie came up to John.

"Let me feel of him," she said.

The puppy wrinkled its nose at her, and sniffed at her fingers.

"Hit's soft, ain't it?"

John was ready to throw down the wood and run back with Georgy. He looked at his sister. "Hit's s' soft," Bonnie said again. John saw that she had tears coming in her eyes. He straightened up from rubbing his face against Georgy's nose. If Bonnie cried he had to be a man. They together could do no less than Abraham who said, "Here am I" to the Lord. He could hear himself saying "Here am I" on top of Thunderhead, and the Lord would feel that John was a man after his own heart, and the Lord would bless them and all their kin.

At the divide over Thunderhead where the trail crossed they stopped to gather stones and build an altar. They built it up slowly. Just above them at the left was the peak of Thunderhead. Now it was half covered with some clouds. They might have gone up into the clouds but the cleared place at the divide was better for a fire, and it was almost the top. Bonnie could not remember whether the Bible had said Abraham went right to the top of the mountain or to a cleared place. The brush was too thick on the peak for a fire, that was certain. Thunderhead had no bald spot, nor a rocky top as some mountains had.

"There was a ram," Bonnie said when they were nearly through building the altar, "caught in a thicket." She looked for a thicket. No laurel grew close by and the blackberry vines were below in the valley. Perhaps they had come up too far, too far away from the thickets. Yet it had to be on a mountain.

"Maybe the Lord's in that cloud," John said. The clouds had come down over the divide. They had become blacker and made a solemn darkness around the top of Thunderhead. The altar of rocks was already high—high enough. It sloped up. On the top they piled the splinters crossways with some dry leaves underneath.

John kept looking at the clouds. "Do you think," he whispered to Bonnie, "he's forgotten us?" His voice now was frightened and mysterious.

"No," Bonnie said. Her voice was low and mysterious, too, as if she was already in the presence of the Lord. "We needn't hurry too fast. Maybe he can't see us yet."

They had forgotten a cord with which to tie up the sacrifice. John broke one of the strings that held up his jeans. Georgy squirmed in rebellion at having his feet tied together. Finally they had him there. He lay on the wood, helpless. And his eyes reproached them. His nose that sniffed so cheerfully when he was happy was quite still. Bonnie stood on one side of the altar and John sat on a rock beyond it. The knife lay on the ground between them, and by it the heavy red flame at the end of the stick of fat lightwood sent up a jet of sooty smoke toward the sooty clouds. But no voice came from the clouds telling them to look for the ram.

"Maybe," John whispered, "we've got to start before He comes."

Bonnie nodded, but she did not make a move to take up the knife. It lay between them, hatefully waiting for one of them to pick it up and plunge it into Georgy's heart. They could see where the heart was. It was beating in and out in his belly that was turned sideways on the altar.

If the Lord did come He might be just a second late. So much could happen in that second. The knife would be outside, touching the skin of Georgy's belly and with a push of the hand it would be inside. In that second between if the Lord did not come He would be too late. Perhaps they were not favored by the Lord like Abraham. Perhaps the Lord wanted them to sacrifice—to go the whole way. It came over John that if they went on the Lord would surely make them sacrifice. He was a jealous God and they loved Georgy. He was a jealous God.

Suddenly John got up. Bonnie gave a whimpering cry and turned away her head. But John took the puppy in his arms.

"We ain't a-going to do it. We ain't a-going to do it," he cried shrilly. He took the knife from the ground and began cutting the cords from Georgy's feet.

"Look, Bonnie. We ain't a-going to."

"No, we ain't," Bonnie said. "No, we ain't." She spoke angrily and it seemed that she was talking not to John but to the Lord.

As they stood over Georgy watching him make unsteady movements with his feet, the rain that had been threatening began to come down. They hurried down to a great rock that bordered the trail and huddled close to it. The black clouds came lower. They covered the whole top of Thunderhead. Wind came up and blew the trees so the smaller ones bent almost to the side of the mountain, bowing and scraping to each other. Down in the valley where Ora lived the sun was shining, but icy rain and wind covered the mountain top. John and Bonnie hugged close together under the rock with Georgy warm and snug between them. And then the lightning began. It was bad lightning for a spring storm. It came darting along the path like the forked tongue of a giant snake. Just in front of them, down the slope a little way, a tree was struck and with a crash split in half. The thunder rattled and banged against the sides of the mountain. It went away and came back with the lightning to rattle and bang again. At the terrible noise so close, Bonnie pushed her head back against the wall of rock. Her face looked green in the pale dark made by the clouds, and then it was blue in the lightning. John hid his own face from her down against the puppy's warm fur.

And then as suddenly as it had begun the storm left the mountain. The thunder rolled away like a wagon down a rocky road, the sound of it getting fainter each moment.

The two small figures walked down the trail. Their clothes were plastered flat to their bodies, and Bonnie's hair was in wet strings over her face. But her cheeks were rosy now she could reach out and feel Georgy.

"Let me tote him," she said. She held Georgy close up to her wet face. To have lost something, parted from something loved, and then to have it again made her feel something like God. She felt big and powerful as if she could reach out and take the whole mountain in her arms.

8

JOHN dipped the wash pan into the black iron pot. It was early morning of baptizing day. Emma had been there before him to light a fire. He and Bonnie must wash all over with hot water. For their brother Basil, her oldest son, was to be baptized. She had a feeling that all of them must be cleansed outwardly on the day that Basil became white as snow inwardly, washed clean of his sins by the blood of the Lamb.

At a protracted meeting that summer which lasted a week, Basil joined the church the second night. The Lord claimed him. Perhaps Basil had always belonged to the Lord. He had certainly attended church regularly every summer since John could remember. Though since he was older, there were times when he got drunk and became anything but religious. Drink made Kirk happy and cheerful but it made Basil glum and ugly for days afterwards. Granpap's defiance of the preacher had made Basil plunge deeper into religion, as if he wished to make up for the old man's defection. He had long talks with the preacher, and afterwards went about looking very important and full of news.

John set the pan of hot water on the wash bench. Off came the jeans and shirt Emma had washed the day before. He hung them carefully on a bush and began to make suds with the homemade lye soap. Disgusted sputtering sounds came from his mouth as he rubbed the suds lightly over his face. They stung his eyes until one hand groped for the jeans and rubbed the soap out.

As a special concession to cleanliness he broke off a soft green twig of sassafras from the bush and cleaned around the navel which protruded a little from his body. Looking down he watched his body curiously. It was not often he saw himself naked, for clothes were made to be worn day and night. The protruding navel, he knew, had something to do with his birth and the fact that Granpap had cut the cord instead of some woman who knew her business. He knew because he had ears with which to listen to the grown-ups talk. He was a little vague about all the details of the business. But it must have been very important, for it had brought him into the world.

To wash the rest of his body John raised the pan high above his head with both skinny little arms and tipped the pan. The water came down on his head and shoulders. It splashed from his shoulders and touched the prominent parts of his body, and trickled along the curved indentation down his back that was like the shallow bed of a stream.

He ran up and down the spring path in the early sunshine to dry. He trotted like the preacher's horse, as it came up the road to church. At the end of the trot he halted at the sassafras bush and nibbled at the leaves. His upper lip curled back and his teeth clicked together, except where two were missing. Reluctantly he put on his jeans when he heard Emma calling.

At the cabin Emma looked him over and was satisfied. With his hair slicked back with water, the boy looked as clean as a peeled hickory.

Basil was having trouble with his shoes. Preacher Warren had given him an old pair of his own. The day before to make them bright and shining Basil had taken some molasses and mixed it with soot from the chimney into a black paste. Rubbed with the paste, the shoes looked quite new. In his pride Basil had put the shoes on when he got up, though he would have to take them off later to walk across Thunderhead. From the very first moment he put them on the flies began to settle on the molasses. Basil shook one foot and then the other. Some of the flies left the shoes, but most of them were stuck fast. Those that had left came back again and settled so that their legs were caught in the mess. And after getting stuck from their own foolishness they buzzed their distress and struggled frantically to get off.

Their distress was not greater than Basil's. At last he was forced to scrape off the whole mess, flies and molasses together, with a stick, and wipe the shoes clean with leaves. He still looked harassed as he went up the trail, with the shoes in his hand and the bundle of baptizing clothes slung across his back. Kirk did not go with him. He waited until Basil was out of sight and struck off to the left, making for the short cut over Barren She Mountain.

On the meadow side, near Laurel Creek, the gray cliff of Barren She Mountain was split open from top to bottom. In the space between the two walls there were enough jagged projections to make a rough stairway to the top. From these the trail led to the McClure cabin. This short cut was a hard climb both ways and few people used it from the south side unless like Kirk they wished to pass the Hawkins' cabin that was at one side of Swain's meadow. But there was an important reason for the use of the trail from the north on the meadow side. In a little hollow halfway up the mountain there was a small still. The narrow stream that ran by this still dripped over the face of the cliff. Occasionally when some careless person dropped sour mash full of carbonic acid and alcohol into the stream the stink was strong enough to make a pig squeal. Sometimes cattle pastured in Swain's meadow had been known to get drunk from licking the water that came over the face of the cliff. This had happened perhaps once, only. But the tale went around and even the children knew where the still was located.

Because of it Emma was sorry to see Kirk taking the short cut. She knew he had begun to drink, and she meant to say nothing against it. He was almost a man. But on this day when his brother was to be baptized she wished for Kirk to be sober and thoughtful. She, herself, went about looking sober enough for both of them as she prepared the lunch. Her two oldest were grown men—almost. They were going different ways. And where those ways would lead them only the Lord could tell.

Across from the upper end of Swain's meadow, Laurel Creek made a bend around the base of Little Snowbird Mountain. At this bend was Fraser McDonald's cabin. Just before it was the old ford. Now there was a rough log bridge built across. The road that led from this bridge went past Fraser's cabin and followed the creek around the base of Snowbird until it turned into a sledge trail further on. About a mile beyond Fraser's a sand and rock beach in the creek sloped down into deep water. This was where the baptizings were held.

Baptizing day came early in August. Whether a person was religious like Basil, or defiant like Granpap, they all attended Baptizing. It was an occasion for neighbors and kin who had not seen each other for a year or more to meet. People came from miles around, some even from the distant South Range neighborhood. In some way the news traveled that on such a day there would be baptizing on Laurel Creek; and the poorest and most isolated tied up some corn pone and cold potatoes in a cloth and set out before day to reach the place in time.

On the other side of the creek a low hill rose up almost from the water. Behind the hill were higher mountains enclosing the place. On the beach side there was more room. Little Snowbird had a gentle slope at the bottom with few trees and some thickets of calico plant and laurel scattered between the rocks. Between the road and the creek there was a wide bank covered with green grass. This was a favorite place for those who had brought lunch. They could use the flat rocks for tables and sit around in comfortable family style. Those who did not have jugs of cider went to the creek side and drank.

Granpap, who had accepted something stronger than cider from a neighbor, nevertheless took a drink of creek water. He came back to the place Emma had selected for their lunching place and spoke to Basil who was eating his piece of corn pone and bacon.

"Now," he said to Basil, "the preacher can't baptize ye. I've swallowed the creek, holy ghost and all."

Basil did not answer. With his bread in one hand and the bundle of clothes in the other he walked away up the road toward the place where the men were to dress.

"It was ugly of you to say that," Emma reproved Granpap.

"Shucks, Emma," Granpap said. "He knowed I didn't mean anything."

"You should talk better before the young ones," Emma went on. "It's you that helps Kirk in his bad ways."

Granpap was silent. He would not defend himself too much before a woman. Emma began again to wonder about Kirk. He had not appeared for dinner. She was keeping his part of the lunch and wanted to find him. Jesse McDonald, Fraser's son, passed and she called him.

"You seen Kirk?" she asked.

"No'm," Jesse said, and went over to the Frank McClure group where Sally was helping Ora with the younger children. Sally was faithful that day for she was to be baptized. She was full of a spirit of helpfulness. Jesse did not tell Emma that he had been looking for his friend. Kirk had vanished. And since he could not find him among the company, Jesse had decided that Kirk must have gone to visit the still again.

"Come along, Son," Granpap said to John. "Maybe we can find him."

They walked off together, John tagging along at Granpap's heels like a faithful puppy. Emma and Bonnie joined Ora McClure.

"Now, you run along, Sally," Ora said taking a sly look at Jesse who was hanging around, waiting to get a chance to speak with Sally. "You run along, Sally. Emma'll help me. But remember, you're going to be baptized with water to-day."

Sally blushed almost to her fingers' ends. Sometimes her mother said the most indecent things. Sally could bear it very nicely when other girls whispered with her and they spoke of experiences that were ahead of them. But when her mother said them she was ashamed, especially when Jesse McDonald was waiting as she well knew to walk down the road with her until it was time to dress.

"No," Sally said firmly. "I'm a-going to stay right here." And she blushed again for Jesse was looking at her steadily.

"You go right along," Ora said, sorry now that she had confused Sally. Taking him all in all, Jesse was a good boy, the son of a good father.

"But," Ora said to Emma when the two had stepped off up the road, "I hope she remembers she's a-marrying with the holy ghost to-day."

"She's a good girl," Emma said, and Ora nodded. She had raised her child right, in the fear of God and man.

Granpap wandered about with John at his heels. People were scattered along the banks in groups and on the side of the hill there were others. Now that dinner was over there was a breathing spell until time for the preacher to come. He was having a regular table dinner at Hal Swain's.

The sun was very bright and the women's dresses made fine irregular patterns of color. Up on the hillside some rosepink calico plants were still blooming and there was wild honeysuckle, a rich orange. The dresses seemed to be growing there just as the flowers and when a woman moved it was as if a plant got up and made a new place for itself or joined itself to another to make a new color against the grass or the gray of some rock. Not all the dresses were bright. Some of them had been washed many times and were faded. And among the older women were several wearing dark homespun or flannel. Granma Wesley wore a brown homespun dress, dyed with walnut juice. Her mother had woven and dyed it. At a distance it did not stand out as the flimsier but more colorful dresses of the others. But it was carefully woven and sewed with small stitches.

The old woman walked in front of Granpap and John across the road. They could not see her face for she had on her sunbonnet and she looked neither to the right nor to the left but straight ahead as if she was making for some goal. Behind her walked Sam Wesley's young daughter. Her waist was blue calico. But the skirt was homespun, dyed red with pokeberry juice, and around the bottom were bands of blue and yellow woven in. The child was twelve years old and the skirt dragged on the ground, for Granma Wesley would never allow her few pieces of homespun to be cut.

Granpap watched them. "Pore old Granma," he said. Since she had risen from her sick bed Granma Wesley had not been exactly right in her mind. She wandered about looking for her sheep. She could not or would not believe they had been killed. Just as soon as he could make the money Sam planned to buy two others exactly like the old ones. He hoped that would ease her last days on this earth.

"We'll go to the bend," Granpap said to John. "Maybe Kirk will be a-coming along from Fraser's." The old man did not sound very hopeful. Like Jesse he had his own notion of the place where Kirk might be found.

Down the road near the bend, drawn apart from the others as if they did not belong, or as if they felt they were too good, was a group of people. The men had not left their wives and children to mix with the other men along the road, and the women sat listlessly on the bank of the stream as if they expected no company and wanted none.

These people were from near South Range and Granpap knew them. On one side they were kin of the rich Tates who had taken Granpap's land. But the Tates did not recognize them as kin. This branch of the family had intermarried with the McFarlanes. They lived in a little settlement on Pinchgut Creek, ten miles from South Range. While Granpap talked with one of the McFarlane men, John stood behind the old man and looked around his legs at the people. They paid little attention to him.

A dog barked at him and one of the children about his age opened its eyes and peered around Granpap to see this boy of six or seven who had come so near. The child had a pale face splotched with red. Its hair was whiter than John's, and its ears were larger than any John had ever seen on man or child. He went closer, edging around Granpap's knee and saw that the women and men, too, had mottled faces and big ears.

Granpap spoke about them as he and John got on the road to go back the way they had come. Years before, the first Tate that made money had driven the McFarlanes off the land. The McFarlanes had gone far up a mountain into a cove by Pinchgut Creek. Later the same Tate had driven some of his own kin away and the McFarlanes had taken them in. Way up there on the creek they had married each other till the Lord only knew which was brother and which sister. And the result was before them. The Tate-McFarlanes had pop eyes and skin that would bleed if you took a straight look at it.

The rich Tates got richer and the poor ones had come to this. It seemed that the Lord took pleasure in shearing his poor sheep and fattening the rich ones. Maybe he did it on purpose so that in heaven the sheared ones would enjoy their riches more, and in hell the rich would burn better for their fatness.

To Preacher Warren all the people in the company were pinch-faced and uninteresting. As he tethered his horse and got his bundle of baptizing clothes from the saddle bag, he felt a load in his heart because as far as he could know he would be doing this very thing summer after summer. He longed with his whole soul to live in town, where his children might grow up in the proper manner, and he might have a congregation of live people. In the whole place only Hal Swain and his wife Sally knew how to live. Preacher Warren felt grateful to them, for if it were not for those two he would have no salary from the community. The occasional pennies and nickels dropped into a hat on Sundays hardly counted. Sometimes resentment filled his throat when he thought that at dances the collections were larger than at church. But he was ashamed of such resentment and when it occurred prayed to his Lord to cleanse his heart of the secret sin.

His early life had been pinched, and he wanted something more . . . a church with stained glass windows, a baptizing pool under the platform and a regular Bible rest where his big Bible would stay from week to week. If he had met John in the road he would have seen just another pinch-faced child with a careless walk, who would grow up to be a careless, slovenly man, living on the lusts of the flesh—his woman or his women, his drink and his food.

As the preacher left his horse some girls came out of the bushes at the side of the road. One of them had her dress still raised. And as she saw him and dropped it hurriedly the others giggled. As they ran down the road he heard them laugh. They were all like that—lewd, coarse. He wanted refinement and reserve. And he had not found it among his own people. He thought of those he was to baptize that day. Sally McClure, Minnie Hawkins, Eve McDonald and the Wesley girls, three boys beside Basil McClure. Of them all, boys and girls, Basil was the only one he felt he could count on.

Sally Swain and Hal arrived soon after the preacher. Sally took up most of the buggy. She was a long time getting out, but once on the ground her feet were light and energetic. For a time she rummaged in the back of the buggy handing out certain bundles to Hal. These they carried to a place further down the road where four trees some distance from each other made an almost perfect square.

Soon Emma, Ora, and several other women were there helping Sally put up the sheets. They were making a dressing room for the girls. In this space the girls were to put on their robes made from unbleached cloth sold at Swain's. Sally furnished the safety pins, and along with them she gave advice. Before the girls were half dressed everyone was wishing her out of the way. But they were too shy to speak, and all of them owed money at Swain's. They knew that Sally was really good-natured. Yet everyone felt like saying "Why are you here?"

"Pin Sally further up on that side," Sally Swain called to Ora. "Or she'll trip sure as gun's iron."

"Here, Eve," she called to Eve McDonald, forcing her to leave her mother's fingers. "That'll never do. You look like you was sent for and couldn't come." And she took the whole robe off, leaving Eve naked except for some flimsy drawers. Eve hid her face in her hands. She might have said the coarsest words to Sally Swain if she had the courage. She knew them. And she was not afraid of being naked. Only Sally Swain's pudgy hands tearing the robe off seemed to violate her, and she wanted to hide herself from the others.

When Emma and Ora came out to take their places on the bank everyone had settled down except a few men who were still talking in a little group on the road. As soon as they saw the preacher coming down from his dressing place in the white baptizing robe, they too walked slowly to the bank and before the preacher reached the creek had found themselves seats in the grass.

Preacher Warren walked sedately through his flock, stood a moment on the bank, then picked his way carefully over the rocky beach. He entered the water up to his knees. Everyone was still. There was not a breeze. Nothing moved except the water that flowed over the rocks and tugged at the ends of the preacher's robe. He was forced to stand with his feet wide apart, for the current was not weak and there were slippery rocks on the bottom.

Facing the flock he gave out a hymn and the people sang after him line by line.

"There is a fountain filled with blood,
Drawn from Immanuel's veins,
And sinners plunged beneath its flood,
Lose all their guilty stains.

"Savior wash me in the blood,
In the blood, in the blood of the Lamb,
And I shall be whiter than snow."

The beginning of the song was a signal. The girls came out from the curtained place and walked slowly in single file toward the preacher. And down the road came the boys with Basil leading. As the song ended they were standing on the beach facing the preacher. The five girls stood in their cream robes with hair combed out down their backs. The young men had new jeans and white shirts—all bought at Swain's at a special price.

The preacher spoke some words to them. Three words, he said, they must make the ideal of their lives. These words were temperance, soberness, and chastity. The girls must be temperate in speech. They must not be coarse in language or in actions, and must not backbite their neighbors. The men must not look on wine, for "the drunken and glutton shall come to poverty: and drowsiness shall clothe a man with rags." These words, he said, came straight from the Good Book.

Drink had ruined men, and laziness had overcome the women of that country. So that they went about in poverty and sometimes even in rags. On earth, he said, they must prepare for their heavenly home. And in the heavenly home all was pure and fair and refined. So all must become pure and fair on earth in preparation. They must work and save and live better. If they did this the Lord would bless them and welcome them into his everlasting home. Amen.

The preacher beckoned to Sally McClure who was first in the line. She went forward, feeling the way with her toes for she had walked the creek barefoot before and knew how treacherous the rocks could be. It would be a disastrous thing, remembered for years by the whole community, if she slipped and fell.

Leading Sally by the hand, the preacher backed out into the water until he was up to his waist. Sally shivered as the cold water struck her body. And she was shivering partly from excitement already, for she knew the eyes of the congregation were on her. At a certain spot, when the water was just above Sally's waist the preacher turned her toward the congregation. He put one hand behind her head, the other on her forehead, and saying the mystic words, dipped her until she was completely covered with water. She came up coughing and he held her until she recovered and could walk to the edge of the creek. There Sally Swain met her with a blanket from the store and covered her. This covering was for warmth and also for modesty. The wet robe stuck fast to the young girl's body.

Minnie Hawkins was next in the line of girls. She had just reached the preacher and was ready to be immersed when a low sound went up from the congregation. The sound was like a hive of bees beginning to swarm. It swelled in places and as it died down in one place grew louder in another. Minnie tried to raise her head, for she heard the commotion distinctly. The preacher paid no attention and held Minnie's head firmly under his hand. These excitements sometimes happened and he had found it best whether in church or outside to pay no attention, but to let the excitement pass off of itself.

His back was turned and neither he nor Minnie, whose head he held fast, could see Kirk McClure sitting astride a horse on the opposite bank of the stream. Kirk had ridden up so quietly no one had seen until the horse's forefeet were already in the water. He must have been waiting behind a thicket for the moment when Minnie Hawkins went in.

He was riding the preacher's horse. Everyone recognized the saddle bags. Kirk began to cross the creek. No one ever found out what he had expected to do. Perhaps his coming was simply a show for Minnie. The water came up to the horse's belly and in places above it. The horse slipped on the stones and splashed the water over Kirk. It glittered over him in the afternoon sunshine. All this took only a moment, that moment when the preacher laid his hand on Minnie's forehead and began saying the words over her. At that moment Kirk reached them. He had on his old felt hat, turned up in front. Leaning across the saddle he took the hat off with a flourish right under the nose of the preacher. Minnie saw him as he had meant her to. She jerked away from the horse and rider with a single startled movement. And she slipped on the rocks. As she slid into the water both her hands grasped at the preacher's robe. His feet teetered on the round stones and in another second he was under the water with Minnie. The two scrambled and fought under the water and might have choked each other if help had not come. At first people were too shocked to move. They were shocked into a stillness like death. Even Kirk sat on the horse without moving, a dazed look on his face. But he was the first to get in the water. And it was Kirk who forced Minnie's arms from around the preacher and set them both on their feet. Before the men could reach them, Kirk had swung the horse around and splashed out of the water. He rode through the excited crowd of people on the bank and galloped up the road.

It was some time before the baptizing could proceed. The preacher was helped on to the bank and sat there panting until his breath came regularly again. Sally Swain wrapped Minnie in the blanket and took her to the dressing place.

There was so much excitement, it was not until the next day people began to ask themselves and each other whether Minnie Hawkins had actually been baptized. The preacher had begun the words, but no one had heard him finish. And he never told anyone. Since he never again asked Minnie to join the church, many people came to the conclusion that he had finished the words and Minnie was saved. But others disagreed, and this baptism was the subject of many discussions for years afterward, especially when Minnie herself later became the chief subject of talk in the community.

9

When older girls and boys were baptized they became grown and ready for courting and marriage. Though Kirk McClure had not joined the church, because of Basil's baptism along with his brother he became a man. The two boys began to go out at night courting girls. Basil never went to dances but he visited the girls and was known to be courting Minnie Hawkins.

These days Kirk washed himself at the spring until his face shone. He and Basil did odd jobs for Swain and with some of the money they bought a razor. They had quarrels over it, for Basil accused Kirk of making the blade dull and wanted to force him to sharpen it. Neither of them took very good care of the razor and as John had used it once on a green stick without anyone's knowing, perhaps the blame should have been put on him.

Kirk was very careless. If he made money he spent it like Granpap, only the Good Lord knew on what. Sometimes he slapped all he had made, which was never much, into the gourd for Emma and the young ones. Basil, much as Emma hated to think it, seemed always to be looking out for Number One. And when he gave money for home he always gave it into Emma's hands with an air as if he grudged what he gave. He was a good, kind son and never said he grudged the money. It only seemed that he did—and perhaps it was the other way.

With Basil and Kirk going about their own affairs, Granpap turned more and more to John. And John was happy enough over this. The second winter after Basil was baptized Granpap got up from the supper table one night and said, "Want to go to the store, Son?" He said it to John who had asked forty times before and had always been refused. Did he want to go? It was Saturday night. Men came in and sat around the store on Saturday nights and talked. John would hear men's talk.

The trail had never seemed so long. John ran ahead and looked down at Granpap who was taking the side of the mountain in leisurely strides. It seemed as if the old man was standing in one place, merely going through the motions of walking. John hurried about on the upper trail like a snake doctor zigzagging above a creek, trying to set Granpap an example of hurry. It was no use. The old man kept up his leisurely regular stride, even when they were going down the steep trail on the other side of Thunderhead.

In Swain's store men sat on boxes near the stove to keep warm and to be near the sand box for spitting. Hal Swain stayed behind the counter most of the time, for people came in off and on to buy. In between selling Hal took his place on the box everybody knew as his, the box at the right of the stove pipe.

Many folks were in that night. Fraser McDonald and his son Jesse were there. Jesse was waiting for Kirk so they could go down the creek to see two girls who had come from South Fork to visit some kin over Sunday.

Jim Hawkins, who always let up on his watch of Minnie on Saturday nights, was there as usual. Some said he locked Minnie in the house, but that was nonsense. He only saw that she had gone safely to bed and shut the door behind him. There was no lock on his door. On Sundays he allowed the young men to come and see Minnie while he sat by as a proper chaperon. There was talk that Minnie was not always at home when her father thought she was there. But it was only talk, for no one had ever given proof. As Fraser McDonald said, people would get along fine if they would believe nothing of what they hear and only half of what they see. Only people don't always act in the best way, and so the talk went around about Minnie.

Bud McEachern was in the store. He lived over South Fork, but was staying a few days with Sam McEachern whose bachelor cabin was under Barren She Mountain. Bud was there to have a talk with Granpap. They were waiting for Sam.

"Sure he's coming?" Granpap asked Bud. "Sure he ain't out after a gal?"

"Sure," Bud said. "Sam aims high. Didn't you know? Got a little miss all dressed in lace down in Leesville."

Sam Wesley, just from the hospital in Leesville, spoke up. "He can have her," he said and spat with a twist of his head. "He can have all the gals in Leesville for what I saw of them."

"And what did you see?" Bud asked.

"Clean to Christmas," Sam said, "and back again."

"Glad to get home, eh, Sam?" Hal Swain asked. From his place behind the stove he saw a girl come in the door, and got up to find out what she wanted.

Many girls who lived near came in on Saturday nights to buy something—a spool of thread, some needles, perhaps just to look at some calico. They came in and with one eye on the counter took little sly glances toward the men. And often after the girl had left, one of the young men got up and strolled carelessly out of the back door.

"Glad to get back?" Sam Wesley repeated after Hal had taken his place again. "As soon as I left the hospital I promised my God I'd never set foot out of the mountains again."

He had been taken to the hospital because of a hard fever. When he felt strong again and they wouldn't let him go, it was very trying.

"I said to the nurse," he told them, " 'I want some water the worst way.' And she said, 'You've had a fever so I can't give you no water. It's against the rules.' I was feeling better so I said, 'Where's my jeans?' And she perked up her lips and told me I couldn't have them. It was against orders. And I said, 'You send the doctor here.'

"And when the doctor come I said, 'Doctor, I lied to my God when I let them bring me here. They won't give me any water and I dream at night about a spring of real water running alongside my cabin. Doctor, I've got to go back to the hills.' And he said, 'Well, to-morrow.'

"And to-morrow the nurse brought my jeans. And she said, 'Get up now and I'll dress ye.' " Sam minced his words in a high treble like a girl. John had been staying close to Granpap's back hanging around in the half dark looking like Granpap's after-midday shadow. Now he edged closer to Sam in order not to miss a word of the story. "And I told her," Sam went on, "that no woman has ever dressed Sam Wesley and no woman ever will. So she went out and I got dressed and slipped away. I found somebody to drive me part the way up the mountain. And the first spring I come to welling out of a rock I said to Jim, 'Let me down, Jim.' And he helped me down because I was still weak. And I laid me down flat and drank of that water till my sights was full. And under that tree with the water coming in my mouth

I promised my God I'd never leave the mountains again."

"Reminds me," Granpap said, "of the time when I come back from Georgy. Men, the ugliest woman up here looked like a sweet angel, and the lowliest bush was a tree of heaven."

John went back to Granpap and sat down on the floor at his side. If Granpap was preparing to tell a story about Georgy, he wanted to hear.

"This is the place for me," Fraser McDonald said quietly. "Here I've lived and here I'll lay me down and die."

"And die poor," Hal Swain told Fraser.

"Yes, and die poor," Fraser said.

"You cut yourself off from outside and you cut yourself off from riches," Hal insisted. "People are getting rich out there."

"And there's plenty of poor, too," Fraser said. "I know."

Hal Swain kept on. "You've just got to be a little smarter than the other fellow and you'll get along," he said.

Sam winked on the side at Granpap. Sure you had to be smarter than the other one. Didn't Hal know, along with his Sally, just how to be smarter than the others?

The talk suddenly lost its interest, or else everyone had plenty to think about when it came to the idea of getting riches stored up. Quietness settled down in the store. John leaned against Granpap's box. He was having a hard time keeping his eyes open. So long as there was talk his ears kept his eyes awake. But when the quiet came, the dimness in the store and the heat from the stove made him doze off. Sam Wesley picking on the banjo woke him. Sam was singing a song about a girl and her soldier lover.

"Soldier, soldier, will you marry me,
With your musket, fife and drum?
Oh no, pretty maid, I cannot marry you,
For I have no shoes to put on.

"Away she ran to the shoemaker's shop,
As fast as she could run.
She bought him a pair of the very best shoes,
And the soldier put them on."

The song went on interminably and Sam's nasal voice clanged out the words, with emphasis on the piece of clothing whatever it might be. At last when Sam had sung of every piece of clothing he could think that a man or a woman might wear—he added the women's to give zest to the song—he ended his singing. And it was very sad, for after the maiden had brought the soldier everything he demanded, the soldier in the meanest way said,

"I cannot marry you,
For I have a wife at home."

John was tired and sleepy. He hated the song because it had lasted so long. And he hated the maiden who had run around so crazily. It showed how foolish women could be. No man could have been fooled like that. He would have stopped running to the shoemaker and the hatmaker and the coatmaker. He would have stood up to the person who was ordering him around and asked, "What do you think I am—a nigger slave?"

On the way back it was John who lagged on the trail and Granpap who urged him to hurry. John trudged along behind Granpap. He was disappointed. For such a long time he had envied the boys when they went with Granpap to the store at night, and now he had been there it hadn't seemed very unusual.

The next morning, however, the visit seemed more of an event. John remembered that no women had been sitting around the stove. And for the first time he had been away from Emma and Bonnie. So he swaggered around the cabin pretending to Bonnie that wonderful and mysterious things had happened the night before, things that she must never be told.

10

THE spring was under a cottonwood tree about fifty feet from the cabin. Some ferns grew around it and deep down at the back the roots of the cottonwood showed up through the clear water. To the right of the tree and just a little way back a fire burned under an iron pot. Near enough to this for convenience was the great round stump where Emma and Bonnie pounded out the clothes when they washed.

Emma was standing on the far side of the spring watching Granpap at work. It was summer time again and Granpap had gone back to his conniving with the McEacherns. But now there was a different situation. He was sprouting corn at his own place where before he had sprouted it somewhere else. And he had decided to peddle the liquor for the McEacherns. At least he had decided to take turns with Sam at driving it to the outside. Sam had made a fair proposition, and Granpap was tired of hiring a steer from Swain. He wanted one of his own.

Emma looked at her father. He was leaning over a bench under a rough shelter of saplings covered with walnut bark. With a hammer and nail he was making some small holes in the bottom of a large new pan. Emma wanted to speak, but Granpap was so intent on what he was doing she hesitated. For awhile she waited and then the words in her had to be spoken.

"I heard Kirk ask if he could go with ye," she said in a low voice. She felt very shy and hesitated again, before she went on. "Are ye going to take him?" she asked.

"Maybe," Granpap grunted.

"I want ye not," Emma told him.

"He'd be a help," Granpap said.

"And maybe go to his death."

"And if he does he's chosen his way. Kirk's a man."

"He's eighteen come next fall."

"And a man."

"And I'm a woman and can't keep him. I know."

"No. Ye couldn't keep him from Minnie though you wanted."

"Whether I wanted or not, his drinking kept him from Minnie."

Jim Hawkins had ordered Kirk from his cabin on a Sunday because he had gone there drunk.

"Hit's Basil now," Granpap said, working over the pan. He hoped to get Emma's mind off the trip Kirk wanted to take with him.

"You don't have to tell me. I know Basil's there every Sunday for supper. Jim Hawkins hopes to get a steady boy like Basil for Minnie."

"Some say Kirk and Minnie have been seen up Little Snowbird," Granpap went on. He was leaning over and Emma could not see the triumph in his eyes. He was getting her off the trail as surely as if he was an animal and had walked into a creek to get the hounds off his scent.

"If they have," Emma said shortly. "I don't know hit. But I do know Sam McEachern brags she's his girl.

"And that's another reason," Emma went on, catching the scent again, "him and Kirk oughtn't to be together. They'll be sure to fight. I wish you'd leave Kirk, Pap. I wish you'd stay yourself and not fool with all this." She pointed to the two bags of corn that leaned against the bench.

"We've got a right," Granpap said, "to make money in the best way we can. You need the money—you and the young ones. How much would the bags of corn bring me if I sold them to Swain? Made into whisky I get more. We need the money, and we've got a right to make hit."

"I'm not a-talking about rights," Emma insisted. "We've got a right. But the Law's got the power."

"We've got the hills."

"Yes. But hit's not like it was. Seems every year the outside creeps nearer. Look at that peddler, Small Hardy. The first time he come was some winters ago and now he comes every spring and always talking about the outside. And if the outside creeps nearer, the Law does, too."

Granpap opened one of the sacks and began pouring corn into the kettle. After all, the best way to close a scolding woman's mouth was with silence. Emma stood sullenly beside him.

"I'd rather starve," she said. "We can eat corn pone and potatoes."

"Shet up, Emma," Granpap said and Emma hushed. She hadn't heard that hard tone from him since she was a girl of sixteen and almost married. Lately he had been quieter and more lenient. The tone hushed her voice in her throat. She turned away and went over to stir the fire under the black pot.

Granpap took the gourd dipper, ladled out some of the warm water from the pot and poured it over the corn. A cloth was lying on the bench and he wrung it out in the pot and covered the vessel. Emma should be satisfied he didn't often drink at home. But if you ever let a woman have half a cob she wants all.

"Watch the corn, Emma," he said and walked away toward the cabin. He had spoken to her as if she was a child.

It was late afternoon and there was mist in the air. A long way off, clear across the south, the big range rose up and down. Mountains piled up, wallowing over each other. They were heavy blue in the mist with black shadows that showed where a hollow came or there was a distance between them. Looking over there, Emma felt heavy and sad and regretful of her childhood spent at the foot of South Range. Pap had been fierce then; he was, still, when he got roused. But there, once he had threatened to knife her when she was fourteen and slipped out with a boy. She had slipped out of church.

It was a church like the one at Swain's Crossing, but larger because that was a larger settlement with the cabins closer together. She would never forget the time she and Ora joined the church. They were sixteen and attending a revival. They had come with Jim and Frank McClure who were sitting with the men across the aisle. The preacher was praying and she and Ora were leaning over side by side. Ora began it by scratching under her arm. Sometimes razor-back hogs slept in the church and left fleas. Ora started scratching. Then Emma felt a bite on her leg and began digging on her own account. Ora turned her head to look at Emma and Emma looked out of the corner of her eye at Ora. And right then Ora giggled out loud. That started Emma and soon they were laughing, but silently, so their shoulders shook with the effort to keep from making sounds. When the prayer was over they could not stop and the preacher thinking they had got religion and were mourning for their sins came and accepted them into the church. That made them quiet enough, for everyone looked as they shook hands with the preacher.

Going home the boys were very solemn toward them both, thinking they had come through. Jim said, "You two sure did get it hard." All the way Ora kept pinching Emma, but neither of them would own up to what had really made them get religion. The next night Jim and Frank walked up to the preacher, and lo and behold all four of them were baptized that summer. And in the fall Ora married Frank, and Emma, Jim McClure.

Children were born and some of them died. Death came like a storm. You couldn't do anything about it. Emma's own mother had died at her birth. Granpap's second wife had several children before she died, too. They had mortgaged the Kirkland land to Hugh Tate who had got hold of three mountains over there and a big valley through mortgages, and they had lost the land. So the Kirklands were wandering outside somewhere and Pap had come to stay with her. And she was glad. He was a good man and what man didn't want to be head of the house he was in? This was only right. Yet she would still fight to keep the boys from going with Granpap.

Basil would be easy. He had what the preacher called a conscience. And it worried him to death. If he had done something wrong he would come and tell about it. He was a good boy.

Emma pushed the sticks with her bare foot closer under the pot and the fire burned up. Then she remembered that the water must be just warm, not like the water she used for boiling the clothes. She picked up a dead stick from the ground and pulled the fire away from under the pot. It went on burning on the edges of the pile of coals. She saw it reflected in the spring and went over to look. The slight mist in the air made the spring smooth and glassy. Emma could see her face. It was thin and brown with brown eyes like Bonnie's. The cheeks were hollow and drawn down, but the nose lifted them up. It was so firm and proud. Her mouth was big and generous and it was sad. The nose said, "I will stand up for what I need." But the mouth below it said, "I don't know what this is about. I don't understand."

Jim had liked Emma's hair. When some of it got away from the tight knot at the back it curled around her face. Maybe, Emma thought, she needed another man. But then she had her young ones. The two oldest were getting beyond her but John and Bonnie were still where she could scold and sometimes love them up a little. The fire flared up for a moment and it looked as if down there in the spring her face was burning up. She put her big gnarled hands against her face, to hide out the sight.

She left the spring and lifted the cloth from the deep kettle. The corn had already softened a little and its sweet smell came up. As Granpap had done, Emma poured some of the warm water over the corn. She listened while it dripped through the holes in the bottom. Wringing out a cloth in the pot, she spread it across the kettle. She was watching the corn and feeling the sound of the regular drip from the bottom of the pan when Granpap returned. He did not speak, but stood for a while looking out over South Range. Presently without looking at Emma he said carelessly, as if he was asking for another cup of coffee at supper.

"I'll not take Kirk this time. But next year he's a-going if he wants."

This was all Emma needed. Next year must take care of itself.

11

How big the dark room seemed to John when he went to bed alone. Sometimes at night when Granpap and Basil and Kirk were away the boy wanted to climb in with Emma and Bonnie instead of going to his own place. But he had his code about what a man could rightly do. He would betray himself and his code if he went back to sleeping with the women. And Kirk, who had begun to let John tag along on occasions, would once more think of him as belonging with them. So each night when the others were away John lay alone on his straw bed until he fell asleep or until Basil or Kirk arrived. Sometimes the fleas kept him awake. Recently they had been worse, because on the evenings when Granpap was not expected John took Georgy in to sleep with him.

The night that Kirk and Basil went to meet Granpap John shut Georgy out. He could hear the pup whining at the door. Now he was sorry he had kept him in the bed at all. For the fleas were very bad, and he was afraid Granpap would complain about them to Emma. He did not want the others to know he had kept the dog with him. Of course if they did find out he would not be ashamed before them. He would do as Kirk had done that morning when Basil tattled. He would say he had a right and stand up to what he had done.

Since he had joined the church and even before that Basil would creep around being sorry and ashamed if he had done anything he felt to be wrong, like taking a swallow of drink down his gullet. An example of this was the thing Basil had done that very morning. The night before, as John knew from listening, Kirk and Basil had come home drunk from the small still. Kirk was giggling as he stumbled around John's bed, and Basil was angrily trying to quiet him. He was anxious for Emma not to know. Yet in the morning he repented and accused Kirk of having tempted him to the drink. And what did he do but go and tell Emma all about it, so she, a woman, had to know about Kirk, too.

Sometimes, big and strong as he was, Basil seemed almost like a woman. And John felt contemptuous of women and of any kind of womanish ways in a man. He was tired of having Bonnie hang around. Two days before he and Basil and Kirk had found it necessary to slip off from her, so they could go hunting.

The boys had taken two guns, Granpap's and Jim McClure's, and gone out to shoot the cotton tails off rabbits. If a man could hit the round white spot that was a rabbit's tail while the little animal was leaping ahead through the woods, he was put down as a fine shot. And he could wear the tail on his hat, or give it to his girl. But the trip had been useless. One or the other of the boys should have proved himself. And they both missed. Granpap would have succeeded, for like his father Granpap was a fine shot. There was a story about Granpap's father. Once when squirrels were as plentiful as chestnuts in season through the hills, Granpap's father had seen about forty of them swimming the old South Fork single file with their tails high up; one tail right after the other above the water. He had stood on the bank and blown their tails off with one single shot from his gun.

In a half-sleep dream John saw all the fleas that were biting him lined up in a row. He took the gun from the wall and with one shot killed them all. And Granpap said, "For that, you can have the gun." Georgy woke him out of the dream, and he cried out "Shet up" for the hundredth time. He turned over and pulled the quilt up to keep out the cool night mist that came in through the wide cracks between the logs. He must have slept heavily when he did get to sleep for he woke to hear Kirk talking. The boys were already in bed. John felt over in his bed for Granpap, but the place was empty.

"Yes, you do," Kirk said very loud to Basil. "You want to slobber out your misery on some woman's breast. If it ain't Ma it's Minnie Hawkins."

"You say that because you want Minnie yourself." Basil's voice was harsh and ugly.

"If I want Minnie I'll get her, you God damned baby."

Basil's voice rose up in a kind of quaver. "You call me that and blaspheme God. Ye can't do hit."

There was a sickening thud of a blow—then another. John raised on his elbow and stared into the room. He could see nothing. But he could hear. He heard the two over in the other bed straining at each other. They sent short panting breaths into the room. John's elbow trembled under him. He sat up straight in the bed. The sweaty bodies struggling in the other corner creaked against each other. They made a sharp sound like crickets chirping. And every few moments came that other sound of a fist against a body. Both the boys were cursing. The words came singly as if they were forced from the mouths along with the breath. Then it seemed that the breath was gone, for there was silence except for the continual sound of the bodies scraping against each other. This half silence when there seemed no breath in the room lasted for a moment. At the end of that moment the bodies crashed onto the floor. A grunt came from one of them as if a last breath had gone out of a body with a heavy sob.

"John," Basil's voice said. "Call Ma. Get the lamp."

Emma was already up, with her skirt on over her cotton "body."

"Can't they ever stop this quarreling?" she said leaning over to get a scrap of paper lit at the fire. The paper flamed up weakly then shrivelled and died out. John took another piece from Emma's hand and lit the lamp.

Emma held the lamp in both hands. John knew why she did this. When he had touched her back there he had felt her hand tremble. He ran ahead into the other room. Emma was soon there. The light came down from the lamp and spread across the floor at the place where Kirk lay. He was lying with one cheek flat on the floor. His fair hair shone in the light except at the back where there was a black stain. Basil stood by the bed. He looked at Emma and Emma looked at him.

"He cursed God, Ma," Basil said.

Emma walked swiftly to Kirk and set the lamp on the floor beside him.

"Bring a pan of water," she said to John. She lifted Kirk's head in her arm. It hung back like a young baby's and Emma shifted her arm to bring it up further. With her left hand she felt the wet spot. Blood seeped down on her bare arm, but she made her fingers go further into the hair, feeling the scalp. The bone was sound.

John put the washpan of water by Emma.

"Now hand me a quilt and hold the lamp high," Emma told

him. Basil wanted to be of use. He lifted the quilt from his bed and held it out to his mother.

"Fold it up," Emma said sharply, "and lay it on the floor." When Basil had done this and stepped back, she laid Kirk's cheek carefully against the quilt. Bending her head and lifting her arms, she slipped off the coarse shift. Her back was to John, but Basil, standing in the shadow, saw his mother's naked breasts and he felt ashamed for her. Emma did not seem to care. She bit into the shift and tore the cloth lengthwise. The noise of the tearing startled John. It was like a gun shot in the still room. Emma bit again. She grasped the cloth with her strong fingers and brought her arms out wide above Kirk's head, as the cloth split. With what was left from the strips, she washed the wound carefully.

"Get up on the bed," she said to Basil, "and reach me some cobwebs from the corner."

She laid the cobwebs against the place and hurriedly wound the two pieces of cotton cloth around Kirk's head.

"His eyes are opening," John said. Blood was still coming from the wound, dyeing the bandage, but Kirk's eyes were quivering open. Seeing this, Emma took up the pan and went outside. John set the lamp on the floor and sat down to watch.

Emma brought back fresh water in the pan. She had slipped on the waist to her skirt and it hung loose outside. With the rag she bathed Kirk's face, pushing back the heavy light hair slowly from his forehead.

Presently Kirk raised up a little, lifting himself from the shoulders. In a second he sank back again. Emma and John, with the lamp between them, sat on the floor looking for Kirk's eyes to open again. Basil, sitting on the side of the bed, watched anxiously. He did not want his brother hurt. Yet as soon as Kirk had raised up, he felt an anger at his brother again. Now that Kirk's eyes were closed he was anxious and sorry about the whole matter. He knew that Kirk went off with Minnie on the sly, and half suspected that Minnie liked Kirk best. But quarreling with his brother was against his religion. He had told the preacher about their quarrels and the preacher had read something from the Bible. "Behold," the preacher read. "Behold how beautiful a thing it is for brethren to dwell together in unity." And Basil felt that it was a beautiful thing, and would make up his mind not to quarrel again. Then suddenly this anger and hate came up between them.

Kirk opened his eyes wide and looked at Basil. When he saw his brother his brows came together. He raised himself up with hands clenched on the floor on either side. "You," he began.

"Lie down and shet up," Basil said.

Emma touched Basil's leg. "That's enough now, Basil."

"I ain't a child, Ma." Basil drew his leg away from her touch. "I'm head of this family."

"I'd like Granpap to hear ye," Emma said. She tried to make her voice sound as if she didn't care much about the whole thing. As if she was making fun of Basil and Kirk.

"Granpap's a Kirkland, and I'm a McClure. And I'm oldest. So long as I'm here Kirk can't profane the name of God in this house."

"Hit's enough, I tell ye." Emma could see the hate coming up in Kirk's face. "Basil," she said, "take that lamp and lead the way to the other room. Now, John, you get under that arm like me." Kneeling beside Kirk she lifted his arm over her shoulder. John would not be much support but she had to keep Basil and Kirk from touching.

John lifted himself as high as possible when they had got Kirk standing and he did help, for he could feel his brother's weight on his shoulder as they walked slowly through the passage and up the steps into Emma's room. Basil set the lamp on the table and helped the others get Kirk on the bed. He hung back in the doorway until Kirk was covered, then returned to his own place.

He was already troubled in himself about Minnie. All the men knew by this time that she was with child, all but Jim Hawkins unless he suspected and would not let himself see. When Jim Hawkins did find out he might accuse him, Basil McClure. In reality the child might be his, if one time could make it his. But there had been other men. Basil was not taking the blame unless the blame was his, and that could not be proved. He did not want Minnie any more as a wife. She was a whore, had proved it. Yet he did not want Kirk to have her either, not so long as he was there, and could see them together. For, much as he despised Minnie, he still wanted her.

In the other room Emma pulled a chair up beside the bed.

"Better go on to sleep," she said to John. But he stood at the foot of the bed and watched Kirk. Emma did not urge him to go, and presently she made a place at the foot of her bed for him. She lifted Bonnie toward the head, so there was a small place at the foot. He lay down and went to sleep with his knees strained toward his chin. One skinny arm lay outside the bedclothes, and the hand was clenched into a small fist. She undid the fist and pressed the fingers out straight. When Kirk moved she lifted the covers back to watch his face. Usually Kirk was so full of life even his family had come to think that he could do nothing but laugh, and make fun. Now his face was set in rigid stern lines. It frightened Emma at first, but his regular breathing reassured her. He was sleeping.

The next morning Basil came in for breakfast. Emma waited on him and tried to say some words. But he had only yes or no to give her. Kirk was sitting up in bed. The bandage, passed crossways over his forehead, made him look jaunty, as if he cared for nothing and nobody. While Basil was at the table he pretended to have a banjo in his arms and began singing.

"John Hardy was a brave and a desperate boy
And he carried his gun ever' day,
And he killed a man down in Johnson Town,
And I saw John Hardy getting away,
Pore Boy."

He said "Pore Boy" in such a way, and gave Basil a look.

Bonnie hung onto the side of the bed, looking up at Kirk and listening to the song.

"They arrested him down at the bi . . ."

"That's enough, Kirk," Emma said. "Hush!"

She was glad Basil did not sit long. Kirk looked as if he was ready to devil anyone who came near, anyone he felt like deviling.

Bonnie liked having her brother there in bed. She took his corn pone and fatback over and three cups of coffee one after another. Kirk would not eat, but he wanted the coffee. And after he had the three cups they could not keep him in bed.

About midday he was sitting on the log below the door. Emma was inside, getting ready to wash the clothes.

"Ma," Kirk said quietly and Emma came and stood above him. She looked up and saw a man riding down the trail. They watched every turn and dip of the trail that brought the horse and rider in sight. When the horse came over the last rise they saw that the man was Hal Swain.

John and Bonnie appeared from somewhere and sat in the yard. Emma heard Basil come through the back door and pull out a chair at the table behind her.

"Well," Emma said. "Hit's time Hal came to see us."

Kirk moved his shoulders impatiently. She was quiet for a little while. She felt that Kirk did not want her to speak. Then in spite of her words came from her mouth again.

"Maybe he's come to say we can have the cow cheaper."

That, she knew, was a foolish thing to say. For Hal could just as well say the same thing over the counter at the store to Kirk or Basil—or Granpap.

Hal rode into the yard and slowly got down from his horse.

"Come in," Emma said. "Hitch the horse, Johnny." And she stood aside to let Hal come into the house.

John slung the bridle over the limb of a tree and hurried into the cabin. The others were already inside. Kirk was on a chair opposite Hal. Emma and Bonnie were standing close by. Basil sat by the table.

"How's everybody?" Hal Swain spoke smoothly like a preacher, and with confidence as if he knew something. He did know something, for he could read anything from a government letter for the post office to passages in the Bible.

"Well," Emma said in answer to his question, and then added, "Kirk hurt his head."

"Had I better look?" Hal asked. He had medicines on the shelf of his store and sometimes he doctored.

Emma undid the bandages. "Lost some blood," Hal said after looking at the wound. "But he'll mend soon." He wound the bandages back, somewhat better than Emma had done them. But he left everything as she had fixed it the night before. "Wash it to-night," he told her, "and put on more cobwebs."

He sat down again. The eyes in the five faces looked at him. He felt the eyes, but kept his own fixed on his hands. He looked at their backs and then at the palms as if he was reading them as he would a book.

"I see your corn's shucked," he said at last.

"John and Bonnie helped," Emma said.

"Many potatoes this year?" He turned and spoke to Basil.

"Some," Basil answered him.

Again Hal looked at his hands. He examined his right thumb nail carefully as if he was a boy who had bored a hole there to measure the time till the sow would litter.

Then he cleared his throat. "Well, Emma," he said and hesitated. "Well, I reckon the Law's got your pap."

"I was afeared," Emma said, "hit might happen."

Basil got up and walked out of the back door.

"Yes," Emma repeated. "I was afeared." Her heart felt as heavy as a full bucket from the spring.

"He's got plenty of friends," Hal told her. "You ain't to worry, Emma."

"No," Emma said looking at the floor. "Hit's no use."

"He sent you this," Hal said and stood up to reach in his pocket. He laid some change on the table.

As soon as Hal's horse turned the corner by the spring on the way back to the Crossing, Basil came in.

"Hit's a disgrace," he said.

Emma raised herself. "Hit's not a disgrace, Basil McClure, unless you make it so."

"Granpap's broke the law."

"For you and the others, to get money to feed ye."

"He had a right," Kirk said, looking jaunty under his bandage, and very sure of himself.

"Hit's a disgrace," Basil repeated. "Up at the settlement they'll look at us and say, 'The law's got Granpap Kirkland.' "

Emma looked at him. "And there'll be plenty to say he had a right," she told Basil.

12

ORA and Frank McClure came over that night. Frank wanted them to know that he could borrow a horse from some kin near South Fork and one of the boys could have it for going to the trial.

Ora had some news for Emma. When they went out in the clearing to squat she said, "Minnie Hawkins is with child."

"No!" Emma said, and then, "Well, hit's to be expected."

"She's been a-hiding it under her dress. But now hit's talked over at the store."

Emma was quiet as they walked to the cabin in the dark. And she wondered who the man was. It might be one of her boys and if so Jim Hawkins had a right to make him marry. And she knew Minnie would not be good for either.

Even while she talked to the McClures she wondered about this. But the worry about Granpap was stronger. And there was the matter of deciding which of the boys should use the horse. Frank said let them both go, taking turns walking and riding. Emma, though she would not say it, wanted Kirk because Basil would not feel with Granpap. But Basil was the oldest.

Basil settled the matter himself before the trial. He came home from the settlement one Sunday night and got his few clothes together in a bundle. "I'm a-going, Ma, first thing in the morning," he said.

"So soon?" Emma asked. She thought he meant the trial.

"I'm a-going to school," Basil said. "The preacher got a place for me in the church school across North Range. I can make my way and learn, too."

"And not have a disgrace," Emma said, and at once she was sorry for her spiteful tongue. But she could not forget all that Basil felt about Granpap, yes, and said.

She got up next morning and gave Basil coffee before he

went. Standing at the door she watched him go off on the path and without wanting to she yearned after him. He was her first, born when she was no more than a girl. And he was going off stiff against her and Kirk. It was early and there was only a half light, gray and dreary—a hopeless in-between time when the dark had gone and there was not any sign of the sun. It felt as if the sun would never come up. Emma listened to Basil's steps until they died off somewhere on the second lap of the trail.

Kirk rode the horse to the trial. Emma and the children walked with him to the McClures', where he would get the horse. Emma carried a bundle for Granpap tied up in a red handkerchief. There were some real flour biscuits she had made and a store shirt bought at Swain's. Most of the money Granpap had sent by Hal Swain had been spent on these things—the flour and the shirt—but they had to send Granpap a message, and the gifts said they were thinking about him.

All morning Emma helped Ora string dried apples and grabble potatoes. The children worked with Young Frank in the corn patch high up on the hillside. Big Frank had gone to Swain's. He had been promised a seat in Swain's wagon if he got there in time. Swain had said, "First come, first served." Most of the men in the settlement wanted to go down for the trial, partly for the excitement, but mainly because they wished to show Granpap faces of neighbors and kin in the court.

During the long late afternoon Emma and Ora sat in the doorway watching the children, who played Ant'ny Over with John's ball. All of Ora's tribe except the baby played. John, Young Frank, and the next oldest McClure played against Bonnie, Sally, and Ora's four others.

Sally called "Ant'ny" from behind the cabin and when the boys who were in front of Ora and Emma heard they called back "Over!" and the ball came bouncing over the roof because Sally could never learn to throw it high. Young Frank caught it and the three boys scurried around the house so that Young Frank could hit one of the other side. If he did this then the person who was hit would be his captive.

Emma could hear Bonnie laughing before she came running around the right side of the cabin. Her hair was down and flying back behind her. She was the first. Behind her came Sally and then the four young McClures, the last toddling along on his short legs. He did not look very formidable, but he got in Frank's way just as he was throwing the ball at Sally, and the ball missed. The dogs ran in circles barking at the children, and with their own pleasure in the excitement. And the children laughed and shouted. Sally and Bonnie yelled at Frank.

"You're no good."

"You couldn't hit a dead possum."

"Look at that little toddler," Ora said, pointing to her next to youngest. "Running along, a-laughing—not knowing that trouble and sorrow are ahead of him."

"Hit's best they don't know," Emma said. She was glad to see John and Bonnie playing—yet she felt a disappointment that they could be so happy when they knew that Granpap might be put away for a long time if the trial went against him. They could forget so easily.

About dark Emma called the children to go home.

"Kirk might be till to-morrow," she told Ora.

"You're welcome to stay," Ora said.

"I know." And Emma did know. But she wanted to get back to the cabin where she was on her own familiar ground. On the trail she walked along slowly. John and Bonnie kept close to her and she felt warmed because it seemed they were remembering Granpap again, though they did not speak. The rustling and panting of the dogs chasing imaginary animals in the bushes made sound for company, and this was enough. She did not wish to talk.

At the cabin Bonnie and John would not go to bed. Emma sat down on the door log.

"Get my shawl, then," she told Bonnie, "and bring a quilt."

She was still hoping to see Kirk and Granpap come along, Granpap riding the horse and Kirk walking behind. They were like this in her mind while she tucked the children up in the quilt. The shawl she drew close around her shoulders and held it with her arms crossed. Bonnie leaned against her, and on the other side of Bonnie John sat upright against the house with the corner of the quilt behind him.

Presently Emma's tongue was loosened. She had tired of peering into the dark and listening for a sound up the trail.

"When I was a little girl," she said, "Granpap used to tell about the Civil War." It comforted her to think of her pap back there and to talk about him. "He used to say as far as he knew there wasn't any civil kind of war. Not that he knew about.

"He said they was miserable, just miserable. He fought most two years. The last year there was a rich man's son, one of them that owned slaves before they was freed, and he was one of their army and only sixteen. He had a slave to take care of him like a nurse. And the slave had stayed on, taking care of the boy even after he knew he was freed. By that time, toward the end of the war, nobody, rich or poor had anything to eat.

"The soldiers used to sit around a campfire at night and the rich man's son had a book called 'Lee's Miserables.' He'd read to them. The General that owned the army was named Lee. And after hearing the book the soldiers called themselves Lee's Miserables. Granpap said he used to get s' hungry. . . . Once he was a-scouting and he came across a little nigger. The little nigger was eating a piece of cornbread. Granpap said snot was running from the little nigger's nose on the bread. But Granpap hadn't eaten a thing for two days. He took the bread away from the little nigger and ate it. And it was the best meal, he said, he ever had."

Bonnie raised up. She was almost asleep. Perhaps she had been asleep. She had heard the story before. But so had John heard it. Yet he was never tired of hearing it again, or of asking his own questions.

"Did he come?" Bonnie asked.

"No, but maybe he will. Maybe hit's why Kirk's s' late. They had to take turns one a-walking and the other a-riding."

About daybreak Kirk returned. Emma was propped up against the door and Bonnie was lying against her. John had stretched out on the ground with only a piece of the quilt over him. They were all wet with dew. Emma waked up at once. At once she looked into the dark behind Kirk.

"Ye alone, Kirk?"

"Yes, Ma." Kirk's voice came lost and hollow from the half dark.

"Come in and have coffee," Emma said. The strain was over and she could wait to hear the rest. Granpap had been put away.

Kirk brought in wood. His head hanging with sleep, John followed Kirk to the woodpile and back again. Bonnie stayed close to Emma. When the fire was built up they sat around it to warm up while the coffee boiled.

"He got two years," Kirk said.

"Two years," Emma repeated. "Hit's s' long."

"He stood up in court and talked to the judge," Kirk said. "He said he'd fought in the Confederacy, and he'd done his duty and had a right to make money when his folks needed money. No government could take that right away."

"Did he say that?" Emma asked. "Right up to the judge?"

"He did," Kirk told her. "I heard him."

"Hit won't help him," Emma said shrewdly. "But I'm glad he did it."

"Hal Swain said," Kirk told her, "he'll be out in a year. Hal Swain's in politics outside. He was acquainted with some of the men down there. He knew the judge."

Emma looked away to the window where light was just coming in. The pot of coffee boiled over and she got up to hand the cups and pour it out.

"Did you see him after?" she asked.

"Yes," Kirk said. "For a little."

"Did he say anything about the McEacherns?" Emma asked.

"No."

"I never did trust them," Emma said. "I believe right now Pap is the one suffering for the lot. I believe they sold him out."

"He didn't say."

Kirk pointed to a package on the table. "He couldn't take the shirt," he said.

Emma opened the package and held up the shirt. "I'll save hit, till he comes," she said. But she saw that Kirk's eyes were on it.

"Maybe we'd better not—maybe you'd better have it while it's new." She held it out to him.

"Save it for him," Kirk said roughly and pushed her away. She saw the wanting in his face.

"Now you take hit," she insisted putting it on his lap. "Maybe when the time comes we'll have money to get Granpap another."

Kirk reached into his pocket. There was a rattle of change and he pulled out quite a handful and let it roll on the table into a pile. John and Bonnie watched every move of his hand. They had never seen so much money at one time.

"Neighbors and kin took up a collection," Kirk said. "Granpap said ye must buy a cow."

The money was there. And it was important. The cow would be important. But this direct message from Granpap was what Emma had been wanting. It was a great comfort.

Presently when Bonnie had gone to sleep and John was out getting wood she asked,

"Did ye see Basil around?"

"No."

"Seems like he might have come down. The school ain't far, is hit?"

"Hal says about twenty miles."

"And down hill all the way," Emma said. "He could have walked it in the time hit takes to have a good meal."

"Well, he wouldn't."

"I know. He could but he wouldn't. I wish he was different."

"He is different."

"Different from us. I don't know where he gets what he's got. And I don't know why I don't like hit. He's steady. Not like you. You're s' reckless."

"No more than others. No more than Granpap."

"Granpap's not near s' reckless as he was. And maybe you'll calm down later."

13

KIRK brought back a souvenir from outside. "When court stopped for dinner," he said, "Granpap's case hadn't come up. I was wandering round and a man in a closed-up wagon called me. 'Want your picture took?' he asked and I said no. He looked at me and then he said. 'If you'll hold my horse while I get some dinner I'll do you for nothing.' So I held the horse, and he took me."

Emma held the photograph up before her. It was not very clear. But it was Kirk with his hair slipping over his forehead, though the gay, careless look wasn't there. He was stiff, and solemn as an owl.

"Hit favors you and again it don't," Emma said, fingering the piece of cardboard.

"Hit's me all right, Kirkland McClure. The man wrote my name on the back."

Kirk took the picture and turned it over. Sure enough on the back was written a name.

"So that's your name written down—Kirkland McClure." Emma spoke the name as if she was reading. Going over to the chimney shelf she put the picture against the salt gourd. While she stood there admiring it Kirk spoke some words.

"What did you say?" she asked. He repeated the words with elaborate care.

"There's a sight of room here—with two gone."

Emma turned and faced him. What was he getting at? He wanted something of her—that she knew.

"Minnie's pap has turned her out," Kirk said.

Emma had no word to say. It was to be expected that Minnie's pap would do just that.

"When a girl like Minnie," Kirk said, looking at the floor, "gets out on the world there're plenty of men waiting round like buzzards over a carcase."

"And the carcase has got to stink before the buzzards smell hit," Emma said.

"Sure enough," Kirk answered. "A woman can't be kind to another."

"Ye want her—now?" Emma asked. Kirk did not answer Emma knew the answer to that question.

"Be ye going to marry?" she asked, then.

"Come spring we'd walk down. She's too big now."

"And her carrying another man's child," Emma said.

"She's a gal that draws men and they take her. She needs a man to keep her from temptation."

"Her pap tried to. He didn't seem to do hit."

"Her pap used her bad," Kirk said. "She needs kindness."

Emma held to the chimney shelf. She stood up quiet and still before Kirk. What was he asking? Children didn't know. They could see only their side. Like an owl in the daytime, their eyes were open but they couldn't see. They flew by night getting what they wanted and if they were shown day things they fluttered and twisted away from seeing.

"Sam McEachern is a-hanging round her," Kirk said.

"Let him," Emma cracked out. "They'd do for each other."

"Ye wouldn't turn out a hog that was going t' litter," Kirk accused his mother. "And ye won't take in a gal."

"I've got enough t' do with Granpap gone," Emma said. But Kirk saw that she turned away.

"I'll help," he told her. When Emma did not answer he walked out to where John was digging the trench clean for sweet potatoes on the south side of the cabin. Kirk took the hoe from John and began digging.

"Run along and grabble taters," he said. John stood by the open trench. He had dug hard and long and wanted to finish.

"I ain't a-going to grabble taters for nobody," he said to Kirk angrily. "I want that hoe."

Kirk wouldn't get angry. "Then grabble them for yourself," he told John. "You're going to eat them, ain't ye? Run along." Kirk began to dig long deep strokes. "I'll be ready before you're half finished grabbling," he said, and smiled up at John from under his hair. John had been ready to fight. There were times when Kirk had a way that made people wish to do what he wanted them to do. This was one of the times. Suddenly John was satisfied to go out and join Bonnie in the potato patch.

Bonnie was reaching down into the dirt feeling after the roots with her grimy fingers. The shallow gully between the potato hills already held a number of potatoes, slim ones, and fat bellied ones with long tails. John began on the row next Bonnie at the other end. He spread his fingers and pushed them through the dirt under the yellowing vines. It was a pleasure when his finger tips touched a root. There was a moment of excitement and suspense before the fingers closed around the potato. For no one could tell until that moment whether it would be small or large and round and worth pulling out.

Emma came from the cabin. Instead of beginning at the end of a new row she started just opposite John.

"Remember Minnie?" she asked John, looking across at him from her row. "Minnie Hawkins?"

"Yes." John gave a tug in the dirt and brought out a fat potato. He felt it carefully, then slung it on the pile behind him. "She's little side up, big side down," he said, not looking at Emma.

"Who told ye?"

John hesitated. "I know it," he said.

"He wants to bring her here." Emma jerked her head toward Kirk.

"Why?"

"He wants her."

John could understand the sounds in Emma's voice. Now he understood that she was disturbed. But he could not make out everything. Kirk wanted Minnie and his wanting should make it right for Minnie to come. Yet Emma's voice said it was not right.

"The McClures," Emma said, "have always been people that stuck. If Kirk takes her he'll stick. And she'll ruin him, just ruin him."

"She's a pretty gal," John said. He had heard them say this at church, and he felt himself that Minnie was pretty.

"Too pretty for Kirk's good. He said," Emma went on bitterly, "I wouldn't turn out a hog if it was going to litter."

"No," John said, "I reckon you wouldn't."

It sounded as if John had pronounced judgment on her. She left her row and went back into the cabin. She could not deny Kirk his home, so long as he wanted to stay. And she did not wish to. She did not grudge Minnie the food nor the roof. If it had been any other girl having a baby she could take her in and say welcome. It was Minnie who made it hard. She was lacking in something fine and upstanding. Minnie's mother was the same. Even when she was a woman married twelve years she would go to the store and if a man was leaving with a sledge or on a horse for the outside she would beg him to bring her something "nice." Emma had heard her once. This was no idle talk. If Minnie came she would be like poison ivy climbing around the cabin. Yet if Kirk wanted Minnie, it seemed that Emma must give in.

She went out to Kirk. "I reckon," she said, "if you want her you've got to have her."

"Will you give her welcome?" Kirk asked.

"I'll give her welcome," Emma said and walked away, leaving Kirk standing by the trench and the big mound of dirt. He did not stay there long. She heard a noise out front and there was Kirk walking the path to the trail.

She called him and ran to catch up. He stood and faced her.

"Be ye bringing her to-day?" she asked. She had thought there would be some time between accepting Minnie and having her.

"Ora kept her." Kirk looked across the cabin to South Range. He did not want to see his mother's face. "It's why I was late. I brought her last night. Ora said I'd got to ask you first."

A warm rush of blood went over Emma at the knowledge that Ora had taken up for her and understood. But this was so soon. Yet she had told Kirk "I'll give her welcome," and soon or late it must be.

"I'll cook some supper," she said. She turned back to the potato patch where John and Bonnie were gathering up the potatoes to carry them to the trench. She thought, "With his Granpap just put in jail he had time to think of Minnie. Like dancing on top of a new grave." In a moment she had another thought. "He's young and the young can't see what the old suffer. They're blind. He's blind as a hoot owl."

All the rest of the afternoon while the sun went down further and the shadows got longer, and the white clouds made shadows on the mountains, Emma walked about the clearing and the cabin, helping Bonnie and John, and making supper. Inside her there was unquiet. It was like winds that blew from the north and the south at the same time. She would hate Minnie and Kirk too, and feel cold and hard toward them. Then she would think of excuses for both. The warm feeling struggled with the cold until Emma felt as if a storm had struck her and torn up her roots, so that she was lying helpless, like a tree on the side of a mountain.

14

ONE day in the late fall Minnie's boy child came. Ora sat over the fire with her legs spread out to make a big cradle of her lap for the child. Bonnie and John had gone over to tell Ora it was time for her to come. They had stayed with the children there. Ora reached Emma's cabin just in time. A few moments after Ora arrived Minnie groaned a little, and there was the baby. The child had got its first nursing and Minnie was sleeping over in Emma's bed.

"Come as easy," Ora said. "Not like yours, Emma."

"No," Emma answered. "Mine all came hard. They seemed to dread getting into the world."

"She'll have plenty of milk, being big and healthy like she is."

"Hit's a good thing. That cow Hal sold us is most dry."

"Hit'll be a surprise for Kirk," Ora said and leaned far over the baby to spit.

"I do so hope they'll get a bear."

"Who went along besides Frank?"

"Fraser McDonald and Jesse."

"Four," Ora said. "Hit won't be much for each one. Hal don't give much for hides."

"No."

Minnie stirred on the bed. She gave a great sigh and turned over. The women listened until she breathed regularly again.

"Does she vex ye much?" Ora asked in a low voice.

"No, I can't say she does. She hasn't helped, but she hasn't hindered. She ain't a talking woman and most of the day she just sits over the fire a-waiting for him." Emma smiled. "Hit seems almost like a reproach from the Lord for the thoughts I had of her before."

"Maybe." Ora drew back with a sudden jerk from the baby. "That's right," she said to him. "Wet me up, ye little man child." She held out the baby to Emma. "Hold him," she said, "while I dry out."

In Emma's lap the baby sputtered as if it might come fully awake. Ora leaned over and the two watched the thin bowed legs squirm, and the head move weakly.

"A man child," Ora said. "Look at him. Look at the damage his pappy did, and now he's here t' bring others to sorrow and maybe t' shame."

"Ye're putting all the blame in one place," Emma said.

"Hit's where hit ought to be."

"The way I look at it," Emma said, "hit's not one's fault nor the other."

"You can't kill a bear without a shot in its side," Ora said. "The bear does its part by getting in the way, but the gun does the killing. A man is a danger to every good woman and she's got to know it. . . . A danger to every woman good or bad. I tell my Sally to look on men that they're deadly as rattlesnakes."

"There's good men," Emma said. "Like Frank. And Jim McClure was good."

"I'm not a-talking about husbands, but men and girls unmarried."

"As I look back there was times when I would have been willing if Jim had a'wanted to take advantage before we was married," Emma said. "And afterwards he was kind for a man. I would a'done anything he said. If he'd a'told me to put my hand in the fire and hold it there I think I would a'done it. But he never did. And before Bonnie was born he walked to Swain's a cold November night to get some pickles. I wanted them s' bad."

The baby's red face screwed up into ugly tight knots. Small gasping whimpers came out of its mouth. Emma stood up. "I'll put hit in the bed," she told Ora. "Maybe she'll wake up and give it some milk."

The next day about noon the men who had been bear hunting came down the south trail. John was at the back watching. Bonnie couldn't be budged from the baby inside. She wanted to hold it continually. Emma almost had to smack her because she got in the way with her begging.

Both the young ones were so taken up with their interests Emma had to do everything about the cabin. She cut the wood and brought it in. But she was used to that. Even when the others were there, it took so long to urge them to the tasks she often did everything herself rather than go to the trouble of persuading them.

Since early daylight John had been on the lookout for the men. He went up the trail every few minutes. At last he saw them far up the trail and knew by the way they swung along together that they had a bear. Running through the bushes toward them he could see the poles across Kirk's and Jesse's shoulders. It was a huge she bear. Her feet were tied to the long poles and her head hung down. John felt her. His hands dug into her thick fur and he felt the nipples under the hair.

When they came on a rise and saw the cabin John remembered the baby. He looked at Kirk. The men were laboring, saving their breath for the burden they were carrying. It was no time to speak of a baby. He saw Emma come to the back door. He was afraid she would speak. But she was silent, watching them carry the load around the house to the spring hollow.

The dogs frisked around the carcase and John hung there too, watching and sniffing as if he was another dog. The men let him bring the stone and whet their knives, while they sat and drank from the jug Kirk fished from the bushes, where they had left it on the way out.

The four guns rested against the spring bench, and John took his soap stone there. He spat on the stone and pressed the blade down. With all the energy in his arm he moved the blade in a circle. When the stone got dry he spit again. When Fraser's knife seemed sharp enough he wiped it carefully on his jeans and picked a blade of dry grass. The knife cut straight through. The late sun glittered on the blade. John looked at Fraser. He wondered if Fraser would notice how finely the blade had been sharpened. If he did, perhaps when the time came to divide the carcase he would think, "What a fine boy Kirk's brother is. We will let him choose."

For Fraser being the oldest and the best bear hunter was the leader. He would do the skinning and later hold up the divided carcase for the parts to be chosen.

When Fraser called for his knife John carried it to him and stood by while Fraser began the skinning. Three skillful cuts and the skin lay back. The dogs, smelling the fresh meat, crowded between Fraser's legs.

"Shut them pests up, John," Fraser said. The boy struggled with the dogs. They were very fierce now the blood was dripping and bit at him.

"Here," Fraser said. He sliced off a piece of red meat and put it in John's hand. "Just let them smell that."

John let them get a whiff and started toward the cabin. They followed yapping at his heels. He ran into the other room and left them fighting over the piece of meat. The door opened on the inside, and he had to spend some time getting it shut without crushing his fingers.

When he returned Jesse McDonald was finishing the knives. He was sitting to rest his leg that had been hurt in a fall over a cliff. It was not hurt much for he had been caught in some laurel bushes. But his face and hands were scratched. He had been out on the mountain picketing. When John came up and sat down beside him, he told how he had walked along taking a drink now and then when suddenly the ground went right out from under him. He winked a swollen eye at John. "The wine was good," he said, "and the night was long."

John was impatient with the talk. He had sat there so Jesse would give the knives back to him to finish. But Jesse went right on whetting them and talking. The new drink had made his tongue loose.

"Well, that's over," Fraser said, and hung the huge mass of thick black fur on a bush.

"Fill the pot with water," Kirk called out to John. They kept him busy. John brought laurel sticks for the fire and went inside to get fire from the chimney. Emma looked at him as if she wanted to speak but he hurried out. He had no time for women. At the spring he kept close to the bear. There was a curiosity to see the inside of the great animal, to see the entrails lying curled up inside the body.

"Get some more laurel sticks, John," Kirk ordered.

John looked up at his brother. "If I do, can I choose?" he asked. Kirk frowned. Fraser was the leader. John knew that Kirk was ashamed. He dug his feet into the dry grass and hung his head. He was down before Kirk's look. Yet he would not go back on what he had asked. Fraser was bending over the red inside of the bear, but he heard.

"What does the young one want?" he asked Kirk.

"He wants to choose," Kirk said in a queer shy voice.

"Let him," Fraser said, and John gave Kirk a triumphant look. Fraser had said, "Let him," right away as if he had confidence in John. It seemed hours before the men stood waiting by the divided carcase. There had been some wrangling about the division. Kirk and Frank McClure, wanting to be fair, had said the carcase must be cut into four pieces, since Jesse was one of the hunters. Fraser insisted that Jesse had been careless, and had had no part in getting the bear, and the family had enough with his piece. At last they gave in to Fraser who was very emphatic; and they had to acknowledge that with the carcase divided into three pieces there would be a very large part for each family.

"Get behind the big maple," Fraser told John. "And shet your eyes."

Behind the tree John turned his back on the spring and the men and closed his eyes tight. A leaf from the maple fell on the back of his neck when it was bent. There was the sound of an animal in the grass. Once he heard a sound from the cabin. It was a baby crying, and for a moment he wondered how a baby got there, for his mind was a long way from the happenings of the days before.

Then Fraser's big voice came. "Whose piece is this?" he asked. The names were already in John. He had them ready. Kirk, Fraser, Frank. But for a moment he was dumb with the weight of the decision.

"Fraser's piece," he called. His voice sounded high and excited. He heard it after it had left his mouth.

There was a pause until Fraser lifted the next piece and called again. "Whose piece is this?"

John did not hesitate. "Kirk's," he answered. The next was Frank McClure's.

Then it was time for John to open his eyes and come around the tree to see what his decisions had given each man. Kirk was holding a large forequarter, food for days to come.

The men slowly got ready to go, strapping up their shares of the meat. Fraser and Jesse divided their part, so each might carry a share of the load.

"Come in awhile," Kirk said to them. "Hit's long till dark."

Fraser picked up his gun. "My woman'll think I'm lost forever," he said. "I'd better get home before she gives me out and takes up with another man."

"You'll be welcome," Kirk said, but he knew they were r'aring to get home and have their women cook some of the meat. He and John stood and watched the three go up the trail one after the other, bent over under the weight of the meat. Fraser McDonald's head was entirely hidden behind the black fur he had tied over the hindquarter. The three dogs John had let out followed them.

Kirk's eyes were dreamy with thinking about the hunt and being at the end of it ready for a fine supper in front of the fire. He picked up the heavy forequarter and they turned toward the cabin.

"How's Minnie?" he asked casually. The thought of her was just coming back into him.

"Hit's come," John told him.

15

JOHN was coming up the road from Swain's, a sack of meal on his back, payment for Kirk's share in the bear skin. He did not hurry. Occasionally he passed one of the cabins of the settlement where tow-headed children came to the door and peered at him curiously. The women were inside hunched over the fires or moving around, working. Once he smelled cooking and his stomach contracted. He had eaten early that morning and there had been very little for the meal.

At the place where Jim Martin's children had made a slide down the red clay bank he turned to the right for the trail up Possum Hollow. Before him was old Thunderhead. In the clear morning it seemed close, but he knew the mountain was far away and the trail to its foot upward. The weight of the sack he held with both hands pressed into the small of his back. It made the distance seem longer. He was measuring the distance with his eyes as he stepped on the log footway across Burnt Cabin Branch. Usually he could walk a footway with his eyes shut. On this day from the very beginning he had been in a daze. There were so many things to think about. They had accumulated in him for days and even months. In his own way he was trying to sort out experiences, and to find answers for certain questions that demanded his attention. With back bent under the sack and nose lifted in the air John walked the footway. And then one foot slipped. He tried to balance, but the heavy sack pulled him to one side. He sat down heavily on the log with a leg on each side. He looked around hastily to see if any of the Martin young had caught him in such a position. To his relief the woods were silent. Pulling himself along with one hand he got to the other side of the creek. It was not very high. In the spring when the snows were melting up above, the water sometimes reached the footway. The spring before, Jim Martin's baby girl had drowned just below. Jim was working over the branch, girdling trees for a clearing. The two-year-old girl was playing on the cabin side. He heard her call, but paid no attention. She must have tried to cross the footway; for Zinie, the oldest daughter, coming to look for little Jennie, found her body washed down against a laurel bush below the footway. The water was beating the body against the roots of the bush. As soon as Emma heard she brought John and Bonnie and stayed three days with Jennie doing everything to comfort her neighbor. She laid out the little corpse, and after the funeral cleaned the cabin and washed all the clothes. John and Bonnie stayed with the Martin young and learned all the ins and outs of Possum Hollow. They went to visit Granma Wesley who was bedridden and heard her talk about the fine coverlet she was going to make. Sam's wife let them look at the loom and put their feet on the treadles. The loom was as high as John. It seemed a huge and wonderful thing to him with its treadles that moved the upper part, and the strings that made it look like some large overgrown sort of a banjo.

At the Martin cabin John found Zinie in the yard with the latest baby on her hip. She stood sideways so the baby would be more comfortable. The Martins had a small porch to their cabin and Zinie leaned against it. She was nine and large for her age, yet the baby seemed big for her. He had a cold and as John came up Zinie took the end of his dress and wiped the nose clean. Her eyelids covered her eyes as if she was interested only in her bare red feet. But she saw John.

"Come in," she said shyly, "and sit."

"I've got to be getting along," John told her.

Zinie shuffled her feet in the dirt. "Tell Bonnie to come over." She spoke very softly. Her own voice seemed to frighten her, for when she spoke her face turned red so that the freckles stood out distinctly like speckles on a bird's eggs.

"You come over," John said. He hurried past her up the trail. Just beyond was the chicken coop and to the side the pig pen with the one pig smelling the empty log trough with loud sniffs.

Up at the left he could just see the Wesleys' cabin through the trees. The shed for the loom stuck out at one side. It sloped a little down the hill and gave an unbalanced appearance to the cabin.

Over Thunderhead John stopped to rest on the flat part of the trail. The climb up the other side had been long and tiring. He let the sack of meal down and leaned against a pine tree on the upper side of the trail. Right before him a stream going down hill had cut a gorge in the side of the mountain. Trees and bushes grew down in the gorge. The tops of the trees came slightly above it and over the tops there was a clear view into the valley below. On the near side the floor of the valley was covered with trees that were bare of green except for scattered balsams and pine. Far over on the other side of the valley was the Frank McClure cabin. At the right of the cabin a small figure moved in the clearing.

As John watched the tiny figure a thought came into his head, worrying him like a bat that swoops down close to one's head and then vanishes in the same second that it has come. The tiny dot in the distance seemed insignificant and of no account. Yet it was a person like John himself, and to that person living was very important; just as to John the fact that he was alive was important. The thought darted away almost as soon as it came, and there was a blank. Then another thought came—about the cabin and Emma and Minnie. He had left Emma and Bonnie stringing apples they had sliced and dried on the roof. He supposed Minnie was still sitting by the fire with the baby in her lap. That morning Kirk had gone toward South Range, having heard they were making a clearing for a saw mill over that way. He hoped to get work.

Emma kept the baby with her at night. It slept in the cradle Basil had been the first to sleep in and John the last. Minnie slept in the other room with Kirk and John stayed in his and Granpap's bed across the room from them. He was pondering on those two. He knew what happened in the night, yet he didn't know. And he was curious about things he did not wholly understand.

Kirk had not come back when John reached the cabin. But a saddlehorse stood in the yard hitched to one of the apple trees. In the cabin Sam McEachern sat over the fire with Minnie. On one side of the chimney Bonnie held the baby while it slept. Emma was fluttering around the room doing nothing, just fluttering like a hen when a hawk is swooping around in the air above the little chickens.

When the boy had let the sack fall on the table Emma drew him out into the back yard. Her fingers dug into his shoulder. Out by the rough cow shed she faced him.

"If Minnie starts this," she said, "there's bound to be trouble."

He nodded. She was right, yet he hated her excited voice whispering to him.

"She's a fool, a plumb fool," Emma went on as she usually did when she wished to speak, not noticing nor caring perhaps that John felt ill at ease. "I can bear her not helping and letting me wait on her like a nigger slave. But this . . ." She threw out her hands. "I knew it," she said. "I knew the hog would go a-wallowing back to hit's mire."

Emma's worried voice made the boy turn away from her. He turned away but because of her he felt strained and unhappy. His voice was casual and hard when he spoke.

"Ain't supper ready?" He had taken his time going and coming and it was almost time for the evening meal.

He was walking toward the cabin. Emma kept beside him. "How can I make any food," she whispered, "with him a-hanging over the fire?"

At the door she stopped. "Don't ye tell Kirk anything," she said.

Sam McEachern was already outside, getting on his horse. Minnie sat over the fire, her arms laid along her big thighs. At twenty she was already a large woman, but her round cheeks and wide blue eyes gave her face a babyish look. And she seemed to wish to emphasize this characteristic. For she had a way of sticking her little finger in her mouth when she looked at men that nearly drove Emma crazy. She did this even with John who was only eleven, and Emma suspected that John himself was half in love with her.

Minnie felt injured. She knew Emma had disapproved of her visitor and would continue to disapprove if Sam McEachern came again. Yet Minnie had come under the disapproval of so many people, one more mattered very little. It was what her pap had raised her on, disapproval and reproaches. So she had come to the place where she simply went along her own way. The others seemed to know so little about what happened in her. They could not understand that sometimes with one man, sometimes with another, the heat came up in her and made her dizzy and blind so she scarcely knew what happened.

It had begun with Sam McEachern when she was seventeen.

Sam had seen her along the road on errands. Sometimes he spoke to her and sometimes he did not. But she could always feel that his attention was on her whether he stopped to talk or went past without a word. And she thought about him. One Saturday night he walked in the cabin door. He came in and gave her something she liked and took what he wanted; and they were both satisfied. It was like having a full meal.

Her pap had made her entertain Basil for Sunday visits. She had liked Basil, only Kirk was more interesting. Jim Hawkins disapproved of Kirk because he came drunk, so she had been forced to meet him up the mountain. There had been excitement in that. Now she had Kirk all the time and he quarreled if she talked of going to the settlement. He had become tiring to her except when she needed him.

Emma was stooping to put the pones of cornbread in the ashes on the hearth. She looked up into Minnie's face. The wide blue eyes stared into hers innocently. Emma had meant to speak but lowered her head again. She thought, "Much as Minnie's pap has dinged right and wrong into her she don't know it any more than a blind bat. Kirk will just have to keep her under his eye. He took the burden and hit he'll have to carry."

Yet could she help but carry the burden with Minnie always at the cabin and Kirk away sometimes for days, hunting work? There had been none at South Ridge. But the rumors of a big saw mill coming kept going around. And each time a rumor told of a new location for the mill, Kirk sought out that location. And as if he smelled out Kirk's absence, each time Kirk went away Sam McEachern came riding to the cabin.

Emma had seen Kirk eye the horse tracks when he came home. Because he did not ask whose they were she suspected that he knew. He was drinking more and more. Sometimes he came back at night with bleared eyes and his hair matted as if he had been sleeping for days on the ground.

One afternoon Minnie and Sam sat by the fire a long time. They were very quiet, and Emma sitting across the hearth felt something rise up between them. Then before her eyes they got up and walked out of the cabin. They looked as if they were walking in their sleep. Emma was close enough to touch them as they passed, but she was surprised into sitting still. She sat there for a moment until she heard them walk into the other room.

The sound of their feet in the other room roused her. She got to the door and stood there looking out. Now there was no sound from the other room. The cold wind came across and blew through her. Those two were over in the other room under Kirk's roof. And she knew. She was Kirk's kin, and it was a McClure roof. Emma suspected that the McEacherns had sold Granpap out. They had money. Sam came back from outside with "nice" things for Minnie that she hid away from Kirk. There was a string of beads and a blue silk waist that Emma had seen.

She had kept it all from her son. In spite of herself Emma had taken this burden and she had to carry it.

"Bonnie!" she said. "Put down that baby and go up the hill for the cow. John, you go with Bonnie."

John was warm by the fire. "It ain't milking time," he said.

"Go up, both of ye," Emma said. "Or I'll lay a hickory on your hides." It was not the threat of the hickory, but the heavy sound of Emma's voice that picked them up and sent them through the door to the cow trail.

Emma walked to the side wall. Over the trunk just below Granpap's fiddle, lay his gun across two crotches of a tree. Emma lifted the gun off its supports, and looked to see that it was loaded. Back at the door she stood leaning lightly against the post with the gunstock under her right arm pit and the barrel pointing down. She looked careless and indifferent, as if she were wondering if the clouds across the top of Thunderhead would bring some rain.

The steps sounded again in the next room. Her left hand came down on the gun and she bent her arms so the stock rested in her shoulder. Minnie came first out of the passage and turned to enter the cabin from the yard. She drew back in the face of the gun and gave a little grunt. Emma stood aside.

"Come in, Minnie," she said evenly. "I don't aim to hurt ye."

Minnie sidled to the wall outside and held to it. Emma was looking at Sam McEachern. She edged back in the door. Sam was a big powerful man and if she was too close to him he could take the gun from her hand.

Sam stood before her with his smile that Emma did not like beginning to spread out on his thin lips.

"What's the matter, Emma?" His voice was soft as lye soap.

Emma pointed the gun straight. Sam looked at it inquiringly. He was not a coward.

"Yes, hit's loaded, Sam," Emma said. "And I'll give ye time t' get on your horse and ride out of here. But no more. And ye're not to come back again."

"Now, Emma," Sam began, "I ain't done nothing."

"Walk out of here," Emma said, "and get on your horse." She put her finger on the trigger and aimed at Sam's big breast, on the left side.

"I've got one, too," Sam said and took a revolver from his pocket.

Emma heard Minnie groan. She did not flinch from Sam's gun. If he shot her, he did. Her business was to get Sam away from the cabin.

"Your time's most gone, Sam," she said.

"What I hate most," Sam said, "is an interfering woman."

"And what I hate most," Emma took a step forward, "is a skunk. You get on that horse, Sam McEachern, with no more palaver."

Sam dropped the revolver in his pocket. His big face screwed up at Emma and his small tan-bark eyes blazed at her.

"A man can't fight a woman," he said and walked off. Emma kept the gun on him until he was beyond the cottonwood tree and going up the Ridge Trail. When he turned into the thick trees she lowered the gun.

"Come in," she said to Minnie who was blubbering against the wall. "I wouldn't hurt ye, Minnie."

16

Kirk came back next day. When Minnie was out of the room and he thought Emma was not listening he said to John, "I met Fraser on the road and he told me, 'Look out for Sam McEachern.' "

Emma heard. "Better look out for Minnie," she said.

Kirk looked at her. "Look out for Minnie?" he repeated.

Emma was silent.

"Be ye jealous because Minnie's got a man and you not?" Kirk asked. His quiet voice hit her like a fist between the eyes.

"Did Minnie tell ye to say that?" she asked, but there was no real strength in her voice. Kirk turned away from her face. "I can take care of Minnie," he mumbled.

Emma thought over the words Kirk had spoken. Was she jealous? Was that the reason she had sent Sam McEachern away? She could say to herself it was not true. Partly, yes. Women as well as men had jealous natures and no one could tell where or when they would come out. But if she was jealous it was chiefly for Kirk's safety. She thought about it all again that evening after supper when Kirk sat over Minnie at the fire, reaching to push her throat up so he could kiss under her chin. She wondered, sitting across from them with the baby in her arms, if Kirk thought he was making her jealous. If he did he was not trying to save her any pain. Perhaps he thought of her, for he got up and said, "Come to bed, Minnie," and pulled at Minnie's hand. And the girl went, hanging down her head like a virgin going to her marriage bed.

As the days went by and Kirk was more at home Minnie became so contrary it was surprising that even Kirk could bear with her. At times she would make John sleep with Kirk while she took his bed. At others she would sleep all night in front of the fire, keeping it going, so by morning all the wood was gone and Emma must nag at John to cut more or go out and cut it herself.

One Monday in January when Kirk and John had gone up South Trail to shoot some meat Minnie picked up her hat and coat and started out the door.

"Where ye going?" Emma asked her.

"To the settlement." Minnie hung her head.

"What for?" Emma knew she was nagging. This was Kirk's business and she knew what Kirk thought of an interfering woman. Yet she couldn't stop. At least she could be friendly and perhaps Minnie would be friendly, too.

"There's no call for ye t' go t' the settlement," she said persuasively. "Sit down, Minnie."

"I got to go," Minnie said.

"Who'll feed the young one?" Emma asked.

"He's just fed. I'll be back come nightfall."

Minnie was so determined to go Emma was forced to give in. She left the baby to Bonnie all day. In the afternoon when it cried Emma boiled the fat end of the meat—all that was left—and Bonnie let the child suck on that.

Kirk and John came in with two rabbits. Kirk looked at the empty chair by the fire where Minnie usually sat. "Where's Minnie?" he asked.

"Gone to the settlement."

"What for?"

"No telling."

"Do you know?" Kirk asked Bonnie.

"She said she had to," Bonnie answered.

Without a word and with the gun still in his hand Kirk walked to the door and out along the trail. When Bonnie was in bed and John, worn out from hunting and cleaning the rabbits, was asleep by the fire, Emma knelt down by the bed and prayed. She asked that Kirk would come back safe. He could have Minnie and keep her if she ruined him—if only he came back. She promised to be kind to Minnie so the girl would not wish to leave the cabin again.

It seemed a direct answer to her prayer when Minnie and Kirk walked into the cabin that night. They drew up to the fire for warmth, but neither of them spoke to Emma of what had happened. Later Ora told Emma what Frank McClure had told her. Kirk had found Minnie at the store sitting by the stove with Sam McEachern on a box beside her. Kirk and Minnie had quarreled behind the store counter, for Minnie refused to go back with Kirk. Then Jim Hawkins came in out of the night. And Minnie slipped through the back door with Kirk.

Emma had made a promise that night, and she would not lie to her God. After that Minnie came and went without Emma's watchful eyes measuring her footsteps. The girl would be gone whole days. She took the short cut that led over Barren She Mountain to Sam McEachern's bachelor cabin, and came back looking flushed and pretty in time for supper. Emma said not a word. She and Bonnie washed out an old bottle that had held Granpap's drink and warmed some milk that Emma had pressed out of the almost dry bag of the cow. They tied a small piece of cloth over the top of the bottle and made a hole in the center. Through this the baby could get the milk. It was not a very good substitute for Minnie and the baby fretted. But at least when Minnie was there she gave him all the milk he wanted.

Emma wondered at Kirk. He was gone during most of the days but came back every night. Sometimes he was drunk. She did not know that the night Kirk brought Minnie from the store those two had made a queer sort of bargain. Kirk was to leave Minnie alone during the day and she was to be his at night. Before the baby came, while Kirk was sure of Minnie, he had been at peace for he knew that Minnie would be waiting for him at the cabin whenever he returned. Since the child was born many things had changed. Minnie was ugly and dissatisfied. And then she had left him. He could never forget the desolation of coming back that night and finding Minnie's place at the fire empty. It was like death to come in and find her gone. So he made the bargain with her. She could go to the settlement as much as she pleased in the day, but at night she must be at the cabin when he returned.

He suspected that Minnie was unfaithful, though he would not allow the suspicion to come to a head. Yet he watched Sam McEachern. He was doing odd jobs for Swain and could not be on Sam's track all the time. So long as Sam was at the settlement Kirk was like a hound, always trying to smell him out. If Minnie met Sam it was at his cabin, and Kirk kept away from that place as if it held someone with a horrible disease. If he met a neighbor and said, "Have you seen Sam?" and they answered, "No, he must be over at his cabin," then the unrest and pain stayed with Kirk all day. But if the person he asked said, "I saw Sam over at Two Forks," or, "Sam has took out a load," then he could be at peace. The other man became a sort of partner to him, almost as close as a wife. Without Sam he was miserable. In his presence, or if he knew just where Sam could be found, alone, he was happy. He became haggard and ill from the strain of watching. Most of the money he made was spent on drink, and he ran up credit at Swain's for presents to take back to the cabin for Minnie.

About this time Emma needed some new soft cloth. Bonnie was getting older and *it* had come upon her. For herself Emma could do with any rag that came along, but for Bonnie she wanted the soft cloth. If she went to the store Hal Swain would probably give the cloth on credit. Minnie was at the cabin that day. She had gone to the settlement three days running. Emma suspected from the girl's actions that she had been disappointed in some way. Instead of coming home flushed and excited, she was irritated. Sam McEachern had promised when he got enough money to take Minnie away and she had been ready to go any time. But for three days she had found his cabin empty. So Minnie was sulking by the fire when Emma started out for Swain's.

When she was halfway down the gorge leading to Possum Hollow, Emma saw a horse and rider coming up the trail. The man on the horse was Sam McEachern. He had a sprig of balsam in his hat as if he was a beau going to meet his sweetheart.

Emma waited, standing full in the middle of the trail.

"Where be ye going, Sam?" she asked, looking up into his face.

Sam was not in the best sort of humor. His woman in Leesville, a girl who worked in the factory there, had tired of waiting for him, and during this time when he was with Minnie she married one of the mill hands. She was a pretty girl and Sam had thought she was his own to do with as he pleased. It fretted him that he was not as important to her as he had thought. He was going to see Minnie and it did not help him to a better state of mind to meet Emma on the road. But his voice was quiet and suave when he answered her.

"Just a-riding over toward South Ridge, Emma," he said.

"Be ye going to stop on the way?" Emma asked.

"Maybe," Sam answered her. "The trail's free, ain't it?"

He gave the horse a punch in the belly with his feet and it swerved around Emma. One of Sam's feet in the stirrup scraped her shoulder. How she hated him with his horse and gun and power to ride over her, his power to ride over Kirk. This matter must be settled, she said to herself as she turned to watch the man riding so unconcernedly up the trail. Even the horse's rump as it moved sideways in the trot seemed to mock at her. She was finished with being humble. For a long time she had humbled herself before Minnie, trying to make her happy and contented. She and Kirk had humbled themselves long enough before those two. Emma turned her back on Swain's and followed the horse up the trail, back toward the cabin.

From the spring the cabin looked deserted. Perhaps she had hurried back for nothing. Perhaps Sam was not coming here, but was paying a visit to his brother at the South Ridge settlement.

John came to the door to meet her. He had Granpap's gun in his hands. Bonnie was standing in the middle of the floor holding the baby. It was crying out loud in long wails and then sucking in its breath.

Emma looked at the hearth over John's head. No one was sitting there.

"Where's Minnie?" she asked. Then she saw that Bonnie was crying. It was her breath that was making the thick sucking noise. John looked at Emma with a long heavy inquiring look. He walked over to the south door and stood there watching.

"What is hit, Johnny?" Emma asked.

"Kirk," John said over his shoulder.

Emma went to him. "Where's Kirk?" she demanded.

"Up there," John said, nodding up at the South Trail.

"Who else?"

"*He* came. They saw Kirk coming and rode off."

Sam McEachern.

"Kirk came over the short trail. He got his gun and went. He told me to stay here."

"Come," Emma said and walked out of the door. They had got only as far as the cow shed when the shots came. One came and then two close together. Emma began to run. John kept just behind her, bending low to keep the gun from hitting against the bushes. The bushes caught Emma's dress and flew back in John's face. He bent his head, receiving them against his heavy hair. With his eyes and feet he followed Emma's feet. He could see them moving just ahead on the path. She panted in long heavy sobs of breath. John panted behind her. They were like rabbits with hounds behind them, only their danger and dread lay in front.

Far up on the edge of a bald spot they found Kirk. He had fallen back against some laurel bushes and broken their branches. One branch full of dark green leaves came up between his legs and covered his face. Emma broke away the branch with a thin snap and threw it out of her way. She bent over Kirk and tore at his shirt. With a sudden movement she put both hands on Kirk's shoulders and laid her cheek on his breast. The cheek came away covered with blood.

"He's dead," she said abruptly. Then she repeated it in a louder tone as if she must make John hear. "He's dead!"

John wanted to laugh. Emma was excited. Kirk was hurt, certainly. The blood was there. But they would bind up his wounds and soon he would come to, as he had before when he and Basil had fought.

"Ain't it a pity?" Emma said. She felt Kirk's arms and legs, and began to knead them as if in that way she could get life back into them. "Ain't it a pity?" she kept repeating. For the first time John looked into Kirk's face. The mouth was open, and the eyes looked straight up at John. The boy thought, "Why, he's a-looking at me." When he looked closer he saw that the pupils did not move. They were staring. He remembered the story about the frozen yearling. Its eyes were open and it stared at a laurel bush that grew out of the mountain. Its eyes were open and it was dead. John stooped by Emma and felt Kirk's face. The flesh was soft, but it did not feel alive. The jaws resisted his fingers. For a moment the face repulsed him. He lifted his fingers away and dug them into the earth as if he was grabbling for potatoes. Tears came out of his eyes and ran into his mouth, and he heard himself sobbing. Yet the sobbing seemed to come from up the trail, and not from his own mouth. Emma was not crying.

"We've got to get him back," she said to John. He paid no attention to her.

"We've got to get him back," she repeated to John and shook him. She was impatient because he did not understand at once.

They tried to lift the body and drag it down the trail. But the head leaned against Emma's breast and made her weak, so she had to lay it down again.

"You go," she said to John, "and get Frank McClure and Ora —and send for Fraser." She was panting after the exertion.

The sun had gone down when John came with Frank and Ora. Frank had a pine torch to light up the darkness. They found Emma sitting on the ground beside Kirk. She had laid him out straight and in the light from the pine torch he looked asleep. Emma sat stiffly beside him. She was stiff with cold. Ora and John helped her to her feet. She had difficulty in standing and at first they almost had to lift her down the trail. Frank stayed behind to wait for Fraser and Jesse. Young Frank had gone for them to help bring the body back to the cabin.

17

EMMA begged her neighbors to help her lay Kirk away in the regular burying ground. It would have been easier to lay him somewhere out in the clearing, for the trail was hard from the winter cold and there were places where the water that flowed over the trail from springs in the side of the mountain was frozen into ice. But Ora said if Emma, who was in sorrow, wanted Kirk laid away over the mountain, they should not be backward about helping her to have her wish.

The men knocked a coffin together from the floor of the passageway. Inside the coffin was smooth where many feet had walked over the passageway. The outside was rough with bark and the marks of the ax. The coffin was in the room on the floor. On the day of the burial Ora took the baby to her cabin and left it for her Sally to care for. Emma and the two children looked at Kirk for a last time before Frank nailed the cover down. Emma had lined the box with one of the new quilts and put another under Kirk's head, so he lay as if he was in bed asleep. But John could still feel in his finger tips the stiffness of Kirk's face that meant he was dead and not asleep. And his brother's attention was gone. The face, with the eyes closed now, was indifferent and cold, like a distant mountain covered with snow. And like the bare trees on the mountain it looked stripped. John felt, "It's stark naked." And an impulse came up in him to cover the face. But Frank was waiting with the boards to cover it.

While Ora was gone with the baby, Frank McClure and Fraser roped the coffin to Fraser's sledge. They had brought two steers from Hal Swain's to make the crossing over the mountain. Hal had loaned the steers and some heavy rope. When they had lifted the coffin inch by inch out to the sledge, Emma sat over the fire with John and Bonnie. John felt that Emma wanted him there, and he was torn between the desire to do what she wanted and the wish to go into the yard. Since the body was out of the room they had built the fire high. The logs crackled and spit as they caught the heat and began to burn. This was the only sound in the cabin.

Presently big Ora stood in the door.

"We're ready, Emma," she said and waited for Emma to get up. She had to repeat the words before Emma lifted her head. The men came in to warm themselves before starting out. Jim Martin, coming over to help, had joined Ora on the trail. He went up to Emma.

"Sam McEachern will pay for this, Emma."

"He's far away by now," Emma said.

"Everybody comes back to the hills."

"Hit's what I told her," Frank said. "We can wait. There's time."

"If ye wait long enough by its hole, a snake will come out to sun itself."

The men's subdued voices spread into the small room and filled it. The words echoed even after the men who said them had stopped speaking.

Ora tied the black knitted shawl around Emma's head. "It's s' cold," she said. She had brought her Sally's shawl for Bonnie. The child cried as Ora wrapped her up. Since they had brought Kirk back that night she had cried if anyone touched her. Ora wrapped Bonnie's hands in the ends of the shawl. "You keep your hands in there," she said, "so they won't freeze." Her own head was wrapped in a square of black woolen cloth, fastened under the chin with a pin. She wore an old coat torn at the sleeves. Emma had Granpap's coat on over her flannel dress. The long skirts on the two women dragged behind them on the floor as they took the step down at the door. Behind them the men walked out single file and gathered around the sledge. Frank directed, for he was the nearest kin. Jim was a distant cousin of the McClures. Fraser was no kin, but he was as near in his friendliness as any kin could be. Frank gave Fraser the lines for they needed his skill in the driving. Jim Martin stayed at the back of the sledge with Frank.

Frank whispered to Jim, "He's s' heavy. Hit was all we could do to get the coffin to the sledge."

"There'll be more to help yonder," Jim said.

The steers strained to make a start. Their bodies slanted

forward and their forefeet pawed the ground, but the sledge would not move. Fraser encouraged them with sounds from his throat and Frank and Jim bent their backs to push against the sledge with their hands.

"Here, Johnny," Frank said. He gave John his place and walked to the front. Taking the halters in his hands he pulled with the steers. Suddenly, as if the load had been made lighter, the steers began to move. Frank came to the back again and John walked between the two men. Emma walked behind the men, holding to Bonnie's hand, and just back of her, tall and protecting, came Ora.

After the gap at Thunderhead, though there was not the uphill strain, the anxiety was greater. The steers could not get a hold on the hard ground and their feet slipped again and again. On the second lap the sledge struck some ice and the back slid off the trail and hung above a steep side of the mountain. Emma started forward. Ora held her back, for the men were struggling with the ropes they had tied to the back of the sledge. Ora heard the ropes that held the coffin to the sledge groan and whine as the box slipped and strained at them. She thought, "Suppose the ropes break and the coffin tumbles on the rocks below." She looked over the side of the road at the steep descent that was almost a cliff and she shuddered against Emma, thinking of the terror if the coffin slipped and fell. It happened in a second. With a great heave of their bodies Frank and Jim pulled the back of the sledge into place on the trail, and once more the little procession moved zigzag across the face of Thunderhead. Down in the gorge where the trees were thinned out the sun had kept the ground thawed and the rest of the way was easier.

Young Frank and Jesse McDonald had come to the burying ground early in the morning to dig the grave. They stood by the mound of clay and watched the steers pull their burden up the slope. Beyond them were the four other McClure graves, one long for Jim and three short for the young ones who had died. They were not marked but the outlines could be seen in the dirt where they had sunk a little below the level of the ground. Other people from the settlement had come and were standing on the slope around the fire that Jesse and Young Frank had kept burning since morning. The smoke went up from the middle of the group of people. They turned when they heard Jesse say, "They're coming," and watched the procession. Their eyes picked out Emma behind the sledge. They had been talking of her, and of Kirk and his reckless ways. Everything they said had not been kind. But when they saw Emma their tongues were hushed. As they waited they drew closer together with a movement of compassion toward Emma.

When the procession reached the grave Frank McClure unhitched the steers and led them away far over to one side of the ground. Jim and Fraser stood by the sledge, and Jesse and Young Frank joined them. When Frank returned there were five men by the coffin. One more was needed. As they waited Jim Hawkins stepped from the group and stood by the other men. A little murmur went through the people, like a heavy sigh. By this act, as if he had spoken the words out loud, Jim said he was standing up for Kirk. He said that he reproached himself for driving Kirk from his cabin. And people began to remember how kind Kirk had been to Minnie, and how lucky Minnie would have been if she had married Kirk and settled down.

Hal Swain had his Bible open. While he read the men untied the coffin and lifted it clear of the sledge to the ground beside the grave. Young Frank and Jesse had already placed three long ropes on the ground. When the coffin was in place the men twisted the long ends around their forearms, and getting into place, three on one side of the grave and three on the other, they began to let the coffin down into the open grave. Hal read out loud as they let it down. "And David covered his face and he cried out with a loud voice, O my son Absalom, O Absalom my son, my son. Would to God I had died for thee." He had selected this passage for it seemed to be the one that was appropriate. And it was short. He looked toward Emma when he was finished, for he wanted her to know he had read it with sympathy for her sorrow. She did not see him. Her eyes were on the coffin the men had lowered into the dark hole. The rope ends dropped from their hands. While young Frank and Jesse shoveled on the red clay, Emma bent above them. She heard the clay striking the coffin.

Jennie Martin heard, and she knew this was the sound that was hardest to bear. She whispered to Ora, "Can't we start a hymn tune?" Ora nodded. "What?" Jennie whispered. Now that Ora said yes she could think of nothing to sing. Ora said the first that came to her, "Jesus Lover of my soul."

Jennie sang the first line and her high voice pierced the bleak air above the hill. On the second line other women's voices joined. They were hesitating and uncertain at first. Then some men's voices took up the tune. The people stood on the hillside and lifted their heads and mouths to sing. They were like cattle lost in a storm, who sniff at the air, trying to find in which direction to go.

The song went up in the air. The women's high voices struck the mountain sides and came back. Bonnie cried out loud. Emma, watching the grave, touched Bonnie on the shoulder with the palm of her hand, as if she was saying with it, "Hush, hush." She saw Jesse break up a lump of clay with his shovel to make the mound smooth. When it was high enough he and Young Frank patted the mound with the round shovel backs until all the uneven lumps of clay had been smoothed down.

The song was finished and most of the people started away. Some went up to Emma. They said a few words. It was as if they had not been there. Emma was looking at the grave.

Frank McClure touched her arm. "We've got a long way to go, Emma," he said. "And hit's most night. Will ye come?"

Then she followed Frank to the place where the steers were hitched under a tree. While Frank was unhitching them so that Fraser might drive them back to Swain's, Emma asked Ora a question.

"Did Hal write Basil?" she wanted to know.

"This morning," Ora told her.

Emma was silent for a little. The children stood by waiting until she would move. The air was bleak on the hillside, now the sun was lower. A wind had come up and blew through them. Bonnie shivered against her mother.

"You two go ahead," Emma said to John and Bonnie. When John started out ahead of Bonnie she told him to wait for his sister. To Ora this was a good sign. It meant that Emma, who for two days had been so silent, was beginning again to see other people. She was beginning to know that she had other children besides Kirk.

They watched the two young ones go down the road to the

trail. Emma looked back at the mound that curved above the ground. It was black against the evening sky.

"He was a good boy," she said.

She repeated the words, "He was a good boy," as if she was insisting that Ora accept what she said.

"Yes, he was," Ora said. "He was, Emma." Her voice was insistent, too, as if she was speaking to the whole community and to Basil and perhaps even to Granpap who was a long way off in a city jail.

18

Basil wrote that he would come in the summer for a visit. Kirk had laid up credit at the store and Emma sold the cow back to Swain to pay the debt. The cow was as thin as a rail, but Swain said he could fatten her, and perhaps sell for enough to cover the debt and have some credit left over for Emma. John drove Sukey to the store, and there Hal gave him the letter from Basil. It was very short, and before he gave it into John's hand Hal read it out loud twice, and made John repeat it after him, so the boy might tell Emma what was in it. The letter said:

"I am sorry about Kirk, and sorry for you. Remember that the Lord chasteneth those whom He loveth. I must stay until school is over. I will come in the summer. Basil."

Emma listened while John repeated this. Though he left out some of the large words, she remembered the part from the Bible and knew what Basil meant to say. She took the letter and put it away in the trunk with Kirk's picture.

Basil came in the middle of the summer. He rode a horse—one he had tended all winter for the school. And he was quite a gentleman, dressed up in a store-bought suit. True, it was patched in the seat of the breeches but only a small patch where the teacher who had given it to him had worn it out sitting at his desk.

In the saddle bag Basil had a Bible for Emma. At night they lit the lamp and sat around the table while Basil read to them. He read about the making of the world. Sometimes he skipped a word if he couldn't make it out; so the reading went something like this:

"In the—be-ginning God made . . . the heaven and the earth. And the earth was waste and . . . and darkness was upon the face of the deep; and the spi-rit of God moved upon the face of the waters. And God said, Let there be Light."

When the reading was over Basil wrote their names in the front of the Bible on a blank page. First, Emma McClure, then Bonnie and last John McClure. Bonnie wanted his pencil at once so she could copy her name. Basil let her have it and she marked up the table with chicken tracks.

"How are you getting on?" Basil asked Emma in his new careful voice.

"Well," Emma said, "as well as poor folks can. We did the spring planting, but there's not as much planted as before."

"It's another year before Granpap comes out," Basil said.

"Hal Swain has promised to get him out before his time," Emma told Basil. "Hal knows men outside who could help."

"What'll you do," Basil insisted, "if Granpap don't get out? What'll you do in the winter?"

"I thought ye might be coming back to stay," Emma said shyly. She was a little afraid of Basil. He was so dressed up, and he even ate differently, using a spoon to hold the fatback while he cut it with his jack-knife, instead of eating straight from his hands as they all did.

"No," Basil answered his mother. "I'm going on fine at school. And they're good to me. They think I'll come to something. I want to keep on."

Of course he was right. Emma herself would be proud to have him get on in the outside world.

"We'll make out then," she said. They sat around the table. Bonnie scratched with the pencil. John and Emma wanted to hear more from Basil about the school. So they waited for more. Basil had something else on his mind.

"Hal Swain wants to buy the cabin," he said to Emma.

"And the land?"

"Yes."

"Why?" Emma wanted to know. The land she and Jim McClure had cleared and the sides of the mountains that Jim had bought were hers. They meant something to her. But what could they mean to Hal Swain?

Basil could not tell why Hal wanted them. He only knew that Hal would pay half in the fall and as long as he owned the place they could live there rent free.

"The money Hal pays in the fall will take you and the young ones through the winter," Basil said. "The young ones mustn't starve."

"I don't know . . ." Emma said. "Granpap would hate it."

"He'd want you to care for the young ones."

"But he would hate to lose all we have."

"Well, hit's my right," Basil told her. "I'm the oldest. Hit's my right to say we can sell or not sell."

"Yes, hit's your right," Emma had to agree.

"I need the second payment for next year at school," Basil explained. "I need books. But I don't want to go against ye. I want ye to say yes."

He left Emma to think it over.

In the morning to John's surprise Basil got out of bed in a long white shirt that he must have put on the night before to sleep in. John ducked his head under the quilt to hush up a laugh. For Basil looked very queer with the white garment hanging around him, and his long legs showing through the slits in the sides. What else, John thought, would they find Basil had learned at that school?

The day before Basil left, Emma took the picture of Kirk from the trunk where she had laid it after the funeral. Around it was wrapped a piece of black cloth. She unwound the cloth and gave the picture to Basil who held it to the light.

"I wrote Granpap," he said.

Emma had thought Basil would never speak of Kirk. She had waited for three days. At last she had to bring out the picture to remind him.

"Yes," Basil said. "Granpap knows." He looked at the picture again. "He could have done what I'm doing, if he'd wanted," he said.

"He was a good boy," Emma answered quickly. She found herself defending Kirk against Basil. And feeling so she took the picture out of Basil's hand.

"He was a good boy," she repeated.

"Yes, he was good," Basil agreed. "But he didn't have any ambition."

John was looking over Emma's shoulder at the picture. He heard the word that Basil used. It was one he had never heard before. At the moment he wished very much to ask Basil the meaning, but, like Emma, he stood in awe of his brother. So he repeated the word to himself and laid it up to remember at another time when he could find out the meaning from someone else.

When the first frost came, John felt a new sensation. It was a fear and dread of winter. He had known before what it was to lack food in the cold days. But there were the all powerful grown-up people who could somehow replenish the meal sack and fill his belly again. Now, since Basil had refused to stay and was back in the school, the responsibility was on the boy. Emma knew how to work. Often, like all the women she knew, she did a man's work while the men sat and talked. But Jim McClure and Granpap after him had taken the responsibility of filling the meal sack and the fatback box. So for these things Emma, without knowing she was doing so, leaned on John. And John felt her. At first he had wanted to shake her off and shake off the responsibility she put on him. But he found this could not be done, and all at once he accepted the burden that lay on his shoulders as if it was a hump that had grown there. Each day that carried them further into the winter took some of their food. The meal bag was flat. John went about looking quiet and thoughtful. Emma had given in to Basil about selling the land, but the money had not come from Swain.

"What would ye do, John?" Emma asked. They had only Basil's statement when he was there in the summer that he meant to sell, and that Hal would give them a first payment. That was very little to go on. It would be hard to go up to Hal and say, "Hand us the money, Hal," for Swain might well tell them he had decided not to buy, or Basil might not have sold. It was all very vague.

They still had potatoes and a few cabbages, though these were half rotten. If the winter had been severe, with heavy snows, there would have been no hope for them except in going to Hal. And toward the last of the winter when the food was gone this became their only chance to survive. The potatoes were down to the last layer in the trench. Emma showed them to John. Then John knew he must go to Hal. He must stand up to Hal and ask for the money. There had been much hesitation in him. And it was so easy to put off an unpleasant thing. Emma had been expecting John to go and talk with Hal. Perhaps even she herself did not know that she was expecting the boy to take the responsibility. But there it was. And John knew that he must make the effort. He said to himself, "The day the last potato's in the trench I'll go." That would be two days, perhaps three, in the future. And the future was a long time ahead.

On the second day of John's waiting Hal Swain sent word by Frank McClure that Granpap was free. He would get back on the third day. But Granpap came on the second day. Bonnie and John were on the hillside getting wood, gathering up rotten pieces that had fallen from the dead trees. Emma was down with the baby in the cabin. The young ones had a pile of dead sticks and logs not far above the trail. Bonnie wiped her sweaty little face on her dress skirt. Though the air was cold they had been exerting themselves to get in a large pile of wood for Granpap's coming.

"I'll tote some wood to the cabin now," Bonnie said. "Hit's time for supper." She kneeled down and picked up an armful. "Lay on some more," she said to John.

"That's all you can carry," John told her.

"Hit's not all," Bonnie insisted. "Now, John, you lay on some more." When he had piled up some sticks clear to her chin he had to steady her while she staggered up. He saw her go off down the hill pretty evenly for the load she was carrying, and went back to get an armful for himself. He heard a kind of groan, a queer sound come from Bonnie, and looking down he saw the wood fall out of her arms. She was standing near the trail. He ran down, thinking she was having some kind of woman's spell. He might have known she was taking too much on herself. At the trail he stood behind her and looked where she was looking, up the trail. Coming toward them was a tall old figure. It stooped and walked slowly.

"Hit must be Granpap," Bonnie said. Still they hung back behind a laurel bush until they could be sure. The person did not walk with Granpap's fine stride. As he came nearer they saw it was Granpap, and broke through the underbrush onto the trail. They stood waiting until he came up.

"Why, hit's John and Bonnie," Granpap said and laid a hand on each of them. Except for his slow movements it was as if he had been gone only a little while. His voice at least was familiar, though it had the familiar sound of Granpap when he was smoking before the fire, and not of Granpap who walked in the woods.

Emma saw them from the cabin. She had the baby in her arms and without stopping to put it down, came fast along the trail. She met them at the spring. There they stood, Emma and Granpap, and looked at each other. Emma felt at Granpap with her eyes. She saw that his head drooped and he looked up as a child does when it is ashamed or angry.

"Hit's a long time," Emma said. She was heavy in herself because Granpap was thin and pale as white clay, and his manner was listless.

"Yes, hit's been a long time."

At the cabin when they had got Granpap into a chair, Emma took John aside. "Go to Ora's," she said, "and ask her for the loan of some meal, and a mite of coffee, if she has it."

Granpap had come a day too early. The neighbors had planned to meet him at the store on the next day. He had half expected this, and had fixed his mouth for a drink or two. But when he reached the store even Hal was not there. Hal was up the valley looking at some land, and only Sally was in to welcome Granpap. At the Martins' cabin in Possum Hollow it was the same. Jim Martin was up the valley with Hal. But Jennie gave Granpap a welcome, and a drink of cider.

Emma saw Granpap watching the baby as it lay in the log cradle. In a way, because of its mother, it had been the reason for Kirk's death. But she knew that Granpap would not blame this child for its mother's sins, and would no more think of turning it out than he would think of cutting off his finger. The child needed care, and circumstances had given it to them. So they took it as naturally as they would have taken a child of Emma's.

She knew Granpap was thinking of Kirk. "Kirk's in the burying ground by Jim," she told him.

"Sam McEachern must pay for that," Granpap said. It was what the others had told her, and she answered Granpap what she had answered them.

"He's a long way off."

"Yes," Granpap answered, but not as if he believed this. For when he left Sam McEachern was very strongly established in the community.

Emma took the picture of Kirk wrapped in the black cloth

from the trunk. She unwrapped the picture and showed it to Granpap. Along with it she took Basil's letter. This she knew by heart, and though she could not read, she said the words to Granpap as if she was reading the ink-writing on the paper.

Granpap looked at Kirk's picture a long time. Emma waited for him to speak of Kirk, but he gave the picture back without a word. She told him of Basil's visit in the summer, holding back the principal thing that had happened. She could not tell Granpap that Basil had wanted to sell the cabin.

When John returned he found Granpap and Emma sitting together before the fire. Bonnie was on the floor beside Granpap. She would not leave his side. Behind John came Ora and Frank with all their young ones. Ora had the baby in her arms. John and Young Frank carried some provisions.

"We have all had our supper," Ora said. "This is for Granpap and nobody else." She had brought coffee enough for everyone, that is, if plenty of water was added to the grounds. Best of all Frank brought Granpap a bottle of drink. It was lucky, he said, that he had been to Barren She Mountain the day before. He had gotten the stuff then to take down to the store for Granpap's homecoming. It was just as well for Granpap to have it a little early. Granpap thought so, too. And Emma was glad it was there. The drink made Granpap lift his head. His eyes sparkled and a flush came into his cheeks. It was good to see him look like his old self, or near to his old self again.

Granpap had his good meal that Emma cooked. And what he did not eat the young ones disposed of very quickly. Ora's youngest were everywhere until Bonnie got them onto the bed, lined up in an orderly row. She enjoyed telling them what to do, and making them comfortable on the bed with a quilt thrown over them. She seemed to have a knack for making people comfortable.

No one spoke of prison. They had all shut down their mouths on the prison and swallowed it up. Later when Granpap was ready to talk of it, they would bring it back and chew on his experiences there, along with Granpap, as a cow chews on her cud. Now it was down out of sight.

There was a sound of footsteps outside the door, and in came Jennie Martin and Jim. Later Fraser McDonald and Jesse came. Until everyone got settled in chairs or on the floor, there was a bustle in the cabin, a sound of people moving around that had not been there for a long time. Granpap became livelier every moment. Jim and Fraser had brought their jugs along, too.

John saw Granpap look up at the back wall where the fiddle hung.

"Hand me the fiddle and bow," Granpap said. And John reached up easily for them, he had grown so much in the last year. While the men talked Granpap sat there feeling out on the fiddle. Sometimes he touched a string. Then he twisted a peg and bent his ear to hear better.

Bonnie and Ora's Sally were perched on the trunk. They looked rosy and hearty in the light from the fire.

"Sally's getting to be real pretty," Granpap said. "She'll be having beaus before the year's out."

"Sally's already a-courting," Young Frank said.

"Shet up," Sally called out to Frank. This was too much, with Jesse sitting in the same room.

Granpap spoke to John. "Give me that rosin off the shelf, Johnny."

The rosin was covered with dust. Granpap wiped it on the seat of his jeans, and when he had rosined the bow tucked the fiddle under his chin. Emma put her cup of coffee down on the table and watched. It seemed they were living as they had before, and maybe Kirk had just stepped outside and Basil was in the other room.

The Martins and McDonalds left early. Ora and Frank, who lived nearer, stayed longer to hear Granpap play the fiddle. It was late when Ora got all her young ones roused and was ready to start out. Bonnie and Sally were in a corner giggling.

"Come on, Sally," Ora said. "What devilment are you two a-making up?"

There was another spell of giggling and some whispers in the dark corner before Sally came out and followed the rest. A little later, Bonnie, lying in the bed, half listened to Emma and Granpap talk, and thought her own thoughts. Sally had told how Jesse McDonald had kissed her on the cheek the other night just outside the door. And Ora and Frank were sitting inside. She was afraid they heard the smack, it was so loud. Bonnie thought, "I'm a woman almost." She wondered how it would feel to get a smack on the cheek. Half in her sleep she made a silly little rhyme, "A smack on the cheek is better than to eat."

The next moment she was ashamed of this thought and hid it far down in herself. The shame waked her up.

In front of the fire Granpap spoke to Emma. "Frank says ye've sold the place."

"He told me he wasn't sure it was sold," Emma said. "I asked him. I'm not sure yet."

"He's sure, now," Granpap said. "For he sold his own to-day."

"I thought ye wouldn't be out till next year," Emma said. "I needed the money for the young ones."

"Was hit Basil persuaded ye?"

Emma was silent.

"Ye needn't answer. I know it was Basil."

"It was McClure land, Pap. And Basil the oldest."

"And he's sold his birthright," Granpap said loud and fierce, "for a mess of pottage. What if ye are poor, Emma, if ye have your own land?"

"Basil said so long as Hal Swain owns the land here we stay rent free."

"And what Basil didn't say was this. There's a big saw mill a-coming . . ."

Emma broke in. "We've heard saw mill talk for a long while, and nothing come of hit."

"This time hit's true," Granpap insisted. "Hit's true as I'm living, Emma. Hal Swain and Sally together have bought up all the land around. And they're selling out to the saw mill. Hit's to be on Laurel Creek just below Fraser McDonald's. And nobody knew. Hal Swain began buying up quiet, promising everybody they could stay on the land. Have you got your money, yet?"

"Not yet. Basil's t' send it soon as he gets hit from Swain. I aimed to have it for winter, but it hasn't come yet."

"And I aim," Granpap said, "t' get your part from Hal Swain to-morrow."

"Hal Swain's been mighty clever to us, Pap."

"And to me," Granpap said. "He's a good friend. But you and the young ones must have your rights."

"Basil's a-going t' do right. You wait and see," Emma said. "We'll get that money."

19

EVERYONE had money that late winter and spring. They had got a second payment for their land. Some who hadn't given in to Hal Swain sold straight to the agent of the lumber company. The cabins and clearings were theirs rent free. And there would be no end to ready money, for the mill would need hands to build it and to cut timber and make road and work around the saws.

A vast excitement had come. Behind all men's quietness the excitement shone in their eyes and showed in the way they behaved at the store, careless and free about money. Best of all there would be more dances than ever, and Granpap expected good collections. The McClures would be rich even without the other money for the cabin.

It was queer about that money. Hal Swain said he had paid the first installment to Basil. This was the installment they had promised Emma. Basil already had the second; but Hal had no receipt for the first payment and Basil swore that Hal had given his word to pay it to Emma or give her credit at the store. Granpap demanded Emma's share. At last Basil and Hal, through writing each other letters, arranged for Hal to give Emma fifteen dollars worth of credit at the store or fifteen dollars in cash. Granpap decided for the cash. It was paid into his hand and he gave it to Emma. She put it deep down in a corner of the trunk where she or Granpap could reach down and bring up one of the big silver pieces when it was needed. Some of them had already gone to Hal for payment on food.

The first dance was at Fraser McDonald's. Granpap took John along for company just as he had taken Kirk and Basil when John was no more than a baby. Though it was early when they crossed the bridge and came close to the McDonald cabin, they could hear the sound of animals down to the right under some trees. A horse moved in the underbrush, and the other animals breathed deep as if they were sleeping. There were not many, for most of the people who came used shank's mare, for they had no beasts to ride. Since the money had come, however, several had purchased animals from Swain. A strong light came from the front door of Fraser's cabin. There would be no sales at the store that night, and Hal Swain had loaned the big lamp that hung from the center of the store ceiling. Inside the cabin someone was picking a banjo.

"Sam's here," Granpap said. His voice trembled a little. This was his first dance for nearly two years. Waves of warmth came up in John. His legs shook under him. He was as trembling in his body as Granpap's voice.

The old man marched up the steps across the porch and into the front room. John followed. The room was quite empty of furniture except for the two chairs in a corner for the musicians. On one of them Sam Wesley waited for Granpap. All the other furniture, a bed, a table, and two chairs, had been carried to the back porch. The table was just outside the back door and on it were some jugs of cider and a cup. Anyone who wanted a drink had only to reach out from the room and help himself.

Granpap walked over to the chair and took his place by Sam. He knew just where he must go. John stood in the middle of the empty floor. The room seemed huge to him, though it was a very small one. The boy's knees almost gave way under him and the opposite wall seemed miles away. He was like a young calf that has not yet got the full use of its legs. Through the door at the left he saw girls and women in a bedroom, sitting around the fire and on the built-in bed. They were all over the bed, and a twittering came from the room like the twittering of birds in a laurel thicket.

There was nothing for a boy to do. All the men were out in the yard waiting until the music started. John walked slowly to the jug of cider and poured out a cup. Someone behind him laughed. He turned around fiercely. It was only Sam Wesley laughing at something Granpap had told him. John poured another cup. Granpap was tuning. He and Sam bent over their instruments and tried them out together. They played "Sourwood Mountain" and tuned again.

The tuning was heard. There were heavy steps on the porch. Feet scraped heavily on the flooring and into the room from the porch filed a procession of young men. A girl peeped shyly through the bedroom door. Others who had more courage pushed her out and followed. Most of their dresses were faded calico. They were flowers the rain has washed out. Here and there as they crowded into the room was a fresh flower just opened. Ora's Sally was one of these. With some of the land money Ora had bought Sally a new dress which made Sally a bright yellow flower, fully open.

Sally spun around on her heel and the skirt spun with her. It spread out under the light of the lamp. Everyone could see the ends of Sally's drawers but she didn't seem to know, until Fraser looked at her.

One of the men said, "You could balance a silver dollar on that skirt." Then Sally saw Fraser's disapproving eyes. Suddenly she blushed red, and put her feet together firmly on the floor. With her hands flat against her thighs she pressed the skirt close to them. But she would not let Jesse think that he was her owner to disapprove of her actions. With a shake of her head she walked to the wall away from Jesse. Just before she reached the wall she turned and gave him a glance. Her eyes were dark and bright, as if she had squeezed jimson weed juice into them. Minnie had done this once to show John how it would make her eyes, which had been blue, round black balls. Some of the girls did it each time they went to a dance, and there were some of these who would make their eyes brighter for church. But it was not like Ora's Sally to do such a thing. Her eyes were bright from the pleasure and excitement of being at the dance, and having a fine looking beau who followed her with his eyes.

Jesse gave Sally a little time to wonder if he was going to join her. Then he walked over and took his place deliberately by her side. Gradually other men fell into place beside the girls. Some of them spoke low words that John could not hear and the girls nodded. Others simply took their places, as Jesse had, as if they belonged.

Granpap called out, "Get your pardners." Everyone had partners as Granpap could see, but this was the way to begin. Only John had no partner, and he wanted none. He told himself he wanted to look on. There was no girl there, even Ora's Sally, who could please him. He did not know the steps, and a man had to be very proficient in order to swing the girls in the right direction and not get mixed in the figures. John wished to learn. He wanted to know many things, and this was one of them. So he watched carefully. He walked to the table, took another drink of cider, and pushing the table back little by little made a place for his feet on the porch. There were so many couples, the one just in front of John had to take all the space. But on the porch he was not in the way.

The fiddle and banjo began "Bile them cabbage down," and Granpap's foot tapped out the time.

He called, "First couple out," and Jesse swung Sally to the center of the circle and back to the second couple. Sally with her heels coming down at the right times danced about Lorene Wesley. Jesse sashayed around Lorene's partner. Regularly at the right beat their heels came down on the floor in time with the music. Sally danced around Lorene's partner and there was Jesse keeping time ready to swing Lorene when Granpap called, "Swing your opposites." Then it was "Now your own," and Lorene and Sally turned back to their own partners and lifted their arms to be swung again.

"Second couple out," Granpap sang and Lorene and her partner swung into the middle of the floor and back to take the couple Jesse and Sally had just left. Soon another couple was out, making three groups within the whole group doing the same figure at the same time.

"Lady round the lady and the gent go slow,
Lady round the gent and the gent don't go."

Then "Swing your opposite—now your own."

And after that "Fourth couple out."

The girls' skirts flared out when the men swung them. The skirts were a part of the dance. They emphasized the rhythm, just as the heels coming down together emphasized the rhythm. And everything was done with dignity. Jesse McDonald had a special way of giving an extra shuffle when he reached his partner. It was a real shuffle but so cleverly done he did not lose a step. Other men had fancy steps of their own. And each girl danced in her own way. Lorene always bent her head sideways on the man's arm when she was swung. She looked down at the end of her skirt as if she was a kitten trying to catch its tail. Sally stood up straight to her man with her hands planted firmly on his shoulders. She was the most graceful girl in the room. The McClure blood was in her. All of Ora's bony angles had been softened in Sally by the McClure blood.

Granpap's face was shining with sweat as he bent low over the fiddle. He had no need to watch the set. He called the figures regularly, evenly, without a hitch in time. He had turned on a switch of a machine and set it going. Knowing it well he had no need to give it any special attention because it was familiar and he could tell by the sound that it was running smoothly.

"Promenade all," he called at exactly the moment when the last couple had finished the circle. The partners swung into place, the girls and men coupling their hands crosswise for the promenade around the room.

"Gents swing back" and all the men dropped back. Each left his partner for the man in front who came back to her. "Swing your ladies and promenade all." Then it was "Gents swing back" again and again until each man after promenading with each girl in the circle had returned to his own partner. Only then the music stopped and the dancers fell out of line. Granpap and Sam Wesley mopped their faces. Most of the men filed out of the front door. The cider was for the women. The men had their drinks tucked away in saddle bags or under the porch in jugs they had toted across the trails from their homes.

John helped himself to another cup of cider. As soon as the women came flocking to the table he ran from them to Granpap and Sam who were on the porch. Fraser McDonald was there. He had just given Granpap a jug and the old man leaned back his head to take a good full drink.

When the others went in for the second set John stayed on the porch. It was more comfortable there than standing in the little space between the table and the room. The men filed past him into the room and the music started again. From the porch the sound of the feet was stronger than the sound of the music; the music was only a whine but the feet made a stamping that John felt in his blood. He was one with the stamping feet and the house that shook, he, John McClure. And suddenly he wanted to go in and join with the rest, so that he might put his own stamp on the floor.

The second set was over sooner than the first, for the figure was "Hands across," a very easy one. John had taken enough cider to fill a barrel and it was necessary to make room for more. He slipped around the house and out to the cow shed. It was not until he had begun that he heard girls giggling inside the shed.

As soon as possible he ran up the back porch and squeezed by the table into the room. Some of the men were still in there talking to girls. The party was getting more sociable. The girls by this time were not so shy, and the men, feeling the attraction of the girls, wanted to stay with them after the sets were over. Presently Sally and the McDonald girl came through the front door. They were red with giggling. Sally looked around, trying to spy out the men. She spoke to Lorene Wesley in a loud whisper. "Did you know hits raining outside?"

"No," Lorene said, and went to look. When she saw the clear sky with its many stars out there she knew what Sally meant. She came over to the other girls and the three whispered together and then went off into fits of giggling. They fell into the bedroom, and the other girls, curious and a little hurt at being left out, followed the giggling girls into the bedroom. Soon there was a bedlam of women's talk and laughter in the other room. The men who were left behind looked straight in front. They had guilty faces as if each thought he was the one the girls were laughing about. It made John feel better to see their embarrassed, guilty faces. He took a drink of cider and smacked his lips over it. Then the men rallied. One of them gave a disgusted look at the bedroom door and walked out. The others followed him and John came along at the tail end. He stood on the porch, when they walked out into the yard, for he was still a boy and knew he would not be welcome. But he listened. Out there under the trees they began to talk and gradually their talk and laughter grew louder and more confident. They were telling stories about women, this John knew. How much better their great voices and big laughter were than the silly giggling inside. John slipped from the porch and was going down to hide in the dark so he might be nearer to the men, when Granpap got up from the other end where he had been sitting with the older men.

"Well," Granpap said, "I reckon the young ones are r'aring for another set."

After the fifth set Sam Wesley picked up his hat and took the collection. It was amazing the number of quarters that were dropped in, along with dimes. And there were two one-dollar bills!

When the dance was over and Granpap and John were walking back to Siler's Cove, Granpap spoke to John about the fine collection. "The mill brings money," he said. "But I'd rather have my cabin and my piece of land. A cabin and land is there. You leave it and come back and there it is again. But money goes fast."

20

For a month or longer the jubilation lasted like a prolonged religious revival. Then, about the first of the month, Hal Swain passed certain envelopes through the post office window. The envelopes had printing in the upper left hand corner. They were from the lumber company and the letter inside notified each man that after such and such a date he must pay a certain amount of rent to Hal Swain as the Company's representative. Hal read out line by line to each man the contents of the letter and the amount he must pay.

When they received the money for their cabins no one had thought of this possibility. Hal told them they could stay on their land rent free. They had not remembered that Hal said "as long as he owned." Now the Company owned and it was quite a different matter. They could not blame Hal, for he had been true to what he said. Not one cent of rent had he asked them to pay so long as he owned the land. Some let it stand that way, and accepted what happened. But there were others who swore they would never pay rent for land they had owned and lived on without being beholden to any man. Granpap was one of these. The day on which he was due to pay his rent passed, and he did not appear at the store. It was Hal Swain's duty to collect from those who had failed to pay, but he could not make himself collect from his neighbors. He sent one of the Company men.

Granpap met the Company man at the door with his shotgun. It was useless for Emma to try to prevent him. He could only feel that somewhere in the transaction he had been fooled, and had a right to defend what he felt still belonged to Emma and the young ones. So Granpap drove the Company man away and he went back and reported to Hal.

So Hal had to come after all. He explained to Granpap that the Company would have a right by law to put the family out of the house. Granpap simply pointed to his shotgun. He had given up listening to Hal, listening as one does who is willing to be convinced. After that Hal went back to his store, and Granpap went about with a stern set face that dared anyone to interfere with John Kirkland. Emma was greatly disturbed. She did not know what Hal and the Company would decide to do, but she was sure of what Granpap might do in an emergency. She began to wish they were out of the country.

About this time a dapper young man appeared in the community. He wore a new store-bought suit, a white shirt, always clean, and very fine tan shoes that he must have wiped very carefully every night, for each morning when he left Hal Swain's house, where he was boarding, all the mud that had accumulated on them from the roads during the day before, was gone. Sally Swain had taken him in to board, without knowing what he came for. When she found out, Hal sent him about his business. But he had already been in the community for several days and had visited many of the cabins. Ora met him one day on the trail over Thunderhead. She almost laughed out loud to see the finely dressed little man walking so daintily on the rough trail, avoiding the muddy spots by taking short little jumps over them. She stopped and waited for him to come up the trail. She was standing in the deep shade made by the thick leaves overhead, and he did not see her at once. When he did, she told Emma later, he looked as if he had seen a ghost.

"Do—do the McClures live near by?" he asked.

Ora thought he was looking for Granpap. "Be ye their kin?" she asked.

"No," he said. "Not exactly. That is, I have a message for them. I'm looking for the McClures who have seven children."

Then Ora knew he meant her and turned to go back the way she had come. When she looked over her shoulder the young man was standing in the spot where she had left him. "Come on," she said, and led the way back to the cove.

At the cabin she spoke to Young Frank who was in the yard. "Go over and get Emma and Granpap," she told Young Frank, "and hurry."

Since Frank was not at home it was best to have her neighbors and kin by to hear what the strange young man had to say.

He seemed eager enough to tell them, when Granpap and

Emma were in the cabin. His words fell over each other in a hasty torrent. It was hard to keep up with him.

People, he said, up in that community, were being fooled. The lumber company had promised them jobs, and of course some of them would get jobs. But how long would they last? At most the company would stay five to eight years. When all the big trees had been cut down, then, naturally, the lumber company must move to a place where there were virgin forests.

On the other hand, down in Leesville, jobs, lifetime jobs, were waiting for people who would come down and work in the factories. Anybody could learn to run the machines. And those who did were given a house with a kitchen stove and electric lights.

"Hold on," Granpap said. "They say there's going to be electric here. They're a-going to build new cabins along the creek and put in wires."

"Suppose they do," the young man had his answer ready. "When the Company leaves, the electric lights go with the Company. Outside there you have electricity all the time. Up here, only men can work. Down there women like you," he pointed to Ora and Emma, "women like you can work in the mills and make money. You can send your children to a fine city school. You can buy at the city stores, and cook on a real cook stove furnished by the company."

"And the young ones can go to school?" Emma asked him.

"Exactly."

"They do say hit's a land flowing with milk and honey, and gold growing on trees."

The young man smiled. "Yes," he said. "It's the promised land, all right."

"And they pay high?" Granpap asked.

"Yes, and all the family—father, mother and children—earn money."

"I guess not the mother, when there's a young one like this." Emma was looking at Minnie's baby that was lying in her lap asleep.

"You can always leave him with a neighbor." The young man dismissed the baby with a gesture. "People down there are mighty neighborly."

"Maybe," Granpap said to the others, when the young man

had left them to think it over, "maybe we could all make enough to buy back the land up here when the lumber company's through."

"I'd want the young ones to have schooling," Emma insisted.

When Frank reached the cabin he and Granpap sat for a long time over the coals of the fire, though it was a warm day. They seemed to hold their words of counsel a secret between them and the chimney.

Ora and Emma went out to sit on the door-step.

"I've felt unsettled ever since that rent-bill came," Ora said. "You own a place and then you don't. The land you've owned, one day hit's yours, and another a stranger sends in a monthly rent-bill. Hit makes you want to git up and git."

"We shouldn't have sold," Emma remembered how she had given up the land so easily. It shouldn't have been done. And now it was too late.

"No," Ora agreed with her. "Frank held out as long as he could; but the ready money was too much, I reckon. Then they told him he'd have to sell, anyway, for they was going to run the log train track right across this place where the cabin stands. They said they had a right by law. But I don't believe hit."

"Hit's hard t' know what to believe and what not, these days. Everything's changin' so," Emma said in her quiet still voice.

"Anyway I'm all unsettled." Ora stood up. She looked unhappy and unsure of herself, and that was a very unusual way for Ora to look or to be. "I'll be glad to do something one way or another."

"You'll be glad if we go outside?" Emma asked her, looking up into her friend's face.

"I'll be glad to do something, one way or another," Ora said.

"One thing," Emma repeated. "The young ones can get schooling."

"Yes," Ora said vaguely. Emma's words did not mean very much to her. She was concerned mainly with her own feelings. She felt like a tree torn up by its roots, especially since she knew another child was coming. She wanted to be planted again. If Frank and Granpap decided to stay around Swain's Crossing and move over to the valley so they could try to get work in the lumber camps, she was willing to do that. If they decided to go outside and find work in the mills, it would be the same.

When her own roots were planted she could think of her young ones and what was best for them.

In Emma there was a hidden excitement at the thought of change, of seeing a city, and living there. The young man had said, "There, the streets are full of houses, mansions." Others had told her about them, and about the engines and automobiles. The outside had come so much nearer in the last few years. It could not be ignored any longer. Her good sense told her that the picture she had might not be true, but some of the things she liked to believe. She was glad when Granpap came out and said, "Hit seems like the best thing to do is go to the outside."

For the next day or two Bonnie and John, though they said little, ran about, Emma said, as if they were chickens with their heads cut off. With a sharp stick Bonnie practiced doing school lessons on the ground. Anyone could see they were simply marks without any meaning. But they meant something to Bonnie. She brought Minnie's baby and showed them to him, and he gurgled some to show his appreciation, and made some real sounds, which, according to Bonnie were words. But Emma knew the child was late about talking, and perhaps this was a beginning. Sometimes one that began late learned faster than others that began early. She was glad anyway to hear the sounds that were like words come out of the child's mouth, for she had thought it might turn out to be lacking.

After the first day, John was quieter than Bonnie. He was in his own way preparing himself for the adventure.

One evening while they were sitting in the cabin, before the doors were shut for bedtime, they heard someone walking on the trail outside. The steps came nearer. They were not Frank's, for his were long and light. This person walked with a quick, heavy tread. He walked on the block and stood in the doorway, looking back into their faces. It was Jim Hawkins with his scraggly beard and one eye. He hesitated in the doorway, waiting for an invitation.

"Come in, Jim," Granpap said and motioned to John, who slid from his chair to the floor.

Jim sat in the corner and slowly lit his pipe.

"Hit's a fine evening," he said, and looked around the room until his eye found the baby that Bonnie was holding in her lap.

The others waited for him to speak again.

"I hear you're traveling." He looked up at Granpap who sat beside him.

"Hit looks like it."

"To stay?"

"I'm aiming to stay from the hills no longer than need be," Granpap told him.

Jim pointed to the baby with his pipe. "I was thinking that young one over there—hit might hamper ye some."

"I don't know," Granpap told him. "Emma thinks a lot of the young one, and Bonnie thinks of hit as her own by now."

"Would hit grieve ye much to part with hit?"

There was a silence in the room. All of them were thinking, "Jim has come for Minnie's young one."

"Hit's mine," Bonnie called out suddenly, and hugged the baby in her arms. "I raised hit."

"Bonnie!" Granpap called out to her.

"Is it true, Jim? Do ye want hit?" Emma asked.

"I thought, maybe you'd better let me take hit, since you're going so far."

"Could ye care for hit?"

"I cared for Minnie, when she was no bigger."

Emma and Granpap looked at each other, and Granpap spoke.

"I reckon hit's Jim's as much as ours, Emma."

"Yes," Emma had to agree. "I reckon so."

"Shall I take hit to-night?" Jim asked.

"No," Emma said, thinking of Bonnie. "We'll bring hit over to-morrow, hit and the cradle."

And the next day Emma, Bonnie, and Ora took turns carrying the baby and the cradle over the mountains to Jim's cabin.

Bonnie cried all the way down the valley, until Emma promised to take her by to see the Wesleys' new baby. Emma felt the loss, too. They had worked hard to make the child thrive. But it was best for Jim to have it. He was a lonely man, and since it was a boy child he would probably raise it with more sense than he had ever used on his girl.

They visited with Sam Wesley's wife for a little while and Bonnie was allowed to hold the new baby for a moment. On the way out they passed Granma Wesley's loom. The old woman had died the winter before, but the loom was still there with the half done coverlet. Emma saw it, and a thought came into her. Down in the factories they must all know how to run a loom, like this one, only, as the young man said, out there they were run by machines. She wanted to try her hand at the loom, but she hesitated to ask Sam, for it was not good for someone outside a family to ask the use of that which has belonged altogether to a person recently dead.

She touched the loom and looked at Sam. "Could I try how it works, Sam?" she asked him and watched his face.

"Why, yes, Emma," Sam told her.

He showed them how it worked. Ora and Emma took turns sitting on the high bench at the loom, and Bonnie crowded up to see. Sam showed them the warp beam from which the threads came down in a thick orderly stream, each one held in its place by a wire contraption. He moved the heddles so that the threads of the warp opened like the palms of two hands joined at the wrists. Through this opening he threw the shuttle, click! Then the reed pressed the shuttle thread into place and when he touched the treadles with his feet the threads of the warp passed each other and made another opening for the shuttle to pass through again.

"In the mills," Emma told Sam, "they have a machine to work it all. You don't have to use your feet, only your hands. Hit ought to be easy."

Sitting at the loom she worked the heddles as Sam showed her, and she thought of herself sitting in a factory beside a quiet machine working it easily, talking to the other women who would be working at the machines beside her. It would be a very neighborly arrangement, as if neighbors had gathered to sit around and talk at a quilting. And she would get money for her work.

Her eyes were bright and her cheeks touched at the top of the bones with a red flush. She knew that if Emma McClure was given the opportunity she could learn how to work the machines. It was silly, and she knew that, too, to think of money growing on trees, but she couldn't get it out of her head. If she worked hard, bright, shining dollars would pour into her lap, and with the money she could buy new clothes for the young ones, and books for school, a fiddle for Granpap, and perhaps for herself a new waist, or a scarf for her head.

21

THE third day they were ready for the journey. Emma sewed the precious dollars that were left from the fifteen into a belt for Granpap to wear. Ora did the same for Frank. Some of the money was kept in pockets for immediate use. Together Granpap and Frank bought two steers and planned to haul what goods they had to the town on Frank's sledge. Later they would sell the steers in the city, or sell back to Hal Swain.

Hal was now a big man. The Company had bought his land and store. They were to put up a new large store further up the valley at the place where the cabins and the mill were to be built and there Hal was to run the store on a regular salary, and get something out of every purchase made. He was to be the representative of the Company until all the officials and engineers came. A woman from town was coming up to teach his children.

All this did not go to Hal's head, and make it bigger than it should be. He was still kind to his neighbors when it did not interfere with his carrying out his work. He was ready to do anything to help Granpap and the others go to the city.

He got up at daybreak to see them off when they left for the city. They had prepared for a long journey. If Hal had been driving his two horses, the journey would not have taken him longer than a day, and less than that. But Granpap and Frank, with a sledge loaded down, and young ones who would get tired on the hot road, would be lucky if they made it in three days.

As it went around the long curves of the mountain road the procession reminded Ora of Kirk's funeral. She did not say so, for it would be a mistake to make Emma think of such things. It was a fine morning, clear, and the sun shone straight at them as if it was showing them the way. This was not like that gloomy time in winter when they had carried Kirk down the mountain. Up the slope of the mountain the calico plants were in blossom, and in places higher up there were some laurel clusters of darker rose color. It was impossible to see into the valley, for, looking that way, the sun was a bright, white light in the eyes. But a person could look up on the side of the mountain and see the flowers. The clusters were still wet with dew, and with the early sun striking them, they were like pink sunburnt faces covered with tiny sweat drops.

Emma thought of them like that, and then she turned away to watch Granpap, Frank, and the two older boys manage the sledge, which needed all their care, around the narrow slippery curves.

The sledge was in front. It was piled up with household goods strapped on with rope. Emma's bed was there, her trunk, and the bed clothes tied up in a quilt. Ora had about the same, though from her cabin, since there were seven children, had come two large bundles of quilts. Sally sat on the back of the sledge with the baby in her arms. Presently Bonnie would take her place there. Ora carried little Raymond when he was too tired to toddle along beside her. The other children walked ahead of the sledge, or lagged behind when they were too tired to keep up. At night they would camp on the side of the road, undo the quilts and cover themselves from the cold night dew.

On the third day, when the sun was in the middle of the sky, as they were walking along Emma looked across the valley from the mountain road. They were still some distance up in the mountains though the road now sloped downward all the way. This meant they were near the valley.

"Hit's like the Israelites," Emma said to the others, "a-going to the Promised Land."

Granpap heard her. "Only," he said, "I hope the Lord don't leave us in a wilderness for forty years."

"Hit's not likely." Emma put her hand out and pointed to the valley. Far off they could see smoke rising up. The air was so clear they could make out white smoke and black, and there, below the smoke, must be the chimneys of many houses.

"No," Emma said. "The Promised Land is too close." She laughed a little as if she was making fun of herself. Bonnie was sitting on the sledge with the baby. She looked up to listen.

"Where money grows on trees?" Ora said, and smiled at Emma.

"Does hit grow on trees?" Bonnie asked. Her voice shook each time the sledge hit a stone, and what she said was not clear.

"What did ye say?" Emma asked her.

"Does hit grow on trees?"

"Well," Emma answered her, "I guess hit don't really. Hit probably grows in the factory and you have to work for it. But I reckon hit's plentiful all the same."

Granpap and Frank knew the city, for they had been there before. But they were acquainted only with the way to the court-house. Hal Swain had told them they must follow the road straight into town and it would lead them to the railroad station. From there they could ask anyone how to reach the mill village.

As they entered the town the road widened out into a street not much wider than the country road they had left. On each side of this street there were dirt sidewalks and beyond the walks unpainted shacks blackened by smoke. The children, who had wandered where they wished along the country road, came closer to Emma and Ora. These two had drawn closer to the sledge. They were feeling bereft, as if just now they realized that the old life was gone from them.

"John," Bonnie said, "look!" From the porches stared children with small black faces. John had seen them already. The town, so far, was a disappointment to him, for the houses here were very much like those in the mountains, except they were made of planks instead of logs. They were unpainted cabins and had big chimneys. Certainly there were windows, but Hal Swain's house had four windows. The young ones here were behaving just as those in the mountains did when anyone passed along the road. These were different, but John would not get excited about them as Bonnie did. He looked at the brown solemn faces from the corners of his eyes, though his legs took him straight along the road. Bonnie turned right in the road and stared until she stumbled over a rock.

At a corner a black woman was pumping water into a bucket. Bonnie was thirsty at once.

"Could I ask for a drink?" she asked Emma, and Emma nodded. Bonnie's face was red and sweaty, and so were the faces of the other children. In the calico dress that Emma had made long before, and that was now too short, though the hem had been let out, Bonnie walked over to the woman. But when she reached the pump she was silent and could only stand and stare. "She wants a drink," Emma said, speaking up for Bonnie.

The black woman reached into the bucket and held out a full

dipper to Bonnie's mouth. The water dripped to the ground from the edges of her mouth. One of the other children left the road and went toward the woman with the bucket and the others followed immediately. In a moment some of the black young ones came out of the yards nearby and stood close to Emma and Ora's young ones.

"Granpap," Emma said, "couldn't we go in for a while and rest?" She pointed to the woman who was ladling out drinks for the children. "She seems real friendly."

"No," Granpap said. He looked as if something was very wrong. "Bring the young ones," he said to Emma. "They can get water at the station."

For a moment Emma did not obey. She saw that the children were still drinking and wanted them to finish. Granpap should understand how hot and tired they were. She would have liked a drink herself.

"They're niggers, Emma," Granpap said. "White and black don't mix." He looked angrily at the small black heads and the tow heads gathered around the pump.

Emma wanted to say "Thank ye," to the woman, but she was afraid to do so with Granpap waiting. Instead she called out for Sally and Bonnie to make the children hurry. She stood helplessly in the road. John could see that something was wrong. He went up to Emma and asked, "What is it?" She was looking back toward the woman who was pumping her bucket full again.

"They're niggers," she told John, and turned to follow the sledge. John went back to Bonnie. "They're niggers," he said and looked contemptuously over his shoulder at the group of black young ones who stood by the pump staring after them.

At the station Granpap herded them into the waiting room and showed them the benches where they could rest while he and Frank watered the steers and got some information.

Emma and Ora sat on a bench, and while Ora nursed the youngest Emma opened the food sack and gave out cornbread to the hungry young ones who pressed up to her. The station room was rather large, and few people were sitting on the benches, so their group was isolated. Emma looked around the room. She wondered where all the people of the town were gone, for she had expected to find many of them here. Two girls sat over in a corner talking with a young man who was dressed like the young man from the factory. The girls had on real hats with feathers that drooped over their faces and bobbed up and down in a fluttering way when they talked. She could not see their faces, which were hidden by the wide hats. Over next the door there was a woman with a child in her arms. They seemed to be asleep, both of them. Emma was trying to pick out a friendly face, one that she could ask where to take the young ones. These, now they had been fed, were looking furtively for some bushes or woods in which to go. But there were only scattered trees around the station and gravel everywhere on the ground. There were no friendly bushes out there to hide behind.

One of the young women from the corner got up and left her friends. She went through a door over which something was written. Emma watched the door and soon another woman came from the outside of the station and entered that same door. Emma looked at the writing above it. If she could read books she would know what that writing said. Ora nudged her with her free arm and pointed to the door. "Hit's got to be done," Emma said to herself. She got up and walked straight through the door over which the mysterious word was written.

The girl who had gone in first was standing at a mirror in there. "Is this?" Emma began. The girl smiled and nodded toward a swinging door.

Emma went back and beckoned to Ora, who brought the young ones. In the large room there were comfortable chairs, larger than any Hal Swain and Sally had in their house. And there was a couch on which anyone who wished might lie down, for the woman who had come in through the outside door lay down on it as if she belonged there. Emma thought to herself, "Someday if I am tired I can come here and rest." She thought then that the station was part of the factory.

They took the children through the swinging door. When the last one had finished, Emma, Ora, Sally and Bonnie spent some time trying to get them all out again and back into the waiting room. For each child wanted another turn at the mysterious string that made the rush of water come down.

The older ones were impressed. "Hit's like the Israelites again," Emma told Ora as they shooed the others into the big waiting room. "Hit's like Moses striking the rock and bringing forth water."

Granpap and John were standing before a picture on the wall. There was much printing on the card around the picture, but Granpap was not interested in that. When Emma went over to say they were ready he pointed to the picture. It was an old man with a beard like Granpap's, dressed in a gray long-tailed suit of clothes with gold braid and gold buttons on the coat.

"Hit's a Confederate," Granpap said.

"Well!" Emma exclaimed and beckoned Ora to come over and look. Soon all of them were standing around the picture, admiring the old man with the fine gray suit trimmed in gold, until Granpap, rousing himself, said it was time to go.

It seemed the journey would never end. They left the station and passed through the straggling edges of the town and on to another country road. Though it was late afternoon the young ones were so tired they found it necessary to stop again and give them time to rest.

They sat on the grass at the edge of the road at the bottom of a rise. Ora's baby was crying and when he kept it up Raymond joined him. The two babies crying made the only sounds that came from the people resting along the sides of the road. The children lay about listlessly on the grass. They were too worn out to protest as the youngest were doing. Granpap and Frank sat together. They had lit their pipes and were watching the steers anxiously. The animals were almost blown. Their sides went in and out like huge bellows.

Sally lay against a sloping bank. She was thinking of Jesse and wishing with all her might that she had let him come down with them, marry her, and take her back as he had wanted to do. But Ora had needed her on the journey and she wanted to see the city before she settled down for good. Well, she was seeing it. . . . She thought, dismally, that it would be three whole months before Jesse would come for her. Even then he might not come, for he had not liked the notion of waiting. He might decide to marry one of the girls up there, Lorene Wesley, or someone else. His work at the saw mill would begin on Monday, and he would be able to care for a wife.

When they began the journey again, Ora sat on the sledge holding the baby, with Raymond beside her. Some of the children, rested somewhat, went ahead of the tired steers and reached the top of the hill ahead of them. Bonnie was the first to see the factory. Emma saw her standing on the rise pointing, then she came running back. "Hit's the factory," she said, and pulled at Emma's arm until they reached the top of the slope.

About two miles away, judging by mountain sight, in the middle of streets and streets of small houses, one exactly the same size and height of the other, sat a huge brick building. As Emma thought, it was like a hen with chickens that have come out of the same setting, all of one size. Only how many hundreds of chickens this old hen had brought forth! Even from the rise they could scarcely see where the rows of houses stopped.

Up from the brick structure rose two huge chimneys, towering into the sky, like two towers of Babel. Smoke poured out of them into the wide open heavens.

Emma felt one of the steers nosing at her shoulder. Then Ora came from the back of the sledge with the baby in her arms.

"Hit's the factory," Emma said to Ora with a catch in her voice.

Ora wondered if it was the evening sun on Emma's face that made it look so queer, almost glorified. The look and Emma's voice made her wish to be very practical and every-day.

"I reckon hit couldn't be anything else," she said. "Hit looks like a working place."

22

THE big doors of the factory, some distance from the road, stood open. A few people, women and men, were straggling one by one into these doors. Granpap halted the steers at the near end where a one story brick building jutted out from the large one even with the road. Here, someone had said, they could apply for work.

Granpap and Frank entered first. Emma and Ora sat on the steps at one side so they would not be in the way of anyone who wished to go in, and Ora began again to feed the crying baby. John and Young Frank guarded the steers and the sledge, and the two girls, leaving the other children to Ora and Emma, walked timidly to a corner that was nearest. Sally had her sunbonnet off and fanned herself vigorously. Bonnie peeped from under her bonnet observing everything that was to be seen.

Across the road there was a large wooden building with a platform in front, like a porch. Two or three young men who were lounging on the platform watched Sally. She was wearing her new calico dress. It was wrinkled and soiled but it could not hide the fact that Sally had a nice figure.

"Ain't that a woman for ye?" Ora asked Emma, though her words were not so much a question as a statement. She nodded her head toward Sally's back. "She knows those pants over there are a-looking at her."

The two girls stood at the corner for a moment, then turned and walked back sedately to the steps. Bonnie was much smaller than Sally, though she was getting to be a woman, and promising to be pretty. Now she had the sunbonnet pulled down over her eyes, as if she was afraid to let anyone see her face. Ora looked under the bonnet when the girls were standing before them. "Are ye shamed of something, Bonnie?" she asked.

"No," Bonnie said, and looked down at her bare feet. Sally had shoes, bought at Swain's, but they had thought it was not necessary for Bonnie to have them. She was four years younger than Sally. "What's that a-rumbling?" Bonnie asked, partly because she hadn't found any words for Ora.

"I feel it, too." For some time Emma had felt a throb in the air, a dull shake to the ground, as if people were dancing a long way off. Now when Bonnie spoke she felt out for the sound as she had often done for sounds around the cabin at night, when she was not sure where they came from.

They all listened, feeling out, like Emma, to locate the cause of the throb.

"Hit's the factory, I think," Emma said. She spoke in a whisper as if she was afraid the factory would hear. "You remember that church song," she went on speaking low to Ora, "that says, 'There's power in the blood.' Well, that sound seems t' say, 'There's power in the factory, there's power in the factory.' "

After she had said it she was a little ashamed as she always was of some of her notions before Ora. But she saw Bonnie look up from under her bonnet as if she understood.

"Yes," Ora answered. Perhaps she was going to say something else, for her mouth was open, when another and very different sound startled them. It was a terrible, earsplitting shriek, as if many people cried out in sorrow, just once.

Sally covered her ears with her hands, and Bonnie's eyes under the bonnet grew round and wide as they did when she was disturbed. The steers out in the road moved as if about to start off. John called out "Whoa" and pulled on the ropes.

One of the young men across the road, seeing Sally's frightened gesture, called out, "It's just the factory whistle," and laughed.

"Look!" Emma said. "Look, Ora."

From the two doors of the factory came streams of people, women and girls, men and children. It was almost more than anyone could bear to see so many people at once. The doors belched them out in two long streams that came together at the road. Here they divided again and spread out across the road, some of them going out toward the long rows of houses, some toward the place where the McClures watched. A few of these looked curiously at the steers as they passed, but most of them hurried on without noticing the strangers. They were sunk down into a sort of sleep, or perhaps they were thinking only of getting home. The late afternoon sun shone right on the factory and made out of its windows fiery eyeballs that watched the home-goers steadily.

"I didn't think there was so many people, anywhere," Emma said, with a gasp, watching them go by.

"I reckon all the houses ain't here for nothing," Ora thought, and then said it out loud, and added, "Hit's a sight of houses."

"And a sight of people," Emma repeated. In herself she was feeling that with so many there might not be a place for her and hers. How could the man that owned the place want more when he had so many already?

She was relieved when Granpap and Frank came out of the office, for they would say if there was a place. But Granpap said nothing at first. He went to the sledge, took the ropes from John's hand and turned the steers, so that the sledge faced the other way.

Then he turned his head toward them. "I feel we'd best go back where we came from," he said in a loud voice.

"What is it, Frank?" Emma asked.

"They told us to wait," Frank said. "And we waited. Then Granpap asked how long, and the man said just wait. So we did. Then he came to us and said, 'Hit's too late. Come to-morrow.' "

There would be no house for the night, then. And the young ones needed a roof over their heads and a little straw or something to sleep on under their bodies. Granpap was waiting, but they could not follow him. They could not turn back to the hills, now they were at the place where they had been promised work. Perhaps to-morrow if there was no work they could bear to turn back, but not late in the evening with the sun going down.

Granpap stood with the ropes in his hands, a boy on each side, waiting. Frank walked across the road to one of the men who had left the factory a few moments before. They spoke a few words, then the stranger came back with Frank across the road. He was a small man and limped somewhat, which made him lag just a step behind Frank as they walked up to Granpap. He was kindly looking, and seemed ready to help, and spoke to Granpap respectfully as someone in the hills might have spoken. The others came nearer and listened as if the words said were something to eat with which they might fill their hungry bellies.

The stranger said there was a place where they could stay for the night. "I'll show you," he added and led the way, limping along in front of the sledge at the side of the left steer. "One of the preachers keeps a boarding house. He'll give you a place to sleep and food if you wish it."

"We were told," Granpap said to the man, "they needed us for the factory. From the way they act hit don't seem so."

"Well," the man said, "I reckon now you're here they've got you."

"Got me?" Granpap spat out. Emma was hushed and strained, fearing that Granpap would make trouble. The man saw that he had not said what was right. "Well, not exactly. But they probably think if you've come so far, you aim to stay."

Emma walked up to Granpap and touched him on the arm to get his attention. "Let's stay, Granpap. The young ones need a bed. Look at them. They're s' tired. And you know Ora ought t' have rest."

Granpap looked behind him and saw Ora with the baby in her arms, and Sally carrying little Raymond, while the others dragged along as if the next step was their last, for with the talk of bed and food being near they had let themselves down to rest, so there was no more fight in them for the present.

"I'll see," he told Emma, but she recognized the sound in his voice that said he was nearly ready to give in. She turned to listen while the stranger talked to Frank.

"You weren't even put down in the Doomsday Book?" he asked Frank.

"No. The man told us 'to-morrow' and that was all."

There was a silence. They walked along on the road between the rows of houses. Smoke was beginning to come out of those chimneys that had been cold before. On the porches that had been empty there were some men and younger children.

"What was that you said?" Frank spoke as if he hated to ask a question. "What was it you called some book?"

"Doomsday Book," the stranger answered. "We call it so around here. I don't know where the name came from."

Frank wished to ask what this book meant to them if it meant anything. Emma wanted to know, and Ora was wondering what it meant, a Doomsday Book. But none felt like asking just what it was. Perhaps they were a little afraid of what the man might say, and so much had happened they could wait for more.

The stranger left them at a corner. "You go to the left," he said. "And it's the third house on the left, the long house."

Granpap knocked at the door. Someone said in a sleepy voice,

"Who is it?" Granpap knocked again and the door opened. A man in shirt sleeves stood before them holding to the knob. He had a full head of tousled hair, and his small blue eyes blinked at them sleepily.

"Is the preacher here?" Granpap asked.

"I'm the preacher," the man said, and passed a hand over his head to smooth down the hair. "Come in," he said. He stepped on the porch and opened another door that led into a hallway. "Come in," he repeated, then as if he was just waking up, "What do you want?"

Up a short flight of stairs he showed them two rooms, each with two double beds. Ora could almost have cried looking at the beds. She wanted to sit right down on one of them, and lie back. "And lie back," she said to herself, "I'd like to lie back right now." But they must wait for the price.

When the preacher told Granpap and Frank they spoke together for a moment, then Granpap put some money in the preacher's hand. When she saw that Ora lay back against the pillow at the head of the bed and closed her eyes.

"If you want supper," the preacher told them, "it's fifty cents and twenty-five for the children." He was very business-like.

The smell of cooking came up the stairs from the kitchen and Emma could see that the young ones were sniffing the smell. Her own nose was not far behind theirs.

"We'll let ye know if we'll eat," Granpap told the preacher.

When the preacher had gone they watched each other. No one dared say, "Let's eat here."

But John spoke up. "My belly aches, smelling hit," he said, and held to his belly with both hands.

Granpap looked at John. "Does it, boy?"

"Yes," John said. "Hit feels like a deep spring, and empty."

"Granpap," Emma spoke softly, "we can do without a meal in the morning."

"Frank?" Granpap asked his question with one word.

"Hit's best t' go down," Frank said.

They had a full meal of hominy and gravy and hot biscuits and meat. But in the morning the full feeling had gone, and the smell of breakfast cooking spread over the house and even followed them through the open front door, as if the breakfast, at least, was hospitably urging them to stay.

23

It was early morning and freshness was still in the air, for the sun was not up far enough to bake everything. The last whistle had come from the factory some time before, but a few late workers passed them on the street. Unlike those who had walked slowly from work the evening before, these late ones hurried along as if the devil was behind lashing them on with his tail.

Granpap had stayed to finish some talk with the Confederate who was going to the reunion in the city.

"He had a uniform like the one in the picture at the station," Bonnie said to Emma, pronouncing "uniform" very carefully since she had just learned the word.

"Yes," Emma said. She remembered the picture very well and how Granpap had stood before it for some time.

John had stayed behind with Granpap but they soon came along. Emma looked at Granpap anxiously. If he got any ideas about going to the city, they were done for. She remembered that he had the money in a belt around his waist.

"He's a Confederate veteran," John said to Bonnie, and Emma listened, because Granpap kept his eyes away from her, and she was cut off from talk with him.

"Was hit General Lee?" Bonnie asked, for she had felt awe for the white bearded old man in the gray suit who had sat at supper with them the night before.

"No, he's the preacher's wife's Pa and he's a-going to stay with his other daughter in the city while the reunion's a-going on. There's going t' be a parade to-day—with uniforms."

"Hit'll cost him a fortune t' go," Emma said, loud enough for Granpap to hear.

"Hit's half fare on the train, Emma," Granpap said. "And in the city they will board and lodge ye for nothing."

"I don't believe big talk any more," Ora put in. She knew what Emma was fearing.

"This talk is true, Ora." Granpap turned and looked at Ora out of his bright blue eyes, and she felt Frank, on her other side, touch her arm. Frank was always a quiet one, and hated especially to mix in a neighbor's business.

"Well," Ora said faintly, but she gave Granpap's look back again.

"Ye ain't thinking of going, Granpap," Emma spoke up quietly from where she was walking just behind Granpap and the others.

Granpap did not answer, but just before they reached the office at the mill she caught up and looked full into his face, and saw by the way his lids came down that he was away in his mind planning something.

"Frank," she whispered and took hold of Frank's arm before he could step into the office. "Couldn't ye talk to Granpap? I'm afeard he's going."

"No, Emma, I can't tell Granpap what t' do."

"Just ask him if he's a-going, then," Emma urged.

"Granpap," Frank said in a loud voice, for when he made up his mind he must say a thing quickly and have it done, "be ye going t' the reunion?"

"I reckon not, Frank," Granpap answered, and there was plenty of disappointed wishing in his voice. "I reckon Emma and the young ones need me right now."

They were right in front of the office door. Here all of them, even Granpap, faltered on the steps as if some wild animal waited behind the door. A man came out and ran down the steps and over the hard ground to the door of the factory. In his hurry he left the door open and with this encouragement they walked through to the room inside.

There were benches against two sides of the big room, a hallway led to the back, and opposite the side wall was a small window like that in the station which was for tickets. Granpap went up and stood in front of this window. Presently a young woman came and said, "What do you want?"

"I want the man that hires," Granpap said in a firm voice.

"All right," the young woman said, and Granpap stood aside to wait. He almost stepped on a little boy who had come in after them through the door.

"Watch out, young 'un," Granpap said very loud. In trying not to step on the child he almost lost his own balance.

The young woman came back to the window. "What is it?" she asked sharply.

"Here's a young one wants something," Granpap told her. He stepped aside again and almost tripped over a dry goods box that stood there. Emma was not always easy with Granpap and sometimes feared him. Now, when he seemed so uncertain, for the first time in her life she felt pity toward him.

"What do you want," the young woman called through the window, for she could not see the child. He was about five years old and was not tall enough to reach up. He seemed to know how to remedy that, for he reached out with his small hands—Emma had time to see how bony they were, like his face—and lifted the box to a spot just beneath the window. Then he climbed on it with a serious and business-like air as if this was his special affair and no one was to interfere. He stretched his neck toward the young woman behind the bars.

"A book of scrip for Mis' Hardy," he said in a high little voice that everybody could hear all over the room.

"Mis' what Hardy?" the girl asked.

"Mis' Fayette Hardy."

She slapped a book on the shelf between them. "Tell her it's her second this month," she said.

"Yes'm," the child answered. He got down off the box, put it carefully in its place along the wall just behind Granpap and trotted out with the book in his hand.

For a long while the window remained empty. Though it was empty, all of them, at least the grown-ups, looked at it anxiously as if by expecting they could make someone appear in the space. And no one appeared there after all, for a man came in through the hallway and spoke to Granpap.

"Yes," Granpap answered his question. "We want t' hire." Frank got up from the bench and walked over to them. The man turned and looked at Emma, at Ora and the baby in Ora's arms. His eyes lingered a moment on Sally and Young Frank, then passed over the younger children quickly.

"Sit down here," he said to Granpap and Frank, pointing to chairs in front of a table. He went back through the hallway and came again with a large book in his arms. This he let drop on the table. Sitting before the open book, the man began to turn the pages. Granpap and Frank sat like two images of stone while the pages turned in the man's hands, over and over. "Over and over" sounded in Emma's mind and mixed in with the throbbing of the factory. She sat forward on the edge of the bench.

Suddenly the man stopped turning and looked up. "Name," he asked.

"McClure," Granpap said at once, and just after him Frank said, "McClure."

"Same family?" the man asked and wrote something with a pen in the book.

"We're two families," Granpap told him.

Then questions popped out of the man's big mouth one after another so fast that Ora and Emma, stretching forward to hear, could not understand them all.

How many of the family alive, how many dead, how many could work, were they healthy or sickly.

"Tell her to stand up," the man said to Frank, pointing to Sally.

Frank turned around in his chair. "Stand up, Sally," he told her. Sally stood up, and anyone could see that beneath the long skirt her knees were bent and shaking.

"Don't be afraid," the man said, and smiled at Sally. He looked her up and down. "All right," he told her and pointed his pen at Young Frank. "Now you stand up," he said. He put down their ages, Sally, sixteen, Young Frank, fourteen, Esther nine years, Hattie seven, Raymond two and the baby nine months. Then it was Bonnie, thirteen, and John, eleven, who must stand. It sounded to Bonnie from the way the man repeated before he put down the name that he had given her another name that was not McClure, and for some time she thought of herself as Bonnie Thirteen instead of Bonnie McClure.

The man opened his big mouth again. He called out to the young woman at the window. "Miss Andrews, ask Mr. Burnett to come in." And in a few moments Mr. Burnett came up to the table. The two men talked together in whispers, and when they finished, Mr. Burnett walked into the back part of the building. There was a curved space between his legs, and his feet met flat, side by side on the floor. He took short steps that carried him quickly out of sight.

The man at the desk said nothing. Granpap and Frank sat before him like figures of stone, and the others waited, almost breathless. If the man would only say something and give them some peace!

Presently a boy came in and gave the man a key. His wide mouth flapped open again, as he spoke to Granpap. But he spoke too softly for them to hear.

Emma heard Granpap say out loud. "Hit's not true. I can walk thirty miles in one day and kill a bear at the end."

The man smiled. His hand went up in the air flat and he said very kindly, "That's enough." But it was evident he meant exactly what he said. Emma, waiting to hear Granpap say more, saw only that he sat in his chair like a stone image. She thought, "Granpap is changed if he can stand that kind of talk." And then another thought, sharp and quick, come. "Maybe all this will change us. Maybe in a year we won't be the same—Granpap or any of us."

As if his interest in Granpap was finished, the man turned to Frank, gave him the key and spoke to him in a low voice. Then he picked up the great book and walked away through the hall to the mysterious place beyond.

Frank got up. "I guess we'd better go," he said to Granpap. But the old man, who was usually ahead of Frank, sat right on in the chair. "Granpap," Frank repeated, "we better be a-going."

Granpap rose up slowly from the chair.

Emma came up to them. "Why was hit just one key?" she asked in a low voice, so the girl wouldn't hear. Frank touched her on the arm. They let Granpap walk ahead. He went as if he could not see where to walk.

"What is it, Frank?" Emma asked.

"Didn't you hear?" Frank looked at her in surprise.

"He talked s' low."

"He said t' Granpap, 'You're too old t' work in the mill, only as a night watchman, and the places are all filled.' "

"Oh," Emma gasped out. "Oh, hit don't seem right." She spoke quite loud then, not caring about the girl, and Granpap had gone outside along with the others.

"And, Emma, he said you must board with us, unless you want the young ones t' work. You must have two elders t' work if you get a house, two elders or four young ones working."

Ora came back through the door. "Are you coming?" she asked them.

"Yes," Frank answered. He hesitated. "You could let the young ones work, Emma," he said.

"No, I can't, Frank. They're going t' school. If I have t' work my hands off they're going t' get schooling. . . . But I didn't think about being a boarder."

"What is it?" Ora asked.

"We've got t' board with ye, Ora," Emma told her.

"Well, Emma, let's go find that house, then we can set down and worry all we want. I want t' set down in a house again for once."

24

"WHERE's Granpap?" Emma asked when she came out of the office.

Bonnie looked up the road and Emma, looking, saw that Granpap was already on his way to get the steers. And she saw that his shoulders were drooped over and that he moved slowly as if his legs had suddenly grown stiff with rheumatism. She wanted to follow him and say, "Ye're not s' old, Granpap. Only a little while ago ye were tramping over the mountains like a young buck, and a-cursing anybody that got in your way."

She turned to Frank, "Frank, tell him hit's all right. Hit don't matter if he don't work."

"I'll tell him what I can, Emma," Frank said and walked up the road to overtake Granpap.

"Emma, we'd better go," Ora said. "That boy is having fits." She nodded to the boy from the office who was stepping impatiently from one foot to the other. He was some distance away as if he thought by going a little forward he could hurry them on.

"Hurry up," the boy said. "I can't wait all day." He must have come from the city, for he was dressed in a fine suit and a white shirt like the young man who had come up to the mountains.

John and Young Frank ran ahead to keep up with the boy and Bonnie and Sally stayed not far behind.

"That boy was a-stepping around so, I thought he must want to go somewheres," Ora said to Emma. "I wanted to say, 'Don't mind us, young man, just step to the side of the road and turn your back.' "

"Oh, no, Ora, you wouldn't."

"Yes, I would, Emma, he had too much sass in his manners. I would have done it in another minute."

As they went further out the red mud became so thick it sucked at their feet.

"Esther," Ora told her daughter, "pick up Raymond and carry

him to Sally. He can't walk any more in this mud. Sally!" she called out. "Wait for Esther."

The rows of houses on each side of the street were silent, as if all the people had deserted their homes. Only smoke coming from some of the chimneys showed there was life going on inside. The houses further out were not so nice as those close to the mill. On the edge of the village they were old looking and some were unpainted. Ora noticed that the pumps had been close together, about every two blocks, at first. Now they walked for some time before they passed another one sitting with its one arm akimbo at a corner.

Then the road stopped abruptly at a field. The boy from the office, having pointed out a place to the two boys, passed them on his way back. John and Young Frank waited at the corner. John leaned against a pump which was there and waved to them, trying to make them hurry. At the left on the side of a slope there were three unpainted houses.

John and Young Frank led the way to the middle house. They stood and looked at it, Ora and Emma tall in the midst of the young ones. The house was square and had a chimney, and a very nice porch clear along the front. In the back yard, just as in the back yard of all the houses, was a tiny outhouse. One of its hinges was broken, and the door swung back, so that inside they could see the slanted seat, with the hole which daylight from the back outlined clearly.

"Well," Ora said, fingering the key, "let's go in. I reckon we've got a right. . . . I'm glad," she told Emma, "the water is near. Did ye notice the pump?"

"Hit'll seem funny," Emma thought out loud, "to get water from one of those."

To Ora Emma's words sounded disappointed and melancholy.

"Why, Emma, hit's not s' bad."

"I sort of reckoned we'd get water out of the wall, like at the station," Emma said. "Well . . ." She stopped speaking.

"Let's go in." Ora went resolutely up the high steps and unlocked the door before them.

They did not stay long in the two front rooms. Bonnie found the stove in the kitchen and called them to look. There, sure enough, just as the young man had said, stood a cooking stove in a corner of the kitchen.

Ora opened the oven door, while the children stood around gaping at the iron box, and peering when they could under the arms of the elders into the dark interior. On a plate of tin John found a piece of iron with a handle at one end. He reached under Ora's arm and stuck the bent piece at one end of the iron into a place where it seemed to belong, and pushed on the handle. The round lid fell off with a clatter and scattered soot in every direction.

Sally, dusting her dress, walked to the window, and Bonnie followed her. But Emma and Ora stayed bent over the stove as if it was a sick person they were trying to coax back to life. It would have been good to make a fire at once, but there was no fuel. Emma stared down at the place where a fire had been once. She saw ashes and a gray end of hickory log with the bark still on. It was smooth at one end where the saw had cut through, and black at the other irregular end where the last fire used by the people before them had not quite finished burning it up.

Looking at the ashes, and the cold round piece that had not finished burning, Emma thought sadly that other people had lived in the house. Perhaps they had been glad to leave this place which she had worked so hard to reach. It made her suddenly angry against those people who had felt so little pleasure in this house. She wished she had those people before her so that she could defend this house, her house, against them. Then it came to her that the house was not hers but Ora's. She turned her back on the dark place with the ashes and went over to Bonnie who was playing with the window, pushing it up and letting it down.

"Don't ye do that, Bonnie," she said. "Ye've got t' remember, this is Ora's house."

"Now, Emma," Ora turned away from the stove, "hit'll be just the same as your house, too."

Emma felt ashamed then. "Yes, Ora, I know hit will. With anybody but you it wouldn't. But I know hit will."

"And anyway," Ora said, "hit ain't mine or yours. Hit belongs t' the mill."

Emma touched the pane of glass with her fingers. "Granpap will be pleased with the windows," she said. "He always did want a window."

She looked out and saw the other house which was only a few

feet away. She did not want to think about what Ora had spoken, that the house belonged to the mill. It made her feel as if all of them belonged to it. There was a sort of suffocation in that feeling and she put it away. She turned to Ora.

"Hit'll need something hung up here, I reckon," she said.

"I never had anything to hide," Ora told her.

"But hit's pretty. Ye can get some goods and make something real pretty."

"Ye want t' dress up a window like ye would a gal?"

"I think where you live, Ora, hit's needful t' have it pretty. Just the same as hit's needful for a gal to look pretty, because . . ."

"A gal's looking for a husband," Ora interrupted.

"And a house is a-looking for people to live in it. A man has got to like looking at a gal, and people should like t' look at their house."

"When a man marries he looks to his wife for satisfactions. When he's hungry and wants supper he don't think whether his wife is dressed up in silk or not. A house is t' give ye shelter and a place to cook and eat. Hit ain't for looks, Emma."

Ora's voice was loud and she looked at Emma as if she wanted her out of the way. And Emma watched Ora out of the side of her eyes as if she hated her. Bonnie shrank back against the window. She wanted to cry, very loud, because everything was so sad, and it was fearful to hear Ora and Emma talking to each other in strange loud voices. The baby, lying in Ora's arms, began to cry, as if Ora's voice had made it want to speak out and say that it, too, was tired of waiting in the blankness of the unfurnished house, that echoed sadly to everyone's footfalls and voices.

Granpap and Frank did not return until close to noon when the sun was almost straight overhead. All were hungry for there had been nothing to eat but some crackers from the store. The salty crackers had made all of them pay frequent visits to the pump so the house from the steps to the kitchen was tracked full of mud.

When Granpap and Frank did return Emma saw at once that Granpap was changed. She thought he must have found a place to drink and was full. Yet he walked steadily enough, and his shoulders straightened out as far as they would go. It was his eyes that gleamed as if he had drunk up a whole still. And, moving in, he urged Frank to pile more furniture on his back, when even Frank thought he had enough.

"Come on, Johnny," Granpap called out to John. "Do your part. Granpap's going to take ye on a journey, if you're good and help like you should."

"What kept us," Frank told Ora, "was a parade. The Veterans were parading down to the station t' go t' the re-union. They had uniforms, and Granpap had to see."

Frank had wanted to see and hear, too. There was a band that the railroad agent had hired and loaned out for the morning with the compliments of the railroad. Granpap had asked all about the reunion.

"They say hit's true that people will take care of ye, board and lodging free, in the city. And Johnny and me will march there. Hit ain't more than fifty miles, Emma."

Granpap, telling his part of the story about the parade, ended up talking to Emma. He was almost begging her to say she wanted them to go.

She did want him to go, if it made such a difference. On the other hand she needed him. So Emma was quiet. She would not say yes or no. Granpap must decide, and she saw that he had decided. Her yes or no would mean nothing in the end. So she became reconciled. The young ones were eating bread covered with beans from a can, and the old ones were not far behind them in finishing up the food Granpap and Frank had brought.

Granpap was full of young energy. He and John took the steers to the store where he had been told wood could be bought, and came back with a load which they piled up under the house. The two who were going away had so much excitement in them the others had to make special efforts to keep up with them. Bonnie followed after John while they were getting the wood piled in place, and Granpap was helping to get the beds up. Bonnie wanted to hear more about the place John and Granpap were going, and what they were to do there. John was not very sure about anything, though Granpap had talked more than usual on the way to the store and back.

"I don't know if we'll go on a train. How do I know? But there'll be plenty of things t' see in the big city and the capitol building that has a governor in hit. And we'll stay with fine folks in a big house where they keep gold in a strong box in the cellar. And maybe we'll git on a train, Bonnie."

"Well, I'm a-going t' school," Bonnie said.

"No, you're not," John told her. "We found out. Granpap found out before. School, hit don't begin for a long time yet. Hit's why Granpap's a-taking me."

When they went up to the house all the beds were made with quilts spread over them, making the place look as if people lived there. Emma's room was to be the back one at the side of the kitchen. There she and Bonnie would sleep in the bed, and as they had done in the mountains before Granpap had built the extra room, Granpap and John would sleep on the floor. When he came back, Granpap said, he would find some hay for a mattress, but even if he didn't, he and John were good soldiers and could sleep on the floor.

Emma and Ora went about the house working, getting the children fed. But they did not look at one another, nor speak any words.

Emma thought, "It'll always be this way. Ora will remember it's her house if I say anything. She can say it belongs to the mill, but she'll think it's hers. Anyway I can have something at my window, and I'll get something pretty with some of that money."

Ora felt that Emma was small thinking that it would make any difference that she had the key. But when Emma went out of the door to walk part of the way with Granpap and John, Ora felt sorry. She knew it was not easy for Emma to see them go.

Emma stood on a little rise and watched the two walk away from her. Granpap walked like a young man. The people at the mills were fools to think he couldn't work. A man who could walk fifty miles to the city and back was not too old to do a man's work anywhere. John looked back at Emma once, but Granpap went straight ahead, as if he could not hurry enough to get where he was going. Emma could see the mill some blocks away and thought she could feel the soft throb of the machines. Granpap and John were going away. But they would come back and all of them would be part of the mill, and part of the village. They were fixed, now. She walked slowly back to the house, climbed the steps, and wiped the mud from her shoes before she went inside to the others.

25

THE flat road that stretched away toward the city was a curious thing to John. Before this the ground had come up to meet his steps, or going down a hill, it had dropped away from beneath them. Now at each step it met his bare feet at the same place. For some reason this tired him out.

"Left! Right!" Granpap said, was the way to walk along a flat road. Sometimes in the army when they marched at night so the enemy wouldn't know where they were, about half the soldiers would be walking in their sleep. Only that Left! Right! kept the feet going when the head didn't know whether the feet were stumbling over a rock or toad-frog.

At some places the road crossed the railroad track. Then John looked up and down for the engine. It never came, but there were times when the road led through woods when he heard a rumble and Granpap said that was a train going by on the track. Toward late afternoon they stopped to rest and get water at a station. People were on the platform and there were trunks further down. All seemed to be waiting expectantly like a hunter waits behind bushes for the bear that the pickets are driving that way.

John saw the black man who stood by the trunks on the platform wave his hand. The man called out, "Raa-a Ro-o-de," in a big strong voice that went up into a peculiar sort of shriek at the end of the words. There was a rumbling on the tracks. Around a curve came the big engine. John knew that it was an engine and there was no need to fear. Yet the huge beast-like thing belched out smoke from its horn so fearsomely, and moved so swiftly upon them, it was hard not to fear. John moved behind Granpap as it came even with them and slowed up. Looking cautiously from behind the old man's back he saw the great bars go round and round pushing the wheels. The thing breathed like a winded steer until one expected to see its sides move in and out with the breathing.

"Hit's a fine sight," Granpap said, looking hard at the engine. The wheels had stopped going round, but it kept on puffing, and little jets of white smoke went up from the top.

"Did hit scare ye?" Granpap asked. "Hit's safer than those automobiles we saw on the road. Hit runs on a track."

John came forward and stood just in front of Granpap with his feet apart and his hands deep in the pockets of his jeans. Then, to show that he was not frightened of the monster, he went closer, and looked it over from top to bottom. Up in the little room a man in jeans was feeding coal into a red hot mouth. Under the body between the wheels there were many parts mixed in with each other like the inside of an animal. John made another step toward the engine and stooped down to have a look at these. In the beginning he had gone there to show Granpap he wasn't afraid. Now he was intensely curious about the pipes and bolts and rods. If the thing would stay long enough he would like to get underneath and feel the parts with his hands.

He heard Granpap say very loud, "Look out!" but did not even think that the warning was for him. And almost in the same second a jet of steam hissed into his face from the bowels of the engine. The steam surrounded him so that he thought for a moment that there was no more John left, only a spirit hurrying away somewhere in a cloud. He could see nothing except the white cloud-like steam, and his face burned. Then a hand pulled him out of the cloud, just as another jet of steam came.

"Are ye hurt?" he heard Granpap asking while the white cloud was still around them. "Are ye hurt?"

The engine blew angrily at them before it drew away. He could not see Granpap yet, and he thought the cloud was still around them. Granpap saw when the last car had gone by that the boy had his eyes closed tightly. His face was turning a bright red.

"Open your eyes, Son," Granpap said and shook John with both hands.

John opened his eyes and saw Granpap's beard just above.

"Are you all right?" Granpap shook him again, less roughly this time.

John's face had begun to hurt like a boil.

"Hit burns," he said.

They crossed the tracks and walked down the road again.

"We'll find some clay," Granpap said. "Hit's cool and healing."

He watched the boy anxiously, and almost casually he watched the bank that was sometimes high and sometimes low at the side of the road. Presently a streak of gray showed where the clay was near the surface. Granpap dug into the clay and kneaded a handful in his wiry fingers before he plastered it over John's face.

"Now, you're a plumb sight," he said. "If you could just see yourself you would laugh." He was torn between anxiety about the boy, and the feeling that he must get all right, so they wouldn't need to go back and miss the reunion. It would be almost a disgrace to be forced back when they had started with so much confidence. And Granpap had something to prove by this trip. He must prove that he was a young man, young enough to walk fifty miles to the city and fifty miles back.

The clay on John's face was cool, but the sun and air soon dried it out, and they had to look for more. This time John would not let Granpap put it on.

"I'm not any young one," he said. "I can fix hit."

"Ye're a wounded soldier," Granpap said and this made John feel very fine, because there was approval in the old man's voice and some admiration, as if John had done something especially fine and outstanding.

Presently, it was necessary to rest. They sat on top of a bank on some pine needles and leaned against a rail fence that marked off somebody's land there.

"We'll find a house," Granpap said. "And maybe they'll take us in. There must be farms along here off the road, and we'll get the woman to put some lard or whatever she has that's best for a scalded shoat. . . . For hit's what ye look like," he told John, "a scalded shoat."

They walked on for a time looking for a road. Then Granpap selected one that led off to the right. It had wagon ruts deep in mud and was so narrow the green trees met overhead.

"Hit looks like a pore man's road," he said.

About half a mile up they found a ramshackle farmhouse. A woman came to the door. Her skirts were tucked up about her waist. The first thing she did when she saw them was to let the skirts down hastily.

"This boy got scalded," Granpap said. "Could ye fix him up with something to ease the pain?"

The woman looked at them. "My man's out in the fields," she

said. "He'll be in soon." She seemed to wish them to feel that there was a man around if they meant any harm.

"If ye don't want us to come in we won't," Granpap told her. "But we'd be glad if you could help."

"I've just come from the fields," she said, and her face, full of sweat and dirt, showed that she had been somewhere working hard in the sun. "But if you'll come in, I'll try to fix the boy."

The clay was hardened on John's face and they had to pick it off in pieces. The woman heated some water on the cook stove and washed the face with warm suds. Then she spread on lard with some yellowroot juice mixed in.

There was a sound of feet on the tiny back porch, and a clank and clatter, then another, and two more. John knew that sound. He had made it himself when he dropped the hoe on the cabin floor after a time at weeding the corn patch. He had time to think, "These folks must be rich with four hoes," before the door opened and they came in. Behind the father came three children, a boy about John's age and two girls, younger. The father walked heavily across the room. His shoes were thick brogans that made the dust come up from the floor. At first he did not seem to notice at all that there were strangers in the kitchen. He went to the stove, lifted up a lid and spat his tobacco into the fire where it sizzled in the heat. He watched it until the sizzling finished, then turned to face them. The young ones were already watching the strangers. John must have been a queer sight with his face plastered with lard.

"Good evening," the man said, looking at Granpap and then with a long stare at John.

John knew what a person must do in a stranger's house. He must explain his errand as soon as possible, to avoid misunderstandings.

"Good evening," Granpap said to the farmer, and when there was nothing said he added, "I'm a Confederate Veteran and going to the re-union in the city."

"This your boy?"

"I'm his Granpap."

The man's face was blank, almost like a dead face. It made no response.

"The young one got scalded up the road," Granpap said. "From an engine. We'd like to stay all night, if hit's convenient."

The man's lips opened a little way and he said some words to the woman without looking at her.

"We can put the boy and his Granpap in with John," the woman said.

John looked up quickly at the woman. "What?" he asked.

"His name is John," Granpap said, pointing to John.

John looked at the boy who had his name. They stared at each other. He had never before seen a boy with his name. Here were two Johns in the same room and if that was true, then nobody knew how many other boys named John there might be in the world that was getting so big. It was depressing and not exciting any more to get into the world. One could not know where to put his finger and say anything was sure or knowable. It felt as if a big mountain had come and sat upon him.

At supper John ate only hominy and fatback gravy, for he could not chew the meat without pain.

"We'll have chicken to-morrow," the woman said, "since it's Sunday. And I'll fix you some soup." She had a bright little voice like a sparrow's chirp. "We've got a few chickens," she told Granpap.

"I reckon we'll have t' leave early in the morning," Granpap answered her. "The re-union begins on Monday."

He wanted to tell the woman and man that he had money and could pay, but he didn't know how they might take it. Perhaps, in the morning, he could just leave money on the table without saying anything.

"Must you go?" The woman asked. Since her husband had accepted them, she was really enjoying the unexpected company.

"I reckon we must," Granpap told her.

"My Pa was a veteran."

"Sure enough?"

"Yes, but he's dead now. But so long as he lived he went to every re-union."

"Is hit true," Granpap asked her, "they take ye in and board and lodge ye free?"

"Yes, it's true. My Pa once stayed with the mayor of the city where they had the re-union. It was a mistake, and he was moved after the first day. But he said the second house was just as good. He died last year and I was broke up, because he had lived with us for his last two years on earth. Before he died he said to me,

'Don't grieve, Mary. Just remember, your life's going on, and you've got to live it.' "

"Yes," Granpap said. "Hit's something we've all got to face, sooner or later. Life goes on whether we're there to see hit go or not."

Granpap's voice took on the woman's tone of sadness, but he spoke the words as if he said them only in politeness, as if he felt, really, that life needed him and he was in it up to the brim.

The woman went on talking. Except for the sadness in her voice when she spoke of her father, her voice kept up its chirp. It was like a twitter of birds, and it said over again, no matter what the words she spoke were, "Well, life's going on, well, life's going on . . . chirp-chirp."

And when she and the two little girls had cleared the table and were washing up in the kitchen, they kept up the sound among them. And it was a good sound, coming from the kitchen into the front room where Granpap, the farmer and the two boys sat.

The woman brought a jug from the kitchen and four cups she had washed clean of coffee grounds. When Granpap saw the jug his eyes lit up. John could see them light up or perhaps it was the way Granpap raised his head as if he was sniffing that made the light from the lamp shine in his eyes. It made John remember what Emma had whispered to him just before they left. "Watch Granpap," she said, "that he don't drink too much." Well, he had shaken off that responsibility very easily. It was not right for Emma to tell him to watch Granpap. John would not take the responsibility Emma had put on him. He would do what Granpap would wish him to do, let well enough alone.

The man poured John a half cup from the jug and his own John a half cup. The two men took theirs straight down, and had more. John swallowed his at one gulp, but the man did not offer him more. Inside his throat the liquor burned him like the scald on his face, and when it reached his belly it burned again; then the burning died away and left a very fine quietness, like sleep.

"You growing cotton?" Granpap asked the farmer, whose name was Mister Sanders.

"What there is of it."

"A lot of cotton seems to be around these parts."

"Yes, it's about the only thing we grow to sell."

"In the hills we grow corn, mostly."

"Cotton's the only thing for farmers in these lowlands. And that is hard come by with little return."

"Have another?" he asked Granpap.

"No," Granpap said. Yet when the man still held the jug over his cup he said. "Well, I believe I will."

The man poured out a full cup for Granpap and another for himself. When he drank he coughed and sent a scattering of drops from his mouth. Some of them came on John's forehead and touched it near the hair where it was not covered with lard. He wiped them off with his sleeve, and the rough sleeve rubbing against the burns made him uncomfortable so he was roused and heard all the words that were spoken.

"Do ye own?" Granpap asked.

"No," the farmer said. "I'm a renter. My Pa owned near a hundred acres around here before the war, with about thirty of good low ground near a pond and swamp. Before that my Granpa had owned more land but sold some to a big slave owner. After the war one of these Southern Carpet Baggers got hold of the rest of the land. . . ."

What was a Southern Carpet Bagger? John wanted to ask that question even while the man went on speaking. He wanted Granpap to ask, but Granpap had nodded as if he knew. He tugged at Granpap's sleeve. "What's a Southern Carpet Bagger?" he whispered.

"Sh," Granpap said and kept his eyes on Mister Sanders.

"What does he want?" Mister Sanders asked.

"He wants t' know what a Southern Carpet Bagger is," Granpap said, and there was an inviting sound in his voice as if he was asking the man to tell.

"Well, you know what a Northern Carpet Bagger was. Do you?" he asked John.

"No," John answered him straight out.

"They came down here during Re-construction and made money off the prostrated South. There are two in the Capital now, two brothers named Forbes. They came down and had niggers elected to the legislature and the niggers passed laws that made money for the Carpet Baggers. Those Forbeses are the richest men in this state right now. And there were plenty of Southern whites that joined in with the Northern Carpet Baggers to make money.

And they did. And one of them got my Pa's land by closing a mortgage. Now I'm renting from him."

There were other things John would have liked to ask, but he knew that for the time he had said enough. And Granpap spoke at once.

"What did ye do to him?" he asked the farmer, and there was an excitement in his voice as if he expected to hear a story of a revenge that suited the crime of taking a man's land away from him.

"Nothing," the man said. "There wasn't anything to do except pay what I owe. I owe him last year's rent, most of it. Last year we had late rains and early frost. It was a bad year."

The woman came in from the kitchen with her two girls. They sat down close to the fireplace as if there was a fire there and they were warming themselves, though it was hot and close in the room, and mosquitos that had come through the windows were swooping around whining their little aggravating tunes.

"Hit's bad when you lose your own land," Granpap said.

"Well," the woman joined in, leaning over to rest her back, tired from cooking and working in the fields, "at least we aren't share-croppers."

"No," her husband told her. "But it might be that next."

"Mostly niggers are share-croppers," one of the girls piped up in a sparrow voice like her mother's. She gave her piece of information which she knew to be true from hearing it said so much, and the strangers looked at her. She wanted them to look, to pay her some attention, but when the old man and boy stared she became confused, and hid behind her mother.

John and Granpap got very little sleep that night. After the lamp was out the mosquitoes came in droves, and were not at all bashful about lighting on noses and foreheads and legs. There was a long fight, and it was against John from the first, for the insects could light on his face since the lard was rubbed off on the bedclothes and he could not slap there for it would hurt the burns too much. Granpap in his discomfort let out some curses, and when the other John heard these, he followed Granpap's curses with some of his own. There were sounds of slapping and whispered cursing in the dark room for a long while. Then, worn out with the fight, they dozed off.

It seemed only a moment to John when he woke up with a bad

sickness in his belly. Granpap took him hastily out of doors, so that he might not make too much of a mess in the house of a stranger. It was shameful and disturbing for this to happen.

But it was more disturbing to find that John could not get out of bed the next day. His legs simply would not carry him.

While the Sanders family went to church Granpap sat by John.

"I'll have t' carry ye back t' Emma, if ye don't get better," he told John.

He was wishing for Emma, though the woman, Mister Sanders' wife, had been more than kind. But it was best for the boy to be with Emma, if he was going to be sick. He looked so pale lying flat in the bed, and so thin. There were dark yellowish circles under his eyes. And lying there, with the fair hair off his forehead, and long bone of his face showing up, he looked like Kirk. For the first time Granpap saw that John favored Kirk and was not like Basil who had squarer bones along his jaws.

At dinner time John had some chicken soup and sat up in bed. But when he tried to walk his knees gave out from under him.

Late in the afternoon with two more cups of soup in him, he was able to get up and walk down the road with the others to one of the cotton patches.

The patch was in full blossom, for it had been an early year.

"We planted the last of January, this year," the farmer said. "And this far it has been a fine crop."

It looked a fine crop. The cotton plants, full of green leaves, grew straight and healthy in long even rows. They were quite full of blossoms, as if a whole flock of red and yellow butterflies had settled between the green leaves to rest.

"Emma would like this," Granpap thought. He had been thinking about Emma all day at different moments, and in the night when John was sick. Out loud he said, puffing at his pipe, between puffs, "hit's right pretty," because he was thinking of Emma.

"I ought to make two bales out of this and the others," the farmer told them. "If we can get the weeds out, and there's not an early frost."

There were plenty of weeds in places and they looked as healthy as the cotton plants though not so high. Across on the far side of the field the ground was chopped clean of weeds, and there the rows of cotton looked clean and upstanding as if proud of themselves.

The farmer looked at the rows, and anyone could see he felt a pride in the work done. "But," he said, "by the time we weed one patch the other is grown up again. It takes the whole family, and then we don't get done what needs to be done."

"We can do it," the woman said. "So long as the Lord gives us strength."

They walked back in the quiet evening on the narrow road. The evening sun came through the leaves overhead and spattered the ground with bright spots and shadows.

Granpap was thinking he would leave some extra money from the belt around his waist for the woman when they left. She had been so kind. And he would make John say "Thank ye" for her kindness. It was only right. He spoke to John who was walking along beside him.

"If your belly has done a-cutting capers," he said, "we'll start off at sun-up to-morrow."

John looked up at Granpap, and for the first time since the accident he was able to stretch his mouth a little. "My belly," he said, "hit's done." His legs felt so much stronger and there was a happy, excited feeling where the pain in his belly had been. He wanted to go on right away toward the city and all the wonders that were promised.

26

THAT Saturday night Ora's family, Emma and Bonnie were together in the front room of the mill house. The lamp was lit and set on the chimney shelf. Over in one corner the bed, with Ora's best quilt on top, made a place for the younger children who had gone to sleep.

Bonnie and Sally pushed the young ones close together so that there was space on the edge of the bed to sit. On this first night all wanted to keep together. And they talked little and then only in low voices as if there was someone sick in the next room whom they were afraid to wake.

There were two windows, one that opened on the porch and one at the side, and before those windows they felt exposed. They had been accustomed to cabins where doors shut out the night every evening at sundown. Now there were the blank spaces through which the darkness outside stared in at them. And there was a feeling that the dark had eyes. And the sounds—the creaking of a joist, someone passing on the road outside, the short scraping that the stove pipe made settling into place—were unknown and mysterious.

Even Ora felt uncomfortable, and when Frank walked into the kitchen she followed him. It was better there. The fire was not quite dead in the stove and it made a little glow in the room. Standing near Frank, there by the stove, with the quietness and strangeness around them, Ora wanted to put out her hand and touch him; but they had not touched for so long except in bed she could not bring herself to do so. She thought of Emma who had been sad all the afternoon and evening. They had been set against each other since early in the day, and even Granpap's going had not brought them together again. She felt now that Emma was right about the curtains, not because they would be pretty, but because a house with windows needed something across them at night to hold in the light and shut out the dark.

"I think," she said to Frank, wanting to talk with him and

perhaps in talking draw closer, "maybe we'll have t' get some goods to put over the windows."

"Yes," Frank answered. He said nothing else, and made no move to say anything more intimate.

Ora went into the front room. It was useless to wait in there for Frank to say more. He was simply not a talking man.

"Emma," Ora said, "soon as we can we'll get some kind of covers for the windows."

She saw Emma's face soften up where it had been hard before, not hard with meanness, but hard with worry.

"Hit'll be nice," Emma said, but it seemed not to mean anything to her.

Ora went to the mantel shelf, "We don't need to use so much oil," she said and turned the lamp wick down until there was only a tiny light. With the turning down of the light the whole darkened room became a part of the dark outside, and gradually the heavy, sad feeling in the room lightened. Like birds when early morning light comes, Sally and Bonnie began to chatter, only this was dark that had unloosened their tongues.

Sally, thinking about the mill, and about working there all night, took herself back to the hills. She dreaded the work in the factory, and the work at home when during the day she must have charge of all the young ones while Ora took her turn at the mill.

"I wish I was back up there," she said.

"Do ye?" Bonnie asked. She could not think of anyone not wanting to stay.

"Yes, I do," Sally told her. "Maybe you don't, because you're t' get a schooling."

"Maybe you could get a schooling," Bonnie said.

"I'm too old. I've got t' work."

"Maybe you'll have some beaus."

"I don't want any. I've got Jesse."

Young Frank broke in there. "Yes, ye do want beaus," he said. "I saw ye making eyes at those men at the store."

"I did not," Sally told him, "I did not, Young Frank."

"Ye'll be forgetting Jesse in a week."

"I won't."

"And maybe he'll forget you, as well. Right now he's maybe a-courting Lorene, or . . ."

"Or maybe he's a-courting fiddlesticks," Sally cried out at him. She was trying to be defiant and sure of herself, but it was too much, thinking of Jesse so far away. Sobs began to come up in her throat. They choked her and then came through with tears coming at the same time—sobs and tears together. She lay face down on the bed and cried all over the feet of the young ones who were sprawled there.

"Be ashamed," Ora said to Young Frank.

She went to Sally and patted her on the shoulder. "Don't ye worry, Sally. Right now Jesse is probably a-mooning all over Choah Mountain wishing for ye."

They were sorry for Sally, yet it was somehow satisfying to have her cry like that. It took away some of the loneliness. Her crying woke the young ones, and when the baby added some howls to Sally's and the others began to join in there was so much to do for a time it was not possible to think of other things. Emma helped Ora get the young ones into the other room. They put Sally and Bonnie in Emma's bed so that Sally, if she cried again, would not disturb the children.

Emma stayed in the room. She was ready to get in the bed herself, for it had been a tiring day. Ora hesitated at the door with the lamp in her hand.

"Do ye want the lamp, Emma?" she asked, for Emma's lamp was still tied up in some old jeans in her trunk.

"No," Emma said. "I'll just get right in with Sally and Bonnie."

Still Ora hesitated in the door, holding the lamp up high, and looking into Emma's face.

"What's a-worrying ye?" she asked. "Is hit something special, or just for Granpap and John?"

"Granpap'll care for John," Emma said as if Ora had said something ugly about Granpap.

"Well," Ora was impatient with Emma for wanting to keep hard and angry, "well, I'll take the lamp back to Frank, then." Yet she waited longer, but turned her eyes away from Emma.

"I know Granpap can take care," Emma said low as if she was speaking to the floor at which she was looking. "Hit's just that I can't picture them anywheres. If I could picture them hit would be better. And then—there's something else. I clean forgot to get that money from Granpap. He's got all we have in that belt around his waist."

This was something real to worry over. It was something so definite that Ora could not keep it out of her mind. And all next day she reassured Emma if for a moment she saw Emma looking as if the worry had come over her again.

"He knows how much store ye set by hit," she said.

"He knows," Emma answered. Then she added, "Sometimes he forgets."

The day was quiet and still, for it was a Sunday. The young ones out in the yard stared back at the children next door on both sides. Sally and Bonnie sat on the front steps and watched the children, and got stared at by all the people who passed. Not that the staring was open, but they could see that eyes were turned their way, especially in the afternoon when people came from other parts of the village to take Sunday walks on the country road. Most of these were couples, young men and women, and Sally looked after them with wishing in her eyes and on her face.

"If Jesse was here," she said to Bonnie, "we'd walk down the road like that."

"And would ye kiss?" Bonnie asked, half in fun, as the grown-ups teased Sally.

"Hit's what we'd go for," Sally told her, trying to make what she said sound as if it was a joke. But each couple that came made her arms hurt with wanting Jesse; until she could not bear the sight of them and went inside.

That night while they were in the kitchen at the supper table the front door opened. The person who opened it came in the door as if he belonged. His boots sounded confidently on the floor as he came through the dark front room toward the light in the kitchen.

Emma thought, "Hit's Granpap come back," and she stood up ready to welcome him. No one else moved. They sat with eyes raised up watching the doorway. "Hit's Jesse," Sally said. And sure enough it was Jesse, six feet of real mountain flesh, standing there looking at them—no, he was looking at Sally. It was good to see the way she got into his arms. This was not a coquettish Sally or one holding back for manner or bashfulness.

No one said anything against it when Jesse told them he had come for Sally, and they must get married the next morning.

Only Ora asked if they couldn't wait until night when all could be there to see them married.

It was necessary for Jesse to be at work Tuesday morning. The only reason he had been able to follow Sally was that a piece of machinery had gone wrong at the saw mill and his work was put off one day. But he must be there when the Company said, or else lose his place. Too many other people wanted it.

"Maybe the man at the office would let ye off for the morning," Emma suggested to Ora and Frank. No one, not Frank and not Ora took up that suggestion.

"Hit'll be enough," Ora thought, "to have to tell them at night about Sally not working."

Jesse and Sally left them to think it out. They were anxious to get outside on the porch or the road where there was some friendly darkness.

Ora looked at the others. She wanted to say, "How can I work when there'll be nobody here to care for the young ones in the day?" And Frank wanted to speak out, "How can I care for ye all?" Yet they sat without speaking around the table and looked at Sally's place, and none of them would have thought of saying, "Sally has got to stay," or, "Let her wait. She's young."

Only Ora spoke out loud as if answering all their secret objections. "Sally is ripe for marriage," she said.

And when no one added to this she spoke again, "Hit's best she's going now, for she'd go sometime soon."

Frank went out to water the steers and came back again.

"They can take the steers," he said, "and keep ours."

"And leave the sledge," Ora suggested. "They won't need hit going up, and can climb faster without. Jesse is young and strong and can make another."

At sun-up next morning with the first whistle blowing, Ora, Frank and Emma stood at the bottom steps with Sally on the porch above them. Each of them had lunch done up in a paper.

Frank said, "I reckon we'll find ye gone, Sally, when we come back this evening."

And Sally said, yes, she reckoned they would find her gone. Then she went back into the kitchen, where she had already said good-by to Ora, to cry.

She and Bonnie got the young ones up and made them some breakfast. Ora had nursed the baby before she left, and Bonnie knew from taking care of Minnie's child what to give it to eat, now it could not have Ora's milk all day.

Jesse came for Sally at eight. They found a preacher, and went through the proper words that made them man and wife.

Back at the house Jesse harnessed the steers and drove them without the sledge. Sally walked by his side in her wrinkled calico dress, very proud. They used the country road because Jesse had found that it was a short cut to the road that went up into the mountains.

Bonnie stood on the steps and watched them go up the road. She would never forget that she had seen them like this, and that she had seen Jesse kiss Sally in the front room. When they were out of sight she clung to the post by the steps and pressed her cheek hard against it. A sound inside the door made her spring away, thinking she heard Young Frank. It was Little Raymond, and he made her remember that for the present she must take Sally's place.

27

GRANPAP and John reached the city in the afternoon. They were tired, and the hard streets of the town did not help the tired feet to get along very fast.

"We've got to find re-union headquarters," Granpap told John, for that was what the veteran said must be done as soon as they reached the city.

Around a sharp corner they entered a long street of brick buildings, some of them six stories high. Stretching his neck backward, John counted the stories, for he could count up to ten, or even more when it was necessary and he was willing to make the great effort. From one of the buildings to another hung streamers of red and white and in the windows were flags. It was a sight for a person to remember, the street white in the sun and clear down its length the red and white bunting and the red flags with some blue and white on them. "Hit's the stars and bars," Granpap said. "Hit's General Lee's flag."

The street was full of people, women and girls in fine clothes and men dressed in gray with white beards or gray ones. And there were young men in caps. Almost at every step they knocked into someone, or a person stepping hastily to get somewhere brushed against them. Granpap caught John's hand in his and held it tight. Under the other arm he held the quilt Emma had given them in case they had to sleep out at night. At times people who had brushed past turned round to look. But no one stopped long enough for Granpap to ask, "Where are re-union headquarters?"

"Just hold out, Son," Granpap repeated more than once.

At a corner some people had gathered together. They were watching an old black man. Here, Granpap thought, where people were still he might be able to ask the way. The black man wore a curious sort of uniform. There was a pair of pants with a red stripe down the sides, and a gray coat like the Confederates. On his head was a cap and in his hand he held a broom. Some of the boys who were there called out to him, but the grizzled black man paid no attention to them. He swept the sidewalk carefully over and over in the same spot; then without any reason he suddenly knelt down and aimed at the automobiles that were passing in the street. He yelled, "Boom! boom!" as a child does who is playing that he is hunting wild beasts. Suddenly he jumped to his feet again and swept the sidewalk before the people who were passing.

A man dressed in Confederate gray asked another, "Who is that?" And the other man said. "He's an old nigger who used to drive a hack around here. Now he's crazy and comes up to the main street every day at the same time. He's harmless so we let him alone."

The man in Confederate gray kept on watching. Granpap let go of John's hand and touched the man. "Can ye tell me," he asked, "where the re-union headquarters are?"

The Confederate looked at Granpap and then he looked down at John.

"Are you a veteran?" he asked of Granpap.

"Yes, I'm a veteran."

The man pointed down the street to a big sign that hung over the front of a building.

"Go right in there," he said.

In the office they asked Granpap some questions—what camp did he belong to? Where had he fought? When it came out that he had walked fifty miles to the reunion, the man behind the desk was very kind. He arranged for them to stay at a certain place. They were sent to this house in an automobile. John and Granpap together rode through the streets in the automobile that took them smoothly up to a fine white house that sat back on a big plot of grass. A woman dressed in the finest silk met them at the door and led them upstairs to a room.

The room was as large as a house in the village, and in it was a bed big enough to get lost in. A door at one side led into a small room where they found water. Granpap walked around on tiptoe, and even then he left a track from the mud that had dried on his boots. It was a good thing John had had some experience in the station, and that Granpap knew something of what people did in cities. Yet Granpap was not at ease. "It would have been better for us to sleep out," he kept saying. John did not entirely agree. He wondered if Basil had seen such houses, and if that was why he had said in such a scornful way, "Kirk hadn't any ambition." Was it ambition to want and get a house like this and fine food and clothing and perhaps an automobile? For the first time John thought of Basil with respect, as a person who had found something that none of them knew about, a secret of living that not even Kirk had known.

A Negro girl dressed in black with a white apron came up and said, "Supper is ready."

Granpap let John go first. As he walked down John saw the woman who had let them in talking to a young man in the hall below.

She said, "You must take them." As if the young man had been saying he didn't wish to do what she wanted. Then the woman added, "We'll send them to one of the barracks tomorrow."

The young man looked up and saw John leaning over the banisters.

"All right," he said, "but I don't promise to bring them back."

The woman met Granpap and John at the foot of the stairs. "We have supper made for you alone," she said, "because we thought you would like to get to the meeting early."

"Hit's mighty clever of you," Granpap said, "to take us in."

"Why, I'm glad and proud to honor our veterans," she said very graciously. "Especially one who has walked fifty miles to attend a reunion."

After supper eaten by themselves in the huge dining-room, Granpap and John were taken by the young man to a great hall on the main street. He put them in some seats halfway in the middle of the hall, and stopped long enough to tell Granpap the name of the street and the number of his house. Granpap repeated both of them after the young man.

John was already looking around, making himself familiar with everything in the hall. It was early and there were few people in the place. The seats went up from a platform in the center until they reached far up the sides of the building at the back.

"Hit feels like we're sitting all alone on the side of a mountain," Granpap said. And it was something like a mountain covered with many flowers in the spring, for the whole place above and around was hung with red and white, and there were flags everywhere, crossed and single and in bunches.

"What was the name of that street now?" Granpap asked John.

"I don't know the name." John tried to remember, but he had not been listening.

"I do remember the number was Nine O Nine, but the name of the street don't come to me." Granpap felt around in his mind. The excitement had made him a little scatterbrained. If he could get hold of a drink it would clear up his head, and bring the scattered brains together.

"Nine O Nine," he whispered to himself, and repeated it, trying to make the name come and join itself up to the number.

"I'll think of hit later," he said at last out loud to John. "Hit just escaped me. But I'll think of hit later."

"What?" John looked at Granpap. He had already forgotten about the missing name. There were so many other things to see and think about. People were coming in now. All through the middle of the building there were veterans with gray uniforms. Toward the back, if John strained his neck he could see light dresses of women and the dark clothes of men who were not veterans. But all around him and Granpap, in seat after seat stretching in a wide circle, one above the other were veterans in gray uniforms or veterans with white beards in regular suits or in jeans, but mostly they had the gray uniform so that all that lower part of the hall was made up of rows of gray uniforms and gray beards with some gold braid glistening in the lights that shone down from above. And the sound of talk was over the whole place, a great buzzing like a thousand mosquitoes; and to John the talk had a tune, though it was a tune all on one note or perhaps two, and it was not irritating like the tune of a mosquito, but friendly and natural.

The platform had been quite empty except for many chairs that sat in rows waiting for people to come and take them. It seemed that these people were waiting purposely until the last. For the place was completely filled when the band that Granpap had pointed out down in front of the platform began to play some music. From the sides of the platform, from behind curtains, came the people meant to sit in the chairs. And they came all at once, as if they had been waiting for the music.

"Hit's Dixie," Granpap said and pulled John to his feet.

The people who came out on the platform were a fine sight. There were men in gray uniforms with enough gold braid to make a harness and young women dressed in white with wide red ribbons running catacornered across their waists in front. They trailed out and stood together on one side, while the men in gray went to another side.

As the band finished playing a preacher came out to the front of the platform and everyone bent his head while he blessed them. Then with a great swish, a sound like many skirts being drawn aside, the people sat down.

A man on the stage who was not a veteran, for he was dressed in dark clothes and had no beard, got up and made a short speech. When he had finished people clapped their hands together. The clapping sounded like rain dropping on a roof.

One of the veterans in gold braid got up and said he wished to introduce the sponsors and maids of honor. He spoke names and as he spoke them two young women would get up and come to the front of the stage and bow. Then people clapped again, and John felt the chill run over him that always meant rain was coming down outside, for the clapping made him feel he was back in the cabin with rain pouring on the roof.

Next the veteran got up and said the speaker who was coming was one whom they all knew: Congressman Hellman. Granpap leaned down to John. "He's the same that Hal Swain knows," he said. "He helped get me out of jail that time."

Granpap clapped his hands together when the man came out to the front of the stage. The Congressman was a tall man with gray-black hair brushed back from his face in a pompadour. This made him look taller. He stood waiting for the applause to stop, and there was plenty of it, so he had to wait a long time.

"My friends," he began and spoke to the great crowd warmly and confidentially. At one minute he made them laugh, and at another he forced them to silence by his loud whispers. Only toward the back where the other people sat there were some voices that said, "It is shameful!" at some of his words.

There were times when John could receive the words of another person so that they were carved into his mind as a boy might carve a rabbit or some other figure on a piece of pine bark. Now he leaned forward along with the veterans and received the words of Mister Hellman. He could not understand them all, but what he did not understand he left until another time, as he had left the word ambition that Basil had given him until a time when he could fit it into a place where it belonged.

The Congressman said, "I have a rough outside, my friends. God did not make me of silken material to bamboozle men, but my heart beats warm for the people." He said the majority of veterans in the hall were of the people, the farmers and factory workers, and it was to them he wished to speak.

"He means us," Granpap whispered, but John scarcely heard. He was listening to the other words that came from the platform.

Mister Hellman continued, "I am for Race Domination. The Creator in his wisdom made the Caucasian race of finer clay than he made any of the colored people."

"Hit's why I told ye," Granpap whispered again, "not to mix with the niggers." It was very irritating to have Granpap whisper like that, while the man on the stage was saying such fine words.

The speaker went smoothly from one sentence to another. The words spilled from his mouth and sometimes his voice was loud and sometimes it was low and solemn.

Promoted by enterprising Southerners and friendly industrialists of the North, he said, the mills had come to the South. Not the blue-bellied abolitionists, but the industrialists were friends of the poor whites. The Congressman read from a paper something about the industrialists: "With a shrewdness that will command the admiration of every practical business man, the industrialist engages in nothing that will not swell the dimensions of his own purse, yet he is always solicitous to invest his capital in a manner calculated to promote the interests of those around him." "And he does promote your interests," the Congressman cried out to them. "The Northern industrialist has come to us on a mission of peace and promise. The Southern industrialist and Northern together have bought the cotton of the poor farmer and put it to work in the mills. Here in the mills they have given employment to the free white and paid him well for that labor.

"And this recompense is your due," the Congressman went on. He came close to the edge of the stage and spoke confidentially to the veterans before him.

"Who," he asked, "saved the South during Reconstruction? It was you, the men, the rank and file, the common people. Before the Civil War members of the aristocratic oligarchy rode in their carriages, and lived like kings, while you, whose boots they were not fit to lick, were crawling in the mire, seeking dishonored graves.

"During Reconstruction you proclaimed the triumph of Democracy and white supremacy over mongrelism and anarchy. Now you have made a New South, a South of prosperous farms, of smooth-running factories, a South in whose bosom you rest, where your children receive free education, are taught the beauties of religion, where you possess peaceful homes, and the freedom to work."

As he sat down, mopping his face because of the great heat in the building, the band began to play so that the sound of music went up with the sound of clapping. Two men on the platform went over to Mister Hellman and shook his hand, then three others followed them. But the white haired old general, and the others near him, sat quite still.

When there was quiet again the general came forward and spoke. "We have with us," he said, "a girl who is the daughter of one of our veterans. She is here to speak for the women of the South."

28

From somewhere at the back came a young girl. She must have been younger than Sally, perhaps about Bonnie's age. John looked at her in surprise. Here was a young girl trying to speak to this big congregation. How would she do it? Then she began and he saw that she could, that somehow her voice could be heard clear through the great hall, for people sat forward and listened, and there was not a murmur. Only he could hear her voice, and along with it the heavy breathing of the old men. They leaned forward toward her, and seemed to swallow what she said with their open mouths, and at times when she spoke more fervently tears rolled down their cheeks.

She told them her father was a veteran and she had come to speak to them because she had been taught to love them from the time she could understand. She had been taught, along with her prayers, to love the South, and the men who had bled and died for the South.

"Upon your breast," she said, "you wear a little iron cross. It is not the ruby-gemmed cross of the Czar of the Russias, nor the Emerald Cross of Britain's King. It is not these, but it is greater than all of these. It is made of a brave man's blood and a brave woman's tears, fused and welded in the red furnace of four years of want and grief and battles and graves, and from that union of blood and tears the South we know and love was made."

She stood on the stage by herself, that girl, and moved from one side to another as if she was at home there. She held out her arms, and talked to the veterans before her, and they listened as if they could not bear to miss a word she said. She told them of her love for them, and they loved her for saying it.

She said, "There are those who say you thought you were right. I say you knew you were right, and through the long years the truth shall be written and shall remain where it belongs. You call your scars ugly? They are not ugly. They are symbols of beauty whose meaning will be enrolled with the years, and that wooden leg is as holy timber as the cedar built temples of old."

And at the end she said some poetry like a song.

"There he stands like a hero, see!" She said this and pointed with one hand into the mass of gray uniforms. . . .

"He bore his rags and his wounds for me.
He bore the flag of the warring South
With red-scarred hands to the cannon's mouth.
As my sire saw him, so I see to-day
The red wounds gleam through the rags of gray."

The girl came to the very edge of the platform and reaching out her arms stretched them toward the men in front as if she wanted to take them all into her arms at once.

"Soldier, you in the wreck of gray,
In the brazen belt of the C. S. A.,
Take my love and my tears to-day,
Take them, all that I have to give,
And by God's help, while my soul shall live,
It still will keep in its faithful way
The campfires lit for the men in Gray,
Aye, till trump sounds far away
And the silver bugles of heaven play
And the roll is called at the Judgment Day."

When she finished there was a roar like rocks falling down the side of a mountain. The whole congregation stood up. John climbed on his seat to watch. He saw an old man in gray climb on the platform and hang something around the girl's neck. The general on the platform went up and kissed her. Then, as if he had set a fashion, other old men climbed on the platform and began kissing her until she was surrounded and no more could get there. One old man came to the edge of the stage and called out to the others. "Let's give her the rebel yell," he said, and held up his arm. There was a sudden quiet. Then came a long weird sound as if the whole congregation was threatening someone in anger. The sound hung over them ugly and shrill and threatening, then up it went into a terrible shriek that shook the hall and the flooring beneath, so that the seat on which John stood became unsteady.

The band began to play Dixie again and everyone started going toward the doors, though the preacher was at the edge of the platform waving his arms. He wanted to say a prayer, but the meeting was over and he had to stop waving his arms and just say the prayer to himself.

Granpap said, "Let's go that way," and pulled John against the crowd that was moving toward the doors. "I want to see the Congressman close," Granpap said. They could see him on the platform just outside the circle of people who were around the girl. He was speaking to everyone who came along. And there seemed to be plenty who wanted to shake his hand. He had a fine way of doing this. He would take the other person's right hand in his and lay his left hand on that person's shoulder. Then he would slowly shake the hand that was in his and his mouth opened as if he said kind words. Granpap and John could see him, but there were too many people between them and the platform, so that when they reached it Mister Hellman and most of the other people had gone. Only the preacher was still there, waiting perhaps for the last one to leave the building, so that he might keep God's blessing in the place as long as anyone was there to receive it.

The only thing to do was to turn and follow the great crowd out of the building. Granpap kept thinking, "If I could find a little drink or two, I could remember the name of that street," for he thought they must now go back to sleep. Just outside the building a man on a chair was calling to the veterans as they passed. "Gather around the campfires, boys," he said, "and fill your canteens. The drinks are on the Congressman." So the evening was not finished.

All down the long main street there were bonfires sending up sparks and smoke. The street was very wide and the sparks died out long before they reached the buildings. But as they went up with the smoke they seemed to be twinkling eyes that said, "Have a good time, old men. There's nobody to watch you but us, and we—are—going—out in—a minute." They went out and others came up from the fire to take their places and say the same thing.

Granpap pushed along with the other veterans. The crowd was like a gray stream pushing sluggishly along, held back by its own weight and the evenness of its bed. At places where the bonfires were sending up sparks, part of the crowd broke off, circled the fires and settled there. Granpap and John, who were on the outside of the crowd and at the end, were among the last to reach a fire.

Near the fire men were sitting in little groups, talking or singing in low tones. Just opposite the fire was a lighted store, and here they went to refill their bottles or canteens.

Granpap had no bottle but he sat down with one of the groups and began to talk. First someone asked him about the boy and that started a conversation. When one of these men held out his bottle to Granpap the old man was not backward about taking a drink.

Far up at one end of the street the white columns of the Capitol building showed in the street light, and the red flare from the fires lighted up the rows of steps that came down from the columns to the ground.

"The Governor's giving a ball to-night," one of the veterans said, "for the higher-ups, the generals and such and their ladies."

"Like the ones on the platform to-night," Granpap said, as if he knew.

"That was a fine little 'un that spoke," one of the old men said.

"Well," Granpap told him, "I don't hold much with women a-speaking."

"It wasn't a woman. It was a girl," another said as if he was angry at Granpap.

And another one said, "When she told us, 'till the silver bugles of heaven play,' by God I heard the bugles sounding in the sky."

"The Congressman was good, too," another spoke.

"Hit was downright ugly for him to speak so about aristocrats before the General and those others," one veteran, who had been quiet before, said.

"Hit was right and proper," another spoke angrily.

"And I say hit was improper."

"When the Congressman says we saved the South, then he's right."

"Maybe he is, but when he speaks like that he don't speak like a gentleman."

"He speaks for the common people, and when he says we saved the South he's right."

"He is right," someone on the outer edge of the group spoke, as if the other voices had just roused him from a sleep.

"We saved the South from the black menace."

"We did that!"

No one had offered Granpap a drink for some time. "I'm going over to that store," he said to John, and got up on his feet. John saw Granpap walk unsteadily toward the store that was so full of light. John roused himself and followed Granpap. Inside the store men were drawing their drinks from barrels propped up on the counters.

"Granpap," John said, going up to Granpap and catching at his fingers, "can you remember that name now?"

"Name?" Granpap asked. He seemed already fuddled, and no wonder. He was filling the tin cup time after time at the spigot. "Name? I don't remember a name. Yes, I do. Hit's Nine O Nine, and away down south in Dixie." He let out a whoop, like the rebel yell, and taking a last drink, pushed John on to the sidewalk. The push was in fun, and Granpap had meant it so. It was not his fault that the arm behind the push was very strong. It sent John right on to his behind flat on the walk. Some people around laughed, and that made it worse. Granpap came out and tried to pick John up. He fell down himself, and someone else had to come and set them both on their feet. Granpap leaned on John then to keep his feet steady and they got back to the little group. The old man sat down on the ground hard, for he had miscalculated the distance, and John was glad that Granpap, too, had gotten his backside hurt. He knew that to-morrow Granpap would be very sorry about pushing him, but for the present he felt angry and resentful. And he was very tired.

"Let's go, Granpap," he whispered.

"No," Granpap said. "Don't ye hear the man's talking. Listen to him, now."

"And election night," the veteran who was speaking said, "six white men stood in front of the polls and dared the niggers to go in and vote. We stood there, each with his shot gun. And the next day we were all in jail, courtmartialed for having firearms. But the niggers hadn't voted."

"It was the same in our county," another man said. "Only there we had the Ku Klux Klan. When the Ku Klux in another county wanted some niggers scared out of that county they let us know by secret messenger. We dressed up in our white robes with robes over the horses and rode up to the nigger's cabin. Under the robes were long rubber pipes. We made the nigger come out his cabin, and we said, 'Nigger, we're dead Confederates come back from hell. And it's hot down there. We're thirsty.' And we made him draw water from the well, bucket after bucket, and as each bucket came up we poured it down the rubber pipe. Then we said to the nigger, 'Get out of this state by sun-up,' or if we didn't want him to vote, we said, 'Stay home from the polls or by sun-down to-morrow you're a dead nigger.' And he did just what he was told. And the Ku Kluxes who lived in that county could prove to the northern militia that they had been at home peaceful that night, or at the store playing checkers, or at church. And that's how we saved the South."

Further up the street some veterans around a campfire began to sing "Tenting on the Old Camp Ground." Their voices sounded crazy and hollow as if they were really spirits come back from the dead. People were leaving the campfires, one by one, or in twos. It was getting late. From up the street on the steps of the Capitol Building came the sound of a bugle. Granpap stood up listening while it played.

"Taps," someone said in a hollow voice. "Time to go to sleep."

Granpap started toward the store again without paying attention to John, who followed right behind.

"Hadn't we best find that house?" John asked.

" 'Nother drink," Granpap muttered, "and we'll tent on the old camp ground."

The man was closing the store and would not let Granpap in. He stood before the half open door barring the way.

"I'm a veteran," Granpap said to the man. "I'm a veteran and I've got a right to a drink. I fought for the Confederacy. I fought and bled and died."

"Go home," the man said. He must have been sleepy and tired, too, for he sounded very cross. "Go home, old man. And take your son with you. He should be in bed."

"Yes," Granpap said. "My son—my son."

He looked around for John and finding him right there close to his hand he spoke to the boy crossly as the man had spoken to him. "Go home," he said to John. "Go home." And he put one hand on John's shoulder to urge him along.

With Granpap's hand on his shoulder John walked up the street in the direction from which he thought they had come. The streets were almost deserted, and the bonfires were low.

Only a few stragglers were left on the street. Their boots sounded on the pavements. If Granpap, leaning on John's shoulder, had not moved so slowly and unsteadily, John might have caught up with one of those and asked for a place to stay. Granpap's weight kept him back. The sound of steps on the pavement going off in the distance rested on him like another weight. They were telling him, "Left! Right! You're left alone with Granpap."

He forced himself to walk as far as possible, down the street and around a corner, then down that street, until Granpap came to rest against a stone fence and would not move. Finally the old man slid down to the ground and stayed there. There was nothing to do but sit beside him and wait until he would sleep off the drink. He was snoring already loud enough to wake the people in the houses that were back from the sidewalk. At least John felt so, for the snores sounded like shouts in the street, which was already still with an early morning quietness. Granpap lay sprawled on the ground, his pale face turned up so that the street light shone full down on it. His beard moved gently with a breeze that had sprung up with the early morning. The beard that looked so majestic in the day when Granpap was standing, now appeared scraggly and worn out. The scars across his right cheek pulsed up and down with his breathing.

John waited for the first light, and when that came he shook Granpap awake.

Still they could not remember the name of the street where they had left Emma's quilt in the woman's fine house.

"We could go back to that office," John said, but he did not want to go.

"No," Granpap answered. "Hit's a good thing not to go." He looked away from John and would not meet his eyes. "Hit's better not to go back there."

Now that the old man was steady on his feet they walked back to the main street. All the stores were closed. They sat with blank fronts facing the bonfires where some embers still showed through the blackened wood and gray ashes.

"We'd best find the station," Granpap said. "And take a train back. I've got some money in that belt. Emma would like us t' get back as soon as we can. Would ye like to ride a train, John?"

"Yes," John said. He would like to do that. But at the time he could not feel that anything was very good. He only wanted to sleep, and forget about Granpap in the night. But Granpap wanted him to say he would like the train. He wanted him to feel an excitement about it.

"Hit'll be fine," he urged. "Ye can tell Bonnie and all that ye rode fifty miles on a train."

"Yes, hit'll be fine," John said. "Let's find the station."

"But I don't know what I'll tell Emma about that quilt. She'll take it hard we lost it."

29

It was just daylight. Emma hesitated on the walk, while the people hurrying into the mill passed around her and Ora and Frank as they stood together. The people entering the door of the mill seemed to Emma as if they were corn being fed into a hopper to be ground up.

Emma saw herself going in and coming out crushed and different from what she had been.

In the mountains she had thought of round silver dollars dropping into her lap, and of buying good food and fine things in the stores. But the people she had seen did not look as if they were used to many dollars. The women looked anxious about the mouth and fearful of something, and the men walked doggedly as if this was something they had to do, and they were going to get it done, simply for that reason. The young children in the pale early morning light showed up sad and pinched about the face, and thin in their bodies. Emma made up her mind further, looking at them, that Bonnie and John and Ora's young should go to school.

But she would not let them make her give up the thoughts she had had of the promised land. She said to herself, that she, Emma McClure, could make money if she tried hard enough. If she worked hard and gave the best she had to the mill, in some fine way she would be recompensed. Perhaps all these people had failed to give their best. Perhaps they were lazy.

"I'll work hard and show them what I can do," Emma thought. She started forward just as Ora was about to touch her on the arm and wake her from that dreaming state that Ora knew so well as part of Emma. As they went through the door they heard the whistle blow.

Frank was to find the finishing room where he was to work as a beam hauler. Ora and Emma were spoolers. The finishing room was on the first floor. They left Frank there and walked up the stairs to the place where they were told to find the spool room. Emma found it hard to get up the stairs, for her knees had given way with the sound of the whistle so close. Ora stepped hard on the stairs, but it did little good, for the sounds in the mill kept her from getting any confidence from her own firm steps.

They stood in the doorway of the spool room, quite alone, not knowing which way to turn. Here the floor shook to the machines. This rumble and shake was as different from the throb outside as the sound of a stream when there is little water is different from the sound when the stream is fed by snows and becomes a torrent coming down the mountain.

A man came up to them. "Are you the new spool hands?" he asked. Ora nodded.

"Come this way," he said and led them between frames filled with long rows of spools and bobbins. The bobbins revolved and were emptied of thread onto the spools. The machines whirred and the spools turned with little jerks as if in a dance. At a place in the middle of the room the man stopped.

"Here," he said to Ora, "you stop here."

He called a girl who was at one of the other machines. She came over to give Ora lessons in running.

Then the man, who was the section boss, led Emma away. She followed him with her head bent over. He stopped at some machines next the windows that looked on the streets. Emma raised her head and for a moment she saw the street outside, and having left Ora and being alone, she wanted to run from the room and get on the street. If she could get there she would be free. She felt this in that moment, but her feet standing on the floor by the machine refused to move in accordance with her wish. In another moment the man was showing her which machines to manage, and another woman was telling her what to do. The man was gone.

If the thread broke she must immediately stop the machine and knot the broken threads together. There was something to learn about starting the machine and stopping it. And there was the special twist of the thumb and finger that made the knot in the thread. To keep the machine going and the threads intact meant walking up and down in front of the spools with eyes always on the thread that traveled with little jerks from the bobbins to the spools.

The girl left her, but had to come back. It was so easy, watching her, to think of twisting the thread in the right kind of knot.

But it was very hard to do it. Thinking and doing were very different.

"I'll never learn," Emma said.

The girl was very kind. "Yes, you will," she said. "But you better remember. When the machine stops, pay stops. So you better learn quick."

The spools and bobbins jerked in their little dance. They made Emma's eyes burn. She raised them a moment. In that time she saw Ora's head across the room. The frames were high but tall Ora was higher. Her head moved along, and Emma saw it cut off below the eyes by the frames, with the eyes down, watching. She jerked her own eyes back to her machines and began the walk again. One of the spools and its bobbin were whirling on their rests, which meant they had parted company and she must tie them together again. Seeing Ora made her think again of Sally. Perhaps the girl was just now going by outside with Jesse, traveling to the mountains. Emma would have liked to look out of the window, but there was no taking time from her threads.

When the bobbin was empty and a spool full she must put on a full bobbin and an empty spool. She watched the box on wheels in which were put the full spools that the girl had told her must be taken to the creels. The box did not fill very fast. That was because she had not learned to watch the frame with eyes that saw, or tend it with fingers that knew. If they would just give her time, though, she would be the fastest among them.

The twelve o'clock whistle blew sooner than she had expected it. There was so much to learn the morning had passed quickly. Emma joined Ora at the door. The section boss met them there.

"How far do you live?" he asked. They told him. "Better bring your lunch to-morrow," he said. "You'll have to be here at a quarter to one."

They had no time to speak much about Sally at home. Bonnie had food for them and they gulped it down, for it had taken some time to get out to the far end of the village where the house was. After the quick dinner Ora gave the baby some milk, but had no time to let it finish nursing. She left it crying in Bonnie's arms.

In the afternoon Emma's fingers began to learn. But she must work a long time before she could do as well as she wanted. Now she noticed the young boys, like John, who pushed the boxes on wheels, to her place. She saw the black woman who swept that side of the great room. But she said nothing. They went about their work quietly, without a neighborly word, and she kept to her work, because it took all of her time. She was fully concentrated on the thread. That was important. That and nothing else.

At night she and Ora met Frank outside, and they stopped at the store to buy food for supper, before they joined the stream of people going down the street. These people looked neither to the right nor to the left, enjoying, but went straight ahead. And those three, Ora, Emma and Frank, looked neither to the right nor to the left, but walked straight, wanting to get home for supper and rest, and to see that nothing had happened to the young.

Only some of the young girls, like Sally, walked slowly and talked and laughed to each other.

"At that age," Emma thought, hearing them, and looking up for a second, "you can be happy anywheres—in any kind of place."

Now she felt old and not new as she had when they first started out from the mountains. She thought of the man who had watched her, the section boss. Even when he was at a distance, she could feel his eyes on her, a sort of burden. She felt the burden of the spools and the thread; the sound of the machines was still in her ear, and she could still feel the throb of the floor going through her feet into her body, making it ache.

30

By the end of summer Emma and Ora had both learned their trades well. They were good spoolers. The first week Emma made only a few cents. Now she and Ora filled their boxes quickly, yet the amount that came in on their pay checks seemed very inadequate for all the expenses. They had bought a few extra fixings. There was a bed for Granpap and John paid by instalment, and an alarm clock. The man came around regularly every week for his dollar. They took out insurance, and the insurance man never failed to come for his toll. The electricity was a fine thing to have in the house. It was still a new experience to twist the button and get light. But the pay for electricity took something every week from the pay check, more than would have been given for oil.

Frank had been put in the slasher room, to run the warp through a starch bath. The hot starch made a vapor in the room, and when a draft came in from an open door or window Frank often got a bad cold. Ora was anxious about him.

"Hit's nothing," he said to her when he got over a spell of coughing. "And hit's a good place to work." Even when he had a very bad cough he went on working, for he had heard from others that the management did not like people who stayed out on account of sickness. And since they were docked if five minutes late, a day's absence would take too much off the check.

Young Frank was working at hauling spools, but he had been promised that he might go to school when it opened. When Young Frank went in the mills John wanted to go, though he was younger. Emma knew from talking to others that the preacher would sign a paper that he was old enough, as he had done for other young ones, but she felt what people told her was true: "once in the mill always in the mill." And she wanted John to get some schooling. So she asked him, "Do ye want schooling or work?" And he said, "Schooling."

Ora had wanted to do the same with Young Frank and kept him out as long as possible. But one day after work Frank met her outside the mill and said, "They want me in the office."

They looked at each other, and each wondered what was coming. Ora waited for Frank. He came out looking as if he had heard bad news.

"Have ye lost—your work, Frank?" she asked, wanting to meet the trouble.

"No—hit's something else. . . . He says since Sally has left, we must send Young Frank into the mill. He's the age."

"No," Ora told him. "Frank ought t' have his one year at school. That much anyway."

"He says hit's better for him to be working than running around loose, getting into trouble, or eating candy and making himself sick."

"I'd see about the candy and the trouble," Ora said.

"There don't seem any other way, Ora."

There was nothing to do but send Young Frank. Ora promised him and promised herself that at the end of summer the boy must go to school with the others. For he wanted to go. He did not say much; he was more like Frank there. But long before he had spoken his wish, and she wanted it for him.

Granpap and John took long walks during the summer. Sometimes they went part of the way to the mountains. They had a secret together, for neither one had told Emma or the others about Granpap getting drunk in the city and losing the name of the street from his mind. They had blamed coming back earlier than had been expected on John's burns, and to each other they did not speak of that night in the street. Granpap had told Emma, "I forgot your quilt at the lady's house." And Emma said, "Hit was just like ye." She might have said more but she wanted to hear over and over about the house and the big meeting and the fires in the street.

John said nothing to Granpap about that night, but each felt that the other remembered, and it became a secret between them. And John felt something else. For a night he had taken care of Granpap, and since then his feelings toward the old man had changed. There was a difference in their relationship. Now, at times, John spoke his mind as if he was a grown-up person.

Granpap wanted to go back up to the mountains, and it was John who said, "Wait, maybe there'll be some work yet." There was no work yet in the factory. Granpap was angry when they took Young Frank. "Hit seems they want just the young," he said to John. "And the young ought to be out a-playing and enjoying. Hit's like in the Bible where they used to put babies in the red hot arms of the idol. I'm a-getting to believe the factory's an idol that people worship and hit wants the young for a sacrifice."

There was no work for him in town. He knew how to cut wood and tend a garden, but this sort of work was done by the black men. "If hit wasn't for niggers," Granpap said to John while they were sitting at the side of the road, "I could get work; but they want niggers, because the black man charges less than the white."

Granpap found it hard to keep himself busy, and sometimes with the few cents Emma could give him he bought foolish things. Sometimes he went to the restaurant where the McEacherns brought their liquor and, sitting in the Blind Tiger, filled himself as far as the money would go.

Once he bought an ornament for the house to bring to Emma. He felt that it would please her, and it did after she got over the feeling that he shouldn't have spent the money. It was a large piece of cardboard decorated with colored flowers. At the top in gold letters was a sign that said, according to the man who sold it, "GOD BLESS OUR FAMILY." At the left was a smaller sign that said, "MARRIAGES," and under this was space to write the names of those married. At the right was "DEATHS," and at the bottom "BIRTHS."

"When you young ones learn to write," Granpap said to John and Bonnie, "you can write all our names in the places up there. Maybe," he said, for he was feeling mournful before the family these days, "maybe ye can soon write John Kirkland under the deaths."

They hung the picture on the wall in Ora's front room where everyone could look at it while they sat. Emma put her Bible that Basil had given her on the table Ora bought from the instalment man. They covered the table with a clean towel and laid the Bible on top. In this room they invited neighbors who stopped to talk. Not many came. Everyone seemed busy with his own household, especially the women. There was plenty to do at home, without gallivanting to other people's houses.

The Mulkeys lived next door. Mrs. Mulkey was sick with pellagra and sometimes she had spells. Mr. Mulkey worked in the factory. They had three rooms and kept a boarder, Mrs. Mulkey's younger sister Alma. She worked in the factory, in the warp room, so Mrs. Mulkey was at home during the day with the three small children. The preacher came to see her once a week, for she and Mr. Mulkey were both very religious. It was Mr. Mulkey who came over one night when Granpap was playing "Bile them cabbage down" on his fiddle and asked him to stop playing dance tunes. No one had asked that before, and Granpap stopped only because Mrs. Mulkey was sick, and if he worried her it might bring on a spell. The Mulkeys were not alone in their feelings against dance tunes. The preacher—not the one they had stayed with the first night in the village, for he was of another sect—their own preacher, spoke against dance tunes at church, and many in the village did not approve. Granpap fretted because he was forced by the opinion around to give up his playing, and sometimes he got out his fiddle and played anyway, to show that he was not to be ruled.

The Mulkey children ran about just as they pleased because their mother was sick. Sometimes they were very dirty, and always ragged. Mr. Mulkey did some of the cooking, for Alma was lazy and refused to work much, since she was a boarder. Yet she was very smart, for she could read and write well; and it was Alma who had taught Bonnie how to find time on the alarm clock, so that Bonnie could teach the others. Often when supper was over Alma had beaus who took her to the store for soda water or to church. Then the oldest Mulkey child, Annie, who was eleven, washed dishes and cleaned. Most of the time she did the cooking instead of Mr. Mulkey, who liked to talk about how hard he worked at home.

Ora's young ones played with the Mulkey children, though Bonnie had to watch carefully to see that they did not run off and get into mischief, begging at the store or getting wet in the creek, led by young States Mulkey who almost seemed to like getting other people into trouble, and slipping out himself. He was ten, but very large for his age, and his fair face had a big mouth almost clear across from ear to ear. His whole name was Statesrights after someone in Granpap's war.

Mrs. Mulkey was very important because the preacher came to her so often, and occasionally the Company doctor, who owned a drug store in the village. She was a sort of mystery to the Mc-

Clures, for Mr. Mulkey seemed not to welcome company and none of them had ever seen her. They had heard from Alma about her spells. And some days when Bonnie was in the yard she looked at the windows of the house next door fearfully, thinking she had heard a call from the sick woman. She wanted to see, yet dreaded going there, for she knew there were times when Mr. Mulkey had to force his wife back to bed to keep her from walking down the street in her nightgown.

One day Annie, who was a year older than States, came running into the house where Bonnie was getting some dinner ready for the young ones.

"Please come, Bonnie," she begged, "come quick."

Without thinking a second time, Bonnie went right over, running.

"I can't get her back in bed," Annie panted out, over and over. That seemed the important thing, to get her lying down again.

In the front room, where the curtains were drawn to keep out the hot sunlight, Mrs. Mulkey walked up and down. Annie stopped at the door. Bonnie went inside. Her heart was beating as if it was getting ready to jump from her mouth right on the floor at Mrs. Mulkey's feet. Mrs. Mulkey was tall as Ora. She had a long white face with big dark eyes, and her fair hair hung in strings around her face. The long nightgown she wore was not long enough to cover her bare feet. They were long, like her face, and stuck out queerly from under the gown.

She saw Bonnie staring and stopped short in her walking.

"People say I look like a ghost," she said, and laughed a tinkling sort of laughter. "I reckon I do look like a ghost."

She began to walk again from wall to wall. Bonnie went up close to her. "Will ye come to bed?" she asked.

"I was naked, and ye clothed me," Mrs. Mulkey said, talking very sensibly to Bonnie, as she would talk to a friend. "I was hungered and ye fed me. I was thirsty and ye gave me to drink."

Bonnie was trembling. She wanted to run from the room. Yet she knew something must be done at once. All the young ones, the Mulkeys and Ora's, were at the door watching, crowding against each other to see. Bonnie slipped her shaking hand into Mrs. Mulkey's.

"Hadn't ye better go to bed?" she asked, and pulled Mrs. Mulkey toward the bed.

"The Lord is my shepherd, I shall not want," Mrs. Mulkey said. She pulled away from Bonnie, trying to get her hand loose. She kept walking back and forth and Bonnie had to follow. The little girl twisted her fingers around the woman's. She could feel the dry bony hand. It felt as if there was no flesh there, only bones for her to hold.

"The Lord is my shepherd," Mrs. Mulkey said again, and tried again to pull her hand away.

"The Lord wants ye in bed," Bonnie told her. For the first time Mrs. Mulkey stopped trying to get away.

"Do you think He does?" she asked earnestly.

"Yes'm," Bonnie told her. "I know He does."

Mrs. Mulkey's hand went limp, and she allowed Bonnie to lead her back to the bed and get her covered. Almost immediately she went off to sleep. Bonnie watched over her for a few moments, then tiptoed out, shooing the young ones in whispers away from the door.

All those days Bonnie was very busy. She was head of the house during the day, caring for the children. She liked this, yet there were times when she felt ready to run, and on those days she was cross and ill natured with the young ones. As the end of summer came it was better, for she could remember that she would soon be starting school and that thought was enough to make her patient with the others.

Some days she had a big baby on her hands. For Granpap was as much trouble as any when he was at home. He fretted so. And since this fretting was unlike Granpap it made everything about him seem unnatural and wrong.

When no one was looking John made up for Bonnie's worry by helping with the dishwashing and cooking. He even scrubbed the floors when Ora and Emma had no time to do so. Ora and Emma, having to do washing on Saturdays and ironing Monday nights, had little time for scrubbing. It would have been against the feelings of the whole community for them to do scrubbing and ironing on Sunday. Yet in secret they sometimes did this, and probably the other women did this, too, and never told outside.

All through the summer Granpap was worrying Emma to go back to the hills. She reminded him that sometimes in the winter up there they had starved. In the village there was sure money and the store to buy from, near by, and there was the school, which was most important.

The summer went by, and it was almost time for school to begin. Changes had to be made, and many things decided—one of them whether Emma or Ora should go on the night shift. For in order to care for the young ones during the day, one of them must work at night so she could be at home while Bonnie attended school.

A few days before school began Emma came home to find Bonnie crying. She was sick at heart at first, thinking Ora's young, or John, had been hurt.

"What is it, Bonnie," she asked. "Now you tell me."

"Hit's Granpap," Bonnie said.

"What about Granpap?" Emma asked and shook Bonnie again.

"He's gone," Bonnie said.

Granpap had put a piece of bread in his pocket, taken his fiddle from the trunk and left for the hills.

31

"WHERE's John?" Emma asked. She thought at once that John had gone with Granpap.

"Out back somewheres," Bonnie told her. "He was a-crying, too," she said. "I know it. But he ran away."

Emma went through the house where Ora was already getting supper. John was not in the bedroom, and the yard at the back was empty. Perhaps John had run after Granpap and by now was part way up the mountain. She called him, and when not a sound came for an answer she called again. With a flat bang the door of the outhouse swung back and hung on its one hinge. John stepped out and came toward her. He did look as if he had been crying.

"Why did Granpap go?" Emma asked him.

"He said he wanted the hills, and wanted work."

Granpap had said more than that. He had said, among other things. "Hit ain't right, Son, for a man to be asking money from a woman. And this place, hit takes everything out of ye. Down here I'm like a gun shell with the shot taken out, good for nothing but a little noise and some foolish smoke."

"Did he say he was coming back?" Emma asked John.

"He didn't say," John told her.

Ora came out. She had just learned from Bonnie what the trouble was. They stood together talking and John walked around them aimlessly, in a large circle, zigzagging in and out around the two women, like a crazy boy. He was actually befuddled. Part of him wanted to follow Granpap into the mountains, and part wanted to stay and get schooling, and learn the new things that he had not yet learned.

Ora said, "Granpap can take care of himself, Emma. And maybe he's better off in the hills. Right now you'd best come in and eat, and not worry. Frank's in there and he'll say the same. Granpap will care for himself, and not come to harm."

Emma knew these were sensible things, and she knew the truth of what Ora said. The trouble was that she had come to rely on Granpap's presence, as if he was a husband. And except for lying together, she and Granpap had been husband and wife to each other. They had quarreled and got over it. Granpap had scolded her and the young ones, and she had scolded back. And they had rejoiced together. It was more than anxiety that held her to Granpap. They had been through too much together for her to lose him without a heartache.

But he had gone for good. She had to make up her mind to that. They watched for him the second day and the third, and another; but on Sunday evening Emma had to say, "I reckon he's gone for good," and turn her mind to other things that needed her attention.

That Sunday evening Bonnie got everything ready for school. Not that there was much to do, but she pretended that she must be busy getting ready. She had already washed her one dress and Esther's. The dresses hung up clean and ironed on the wall in Emma's room. Bonnie wore Emma's shawl and Esther had an old dress of Sally's, torn and too big, but good enough to wear at home.

John was already wearing his clean shirt and jeans. He was not like the girls wanting to keep his clothes fresh for morning. The important thing to him was school. Ever since the visit to the city he had thought about Basil and what Basil wanted. Basil had gone somewhere and learned books; and people who knew books somehow had a chance to get the kind of things the rich woman in the city had. There was Emma who needed new clothes and some time to rest, and Bonnie who wanted an extra dress sometimes. Schooling, to John, meant living better. He wanted to meet Basil and talk to him about such things. For years when he thought of his brothers Kirk had come first. Now he felt rather scornful of Kirk who had thrown away everything he had, and lost his life for a woman.

Everyone went to bed earlier than usual that night, for there were many extra things to be accomplished in the morning. Bonnie went to Emma's room first. She wanted to be first to bed, and the first up. But someone was there before her. Young Frank was now sleeping in Granpap's place with John. Much as absent ones were regretted, in such a crowded household there was always someone to use the space they had left.

Bonnie heard Young Frank sobbing over in the bed. When she heard that she did not turn on the light. As far back as she could remember she had never heard Young Frank cry, or laugh either, for that matter. He was always quiet and shy.

"Young Frank," she said, and then didn't know what else to speak. She thought he would not answer, but unexpectedly he raised his head and spoke in a loud whisper. She felt that he was not talking to her but to everybody. He talked as if he hated the world and everyone in it.

"They won't let me go to school," he said. "Won't they? Well then! I'll haul spools and I'll work every day like they make me. I'll haul spools and let the old mill shake. But hit can't shake the devil out of me. You watch. I'm a-going to the devil as fast as I can. They can't stop me."

"I'll teach ye, Young Frank," Bonnie said, standing back, almost afraid of him for the first time in her life. He had been so quiet she had never thought of him as having any special wishes. "I'll teach ye at night."

"Teach me! I'll teach you," Young Frank said. He put his head under the bed clothes and would not answer again.

The alarm clock in Ora's room was set for four-thirty in the morning. Emma lay in bed with everybody asleep and pondered on her life that was to come. She wondered about the night work. She would have taken the day work, if Ora had not been big with child. It was the least Emma could do to take the burden of the heavy night work, with only snatches of sleep in the day, for Ora during this time. When the baby was born, then Ora would stay home, and when she got well enough would take the night shift, and leave Emma free to work in the day. Even if she had to work day and night, the young ones were to get their schooling. And that was enough satisfaction. And these two younger ones, Bonnie and John, would never leave her completely as Basil had done.

Emma drifted off to sleep, then woke with a start, hearing someone moving about in the house. The light was on in the kitchen. She got up and went in there. Bonnie was standing by the stove completely dressed in her clean calico, making a fire.

"Did Ora wake ye?" Emma asked.

"No," Bonnie told her. "But I'm sure hit's time t' get up. I think we'd better wake Ora."

"Ora always wakes by the clock," Emma said. "Hit's too early, Bonnie."

"I might be late a-getting to school," Bonnie said. "I know hit's time t' get up."

Bonnie was so stubborn the only thing to do was wake Ora. When the light in her room was turned on the clock said one. Bonnie would not believe, and held it to her ear. Then she had to say reluctantly that it was going. Frank grunted from the bed, hating to be disturbed by the light, and the youngest, lying at the foot with little Raymond, moved and let out a wail of protest. By this time there were stirrings all over the house, in all of the beds.

Emma cut the damper so the fire would go out, and made Bonnie undress. It was very humiliating to Bonnie, and depressing; for everyone was cross with her for rousing them three hours before time. She got back into bed expecting to keep awake, and when Ora came in to call them she thought it was still one o'clock or near that time. But Ora insisted that it was four-thirty and after.

Then there was enough hurry to satisfy Bonnie. Frank, Ora and Young Frank started out first. Young Frank was gloomy. Just before they left Bonnie remembered what had happened the night before. She went up to Young Frank and said low, so the others wouldn't hear and make him feel embarrassed, "I'll bring home my books and teach ye." Evidently he didn't think much of her offer, for he said not a word in answer, and went off behind Ora and Frank, quiet and sullen.

Emma wanted to give John and Bonnie advice about school, but she knew so little about it herself. How could she tell them what to do, or what not to do? They must learn for themselves. Only she saw that their faces were clean and that John had not got his jeans too dirty again.

"When cold weather comes ye'll both have t' have stockings and shoes, and maybe new clothes, if we can manage," she told Bonnie. She knew that they would need coats, and had already planned to cut her own down to fit Bonnie. She could wear her shawl to work around her head and over her shoulders.

Ora's young would need more clothes. Esther and Samson were starting in like John and Bonnie. Though they were younger all would be in the same grade at school. John had shot up during the summer. He was very tall for his age, and skinny; not as strong as he would be later on. His tallness was emphasized as he walked off with the other three.

"He looks like a pine tree," Emma thought, "in the middle of some scrub oaks."

John's tallness singled him out in the line at school. In the morning when the bell rang all the classes lined up in the school yard, two by two to march into their rooms. Many of the young ones in the first grade were no more than six or seven. There were some older ones, but John was the tallest, and even the first morning the boys in the higher grades called out to him before the teachers came to march in the lines.

Most of these larger boys and girls lived on Strutt Street. This was the short paved street that went by the mill. On this street in the best houses with plastered walls inside, bathrooms, gas to cook with, pianos and fine furniture, lived the superintendent, the overseers and other higher-ups. The other people in the village, those who lived on the muddy streets in the small houses, had named the paved part Strutt Street. The children at school who came from this street were dressed nicely. Even in warm weather they wore shoes and stockings. Their mothers had silk dresses, and sent their washing to the laundry.

The first three grades in school were always full. Most of the children after the third grade, or the fifth at most, went into the mills to do their part in keeping the family. The village was called a "good" one, which meant that not many moved on as they did in other villages. Yet even in this one the lower grades were always changing, and sometimes the teachers had to make up new rolls to call on Monday morning. Bonnie found it a very interesting thing to watch for new faces and look for those who had gone away. From the first she was delighted with school. She couldn't have enough of it, and even in the afternoons she lined up the young ones of Ora's family and the two Mulkey girls and played teacher. She went over her own lessons and learned them better by repetition.

Beyond the third grade the classes thinned out until there were only a few pupils in the upper grades. These upper grades had one teacher for all. The pupils were made up mostly of children from Strutt Street. Naturally the boys of these families, who were expecting to go to high school, were more confident than the others. One of them, Albert Burnett, had called out to John that first morning. John was learning in the schoolroom. But there were things he had to learn outside that Bonnie was spared.

The first grade had recess by itself, or John would have had a worse time during that period, and perhaps, it would have been a good thing, so that the nagging of the bigger boys would have come to some kind of conclusion sooner. As it was the nagging went on from day to day. The boys hid behind fences and trees when school was over and called out at him. In the morning when the line was formed they satisfied themselves with such names as "Baby," and mimicked a baby crying. But after school they thought up other and more hateful words. "Baby," they called, "you're losing your diaper," or: "Doctor, is it a boy or a girl."

They said that the first day when he was walking back with Bonnie and Ora's young as Emma had made him promise to do. Bonnie cried when she heard the boys. John saw she was going to speak out at them. "Shet up," he said to her. And after that he came and went by himself. This didn't help. The boys resented John's silence. They wanted to make him cry, or else force him to fight, so there would be a good sound licking.

At last it came to the place where John wanted to stop school. It was not that he was afraid. He was ashamed in the class room of being so big among the others, and of knowing so little. He thought of going to the hills, running away and meeting Granpap. There he would be free and at home. There he could fight on his own ground. He was confused. In the hills families stuck together, but it was man against man. He could not quite make out how to manage with several against him, for the boys who nagged were always together.

And Emma was expecting so much. She had put responsibility on him again. He had to see how hard she worked, and that she stinted to give him and Bonnie what they needed. He would have liked not to see. She had done without herself to buy a coat from the Jew, Sam Reskowitz, who kept a second hand clothing store in the town. His coat was thinned out here and there from use, the wind could come through the worn part; but on quiet sunny days the coat kept him warm and comfortable.

He wished to be a man so that he could get away sometimes as Frank did at night. Frank gave as his reason for going into town that he wanted to get news of Granpap. It was a reasonable and true excuse. But he liked going to the Blind Tiger, the restaurant where the McEacherns took their liquor. There he could have a few drinks and talk with other men, or rather listen, for he talked little himself. One night he found out that Granpap was back at his old job of bringing the liquor down. This was no news to give Emma, so he kept it to himself, only saying that someone had seen Granpap in the hills, and the old man was looking well.

Emma listened to Frank. She was glad to hear of Granpap. Yet during these days she was rather worn out, too tired to think much about his absence. The night shift was a twelve hour shift, from six to six. She took a lunch, and as there was no lunch hour she ate the bread while walking up and down before the frames, watching the spools and bobbins.

The night section boss was not a kind man. Perhaps the night work made him more irritable, yet he wanted the privilege of being as mean as possible, while expecting those working under him to be quiet and even-tempered. He sat near the toilets and frowned when anyone went inside. And he was shameless, for if he thought they were staying too long he called out to them to hurry up in there. He sold a drink that was five cents a bottle and must have made money from the sales, for the drink kept them awake as nothing else could, and many spent all the nickels they could spare or couldn't spare on it.

Emma had heard people say, the last hour of work was the worst on the night shift. She had heard the words, and only learned their meaning when she was there. The eleven hours before were hard but they went by. When the little bit of light showed up in the windows, meaning that daylight was preparing to come, it seemed to make her stiff muscles let down, as if they were lying down like a spoiled baby that won't be picked up until it gets what it wants. Her muscles wanted rest, and they lay down, refusing to work for her. In that last hour or two she had to go on from minute to minute. Her mind had to whip her muscles to make them keep up, as a person would whip a bad child, and the muscles ached under the punishment. Sometimes the person who worked her frames during the day came early, and Emma got off fifteen minutes sooner than she had expected. When that happened she told Ora it seemed the heavens were opened and angels sang around her.

There was not much satisfaction at home. She could not see the young ones as often as she liked. At first she had tried to stay awake in the mornings to talk with Bonnie and John. This meant the loss of two good hours of sleep. Now, on coming home she went to the bed, still warm from Bonnie's sleeping there with Ora's Esther, and fell into it until Bonnie woke her. During the day she must keep herself awake to look after Ora's youngest. When Bonnie got home about two she could sleep again. Then at five she must have supper, get her lunch, and start out for the long night.

Sometimes Emma and Ora talked of going back to the hills. At these times they always remembered the terrible winters, sometimes without food; and the loneliness of living off in a little cabin. They always came back to thinking it was best to stay where they were.

32

THE insults from the big boys rankled in John. If possible he would have liked to take Granpap's gun after the whole lot. Why they kept at him, he did not know. Sometimes they did let up but were at it again, as bad as ever in a few days.

One day he was kept in by the teacher to learn spelling. He was hungry and on the way home hurried along the old road that was a short cut to the edge of the village. He saw the boys behind him and hurried along expecting them to call out. When he understood that they were trying to overtake him he turned. Now he was going to meet them. His fists were bony and small, and the muscles in his arms had not grown as big as they should. But he could not bring himself to run away. Big Albert was in front. In one way or another Albert had made the other boys in the school respect him. If they didn't respect him as son of the Superintendent, then there were ways to make them fear him. He did not enjoy hurting just for the sake of hurting. In that sense he was not a bully. Just as soon as a boy acknowledged his superiority he was very kind and just.

On this day there were five other boys behind him. They came up to John at the grove of trees that grew in a dip between the road and a field on the other side. Albert took John under the armpits, holding his arms above his head, and the other boys caught his legs up from the ground. The bushes on the slope whipped against John and the briars made long scratches on his face. The blood trickled down and was like sweat in his mouth. He kicked out and saw with pleasure that the boys had to let go. He had plenty of strength in his legs. The boys helped Albert with his head and arms, and let his feet drag.

Behind some bushes at the foot of the slope they laid him flat on the ground, face downward. Boys sat on his legs and two on his body above the waist. Then, carefully, they stripped his jeans, so that he was naked from the waist down. He turned his head in the dirt, and saw a bottle in Albert's hand. Some of it spilled as

Albert took out the stopper, and he smelled turpentine. He understood, vaguely, what they had planned to do. He tried to fight again, but the five boys had him flat to the ground. They giggled like girls, high, excited giggles, while Albert leaned over his back.

The burning there was like nothing John had ever felt before. The boys stood up and watched him. He thrashed out with his legs, and fought with his arms, not at the boys, but because the pain was so intense. His eyes were glazed and at first he could not see, but he could hear acutely, and he heard some of them laughing. When their faces became clear, he saw Albert standing at his feet looking down solemnly. The pain gave him strength. He sprang right from the ground on Albert. They came down together. He had expected a fight, but Albert lay still, with blood running from his head.

"Now you've done it," one of the boys said. "You've killed him."

The boy ran up the slope and the others followed. John knew they would bring some of the higher-ups. He must get away. He looked for his jeans and saw them sticking out from under Albert's body. As he pulled them out hurriedly he could see that Albert's eyelids moved as if the eyes were going to open.

On the road he remembered the pain from the scalding and how Granpap had found some clay. If he could find some it might cool the pain. It was like a spur in his back. He did not stop running until he was on the road to the mountains. It was only then, when he stopped at a stream that ran over the road, that he remembered he had passed the house where Emma was, and Bonnie and the others. It did not matter that he remembered. He was going on to the hills.

He slept on the side of the narrow road to the mountains two nights. The burn had cooled down, but he was very weak from hunger. On the morning of the third day when he was sitting down to rest as he had to do every few feet, he thought his eyes were not right when he saw Granpap come around a curve sitting high up in the wagon behind a horse. It was just after daybreak and Granpap would have missed him altogether if he had not stood up in the way.

The old man got down from the wagon. John looked as if he was about to fall over. He was pale and haggard. Granpap reached down in his jeans and brought out his bottle. The drink went to the boy's empty stomach and then to his head, so that Granpap had a very drunk boy on his hands, and had to lift him into the wagon seat. All the way down the mountain he held the boy, and wondered what had brought him up there looking like a scarecrow.

When they reached the restaurant, Granpap took John into the kitchen, and left him for a few minutes with Jake, the black cook. Jake was very kind and gave him some hominy and a cup of coffee. Almost immediately John had to go outside and give it all back, as a present to the ground.

That was the way Jake put it. He said John was very kind and generous making a present to the ground. When Granpap came in John tried eating again and this time the hominy stayed down. Granpap was fidgety. He wanted to get back up the mountain. First, he must hear what had brought the boy up to find him. When John told he understood at once. It was bad, of course, that the mill superintendent was also superintendent of schools, but there might be ways to fix that.

"Hit don't do to run away," Granpap said. Then he noticed that John looked at him, and then looked away, as if he felt something was wrong.

"Hit's best for ye t' stay here," he repeated. "Ye've got something t' do. I didn't have work, and I had to go where I could find hit. Maybe I'll make something, so we can buy a little place somewheres. You've got school, and after that the mill to work in, or maybe something better."

"Do you think the boy was bad hurt?" he asked.

"His eyelids were fluttering."

"Was the blood still flowing?"

"I think so."

"Then he wasn't dead." Granpap thought a little. "Basil's working in the town," he said, as if he regretted telling this. "He's living with Preacher Warren, who's got the church in there. I talked to Basil one morning. He works in the cotton warehouse by the station. I don't know what Basil would do for his folks. This much I know. All the high-ups go to Preacher Warren's church. So the superintendent must go there. You go to the station and see Basil and get him t' ask Preacher Warren to speak to the superintendent."

Then he added, "I'll see Basil myself and ask him this morning if I can. Now ye go right back to Emma. She's probably plumb crazy by now a-worrying over ye."

John had to go back.

During those three days Emma had very little sleep. The first night none of them knew why the boy did not come home. Emma had to go to work, but Frank went up and down the road for miles and called out. He càme in about ten and went out again. There was no sign.

The second day Bonnie came from school with the whole story. John had fought with the superintendent's son and had nearly killed him. Not exactly that, for Albert was back at school that day with his head bandaged. But the teacher sent word to Emma that John must apologize to Albert, or take a whipping if he wanted to come back.

That morning when John walked into the kitchen, Emma stood by the stove and looked at him. She could not move. He was so pale she wanted to cry.

"Why, John," she said, and they were not the words she wanted to say, "look how you've torn your clothes." John did not look at her. "My belly's plumb empty," he said and sat down on a chair, because he was weak.

She gave him food, and after eating he went off to sleep on the chair. She got him into bed, first stripping off his jeans to see if he was hurt anywhere. In between looking after Ora's young she went in to look at him. Now he was growing up he looked like Kirk. She went to the front room and got Kirk's picture from the Bible and compared them. But the picture was not as like Kirk as John was, lying in the bed with the hair back from his forehead.

Emma could not persuade John that he must go back. He would neither apologize to Albert nor take a whipping. She couldn't get it out of her mind that he was keeping something back. He left it that Albert had fought him and he had fought back. And he seemed to feel himself in the right. But she wanted him to have the schooling.

"We've got to do what the higher-ups say," she told him. "Down here hit's what they say that counts."

It didn't matter to John. He would not go back.

Whether Granpap saw Basil and arranged matters, no one knew. On the day after John returned Bonnie came back with word from the teacher. There was a note that Emma was to send back which said that Emma had punished John to teach him not to fight. Bonnie signed Emma's name at the bottom as she did on the reports, and Emma made her cross on the paper. The next day John carried the note to the teacher. Emma had not punished her son. She felt that telling a lie was against the teaching of a church. But she would not give her boy a hiding for something he had a right to do. If the higher-ups demanded a lie she was willing to give them what they wanted, if it meant that John could go back.

To his surprise John found little trouble at school. Everyone knew by this time that he had got his man and gone up into the hills to hide like an outlaw. Because the boys had not dared to tell what they had done to him, John had the best of it. Soon most people forgot. But there was a feeling left with those who kept on living in the village that John McClure was a wild boy and one not easily frightened or fought down.

33

THE mill sat over them like an old hen and clucked to her chickens every day. In the morning she said, "Get up, get up." In the day she said, "Eat, eat," and at night, "Go home, go home." But to Emma, working all night, the mill said other things.

There was a story the teacher told the young ones at school, and Bonnie, playing teacher, told it over to the children at home. "And the ogre said, 'I'll grind your bones to make my bread,' " At first the throb of the mill had been like the throb of a big heart beating for the good of those who worked under the roof, for it gave hope of desires to be fulfilled. A woman, one of the weavers, said to Ora and Emma one lunch hour during the summer, "The weave room has a sound different from the other rooms. It's like the sound of sinners' teeth grinding in hell."

Now to Emma the throb of a heart had changed. She was feeling the grind of teeth. The mill crunched up and down—"I'll grind your bones to make my bread."

Walking before the frames in the night in her stocking feet with her head tied up to keep the lint out, Emma thought about the mill and considered where her work there was taking her. She thought of all she had promised herself. Now Granpap was up in the hills, and Basil was in the town, maybe, because he had become educated, getting the things that she had planned to get for all of them. At first when she talked to John she had thought more of him because he had been lost for three days, and less of what he said of Granpap and Basil. Now it came to her that Basil had been living in town for some time and had not come for a visit to his folks. Granpap had gone back to the hills, but sent word that he would come again, and he remembered her with two dollars.

The money was at home, and in the night Emma planned the different ways in which she might spend it. Of course it should have been spent for necessary things, but she decided to make this something for herself. It made the walking easier, when she planned what to buy. In this way she could escape from her sore feet and the night tiredness.

That Saturday afternoon she spoke to Ora, when Ora had come from work and they were settled around the fire with the pleasant settling that comes from the knowledge of a day and a half of no mill ahead. "Ora, I'd like to go to the town for once. I'd like to buy a hat for church. Will ye come?"

"Go to town like this?" Ora asked. She pointed to her big belly. The youngest child, who had been weaned in preparation for the next one, stood by her knees trying to reach up to her. "Stop that," she said to him. "Hit ain't for you, any more." She dragged him on her lap where he had to sit perched on the end of her knees, so that he might not interfere with the one inside.

"I'm s' tired, Emma."

"Hit'll do ye good, Ora." Emma's eyes had a shine to them. She had never been to town except the time she went to get the coat at Reckowitz's store, and that was on a side street, almost an alley.

"The washing's got to be done."

"For once hit'll have to go. And Bonnie here can care for the young ones."

"I'd like to go," Bonnie said.

She tried to frown and look grieved, but she was so healthy it was hard for her to look sad. School agreed with her. And this was the time when the "first flush of womanhood was creeping into her cheeks." That is what the preacher called it. He said, "It is when the first flush of womanhood is creeping into the cheeks of your daughters that they need a mother's care most."

"Take her instead of me," Ora told Emma.

"No, Ora. Hit'll do ye good. Don't ye want Ora to get a little airing, Bonnie?"

"Yes, but sometimes I want to go to town."

"Well, you'll go one day. I'll take ye."

Ora always looked queer when she was with child. She was so lean and tall the baby stood right out from her. It was not for that reason, though, that Ora and Emma walked down side streets going to the business part of the town. No mill people, even the young ones with beaus, liked to walk on the streets where the fine houses stood, though that was the quickest way. There was a feeling that the rich didn't want the sight of poor on their streets. Mill hands' clothes didn't go well with the fine houses, and the pleasures of wealth.

"Let's go behind Mr. Wentworth's place," Emma said. "Hit's quicker to town and I'd like t' see hit if only from the back."

Perhaps it was meanness and envy, but most people in the village made fun of those who lived on Strutt Street. Some of the men had got their places by hard work, but all of them licked the boots of the bosses, the managers and superintendent. For there were plenty of hard workers who hadn't risen. The higher-ups had to short the regular hands in weighing and making out the pay checks in order to make as much money for the mill as possible. It was a known fact that the high-ups had to do this as part of their job. But the best ones hated to do this against a neighbor, so it kept them from rising. In the case of the overseer, it was whispered his wife had lived with Burnett once, with him making no murmur against it. This was gossip, and perhaps not true.

Though there was the attitude toward the high-ups on Strutt Street, there was no such feeling toward the really big ones, those who lived in the town. There was interest, and if the man who owned the mill, who lived in Washington, came down, there was excitement. Everybody said he was as common as mill people and spoke to all as if he was on their level. His son, who lived in the town, was the same. This was the young Wentworth whose house Emma wanted to see from the back.

Emma and Ora went down a street and up another side one and came out right behind the son's house. With the lawn it covered a whole block. There were no leaves on the trees, so they could see the large white house, very clearly, with the big central part and a wing on each side. The lawn, blue-green with winter grass, came down to the edge of the sidewalk where it was protected by a stone fence about two feet high.

They stood and looked.

"I reckon one of those rooms is as big as our whole place," Ora said.

"The back yard is clean as if hit was the front."

"Hit must have a hundred rooms . . . and I'd be willing to say . . ."

"Look, Ora!"

The back door opened. A black man in a white coat and dark trousers came onto the porch pushing a baby carriage. He let it down the steps into the yard. Behind him came a black girl, and in her arms was a white baby wrapped up in a warm looking pink blanket.

"Hit's that baby."

"Maybe we'd better go along, Ora."

"I helped give hit that present. I've got a right to look."

"I gave ten cents, and had to tell Bonnie to wait for a tablet till the next week."

"Frank gave a quarter for both of us."

"Wasn't hit pretty, Ora? Gold and silver with a silver spoon."

"Maybe they've got the goblet now in the carriage."

"Let's look if she comes closer."

"Hit must be four months old now."

"Look, he's put the carriage under that tree in the spot of sunshine."

"Did you ever see anything like hit? Hit's like a baby hearse."

"We'd better go, Ora. They're a-looking at us."

"Wait, Emma. She's going to put him in. I can see his feet, in little shoes."

"They're a-looking at us."

"Look at the blankets she's laying on him. They're little, like they was made for a baby."

"We'd better go, Ora."

Someone called the black man from the back window. He went below the window and looked up.

"I've got a right here, Emma. I helped give hit a present."

The black man came toward the street, as if he wanted to speak with them.

"I'm a-going, Ora, and you can stay." Emma started walking away down the sidewalk, and Ora had to follow.

"I don't think he meant anything, Emma," Ora complained. "I wanted t' see more. Maybe the black girl would have let us go close."

Emma walked on.

"They say that baby owns stock in the mill," Ora said, trying to keep up. Emma slackened in her walk now she was some distance from the house.

"I haven't yet exactly known what stock is."

"I don't know myself. But hit seems to mean that ye get money out of the mill."

"We get money out of the mill."

"Well, I think hit means ye get money without working. Like that baby, now. He's got stock and he sure is too little t' work any."

"Maybe. Granpap said Mister Hellman that spoke at the re-union owned stock in the mill, and hit's right I don't see him around working any."

They turned up another street that led toward the square.

"Ye know," Emma said, laughing at herself, "at first I thought stock was us. You know how Hal Swain used t' say he owned twenty head of stock or thirty. I thought hit meant we was the stock and they owned us."

"That was right foolish."

"I know. Hit made me mad, thinking of being owned, till Granpap set me right, because Hal Swain had told him about the Congressman, the same that got him out of jail, owning stock in this mill and others. I know hit's something on paper that brings in money, but still I don't understand."

Now they were just off the big square where the large stores were. Emma stopped before a store window. The window was full of photographs of people. Bride and groom stood together in some of the pictures and smiled happily if a little foolishly at the world. Girls looked over their shoulders coquettishly. In the center of the window was a crayon portrait in a large frame with glass over it.

"Hit would be fine to have something like that on the wall," Emma said.

"Hit must cost a lot of money."

"I'd like to have a big one like that of Kirk."

"Hit's a fine sight. I wonder that anybody can make a likeness like that with a pencil on paper."

"Johnny made a likeness of some apples. The teacher put hit on the wall, it was so good."

"Johnny can make a likeness, I know. He's smart, Emma."

"I'd like t' go in and ask how much to make one like that," Emma said. She turned away. "I reckon hit's more than I could give."

At the corner she stopped very still. "Ora, I'm a-going back and ask the man. I'd like so much t' have Kirk on the wall in a picture."

"You need a hat, Emma, and other things. Seeing the rich must have made you forget you're pore."

Emma did not answer. She was excited now and resentful of interference. Ora followed her back reluctantly. She knew how much Emma needed a covering for her head, and a coat and many other things. Emma might quarrel at Granpap for spending money recklessly; at times she was just the same.

Emma came out of the shop. "Hit's a dollar and a half. I'll send John with the picture on Monday after school."

"Did you give him the money?"

"He took hit. There'll be a frame and a glass, all for a dollar and a half down and fifty cents a week."

"And how much altogether?"

"Hit's none of your mind, Ora. . . . Now, Ora, don't quarrel at me. Hit's so nice t' get something like that ye want, and don't just need."

Ora didn't like it. Emma was getting foolish because the burden of providing food was taken off her. She was a boarder, and some weeks didn't pay, for she hadn't the money. Now she was already in debt to Ora and Frank.

"Hit seems ye don't mind being in debt," Ora said.

"Well, ye don't mind me working nights t' save ye. Working nights makes me want something t' pay for hit."

Emma walked on without speaking another word. People came between them and Emma was glad. She wanted, just then, to be separated from Ora. But Ora caught up and put a hand on Emma's arm.

"Now, Emma, I didn't mean anything. I'm a-getting nervous, I reckon, because my time is coming soon."

She looked down at Emma and saw her face break up almost as if she was going to cry. They walked on close together.

"Hit's funny about that baby . . ." Ora began to talk, but couldn't finish. They were on the square and people were crowding the streets as they did on Saturday afternoons. Long, lean farmers in boots were in town and their women with them; and there were mill people, looking much like the farmers, except the men had no high boots, and the well dressed folks of the town, all were coming and going, passing each other. There were some black people mixed in. Some of these stood together off the sidewalk, talking. The court house was on the side of the square opposite them. It took up one whole side along with the jail, and was set on a lawn like the houses of the rich.

Emma asked Ora humbly, "Do ye think I can get a hat for fifty cents?"

"I should think so," Ora said, "if we look far enough. But I'm plumb tired." She wished to point out to Emma that there were more reasons than one for her quick anger of a few minutes before.

"There's a drug store, Ora. Mrs. Mulkey's sister says when she comes to town with a beau they sit in a drug store and rest and eat ice cream."

"Hit ain't for us, Emma."

"Yes, it is. Ye can rest there. They sit at a table. Hit's just a nickel apiece, and even if it's more, I've got the change."

Ora held back. "Let's go in, Ora," Emma said, and went right through the door. They reached an empty table far back behind the crowded ones. Ora dropped into a chair. Emma stood for a moment, wanting to see if anyone came to tell them not to stay; for the people had looked at them curiously as if they did not belong. No one came and Emma sat down to rest her feet. They waited a long time, and both were strained, waiting. They could not talk at ease.

A boy in a white jacket went to other tables, bringing ice cream and drinks in high glasses. Emma wanted to call him or go up to him but she did not dare before the other people. She wanted to talk so she might keep Ora from noticing, but there was nothing to say.

People got up from tables and others took their places.

"Emma, I'm rested, now. Let's go."

"Well, I reckon we might as well," Emma said. Her voice was high and cracked. They got up and walked through the people, passing sideways between the tables. Emma heard a woman say, "They're mill hands"; and she saw that others stared at Ora's big belly.

"I reckon he just didn't see us," she said to Ora out on the street.

"Maybe. He seemed right busy."

"Anyway," Emma laughed with her words, "you got your rest."

"Yes, I did. And it helped."

"Now we've got to find a hat store."

They peered in windows trying to find out whether the hats were expensive or cheap. Only Emma would turn away sometimes to peer at the people who passed by.

"I wonder if Basil works on Saturday afternoon," she said.

"I wonder if he does."

"I thought young folks like him would like coming to town on Saturdays if they didn't work."

"Likely they do."

Down a side street, a small store had many hats in the windows. The people inside were not finely dressed. They walked through the door.

There was a black hat with a feather.

"Ask her how much," Emma said. Ora was willing but she had to wait until one of the two girls was finished waiting on someone else.

"How much is that one?" Ora pointed to the black hat. It was fifty cents marked down from one dollar.

Emma stood forward. "If I do without the feather," she asked, "would it be less?"

"Forty cents then," the girl told her.

"Take off the feather," Emma said.

"You ought t' have the feather," Ora whispered. Emma stood without saying anything. The feather was green and curled at the end and she wanted it, but her mind was made up. Outside she told Ora. "It leaves me ten cents for church; five for me and the pennies for the young ones. I'll feel better putting in some money for church when I'm wearing a new hat."

The girl gave a black headed pin with the hat, and Emma wore the hat out, with the pin through her knot. Even with the pin it was hard to keep the heavy felt sitting in the right place on her head, where the girl had placed it.

"You'll learn to keep hit on," Ora told her. "And it looks good on ye, Emma."

"Hit'll last," Emma said. "And hit's warmer now, since I'm able to keep the shawl clean down over my shoulders."

She did not care any more for the hat. Even giving up the

feather was not much, for now she could look forward to the end of next week when the picture of Kirk would hang on the wall.

"Hit's funny," Ora said, "how some have such fine, pretty things and others not."

"Yes."

"I never thought much about it before."

"I know, but . . ."

"But I did think to-day or felt hit. You remember when we were seeing that baby . . . you know . . ."

"Yes, hit was the prettiest baby."

"I thought hit was pretty, too. And I felt like it was right for hit t' have everything hit had. . . ."

"Yes, it must be right."

"Yet going up the street, right after we left hit, I started feeling s' mad. Mad at everything and at nothing, because my babies couldn't have a thing. I was s' mad. Hit was why I spit out at ye, that and being tired. I know now."

"There's no use getting mad, Ora. Hit's the way the Lord made things to be."

"I know it. I was just mad without any reason. I just wanted ye t' know, Emma, I didn't mean hit for you."

"I know," Emma said. "I get that way sometimes. Mad at something, I don't know what. Then I have to remember whatever happens is the Lord's will."

"There's got to be pore as well as rich to make up the world."

"And the preacher reads to us, 'Thou shalt not covet.' . . . Hit seems funny, now though, how I thought of money growing on trees and a land of milk and honey."

"Did you really think that?"

"Yes, I did, Ora. I half believed it anyways. And I think now our young ones will grow up to better things. And that's something."

"Yes. That's worth any amount of trouble and sorrow."

They walked past the mill, past the houses where lights were coming on, down to the end of the village. Ora looked up at their chimney. Smoke came out of it with a little flourish in the wind before it blew sideways and joined in with smoke from other chimneys.

"I'm glad Bonnie's got a good fire going," Ora said. "Hit'll be nice to rest by the fire. I'm s' cold by this time."

34

ON Monday afternoon Emma took Kirk's picture from its black cloth wrapping, did it up in a brown paper bag from the store, and gave it to John.

"Hit's the little street off the north corner of the square," she told him, "And you take Bonnie along. She wants to go to town."

"No," John said. "I can't take her."

"Why?" Bonnie asked for herself.

"Because of rails, snails, and puppy dog tails."

"Did you learn that at school?" Emma asked with sarcasm.

"When I have beaus I'll go with them and you can't come along," Bonnie said. "I'm older than you."

"Make Young Frank take ye. He's your beau already."

That remark quieted Bonnie so John got out of the house without any more talking.

Young Frank was following Bonnie around, and people in the house noticed this and teased her. But there was something they did not know about him. Sometimes he found her in a room by herself, and backing her into a corner, would try to touch her leg under her dress. And even in the dark when she was undressing for bed in the room she felt his eyes staring at her trying to make her out. She was sorry they must sleep in the same room. Neither John nor Young Frank would move the bed into the other room where Ora's five young ones slept; for these had a way of getting out of their own bed into the bed with any others who slept near by. Perhaps Young Frank's behavior toward her was what he meant when he said, "I'm going to the devil." Whatever it was he made the whole place uncomfortable for her.

John's coat came down almost to his heels. The cold came in through the worn parts like a ghostly hand feeling its way across his shoulders. On his head was a white cap that was given away at the store.

People in the village said, "They don't want us on their fine streets in town." But John walked right through the street of fine houses. He had a brother who lived in the town, and so had a right to be there. Also that street was the shortest way of getting to the square, and he had no time to lose.

He did not intend to stop even to look at the houses. But at one place a house with turrets at each end had, on the wide front lawn, two dogs, one on each side. They sat in dignified silence with heads erect. It was necessary to find out whether they were real. He stood quite still waiting to see if either of them would move. If he threw a pebble and they did not move then he could be sure they were carved out of rock or wood. He stooped down. A stone came whizzing past his ear, and another struck his cap. Luckily the cap was on tight and the stone just grazed his head. He looked back under his arm. Four boys were standing near the steps of the house. One of them called out "white trash" and another stone came. John walked on pretending that he had not seen them. Casually, as if that was the way he had planned to walk, he crossed the street. An automobile passed behind him and a slow wagon cut him off from the boys. From behind a tree on the other side of the street he looked back but could not see them. Further down three boys were standing on a lawn, working over a bicycle. He felt an impulse to stop and have a look at the bicycle, but he must hurry by these boys so they would not notice him. And probably they would not have known that he was passing, if the other four from across the street had not come. They ran by John two on each side and joined the three around the bicycle. There was some whispering and just as John went by they stood together and chanted a verse at him. He heard each word they said.

"Buzzard flying through the air
Caught a mill hand by the hair.
When he'd eat and drunk his fill
He dropped the trash into the mill."

And this was not enough. When he didn't notice they began again. Without knowing he was going to do so, John turned. "I'll show ye," he said. "I'll show ye to call me a stinking carcase."

The boys stood together and jeered at him again. A man came

out of a side entrance of the church. He wore a black suit and a round white collar.

"Boys," he said, in a loud voice. They did not hear him. He went up and took one of the boys by the shoulder.

"Son," he said. "Son, I am ashamed."

The boys were very quiet now. The man looked at John with kind eyes. "Come here," he said. John wanted to go on his way, but the man insisted. "Come here," he repeated, and John walked up to him reluctantly.

"Boys," the man said. "This boy has done you no harm, and you attacked him. You must tell him you are sorry for your behavior."

The boys looked ashamed, perhaps not ashamed for what they had done, but sullen because of the interference. They slipped away one by one, and the man was left holding to the shoulder of his son.

"Henry," he said, "Tell this boy you are sorry."

"I didn't do it," Henry said. "Not by myself."

"Then you will speak for them all. I am ashamed that the boys of my congregation should be so—so—unmanly."

John wanted to slide away as the other boys had done. Now he felt sympathy for the boy whose father was making a fool of him. It was a silly and foolish place to be. There he was, standing on the lawn, facing those other two, while the other boys stood at a distance and watched. He started away.

"One moment," the man said to him. . . . "Will you do what I say, Henry?" John saw his knuckles whiten on the boy's shoulder.

"I'm sorry," the boy Henry mumbled, and as his father's grip lightened he ducked away.

"I'm sorry, too," the man said. "I am Mr. Warmsley, of this church." He pointed to the church with the cross. "Did they hurt you, before I came out?"

"No," John said, and like the other boys he slunk off. The preacher was trying to be kind, but it was uncomfortable. He wanted to get on his way, for there was the thing he had planned to do.

In the picture store, he asked the man, "How do you get to the station?"

The man gave him directions, and he found the station was not so far from the square as he had thought. He climbed up on the wooden platform of the largest warehouse, and walked up and down trying to look as if he belonged.

He saw the sign on the wall and slowly began to spell out the printed words:

COTTON OIL COMPANY—COTTON SEED MEAL AND HULLS
FERTILIZER AND FEEDS

A man came out of one door and hurried into another. John wanted to ask him a question, but it was hard to go right up and speak out. "He can't kill ye," he said to himself. "What are ye afraid of?"

The next time a man came out he stood in the way. "Does Basil McClure work here?" he asked.

"Who is that?"

"Basil McClure."

"No," the man answered. "Maybe he works at the next warehouse." And he hurried away.

It was just beginning to get dark. Lights were turned on in the warehouses and made squares and oblongs of pale yellow on the floors of the platforms. John jumped from the end of one platform to the ground, and climbed up on the next. The door at the further end was open and he hurried there and looked in. Basil was standing at a desk behind a railing, talking to a man who sat at the desk. It was surely Basil, tall and dark, with square jaws a little too wide for the rest of his face.

A heavy wind had come up with evening. John leaned against the wall while he waited, so the wind would not pass through his coat. They must have it warm inside, he thought, for Basil was in his shirt-sleeves.

A man came out of the door. He wore an overcoat and a hat that hid his face in shadow.

"Basil," John said. When the man turned he saw it was not his brother.

"What is it?"

John did not answer.

"Do you want Basil McClure?"

"Yes."

The man turned and leaning around the door called out, "McClure, here's a boy to see you." He stared at John for a moment, then walked on down the platform to the steps. His feet made quick, heavy sounds on the boards.

Someone said to John, "What do you want?" and leaned down to look in his face.

"Is it you, John?"

"Yes."

"Come along," Basil said.

They walked to the steps, down by the station and up a street.

"Did she send you?"

"No. . . . I came."

"She knows I'm here?"

"She knows."

Basil wore a long overcoat, though it did not reach down so far as John's, but he felt they were like two men walking together in the town. Basil unhooked a gate in a back fence. John had not been invited but he felt that Basil expected him to follow—and he wanted to go. His brother led him through the hallway of a house and up the stairs. As they went up someone called, "Basil," but Basil did not answer. Upstairs he opened the door of a room at the back of the house and turned on the light.

As if expecting John to enter, he held the door open and looked at him.

"Take off your cap," he said. Basil had taken off his own hat as he entered the house downstairs. A fire was laid in the grate and Basil touched a match to it. The paper flared up and lit the kindling. It burned low for a moment then the rosin crackled familiarly. Basil stooped lower and laid on a short hickory log.

"How do you like my room?" he asked looking up; the lines at the side of his jaws showing up in the firelight.

"Hit's fine," John said passing his cap from one hand to another behind his back. He looked around the room, seeing all the details. There was a bed and a bureau, with a large mirror. Against the mirror at its base leaned photographs of some girls. Over in one corner there was a bookcase with a few books. A carpet covered the floor, and on it along with the other furniture sat two chairs, a rocker by the fire and a straight chair by the table.

"Sit down," Basil said. He brought up the chair from the table for John. "This is Preacher Warren's house," he told John. "I rent a room here."

"Hit's a fine room," John said again. Basil looked at him quickly. He saw the boy meant his words, that he was really admiring.

A woman called, "Basil"—from downstairs.

"Wait here," Basil said. He went out, leaving the door open, and a warm smell of food cooking came in the door.

When Basil returned he sat down and as he sat pulled his creased trousers up a little way with a careless gesture. It was a careless gesture, yet had its fineness. It seemed to say, "Look at me, I'm a gentleman, with creased trousers and fine manners."

"Does she speak about me?" he asked John.

"Some."

"How is Bonnie?"

"Well. She's in the second reader now." After a moment John added, "I'm in the second reader now."

"That's good," Basil told him. "It's good that you're both getting an education. It's not hard to learn if you put all your strength into it. And it means you'll get somewhere if you have sense."

"I want to get somewhere," John said.

"If you want to get along," Basil told him, "you must remember that you can't think too much about other people. If you rise in this world you've got to rise by yourself. You've got to save your nickels and study. And—and not see anybody else. You've got to be practical. Then—when you've risen—you can reach down and help others. Do you see?"

"Yes."

"Maybe by the time you're old as I am, you'll be going to college."

"College?"

"Yes, maybe by then I can help you. I'll be glad to help you, Johnny. When I've risen. Now I'm saving for other things. I want my own business. And I know the Lord will bless me for I give him his tithe, a tenth of what I make every month. You tell her that, if you tell her anything. Say I give the Lord his due. You understand?"

The boy sitting on the edge of his chair, nodded. Basil had never talked so, before he left the hills. He had learned much, how to talk and reason. He could speak as well as a preacher, and perhaps he should have been a preacher.

"I've found out one thing, John. I've found that people think a lot of me. Up in the hills I always felt that Kirk was so—reckless—and fine looking—nobody could like me, not the girls, anyways. Now I know that girls like me. See those pictures over there? They're from girls. And I've got letters from them, letters I didn't ask for, saying they think a lot of me. If I read you some of those letters you'd be surprised what girls will say."

He laughed and stretched his arms over his head. "Now all that is over. I'm engaged now, to be married."

"To be married?"

"Not for a while yet. She's Preacher Warren's wife's sister. She taught in the church school, and now she's teaching in the public schools here. We're saving up for a business. She wants me to take all those pictures and throw them away, but I tell her—not yet."

"Granpap is saving up for a farm," John said. He felt that the knowledge of Granpap saving for something would make them all finer in Basil's eyes. He wanted to make Basil think much of them, but had forgotten the way in which Granpap was making his money and that his brother might not approve. In a moment he saw his mistake. Basil's eyes shut for a second and the lines on each side of his mouth went deep into the skin.

"He's breaking the law," Basil said.

For the first time John felt against Basil. It was not right for him to talk against Granpap. "He's got a right," he told his brother.

"He has not. It's one of the first things to learn, you can't go against the law. It's not right by law or religion for Granpap to be doing what he is doing."

John's mouth set like Basil's had done, and a frown came between his eyes. "He's got a right," he repeated. Granpap was good, this he knew. And he knew Granpap had a right to make money in the way he was doing. It was work and no easy work, at that.

"Well," Basil said, "there's no need to worry, for Granpap will soon be finished."

"Finished?" This was a frightening word that might signify jail again for Granpap.

"He'll be through with the work, if you call it work."

"How?"

"The lumber company wants to build a number two camp near South Fork. The McEacherns have been holding out for a higher price for their land. Now they've got it and are moving to the city."

"How do ye know that?"

"How do I know? Because I hear about things that are going on. One way, Hal Swain stops in to see Preacher Warren sometimes when he comes into town."

John sat looking at the floor and at the fire. A silence came up between the two. Between them the flames burned up the dark chimney, and the ashes crackled as their live sparks went out and they settled down to die. John felt it was time to go, that now Basil wanted him to go, but he was not sure just how to leave. Basil looked at the alarm clock on the mantel and moved restlessly in his chair.

"Will they be anxious about you?" he asked.

"Maybe," John said, and stood up. Basil took a money folder from his pocket and selected a bill.

"You went back to school all right?" he asked.

"Did Granpap tell ye?"

"It was me that got you back in school. I asked Preacher Warren, and he spoke to the superintendent of mills over the telephone."

Basil looked at the bill he held in his hand.

"You see, John that's the way people that have got the ambition to rise can help the others. I helped you, didn't I, to get back into school. Because I knew people that had influence. It was the same when Hal Swain got Granpap out of jail. And even if the superintendent hadn't let you go back into school we could have got Hal to see or write Congressman Hellman because he owns a lot of stock in the mill. You see that I helped you, don't you, John?" Basil spoke earnestly, trying to make John understand this important question. For the time he seemed to be begging that John should realize the help that had come from him.

"Yes," John answered the begging in Basil's voice, and he added, thinking that was what should be done, "I thank ye."

"I was glad to do it," Basil answered. Now he was not begging, but somewhat pompous and assured. He opened his folder and replaced the bill. "Here," he said, and gave John a fifty cent piece from his pocket. "Take that to her, and you tell her I'm coming for a visit soon."

John held the money in his hand. It was cold. He could feel the cold round edges making a circle in his palm.

A door opened when they reached the hall downstairs. Preacher Warren came out. He put a kind hand on John's shoulder.

"How you've grown!" he said. "But I would know Basil's brother anywhere."

"Tell Emma," he said, "we're proud of Basil."

"Yes . . . sir," John answered him, and slipped out of the front door that Basil was holding open.

35

BASIL was right. The first of the year Granpap came to the house one evening. He walked in as if there had never been any going out.

First he had to be shown Ora's baby that was a week old. Ora lay in the bed in the front room. She was not very well, for working up to the last minute had done something to make her lame, so that she could not stand without pain and could not walk at all. But she could talk, lying in the bed. She said to Granpap, "I almost had him while I was at work, right there in among the frames."

"I told her she ought to name him Bobbin," Emma said, excited and flushed over Granpap being there again. "But she thought hit sounded like a name for a creature, not a child."

She added, "Mr. Mulkey knows something of learning and his boy is named Statesrights."

"That," Frank said, "is not the name for creature or man."

"Well," Ora told Granpap, "we made a good old-fashioned name. We named him Kirkland after you . . . and him." She turned her eyes to the crayon picture of Kirk that was high on the wall.

Emma moved over to the picture. She had watched before to see if Granpap would notice it. The old man went up and looked at it closely. "Why," he said, "hit's as if Kirk was here in the flesh." The frame was gold, very fine, and he ran his fingers over it.

"And there's glass," he said. "Hit'll keep the dust from getting in." As if everybody didn't know.

Granpap had news of Sally, which was something for Ora to get flushed over, except Ora never flushed but her face became soft as if the flesh had melted into the bones. Sally, Granpap said, was planning to make Ora a grandmother. She and Jesse were living with Fraser until the cabins the lumber company was building got ready. Sally had sent a jar of honey to Ora and a slab of bacon from Fraser's pig killed in the fall.

"They can't well spare hit," Ora said. "But I'm glad to have the lean meat instead of salt pork always."

Emma watched Granpap, for she knew he had something on his mind that was not yet told.

Two days later when she waked up in the afternoon, for she was still on night work until Ora would be well enough to go back, Granpap spoke to her. He had given what money he had saved, as payment down on a place two or three miles up the road. It was off Company property and the young would have to change to a county school.

"I could have paid less, Emma, and rented," Granpap said. "But I want to buy. I want a place that's mine, that's Kirkland land."

"And the young will go on to school?" Emma asked.

"I mean it, Emma."

He had something more to say, but it was a hard thing to ask of Emma. He sat opposite her in the bedroom, where Ora could not hear. Emma looked at her father and saw the way he looked back half reluctant, yet with a shine in his eyes, meaning that he was thinking with joy of the farm.

"There's something I want to ask of ye, Emma."

"Ask hit, Granpap."

"If ye could keep on at work in the mill, maybe we could make the payment next year this time. I could work on the farm; but I know from talking to others that the cotton don't always come out right. Sometimes hit's frost or rains, and ye can't tell. I've got two good clean acres, and sometimes people make as much as a bale an acre. I've heard of it. But the first year, not knowing, I might not make very much. And I must give the man that owns the place now a bale for the use of farm things and as part payment. I figure that if we make two bales, then one will go to us, and you can stop work in the mill."

"I hadn't expected not to work in the mill," Emma answered him. "For what would we do for meat and bread every day otherwise?"

On the same day that Emma moved to the country, Ora moved also to another place in the village. Granpap went ahead and was waiting on the farm for Emma. Ora and Frank moved into a house with three rooms. Ora was well enough to go about, and Esther, now, must leave school and stay at home with the young baby. Ora would go back to work. If Ora hurried she could get back at noon to nurse the baby and cook dinner for all; for the new house was much nearer the mill than the old one.

The farm made a light for Emma. For a long time she had been walking lost in darkness and suddenly she saw light ahead, which meant rest and hope. If they did well on the farm, then, sometime, they could leave the mill forever.

The farm house had three rooms, a chicken house and a shed for animals. In the top of the shed was a place for hay where people who had lived there before them had left some hay for the next ones to come, or because they had gone back to the mills and didn't need it. The stalls in the shed were full of manure that could be used for fertilizer. The horse which the owner of the farm had advanced to Granpap on his crop was a nice animal.

"I can ride it," John said and got astride. Immediately the backbone of the horse, which had seemed rather straight, sank down in the middle so that John seemed to be sitting in a valley between two hills.

"John," Emma said. "You're breaking its back!"

"No," Granpap told her with a shamefaced look. "Hit's just a little swayback. But the back don't matter so long as hit's strong enough to pull a plow."

"We'll have to be right smart every morning," Emma said to Bonnie. "If I get t' work on time and you two get to school." For the county school was three miles further up the road away from the village.

They rose at dawn or before every morning and cooked on the small stove Emma had bought on instalment. Granpap was full of energy. As the time came for plowing he was up and out in the fields just so soon as he could get some breakfast in him. They were very careful and saving of food, so there was not much breakfast, but it was enough to start him out, rejoicing. He was glad to do without, for he hoped that there would be plenty from the farm the following year.

Granpap was not new to farming, but he was new to cotton.

During the early spring when he was preparing the ground and getting the seed planted he often had to go across the road to consult with Moses, the black man who cared for Mrs. Phillip's farm.

Mrs. Phillip's house was only a little way up the road. It was a large place with seven rooms and new white paint on the outside, and green blinds. The black man, Moses, had charge of the whole place, for Mrs. Phillips was away all week working at some mysterious business in the city. She came back usually once a week to visit her children and the farm.

Moses was a help to Granpap that spring. Granpap learned from the black man how to put the cotton seed in the ground with the machine, and many other things. From him Granpap bought five chickens, including a setting hen and a dozen eggs for hatching.

Emma came home at night worn out from her work and the two-mile walk. Sometimes before coming home she stopped at Ora's to rest, for she was feeling weak and sickly. Ora's baby was not thriving. "Hit lacks mother's milk," Ora said. And probably that was true, though many of the babies in the village did without.

"But Esther is a real help," Ora said, wanting to praise Esther, who was in the same room. Emma looked at the little girl appreciatively, and Esther hung her head before them.

"Bonnie works in the fields after school, and cooks supper every night," Emma said, doing her share of bragging. "And John works, too, in the fields."

She faltered a little at the last, for she knew Granpap had to scold sometimes to make John get out his hoe and work. John liked to stay at the Phillips place and watch them there. Robert Phillips, the son, did not have to work much, and it was a bad example for John to see him doing nothing. But Emma kept this to herself.

Bonnie and John had learned to know Robert Phillips at school. He seemed very lonely there, or perhaps he thought himself better than the others. He was a big boy, not tall, but almost twice as broad as John. His hair was black and heavy about his face and below it was a rosy complexion and big eyes with plenty of white to them. His mouth was large and if the younger children at school came around to watch him eat his lonely lunch he twisted his mouth into queer shapes to frighten them.

He spoke to John first, there in the yard, when John and Bonnie were quite new in school. After that those three ate their lunches together, and having this friend made John and Bonnie free of the others, though at times Bonnie regretted that she was cut off from playing "Baa Sheepie Baa" or "Pretty Maids from the Country" with the other girls. Once at recess she went up to a crowd that was playing. She wanted to say, "Can I play with you?" but her tongue was dumb. The girls paid no attention to her, and she stood on the edge of the game ready to cry, yet with her face set, determined that she would not cry no matter what happened.

Probably the girls would have asked her to join them if she had waited long enough. But Robert called her, and she was glad then of an excuse to get away.

Robert said, "Those girls don't want you. They are stuck-up. You'd better stay here. I'll take care of you.

"You better stay here," he repeated angrily.

He told them many astounding things. He liked to see their eyes grow big and wondering. He told them about his mother's house in the city. It had a hundred rooms, and each bedroom had a bath. There was a private doctor, the same who came some week-ends to the country, and they always had music in a big room downstairs.

"Did you live there?" Bonnie asked him once.

"No, I didn't, and don't ask foolish questions," Robert said.

"Moses' wife works there, and I've heard her tell about it in the kitchen." He said this grudgingly.

One Monday a preacher came and spoke to them in the morning in the big auditorium. He told them about the Lord's goodness, and the sins of people who did not thank him every day for his goodness.

Going home that day Robert did not say much. When they reached the bridge he stopped there and looked down into the stream that ran under it. Bonnie was glad to stop. On the sides of the stream there were white and yellow violets, and from the trees yellow jessamine hung down. The deep yellow trumpets filled the air just around them with a startling fragrance.

She sat down at the edge of the stream when she heard Robert speak out loud angrily to John.

"I don't believe in God," he said.

"Why?" John asked him.

"I don't believe, that's all."

"Then you'll go to hell."

"Hell's a better place than earth."

"You haven't been there."

"How do you know I'll go to hell?"

"The preacher says so."

"Then the preacher lies."

Looking up from the violets she was picking, Bonnie saw Robert give a defiant look at John and walk away over the bridge and on up the road.

"Wait for me, John," she begged. But when she caught up with him and they walked along some distance behind Robert she had no word to say. But the words they had said on the bridge disturbed her.

At the steps leading from the road up the high embankment to his house, Robert stopped until they came up.

"Come in," he said commandingly.

He opened the front door and took them into the hallway. There was a scuffling in the front room at the right. He pushed them back and waited, standing in front of them and watching the door. Bonnie heard something dragging slowly across the floor. It made her heart beat up to wait for the unknown thing to show itself.

When it reached the door she saw it was a girl like any other. She had a healthy face, like Robert's. But she came walking on all fours like an animal, and behind her knees she dragged two useless legs, like sticks. When she saw them she sat up, resting both hands on the floor.

"This is my sister, Mary Louise," Robert said. He looked at them as if he dared them to say anything except what he wanted.

"Howdy, Mary Louise," Bonnie said, for she knew that was manners.

"She can read," Robert said. "I taught her."

He reached over and took John's reader and opened it at the back, far beyond the place where John had learned.

"Read that, Mary Louise," he said and handed the book down to her. She balanced herself with one hand, and with the other held the book near her eyes; and read the whole page without hesitating once.

Robert looked at them. Probably he expected them to say words in praise, but they could only look back at him, and with wonder at the girl. He was satisfied with their silent admiration.

"She's smart," he said and gave the book back to John. "Now go back to your room, Mary Louise," he told her, and the girl scuffled back across the door sill.

In the kitchen Robert put food on the table that Moses, who cooked for him, had left in a pot on the slow fire.

"You see," he said to John, "if there was a God he couldn't make my sister like that. They say God is Love, and Love couldn't do anything cruel like that."

"Maybe hit's a punishment," Bonnie said very softly. She was almost afraid to speak out with Robert. But something must be said for religion.

"What do you mean?" Robert stood up. His face was white and his eyes grew round and threatening. They seemed to blow out sparks. "If you mean my mother you can go out that door and never come back."

"I didn't mean a thing," Bonnie said. "Not a thing."

She looked frightened and sorry for what she had said. There was no doubt of that.

"Then it's all right," Robert told her. "But you understand my mother is not to be talked about. I licked four boys at school just for that. Everybody knows they can't say anything about my mother."

36

SUMMER came very quickly. After months of work in the fields, Granpap was bent over like an old man. He had a misery in his back that would catch him in the fields so that he was forced to take a little time off and rest. John and Bonnie, since school was out, worked in the fields all day.

Sweat poured from Bonnie's face into her eyes, as she leaned over the long rows. She came back at the end of the first days exhausted. After that her back learned to bend without aching, though she was always ready for bed at the end of a day out there, and John was the same. They took a bucket of fresh water from the well to the field with them. And Bonnie found that if they tied up their heads in wet rags and put the straw hats Emma had bought in town for five cents over these, the sun did not give headaches. But nothing could keep it from their backs. They had worked in the sun up in the hills. It was never so hot up there even in the middle of the day. There was a saying that the sun beat down. And it was exactly what the sun did on the backs of people working in the fields. It came like a red hot hand across their backs, then went away as if to get strength for another blow and down it came again, a hot fire.

There were Negroes working in the Phillips' fields across the road, for Moses often hired the children of share-croppers to work for Mrs. Phillips. An old Negro woman, Aunt Sarah, bent with rheumatism, brought her five grandchildren to the fields. She laid the baby—its mother cooked for a white woman in the town—on a croker sack between the rows. The other children, even the five-year-old, chopped cotton. Bonnie could hear them when they came to the end of the rows near the road, over there. While she was thinning out the fresh young plants that snuggled together in a row and measuring with her eye in order to leave the healthiest plant at the right distance from the last one, she heard Aunt Sarah urging the young ones to stop playing and get to work. She always threatened them with a whipping from their mother. "Ne' mind," she called out to them, "ne' mind"—in a threatening voice, very high and cracked.

Granpap kept after them just as Aunt Sarah kept after her young ones. When the bright nights came, because of the moon, he took John and Bonnie into the fields to work at night.

Emma wanted the young ones to have some rest. "Hit's easier," Granpap said, "with no sun, and we rest longer in the middle of the day when the sun's hottest."

"But hit's like the mill," Emma said. "We're making the young sweat."

"If hit wasn't here, hit would be in the mill. Better for them to sweat for themselves—for the land will be theirs, Emma, if we earn hit."

Emma wanted to go out in the moonlight when they went to work. She was too worn out for that. It was like a circle, she said. If she didn't rest, she couldn't work, and if she couldn't work, they couldn't eat, and if she couldn't eat, she couldn't work. "So," she told Bonnie, "I've got to have rest."

Then there was the redness on her hands. "I thought at first hit was the seven years itch," she told Bonnie. "You never know if you're touching a place in the mill whether somebody with the itch hasn't been there before ye. So many have the itch."

She wanted very much for Bonnie to understand what working in the mill meant. The farm was their life, but the mill was hers.

"Frank's working in the weave room now," she said. "He's still got his cough. And there's a man next him with the consumption."

She often talked to Bonnie when they cleared up the dishes together, but all the time she knew that Bonnie was living another life and though she tried to listen didn't even hear. Bonnie and John were not even much interested when Emma told them Ora was coming for Sunday dinner. Six of the chickens from the first setting had escaped sickness and hawks and grown big enough to eat, and Emma planned to fry two of them for that dinner. She bought sweet potatoes and rice, and a whole sack of flour, and a can of lard. On Saturday Granpap borrowed a wagon and harness from Moses and driving his own horse (for it seemed his own, though really it belonged to Mr. Ashley who owned the place) he drove into town with John and brought back the supplies Emma had bought, along with some oats for the horse.

Emma had long since stopped paying insurance, but she was still paying Ora a little each week for the board she had not paid. Ora had said, "Shucks, Emma. What's over is over." But Ora was having the doctor for the baby, and needed the money. Now, with Ora almost paid, Emma had hopes of catching up. This was why she felt rich enough to buy flour and lard.

She was almost praying for that Sunday to be full of sunshine and peace, for then Ora could see the cotton in full bloom in the sun. Her regret was that she had no garden of fresh vegetables. Granpap had plowed the ground and she had planted. Then they had all neglected the garden, for cotton was everything. The garden fence was almost gone, and there was no money with which to buy new fencing, so the chickens ate up most of the vegetables that came up, and then laid only a few eggs in return.

That Sunday came in with plenty of sunshine just as Emma had hoped. John and Bonnie, up to now indifferent, became excited about the fact that company was coming and there was to be a fine dinner.

Granpap stayed in bed until late to give his back time to catch up with the week's work. He had coffee in bed just like a rich man, he said, when Emma brought it to him. Emma cleaned up the front room, even washing the floor first thing in the morning after breakfast. The bed there was covered with her best quilt. There was no table yet, but the Bible was on the mantel-piece, and above it hung the picture of Kirk. Two chairs sat in the room, though they would be taken into the kitchen when it was time to eat. Bonnie had brought in some late wild honeysuckle and sweet william. The honeysuckle was a deep pink and its thick stems stood up in a bottle on the table in the kitchen. The sweet william Emma put in a cup on the mantel, and the pink flowers hung over the side of the cup and trailed on the shelf as if they were growing there.

"They'll be late," Emma said to Bonnie. "For hit's a long way the first time you walk it. Now I don't notice so much going back and forth every day like I do."

The family came just as Emma finished cutting out the biscuits. The chicken was ready to fry and the potatoes and rice were cooking.

Ora sat down to rest in the front room and nursed the baby that fretted every minute it was not at her breast. All her young ones stayed nearby, for they smelled the cooking in the next room.

"Keep the young ones here," Emma called out to Ora, "for dinner's most ready."

"You couldn't get them away if you took a stick after them," Ora called back.

"I can't hear ye." The sizzling of the frying chicken in the pan before her was all Emma could hear clearly.

"Hit'll wait," Ora said comfortably.

After the full meal, all the older ones with the youngest went to look at the cotton. Esther and Bonnie washed dishes in the kitchen and ate scraps, though there were not many left. John waited for Young Frank who was hesitating between following Granpap and Frank and staying around the kitchen.

"Want to come with me?" he asked Young Frank. "I'm a-going across the road."

"I want by myself," Young Frank said, and John left him.

Emma and Ora walked some distance behind Granpap and Frank. They had to pass along the road to reach the cotton patch further up.

"He's getting bent over like an old man sure enough," Ora said looking ahead at Granpap who walked as if he was continually looking for something on the ground.

"Hit's his back and leaning over to plow and chop. He don't know when to say stop to himself. Hit's cotton, cotton, day in, day out. 'I'd like to make a bale an acre,' he says. Mrs. Phillip's black man, Moses, says it has been done, but not often. Yet everybody will work themselves sick to try."

"Because it brings in money."

"Yes. And I'm glad except that Granpap's wearing himself out. . . . Look! Ora," Emma spoke in a whisper. "There's Mrs. Phillips."

Mrs. Phillips came down the steps of the white house across the road. She was a buxom woman in a fine white dress.

"You can't see her face for that big hat," Emma whispered. "But she's real pretty, with a bright color. That's the doctor with her. I think that's his automobile, though maybe it's hers, for she's rich."

"And she just comes every week to see her young ones?" Ora asked.

"Yes, she's got some kind of business in town. I told you. Now she's going back there."

"What business would keep a mother away from her young ones?" Ora asked.

"I reckon the same kind that keeps us from ours, making money to live on." This quieted Ora. Only she thought to herself, "If I had a house like that I'd think myself rich enough to stay at home."

John looked back again from across the road. He was waiting until Mrs. Phillips would get in the car and drive away. Then he and Robert would be free to go where they pleased. Frank was still in the yard, and had probably decided to stay near the girls. So, if he liked girls better, then he was welcome to them.

Robert was waiting at the back of the house. He had a special place for them to go. "The chain gang is camped up the road," he said. "Let's go and watch."

It was further than John had thought, for he knew Emma would be looking for him to be there when Ora and the others left. Yet when Robert once wanted to do a thing it was hard to say no to him; and John kept on walking. It was almost sundown when they reached the spot. The gang was camped in an open place near the schoolhouse.

"Come in here," Robert said mysteriously, and dragged John into some blackjacks. They sat down to watch, with no one in the camp suspecting they were there. It looked as if the men had just finished supper, for at one side under a tent a black man in stripes was cleaning tin dishes and piling them on a table to dry. Beyond the tent there were two long cages on wheels, with rows of shelves inside.

"They sleep in those cages, Moses says," Robert whispered to John. "And they're chained together so they can't get away."

About thirty men sat on the ground. Some of them looked to be white, but most were full black. They sat pressed close together and the stripes of their clothes ran into each other and made a long ring of stripes as if the wide black lines were a fence to hold them in. Behind the circle on a sort of stool sat the guard with his big gun under his arm. At his feet were two hounds with long drooping ears. He held them by a chain that gave out a clank when the hounds moved.

The guard raised his gun a little way in the air and pointed with it at one of the black men.

"All right, Sam," he said. "Begin."

Sam stood up. "He's a trusty," Robert said, very low. "You see he hasn't any chains hanging to his legs."

All together the men raised their voices and sang. There were two hymns that John had never heard before. Then Sam began, "Nearer my God to Thee."

This one John knew, and all the men seemed to know it well. Their deep mournful voices mixed with the heavy feeling of night just coming, and went up toward the heavens where stars were coming out.

Nearer my God to Thee
Nearer to Thee
E'en though it be a cross
That raiseth me.
Still all my song shall be
Nearer my God to Thee
Nearer my God to Thee
Nearer to Thee.

When this third song was finished, the guard gave an order and another guard with a gun came from a small tent at the right of the cages. The men in stripes rose up and walked, one behind the other, to the cages. Their black heads became part of the night, but the stripes stood out in the one light that was fixed on a tree in the center. It looked as if only stripes were moving around in the shadows, as they marched toward the cages. But there was the sound of heavy chains rubbing together. Two of the trusties stood aside waiting for the others to pass into the cages. John saw the first cage fill up with stripes lying flat on the shelves, and in places between the bars of the cages he could see white eyes shining in the light from the lantern. There were some murmurs, then again the clanking of chains as the men climbed into the second cage. The voices of guards sounded sharp and rasping.

"Get in there; quick now. Get in there."

Then something went wrong. The guard's voice called out. "Get in there you black ——" There was a scuffle and the guard brought his gun down heavily.

"Bring him out," he called. The other guard and a black man who was unchained stooped and dragged one of the convicts into the light.

"Get a wheelbarrow," the guard said to the other trusty, and the man ran fast to do as he was told.

The guard and the black man laid the convict across the wheelbarrow face down and stripped him to the waist. There was a silence, terrible like that between bright lightning and a heavy crash of thunder, only it lasted longer.

The convict on the wheelbarrow had a gash across his forehead, and the blood dripped from it to the ground. The others were waiting for something, and while they waited the man cried out. "Boss," he said, "I didn't mean it. Oh, Boss, I didn't mean to be impudent. You don't understand."

The white guard came from the tent with a long leather whip.

"Thirty licks," the other one said, the one who held the hounds. "Lie down," he said to the hounds, who began to howl dismally. "Lie down." And he touched one of them with the end of his gun. The dogs quieted.

The leather came down on the back of the convict. The sound of the leather cutting his back went up into the heavens as the sound of the hymn had gone up. And another sound went up. As the leather came down the man lying across the wheelbarrow groaned. The lashes never stopped, for when the white guard tired he handed the whip to the black man and ordered him to go on with the punishment.

"One," Robert counted in a whisper. "Two." And kept on counting.

Groans came from the man on the wheelbarrow. They grew fainter, then there came a groan from the cages, and another. Robert counted, "Twenty, twenty-one . . ." The groans accumulated into one sound. They swelled up until they were louder than the song had been. And they were one groan made of the groans of those who were lying on the shelves in the cages.

John heard them, but he did not see. He was lying face down on the ground with his mouth in the dirt. A sickness had come on him. Like Job of old he wanted to curse God and die.

"Twenty-nine, thirty," Robert said. "Nearer my God to Thee," he shouted out and laughed. Lying on the ground John heard him, and talked with his mouth in the dirt.

Robert leaned over him. "What did you say?" he asked.

"Nothing," John told him. The sounds had stopped and he sat up. He saw the shadows that were the blackjacks all around him. The light in the camp had been turned down and everything was quiet there, except for the noise that people make when they are lying down and have not yet gone to sleep, but are restless or feverish. Looking over John saw that the guard sat under the light with the gun in his hand. At his feet lay the two hounds. One of them moved in his sleep and the chain clanked gently against the butt of the gun in the hand of the guard.

37

THE weave room was close and hot, for no air that might break the precious threads must come in. Weavers stood at their looms wet through with sweat, and often there would be a stirring of people about some section when one of the women, overcome with the closeness, or perhaps by some kind of sickness, fainted. Frank worked at his looms there, so John, who was put in that room as a filling hauler, pushing the boxes on wheels filled with spools, saw him every day.

Bonnie worked in the spinning room as a doffer. It was temporary work, for the doffers were usually boys. She learned to breathe in air that was full of lint, and after the first two or three days did not get sick at the smell of oil. Each spinner had a different mark, and though she was bewildered at first, she soon learned to put the right mark for each spinner on the spools she took from the frames. Her work was very important, for each spinner must get the correct number of spools recorded for the pay check. For every cent counted. Bonnie's head came just to the shelf where the full bobbins lay. She could not see over the long, high frames, and ran from one to another, trying to keep up.

At night she hurried back the two miles, cooked supper and made Emma comfortable. Every day Ora waited outside the mill to ask her, "How is Emma?" Some days she answered "better" and other days "worse." It was like the game, "We've come to see Miss Jennie Jones, and how is she to-day?"

Emma was sick, and Bonnie and John were working in the mill. Their working came about in the most natural and reasonable way; yet no one, least of all Emma, had expected them to leave school so soon.

At the time Emma first became sick several things of special importance at the time, and of later interest, happened to the family.

She had been ailing for some time and one week-day morning did not get up. On Sunday when Mrs. Phillips learned of Emma's illness she came over and brought her doctor.

"She has pellagra," the doctor told Granpap in the kitchen after he had looked at Emma.

"Do you think," Granpap asked, "I'd better get the Company doctor to her regularly?"

"He would tell you the same thing," Doctor Ford said. "I was on the Board of Health once, so I've seen enough to know. And there's nothing he could do. Give her plenty of lean meat, milk, and other nourishing food, and she'll get better."

Granpap told him. "I'm having a hard row to hoe right now. I don't know how I can well do it."

The doctor became very angry, angry enough to frighten Bonnie who was in the corner behind the stove, listening.

"Don't ask me how," the doctor said. "A doctor can't produce decent food for the many that need it. What can I do? Don't ask me."

He went out of the back door hurriedly as if he wanted to shake the dust of the house from his feet. Granpap followed and left Bonnie to ponder on the dreadful word. She knew many children in the village who were afflicted with the disease, and grown up people. Only recently Mrs. Mulkey had become insane. She drove her young ones out of the house. It was said she heard voices talking to her and answered them, and imagined that horrible animals and devils were running around the walls. People said she behaved like a man who is crazy with drink.

If Emma did not grow better, Bonnie thought, she might become like Mrs. Mulkey. She went to the door of the bedroom and listened to Emma talking with Mrs. Phillips in order to reassure herself that her mother was very sane. Emma's voice was quiet and just as usual, though she got somewhat excited when Mrs. Phillips told her that one of the girls who worked for her in the city knew Emma. The girl's name was Minnie—Minnie Hawkins. Minnie had heard Mrs. Phillips and the doctor speaking of Robert and John McClure, and had asked, "Do those McClures come from the mountains, at Swain's Crossing?" And then she had said, "I know them."

The following week Ora and Frank brought Mr. Turnipseed to the farm house. They explained to Emma that the preacher, for whatever money Granpap could give, would sign papers saying that John was old enough to work in the mill. And since Bonnie was old enough already, Ora and Frank persuaded Emma to let both of them work in the mill. They said the children could go back to school later, when Emma was well enough to go into the mill again. Reluctantly Emma had to consent, for if the young ones did not bring in some ready money, there would be nothing for them or anyone else in the family to eat.

That day while Frank and Granpap were in the fields, Preacher Turnipseed spoke to John and Bonnie while they were in the front room with Emma and Ora.

He said, speaking partly to Emma, partly to the children, it was time for them to acknowledge Christ as their Savior. Their mother was sick and how could they pray to God to make her well if they had not professed their belief in Him and His Son.

Standing at the head of the bed, John felt disturbed and angry. He looked on the bed and saw Emma's face with the cheeks sunk in. He saw her hands stretched out palms down on the quilt. They were yellow and scrawny like the claws of chickens, and the fingers were bent as if in working they had grown that way. A great many thoughts had come up in him recently, and he was queerly upset and angry at everyone. Standing there, he wanted to ask, "Why did God make her sick in the first place?" To him it seemed a reasonable question, but to say it aloud before Emma was not quite possible. While the preacher talked, Emma reached her hand up along the bed clothes to touch him, and he could feel her hard fingers worrying at the tips of his own as they hung at his side. But he would not say what she wanted him to. It was Bonnie who answered Mr. Turnipseed's waiting and promised that at the next baptizing she would come into the church.

Mr. Turnipseed had to be contented with that. He got up to go outside, but left Ora with Emma, after giving her a significant look from the door.

He came back again, opened the door, and called out, "John, you and Bonnie come and show me the farm."

When they hesitated Ora said gently, "Yes, you run along with the preacher."

As the door shut she bent over the bed. "I promised the preacher to tell you," she said to Emma. "I don't know what's the right or wrong of it, for you have said Mrs. Phillips has been kind since you have been sick."

"She has been kind. Before last week she paid us little or no attention. But she brought her own doctor over."

"That's hit," Ora said. "That doctor was turned off the Board of Health for not believing in God, and for other things. And Mrs. Phillips," Ora bent over Emma and whispered, "Mrs. Phillips . . . keeps a . . . bad house . . . in the city."

"Is it sure?" Emma gasped.

"Preacher Turnipseed said hit."

"Oh," Emma said. "Oh. Pore Minnie."

38

Sometimes John spoke to Frank in the weave room. Frank walked from one loom to another, watching them earnestly, and when a thread broke he inserted his big fingers in the machines to make the threads whole again.

"My hands are too big for this work," he said to John. "I aim to get somewheres else where a man's strength is needed."

Most of the time he said nothing, but nodded to John when he passed, for the noise was not a thing that many liked to talk against.

Young Frank worked in the spool room. After hours he did just about as he pleased. "Sometimes," Ora complained to Bonnie, "he don't come home for supper even—and he stays out late at night. Hit ain't right for a boy of sixteen."

Now that Bonnie was working Ora treated her almost as a grown up and confided in her, which made Bonnie feel very proud, and sitting by Emma's bed at home she often repeated Ora's words, with a sad, responsible heaviness to her voice as if she felt the burden of them as well as Ora did.

"And he keeps back more of his wages than he ought," Ora said. "I wouldn't mind if I didn't know he was wasting it in gambling. And hit's s' hard to get along. I dread the winters more and more. When spring comes and the young ones can go barefoot, and there's no coal bill to pay, I get plumb excited from relief."

Bonnie and Emma understood well enough Ora's feelings, for they had saved on shoe leather, and they watched anxiously for spring. There was so little money. The first two weeks while she and John had been learning, they got no pay. Two weeks before the instalment man had taken their kitchen stove, for they had fallen behind on payments—so Bonnie cooked on the fire as they had done in the mountains. But spring meant less fuel.

Just as the children took off their shoes and stockings and played happily in their bare feet when the first warm weather came, so the poor, when summer made a promise of coming soon, shed the burden of providing coal and warm clothes and covers, and doctors for the winter sicknesses—with joy.

"Spring is the poor man's time of hope," John Stevens said to John. "These machines can do the work of many men, but unlike men they have no winter and no spring. And they can't reason. Don't ever let yourself think the machines are bigger than you are. For they aren't. If for no other reason there's the reason that you can feel the warm, calm air of spring and say to yourself, 'This is good.' "

It seemed to John that this man and the other weavers were fine beings because they could manage the great machines and produce yards of cloth. He liked the weave room and sometimes puzzled over the sound there, for somewhere before he had known a sound like it. One day, listening intently to the looms he remembered.

He had stood outside McDonald's cabin and heard feet pounding inside to the sound of fiddle and banjo. The feet had come down on the floor rhythmically. They got into his blood. The rhythm had beaten up from the shaking floor into his feet, just as it did in the mill. He thought with pleasure that one day he would be one who controlled those machines.

Because he was thinking of them an accident happened to him one day which might have been very serious. But it was a fortunate accident, since it made him acquainted with John Stevens.

The machines must be cleaned on extra time and the workers had to go early or stay late the day before pay day to clean up. During the week the machines dripped oil. If the weavers stopped to wipe off the oil they lost money, and if they wiped the machines while they were moving there was danger of a serious accident. They did this rather than stop, but made one wiping last as long as possible, so oil dripped on the floors and stayed there.

John was pushing his truck along, listening to the sound of the looms. He did not see the oil spread out on the floor by the weaver's foot. When he slipped his truck went one way and he another, almost head on into a machine. It was John Stevens who caught him in time to prevent an accident.

The boy stood up, trying to hide his trembling, for the belt of the machine had been very close.

"You'd better be careful," John Stevens said, and gave him a shake to emphasize the importance of what he said.

"Will you be careful now? I've seen you around here. You're just about as particular as a cat in a bed of catnip, poking your nose in and having a fit over it all. I've looked every minute to see you roll over on the floor with joy in the looms."

He loosed John and went about his work. And John, ashamed and rather angry, got his truck and went on without a word. Gradually, because John Stevens never failed to notice him, they began to know each other, and sometimes at the lunch hour sat down in the mill yard and ate their bread together.

John Stevens was a small man, but strong, and in spite of a limp, very active. His hands were small so he was better fitted for weaving than Frank. He had been a weaver all his life, and his father before him. The limp came from a badly set leg he had broken in a fall when he was eight years old and had just begun to work in the mills.

"It was a slippery floor," he told John. "That's why I blew you up sky high that day; though I slipped on soap and water, for then as now they have the floors washed while we are still at the machines."

Once John heard him singing at his work, and at lunch asked about the song, and from listening to it on occasions learned the words. While the looms pounded up and down John Stevens sang. His voice came clear under the sound of the looms. Most people shouted trying to make their voices heard above the grinding, but John Stevens knew how to make his clear under the sound, just as people standing on the outside of a waterfall might scream to be heard, but one who stood in a cave underneath could speak with a low voice.

John Stevens stood in the cave underneath. He spoke to his looms, and knowing each part, spoke of them. He liked his machines.

"It's what they do to people," he said to John one lunch time, "that makes me sick at heart."

The song was about factory people, and it was easy to see how John Stevens had made it up while weaving, for his voice, singing it, rose and fell with the rhythm of the looms.

"I lived in a town away down South
By the name of Buffalo
And worked in a mill with the rest of the trash
As we're often called you know.

"You factory folks who sing this rhyme
Will surely understand
The reason why I love you so
Is I'm a factory hand.

"While standing here between my looms
You know I lose no time
To keep my shuttles in a whiz
And make this little rhyme.

"We rise up early in the morn
And work all day real hard
To buy our little meat and bread
And sugar, tea and lard.

"We work from weeks end to weeks end
And never lose a day
And when that awful pay day comes
We draw our little pay.

"We then go home on pay day night
And sit down in a chair
The merchant raps upon the door
He's come to get his share.

"When all our little debts are paid
And nothing left behind
We turn our pockets wrong side out
But not a cent can find.

"We rise up early in the morn
And toil from soon till late
We have no time to primp and fix
And dress right up to date.

"Our children they grow up unlearned
No time to go to school
Almost before they've learned to walk
They learn to spin or spool.

"The Boss men jerk them round and round
And whistle very keen

I'll tell you what, the factory young
Are really treated mean.

"The folks in town who dress so fine
And spend their money free
Will hardly look at a factory hand
Who dresses like you and me.

"As we go walking down the street
All wrapped in lint and strings
They call us fools and factory trash
And other low down names.

"Just let them wear their watches fine
And rings and golden chains
But when the Day of Judgment comes
They'll have to shed those things."

John wrote the song verse by verse on paper at home and brought it to show to his friend.

"I'm right glad you liked it that much," John Stevens said. "I've sung it in mill towns in three states and in the North, too, and people have learned it. I feel good sometimes to think I've spoken to folks at times when they feel the sorrow of working without much recompense."

Once John asked him, "Do you believe in God?" and John Stevens did not answer directly. "It's best not to ask," he said. But later in the day when John passed with a truck full of spools, he stopped him.

"I believe in a Judgment Day," he said.

On the same afternoon Frank beckoned to John. He pulled him close and called out into his ear so loud John felt a scorn for Frank who did not know how to talk under the sound.

"I heard in town," Frank cried, and had to stop for a moment while he turned away his head to cough. But his hand was still on John's arm and the boy felt the shaking from the cough pass from Frank's hand into his arm. "I heard in town," Frank repeated, "Basil's getting married to-night."

"Where?" John asked.

"What did you say?"

"Where?" John stood on tiptoe and reached up to Frank's ear. They were like two deaf people.

"At Preacher Warren's church," Frank called out with his mouth close to John's ear.

When the six o'clock whistle blew John sought out Bonnie. He stood at the left hand doorway of the mill through which she would come. The air was still and damp, for there had been a heavy rain during the afternoon. There was a mud puddle near the door and he watched people step over it or into it as they came out. Then he saw Bonnie's feet in the new shoes she had bought the Saturday before, because her others had split across the tops.

She came from the stream of people when he called her.

"What is it?" she asked him, thinking of Emma.

"Nothing. I won't be home to supper."

"Where're you going?"

"Somewhere."

"I can't say somewhere to her."

"Tell her I'm a-going to the preacher's."

If Emma concluded that he was going to visit Preacher Turnipseed she would have to do so. It might even be best for her to think he had gone to get straightened out about religion. Bonnie walked off at the end of those who were hurrying home, and John turned the other way.

It was getting dark when he reached the church. There were lights in every window, and the vestibule door was open so that the pale yellow glow from inside came out over the steps. John stood at one side of the steps in the shadow. People came along the sidewalk. Though he could not see their faces he heard the steps flat along the walk. He felt very much alone, with the steps going past, as if he and the church together were stranded somewhere in a place that people could not reach.

Presently some began to come up the walk and go into the church. They came on foot and in automobiles, and those who rode left their cars, and walked into the church hastily as if they were expected. The women's skirts made a sound as if a wind was blowing in a pine forest, making the needles swish against each other. John felt the wet bushes around his legs. The wet seeped into his jeans and made them cling around him, so that he was uncomfortable, and wished to move. But there was nowhere to go. He must wait for his brother. He had a right to be there. Was it not his brother who was to be married in the church? Yet at moments he almost doubted if it was Basil's marriage all these people were coming to see. Perhaps Frank had been wrong.

Then he saw Basil step out of an automobile at the curb. He came up the walk with two other men: and all three were dressed in white shirts, black suits, and hats that stood too high above their heads. They wore white gloves as if they were at a funeral expecting to lift the coffin.

John slipped along the wall and as Basil came up the steps stood in the lights that came from the vestibule. Basil saw him at once. He turned his head quickly to the other two men. "Go on in," he said. "I'll join you in a moment." He stood with his back to them as if shielding John.

He was looking down, not into John's face, but at his clothes: and the boy, looking down, saw himself with Basil's eyes. In his hurry he had forgotten that lint still clung to his jeans. He should have dressed for the wedding. The fault was his, for he had not thought of a crowd of people, but only of Basil, and of saying to Emma and Granpap, "I went to Basil's wedding."

"Come here," Basil said and took him by the shoulder with tense fingers. They stood in the corner made by the vestibule of the church and the outer wall.

"We planned to have a small wedding," Basil said in a whisper, and he was panting as if he had hurried from a distance, "with all our kinsfolks present. But Mary's father is a rich man and he insisted on a big wedding. Do you see? Tell Emma we'll come to see her soon. Now you run home. You must be drenched from these bushes. Hurry home now, and get dry, or you'll be sick."

The hand left John's shoulder, and he saw Basil hurrying up the steps into the lighted vestibule. His brother had said, "Go home," as if he was an unwelcome dog. But he could not believe it was the end. Surely Basil, who was so powerful, could say to someone, "My brother is here. We must find him the right clothes to wear; I can't have the wedding without him. Though I see little of him, he is really very important to me."

The organ played very loud music, then quieted down to a soft monotony. People came along the street and stopped to listen. Through the open door of the church they could see the decorations, the flowers and smilax, and knew it was a wedding. Presently there was quite a crowd lining the walk to the church, waiting to see the bride and groom come out. There were some black people, and others who were white. None of them was dressed finely like those in the church, and John began to feel more at home. He pushed between two of them and stood on the walk where he could see and be seen when the others came out.

"Behold the bridegroom cometh," one of the men near him said in a loud voice, when the music swelled up into a triumphant blast. There was the sound of many voices, especially the higher voices of women. Basil came through the door with a woman dressed in white hanging to his arm. They stood in the door a moment, fine and triumphant. The woman's white veil floated behind her against the wooden wall of the church. Someone gave Basil his hat, and together he and the woman who was his wife ran down the walk and into the automobile that was waiting for them at the curb. The car drove off, and others took its place to take in the people who thronged out of the church.

One of the men who watched from the walk said, "She was the homeliest bride I ever see." And another one said, "She was ugly as homemade sin."

The words made John ashamed. But he repeated them to Granpap that evening, when he got into bed, after finding that Emma and Bonnie were asleep.

"Hit's too bad," Granpap whispered. "With Basil getting along so well for him t' take a wife that's ugly. A pretty wife is God's gracious gift to man, but an ugly one tempts him sorely to stray."

Later when John thought Granpap had dropped off to sleep, the old man raised up in bed and spoke again.

"You say he didn't see ye?" Granpap asked.

"Who?"

"Basil. You say he didn't see ye?"

"No," John answered. "I just stood in the dark and watched. He couldn't see me for the darkness."

Granpap went off to sleep. But John was awake for some time. He was trying to piece some things together. His mind was broken up into parts. In one of them he admired his brother, and in another hated him. The parts would not come together, and he went to sleep at last without having made up his mind. But for several days the resentment against Basil was strong in him.

39

For two years more Granpap struggled on the farm, trying to hold on as possible owner. The time came when Mr. Ashley's agent gave him the choice of giving up the farm or becoming a share-cropper.

"I have learned to know what a share-cropper is," Granpap said to John. "I have talked to some and have watched them around here. Share-cropping is the same as slavery. Hit means food advanced, and seed and other things advanced, and at the end of the year the reckoning comes. What's his share goes to him, and what's my share goes to him, for I must take his word for the price of what is advanced. Hit means ruin."

He went down to the mill and tried to find a place as watchman. There was none open to him. So he stayed on the farm and looked on what he had lost. That was the hardest part: to stay and see that all the money paid down in the beginning, and that spent on making the place better, though it was not much, and the hard work he had put into the fields—belong to someone else. He had begun to think of the farm as his own.

Emma was known in the mill as a skillful worker, and when she went down and asked for work she got it. Yet during the two years she had found it necessary to go back to bed, and at last had to give up and stay at home.

There, when it was necessary for her to remain in bed, she lay in the front room alone during the day and looked at the treasures she had accumulated during her years of work. There was the picture of Kirk, which was the most precious. It hung above the mantel-piece, and opposite was the record of Births and Deaths that Granpap had bought in the first flush of their making money. John and Bonnie had written names in the spaces. Under the Deaths there were the names of Emma's children who were in the mountains and the name of her husband. Under Marriages was Basil McClure, and there was a name under the word Births, for Basil, after being married a little over a year, had a son named Basil. It was Frank who had brought them this news, and Emma had immediately taken down the record and had Bonnie write the name, Basil McClure, carefully under the word that she had begun to know by its appearance and position on the record. She wondered, lying in her bed, how many more Births would be put down there before she left the earth.

Under Kirk's picture on the mantel there were two vases she had bought at the ten cent store in town. They were bright yellow and when the sun came in the west window it seemed as if lamps were lit in the vases. If Emma was in bed she watched to see this happen. It was something to look for during the day. Later there would be the young ones coming from work, and Bonnie scolding because she had, perhaps, got up to straighten the house, or wash out some clothes.

Bonnie had grown into a young woman in those two years. When she and John first went into the mill they had become thin and pale, and John had remained so. But with some of the mountain freshness in her, Bonnie had grown plumper after she got used to the mill, and now there was plenty of redness in her cheeks.

She was working in the twist room, and often young men passing by her frames, or in the yard at lunch time, spoke to her. She kept her head down when they did this; but after they went on thinking probably that she was unfriendly, she looked after them shyly, and would have called them back if she had dared.

She was full of energy, and made such a feeling of hopefulness get into the farm house, that Granpap got out his fiddle, something he had not done in years, and played. So it happened that Preacher Turnipseed, coming to see Emma one Saturday afternoon, stopped in dismay, as he told Emma afterwards, at hearing the sound of dance tunes coming from the windows of their house.

On Christmas Eve the church was to have a Tree and Box Supper. At these suppers each girl took a box provided with enough food for two people, and the boxes were auctioned off. Some of the girls were very cunning and spent all their money on decorations for the outside of the box, and put only crackers and cheese or sardines inside. So they hoped to win one of the best looking boys for supper.

They had five chickens left, and Emma insisted that Bonnie

fry one of them for her box. On the Saturday before Christmas Bonnie went to town and bought a roll of crêpe paper for the outside covering of her box. She had already saved up silver paper from chewing gum and what she could find on the floor of the mill from the men's cigarette packages. From this paper, smoothed out very carefully with her thumb, she cut stars and crescents.

Recently Bonnie had grown in stature and this was her first party as a young woman. The night before she sat on the edge of Emma's bed with the yellow crepe paper spread out before her, and the silver laid out on a pillow beside Emma's head where no careless person might disturb it.

"This time to-morrow night," she said, "I'll be there. I wish you could go." She spoke to Emma.

"You make Granpap go," Emma answered. "He never goes from the house except to work in the fields. Hit's time he mixed with people again, for he always liked t' do that. Hit's unnatural for him to stay here all the time, just sitting, like an unfruitful seed."

On the night of the party John went first. He was dressed in a second hand suit bought at Reskowitz' when he first began working in the mill.

"Now, Granpap, you've just got t' go," Bonnie said to the old man. She put her arms around his neck and kissed him on the scars across his cheek.

"No," Granpap insisted. "I'm an old man."

"You can be my beau," Bonnie told him.

"You'll have plenty of beaus with those roses in your cheeks and that light in your eyes. She's real pretty, ain't she, Emma?"

"I think she won't be left in a corner," Emma said, more casual than she really felt. "I want ye t' go, Granpap," she said.

"And leave you here alone?"

"I have been left alone before and it never hurt me. Now, Granpap, if ye don't go, I'll get out of bed and go myself."

It ended with Granpap becoming almost as excited as Bonnie. He washed behind his ears, combed his beard and was ready.

"Do ye reckon I might take the fiddle along?" he asked, and Emma looking at him saw that his eyes were as bright as Bonnie's and she hated to say no to him.

"With Preacher Turnipseed there," she said, "hit wouldn't do. Unless you might play hymn tunes on it."

Granpap drooped at the shoulders. "I reckon hit's better left at home," he said and followed Bonnie out of the door.

When they reached the school auditorium a few young men were already standing just outside the door, in the cold December night. They were waiting until the tree, which was especially for women and children, should get finished and the box supper begin. Bonnie felt that their faces turned to watch her. She held the box closer to her side, so that feeling it would give her courage to walk without fear and trembling up the steps. Yet their looks gave her courage, too.

She stopped just inside the door and put out her hand to touch Granpap who would have gone in at once.

"Isn't it a big crowd?" she asked him.

People were standing in groups, talking, and seemed to fill the whole place. Benches were set against the walls, and on these sat women with small children and with some of them were their husbands.

"Why, Granpap, hit's good to see ye," someone said. And there was Ora, holding the baby with one arm, and reaching out to Granpap with the other. Frank was beside her on the bench.

"Take your box right up there to the front," Ora said to Bonnie.

Turning to come back Bonnie saw that John was standing in the front part of those waiting for the exercises to begin. She felt that he was looking at her with approval, and the blood burned up in her cheeks from his appreciation and from excitement. She returned to Granpap and stood before him while Mr. Turnipseed was getting the young ones together on the floor in front of the tree.

On the platform sat the Superintendent, Mr. Burnett, the three preachers from the village, and a visiting preacher.

When the young ones were settled, and the older ones had found places in a half circle behind them, Mr. Turnipseed stood up on the rostrum. The talking quieted down slowly until there was a silence like church.

Mr. Turnipseed announced that the tree with all its many and fine decorations had been donated by kind people in the town. The entertainment was given by all the churches of the village, so money from the sale of boxes would be divided among them. It was the usual Christmas announcement. It was fitting, he continued, at a time of peace on earth, good will to men, for all denominations to come together as one family in Christ. The speaker of the evening was from a different denomination from any in the village. He wanted to introduce Mr. Warmsley from the town.

Mr. Warmsley spoke in a fine voice. When Bonnie heard it she thought of molasses, brown and thick, pouring from a pitcher and spreading out on a plate. Mr. Warmsley's voice spread through the hall slowly and quietly.

"I have asked Mr. Turnipseed," he said, "to let me speak to you early in the evening, because in my home little ones are waiting for their father to begin Christmas Eve. There, in my home, we have a tree, just as you have one here. Over all the earth it is the same. People of all races, nations, are celebrating the birth of Jesus."

Mr. Warmsley's ruddy face glowed beneath soft white hair. His deep, slow voice reached to every part of the room and created a feeling of good will, so that people listened with attention.

"Why do people celebrate?" he asked—and answered the question. "Because Jesus brought love to the earth. God, the Almighty, gave commandments to men. Sometimes to us he seems a bitter, jealous God who punishes and does not love. But we can never really feel that, when we realize that 'God so loved the world, he gave his only begotten son.' In Jesus Christ he gave us love divine, the love that suffers and forgives, the love that bears all things, the love that these mothers, holding their babies, have for the children in their arms.

"There are times when your lot may seem hard to you. You may feel that you do not possess much. Let me say to you, my friends, that you possess the only true greatness and power. I have been among you and have watched when you did not know. I have seen the dignity in you that rises above worldly considerations. I have compared your dignity with that of the rich. And beside yours their dignity of wealth and possessions is nothing. Yours is the true greatness. Have I not seen your dignity and worth under abuse?

"Let me tell you a story. One day some years ago I was in

my study, which is in one of the wings of the church. I heard cries outside my window and went to find what had caused them. On the lawn were some of the boys of my congregation. They were hooting and jeering. And standing before them, the butt of their jeers, was a boy from this mill. He stood there dignified and aloof as Jesus Christ himself might have stood before his accusers.

"That poor boy, dressed almost in rags, stood up under the lash of scorn with a dignity that shamed those other boys, rich though most of them were.

"And I tell you that some day the rich will see your goodness: and bow before your spiritual wealth that is greater than their material wealth, so that in the end they will endeavor to become like you, simple and good.

"And when this spiritual brotherhood will have been accomplished, the rich will say, 'What is our wealth, that our brothers do not share in it?' And they will straightway share the wealth, so there shall be plenty, and all will be furnished with the necessities and the good things of earth that God has given us.

"Then the spirit of Christ will shine in all hearts like the star on the summit of that Christmas Tree, and all men will acknowledge each other as brothers in Christ and sharers of wealth. Then, my brothers, there will truly be peace on earth, good will toward men."

40

WHILE the minister spoke faces strained upwards toward him, as if they were sniffing in the words he said with their nostrils. There were gaunt men and tired looking women, old before their time. There were boys and girls, wan and stunted of the second and third generation of those who had worked in the mills. They seemed about ten or twelve, but they were old enough to be looking at each other, thinking of marriage. The faces, raised to the light, seemed to have no flesh, but to be made of bone with skin stretched tightly over it.

When the preacher finished and the people turned to each other for talk, their faces showed color and some animation. The town preacher shook hands with his colleagues on the platform and hurried away to his home and children. Bonnie stood near Granpap who was talking with Frank.

"What he said had sense," Granpap told Frank. "If the rich could get the grace of Jesus Christ in their hearts, hit stands to reason we'd all have enough."

"I didn't like so much his speaking about us as being pore so much," Frank said. "If he'd spoke it just once . . ."

"No," Granpap answered before Frank could finish, "hit didn't seem to fit in exactly. But what he says is mighty true. Only all the rich would have t' do it together—for there are so many pore."

"You run along, Bonnie," Ora spoke to Bonnie and gave her a push with her big hand. "Go and mix with the girls. The young men will be in soon. Can't you see how Lessie and Tiny and the rest are watching that door? You mustn't let them grab all the boys from ye."

Bonnie wished to do what Ora wanted. She was not very timid at home, but her greatest desire was to get between Granpap and Ora and hide the fact that she was there at all. Suppose no one picked her out—no one thought her box good enough to buy!

They were giving out gifts from the tree, a bag of candy and an orange for each child. Facing Granpap Bonnie heard the door to the yard open. She heard the heavy steps and knew the young men had come into the hall.

"You go along," Ora insisted. "Mr. Burnett's going t' speak. You go nearer and listen."

Some of the women had gone up front to find their young ones and take them home. People were walking around and talking together. But when Mr. Burnett rose to speak there was silence.

Mr. Burnett said he would not make a speech. He only wished to give them all a Merry Christmas from the management, the Directors, and the President of the Company. Before anyone left he wanted to ask them all to join in singing the Doxology. Bonnie, who had slowly made her way into the crowd of people, raised her voice and sang with the rest. When the Doxology was finished someone began "The Old Time Religion."

Bonnie, singing "It was good for Paul and Silas," heard someone speak in her ear. She turned and her cheek brushed against the cheek of a young man. She looked at him. This was one she had never seen before, but in the short glance he gave it was plain that he was not one who might be speaking to her because he was unwanted elsewhere. He was not tall like the men of her family, but she saw blue eyes, and brown silky hair brushed back from a white forehead, which frowned at her coaxingly, as if saying, "Don't be too hard on me."

"I asked if I could talk with you," he said. "But you didn't seem to hear."

She looked up again, and the flush that had been on her face before came up into her cheeks.

"You have the prettiest mouth," he said, "of any girl here."

"And you can talk the prettiest," Bonnie answered him, "of any man here."

"I don't know just how to take that," he told her.

"I think I'll have to be going," Bonnie said. She felt that she must have spoken the wrong words.

He reached out and touched her arm. "Don't go away," he begged. "I'm a stranger here and need a friend.

"They're going to sell the boxes, now," he added, holding her arm lightly with his fingers. "Wait." She felt each of his fingers touching her lightly on the arm just above her elbow. They were like bolts that held her to him.

They watched Mr. Turnipseed, with the help of one of the boys, lift the table loaded with boxes of all colors to the platform. All the other people had gone from the stage, and in the auditorium the onlookers were settling down on the benches around the room preparing for the auction. They passed Bonnie and her new friend, and some of them, knowing Bonnie, looked curiously at her. She did not even see them, and her voice answering questions seemed far away, as if she was in a cloud on a mountain and heard someone speaking far down in the valley.

"What's your name?"

"Bonnie McClure."

"Will you tell me what your box is like, Bonnie?"

"It's—why, I don't know whether I should say."

"You tell me."

"It's yellow crêpe paper with silver stars."

"Jim," one of the young men from the side of the room called out.

"My name is Jim Calhoun," Bonnie's friend said. "And you're my girl. Don't forget." He pressed her arm and went over to those who had called.

"Come here, Bonnie." Lessie Hampton made a place on her bench, and Bonnie joined the group of girls who were strong in the confidence that their boxes were already as good as taken.

"Is he going to buy your box?" Lessie asked her.

"I don't know," Bonnie answered, for she was not yet certain that what was promised would come to pass.

"Watch out, Bonnie," another said. "Jim Calhoun has a name for being mighty fickle."

Bonnie looked toward the young men and saw Jim Calhoun talking intimately with the others. He had said he was a stranger, but he seemed to know people and they to know him. Somehow it didn't matter.

Mr. Turnipseed brought his fist down on the stand. "What am I bid for this beautiful box?" he asked, holding up a box covered with white paper, and decorated with red hearts.

Someone made a timid bid. Mr. Turnipseed shook the box close to his ear. "Sounds like there's mighty good things in there," he said.

The bidding was slow at first, but it gathered interest with every box sold. Mr. Turnipseed reached for another and then another box. Still Bonnie's yellow one remained on the table. She almost hoped he would overlook it altogether.

As soon as a young man bid in a box he opened it to find out the name of his partner for supper. Bonnie had written her name many times before she had made the writing as she wanted it. The slip lay in her box, on top, "Bonnie McClure," in large round letters.

Some of the young men frowned when they saw the names in their boxes. And this was what she dreaded, that her name would be frowned upon. She would be glad, almost, for Sam Fellows to get her box, if he would only behave as if he was glad to have it. Sam, who was very greedy, had bid in three already, and had three girls around him: but what was more important to him, there were three boxes from which he could choose his supper.

"What am I bid," Mr. Turnipseed said, "for this box, the color of ripe corn silk."

Bonnie saw that the box was hers.

"I can just imagine," Mr. Turnipseed continued holding the box up high so all could see, "I can just imagine the girl who made this exquisite arrangement of stars and crescents. She must be beautiful as the stars, and good and kind as the moon on a summer's night. What am I bid?"

"Ten cents," a boy from the right of the platform called out and everyone laughed. But Bonnie wished to hide her face because of the laughter, and because it had brought her down from a high place where Mr. Turnipseed's words had taken her.

"One dollar," came from the group of young men. Jim Calhoun was speaking. He stood up and spoke angrily looking in the direction of the boy who had called out "ten cents."

Mr. Turnipseed said, "One dollar, one dollar." He held the box to his nose and sniffed at it. "I seem to smell fried chicken," he said.

Sam Fellows looked up from his three girls and three boxes. "One dollar and twenty cents," he called out very loud.

"He's got three. Now he wants more," the boy from the right said complainingly.

"I haven't got one with fried chicken," Sam Fellows called back.

"One twenty. One twenty," Mr. Turnipseed droned.

Jim Calhoun bid again, and Sam followed him. Some of the

other young men, finding that a game was going on, joined in the bidding, until Bonnie's box sold the highest of any—to Jim Calhoun.

By this time most of the girls were gone from Bonnie's group, claimed by the young men who had bid in their boxes. Bonnie sat on the bench, her hands lying loosely in her lap, her face tense with happiness and expectation. When Jim Calhoun came toward her with the box under his arm, while people clapped because the bidding had been so close, she closed her fists together in her lap to keep her hands from going right out to meet him. He was so welcome.

That night, for the first time in months Granpap and John walked together. All the way on the country road in the dark ahead of them, they heard Bonnie and the young man, Jim Calhoun walking, occasionally stumbling in the ruts, laughing, and going on. They heard the young man's low, deep talk and Bonnie's rather high voice answering him.

41

JIM CALHOUN's father was killed in a mine accident in Kentucky, and while he was still very young his mother brought him further south to a mill village where she could make enough money to feed and clothe them. They had traveled from village to village to find better wages until Jim's mother died and he was left alone.

Bonnie and Jim were married six months after they met at the Christmas Party.

"I'm a rover," Jim told Bonnie, "by birth and by life."

"I don't want to rove," Bonnie answered him. "I want to stay in one place and make something of ourselves."

"Anything for you. I'd settle down forever if you want that."

They were fine lovers.

"There are some who are sad, and say life is poor," Bonnie said to her husband. "It seems to me life is rich so long as people have this."

They were in their own room in the farm house, which had new furniture bought on instalment. The floor of the room slanted downwards toward the fireplace, and there were holes between the planks through which the wind came up in winter. But the other rooms were the same.

"Our young ones will have things better," Bonnie often thought to herself, and she did not mean to sit down and expect the good things to come. She must work for them. She thought with pity of Emma lying sick in the front room. Emma had wanted good things, but somehow she had not managed right—and neither had Granpap who worked so hard on the farm and got in the end only feebleness and discouragement. She and Jim, young and happy, could do anything.

Even when Jim left for the war along with many other men of the village, she was sorrowful, but not discouraged. Her baby was coming and with John's help they could keep Emma and Granpap. She could work in the mill, if she kept well enough, until the last minute. Most of the women did this, and though some of them died, Bonnie never thought of death as her part. She was to live and do great things before death came to her in a fine old age, a time too far off for her to imagine. The older people in the village and the preacher were always speaking of death, and there were so many funerals it was no wonder. Many of them thought in terms of death, and many of them said, "What is there to do, except wait and hope for heaven?" Instead of repeating their words, Bonnie said, not in words but in her feeling and actions, "What has life got for me and mine?"

With Jim gone, and the four miles to the mill and back too much for Bonnie, they found it necessary to move into the village. And only Granpap was sorry.

John was glad to go where he might have more company. It was lonely in the evenings, for theirs was the only inhabited place near by. The Phillips house was empty. Robert had gone to war, one of the first, and Mrs. Phillips came one day in a great hurry, packed everything, took her crippled child and left in an automobile on the same day. There was a "For Sale" sign standing in the front yard.

Even Bonnie could not keep John from loneliness, though he was glad to be with her. Her face shone as if inside she was full of a slow, warm fire at which anyone who was cold might get warm. He did not say much to her but they understood each other.

They moved into a house near Ora's in the mill village. John was working as a slubber hand in the carding room. Bonnie had some money from Jim in the army, but she kept at work, because they needed as much as possible for Emma, and because she wanted to save something for the baby.

The Company doctor was visiting Emma. He was also the owner of a drug store and his visiting bills and drug bills took a great deal of money. Mrs. Phillips' doctor had said, about Emma, "She needs plenty of good food, and no doctor." Yet when they moved to the village, with people advising that they get Doctor Foley, and with their own uncertainty, they found it the only thing to do. For they needed confidence that they were doing the right thing by Emma, everything possible that might make her well. The doctor was kind enough to let them run up a bill for drugs at his store, so the bottles on the chair beside Emma's bed were kept replenished.

One thing helped. Wages were higher than they had been.

People said it was because of the war. But the war also took money from them, for rich people from the town were continually coming to the mill to make what they called drives for money, and all in the mill were expected to give their part toward saving the nation from the enemy.

Bonnie planned to learn every trade in the mill so she would become indispensable to the management. When Jim came back they must make something of their lives. She spoke to John about this one Sunday afternoon when he sat in the kitchen while she scrubbed out some clothes.

"What is it you want?" he asked her.

"I don't know. . . . Well . . . suppose we had books around the walls here and hit wasn't hard to make out words like we find it, but we could read together or by ourselves—and could put a shovel of coal on the fire without thinking where is the next coming from—and people could love—like—like Jim and me. Wouldn't it be a fine sort of life?"

"I reckon it would. But hit's not so easy," John said out of thoughts he had had before. Yet he almost believed with Bonnie that things would be better for them: that something good lay ahead.

"Maybe it's not so easy, but I'm a-going t' try," Bonnie said.

To learn the trades in the mill, she went back after supper on the nights when Emma was better, and went through the different departments, watching the night shift work. She visited the mill from top to bottom—from the opening to the finishing room—and watched every process carefully. There was the hopper where cotton from the bale was fed into a great mouth. The lap came out soft and wide, thick as her hand, but so clean and soft she could see through it.

In the carding room they showed her the machine that divided the lap into thick white strands. It seemed as if the machine was a hand that played delicately with the cotton, combing the lap into strands and winding those gently round and round in the tall cans. At the drawing frame she saw the six strands of card sliver from the other frames gathered together by a machine hand that by alternating the fibers of cotton drew them into a stronger sliver: then in another machine this length was drawn and twisted to make a stronger thread, though this rove was still thick and easily broken.

In the slubber and speeder frames the rove or thread prepared in the other frames was drawn and twisted into a stronger cotton thread. It was all a process of making that which was weak strong enough to stand the strain of the weaving.

She stayed in the spinning room, and skipped the spooling room, for that was where she was working at the time. The warp room was the finest looking of them all, and gave her most pleasure to watch. There the threads came from rows of spools lying horizontally on the creel which was a narrow, high rack. The round cylindrical beam was some distance in front of the creel, from which the tiny threads came and wound over the beam, each in its rightful place. The threads came from above, the center, and below, and they were as plentiful as the threads of a new cobweb, yet they stayed apart, and each, as if it knew, took its place on the beam: which, when it was full of threads, would be taken to the drawing-in room where the ends would be harnessed for the looms.

Each night after hours when it was possible to be in the mills Bonnie went back after supper to learn. And when the time came that she was too tired to go, she sat at home by Emma and let the processes pass before her eyes. Often her thought turned to God and she prayed that he would bless her undertaking: to make herself so skillful that she would make a good life for herself and hers.

On Sundays she went to church, and Granpap, who was learning to play hymn tunes on his fiddle, went with her. Brother Turnipseed had promised to find him a place in the mill—and toward the end of summer of the second year of the war, when one of the old watchmen died, Granpap was given his place.

One Sunday there appeared across the front of the church a long cloth sign. Bonnie read the words to Granpap. The large red letters at the top said:

BLOOD AND FIRE CAMPAIGN

and underneath in smaller black letters:

Prepare to meet your God.

Evangelistic Meeting . . . . Speaker—Cyclone Carter.

And under that the date and hour of the meeting.

The revival service came on a week night when Granpap had to work, so Bonnie went alone to the church with a promise from John that he would meet her afterward.

There had been some meetings to prepare for the revival in people's houses, and one of them had been held at their own house. The meetings had come on Sunday afternoons, so Granpap had attended, and at each meeting he became more earnest in his attention to what Brother Turnipseed spoke about—life here on earth as preparation for life after death, in heaven. And Granpap began to like the songs that were sung—one especially made him feel that it was written for him. "I'm but a stranger here," it said. "Heaven is my home. Earth is a desert drear. Heaven is my home."

When Bonnie reached church on the night of the revival meeting it was crowded already. People from all denominations had come to hear the well-known Cyclone Carter. Bonnie found a place in the middle of a bench, toward the back.

There were prayers and songs. She always liked the songs and lifted up her voice earnestly with the others. The evangelist was a tall man who moved around on the rostrum as if he had springs in his shoes. His black eyes were very bright and he was continually searching the congregation with them. In speaking he used his arms, and they, too, when he began to move them in the air, seemed to have springs. He filled the whole rostrum with himself while he talked, moving his legs and long arms about swiftly.

His whole sermon was about the war. Behind him, draped across the wall, was a large flag. First he read from the Bible. Then he spoke of the duties of those who stayed at home from the war. He said not only were the soldiers in danger of losing their lives by the sword and pestilence, but they were in greater danger of losing their souls through temptations of the flesh. And for the preservation of their souls from hell fire, the prayers of those at home must go up to the Throne.

Thank God, he said, there were people trying to protect the soldiers from sin. Near the Capital City, he told them, there was a camp preparing young men for war against the foreign beast named in the Book of Revelations.

"And in that Capital City there was at one time a street of sin, located behind the very building where the legislators gathered to make the laws of the state. Some time after the war had started a committee of Christian men and women, realizing the menace this street was to the boys who were gathered in the camp, had come together and driven the women from this street of sin, and prohibited them from gathering in one place again."

The evangelist himself had visited one of the most famous houses. "After," he said, "of course, *after* the madam and her foul herd had been driven out." There were many bedrooms in the house and each had a private bath. On the first floor he saw a long room, where, he was told by members of the committee, scenes of debauchery had been enacted. As he stood there imagining the foul scenes the room had witnessed, he thanked God that, as the world was being made safe for civilization, so that city was being made safe for the boys who had been sent away with pure kisses on their lips.

At this point something happened that disturbed the congregation. One of the boys who had been listening with intent face while the evangelist spoke of the house in the city, made a sound with his mouth. Perhaps he was trying to imitate a kiss, or perhaps something else. Whatever it was, the sound caused some people near the boy to laugh. There were whispers and glances toward that section of the church. Some people looked with reproach and others moved uneasily. The preacher was not disconcerted. He stopped a moment as if to get his breath, and continued his sermon.

Bonnie, who was sitting near the boy who had caused the interruption, could not hear what the preacher continued to say, because of the whispering and laughter which did not quiet down very soon.

However, at the end of the sermon many people went up to profess Jesus. They shook hands with the preacher and with Cyclone Carter and kneeled before the rostrum.

At the end of the meeting Bonnie went out of the church alone and found John waiting for her. They walked along the streets toward the house where they lived.

As they neared the mill Bonnie asked, "Was Ora still with her when you left?"

"Yes," John said.

"Then let's go down and talk to Granpap. He gets lonely by himself at night—he's so new staying there."

"If you want," John said quietly.

They walked down a side street in the dark toward the back of the mill where Granpap guarded one of the gates.

"I'm thinking of going to fight in this war," John said.

"Why?"

"I don't know. I want t' see more than I see here."

"With Jim and Young Frank gone hit's enough."

"Now we know they get money, hit would be all right. I could send money back."

"Don't talk of hit now. There's Granpap."

The electric light from the gate shone down on the old man. He sat on a stool bent over, and they could not see his face which was in the shadow, but the light picked out the thick gray hairs on the top of his head.

There was darkness around, except for the dim electric light and the yellow squares up above that were the mill windows. The heavens were open and immense: even the mill that was so huge in the daytime looked flat and insignificant.

Granpap got to his feet hastily when he heard them. As they stood before him and he saw who they were his face brightened and he sat down again on the stool.

"So you went to church?" he asked looking at Bonnie, then at John.

"I didn't," John said. "Bonnie went."

"Ain't ye never going t' get right with God?" Granpap asked John. "Hit's better, Son, to do hit in your youth. Give your best years to God, and he will re-pay. 'The night cometh.' I'm an old man and I know." He gave a great sigh.

"Granpap," Bonnie said, "you know you're going to live to be a hundred."

"Now, hit's a queer thing, Bonnie. Hit's the same exactly that Mr. Wentworth said to me. He was here from Washington to-night on business for the Government," Granpap whispered to them, and before going on peered into the darkness on each side. "They took him all around the mill and he stopped and spoke to me just as common as any one of us. He's not a bit stuck up, rich as he is. He asked how I was, and I said just tolerable and getting old. And he told me, Bonnie, just the words you said. 'You'll live t' be a hundred.' He's a fine man, one I'm proud to work for."

As they went from the mill along the street toward home John said abruptly,

"I don't think much of the way Granpap's turning out."

"How do you mean?"

"I don't know. He's lost something—pride or something I valued in him. I miss hit."

"Why, he's just getting old I reckon."

"No. He's lost something—something I hate him t' lose."

"You sound unhappy, John. What's the matter? Granpap's all right—just old."

"I reckon so. I'm restless, I reckon—and can't find anything to satisfy."

42

EMMA did not grow any better. Both her hands and forearms became a bright pink, and were covered with a fine scaling. When Bonnie had her baby there were two invalids in the room. There was Emma, depressed by her illness but cheerful about her grandchild, named for her, Emma Calhoun—and Bonnie, happy with her baby so that nothing could make a cloud for her. She was soon up and waiting on the baby and Emma together, and then back in the mills at her frames.

When Jim came back from the army it was like another marriage for them at first. Later Bonnie found her husband restless, wishing for the army, and hating to go back into the mills. There was no place for him in the beginning and he was secretly glad, though many of the men were angry that women who were paid lower wages had been given their places.

One day Bonnie went to Mr. Burnett and asked him a favor. She was so sure that what she wanted was a good and natural thing, there was no thought in her of being denied. Was she not one of the best and steadiest workers they had? She was very confident of her right, yet it was not so easy to ask her favor when she came face to face with Mr. Burnett in the office.

"Could I go home," she asked him, "at about nine in the morning and three in the afternoon, to nurse the baby?"

From behind his desk Mr. Burnett looked at her in surprise.

"Why, Bonnie!" he said, and smiled at her as if she was a foolish child.

"I'm willing t' lose the money while the machines are idle, Mr. Burnett," she told him earnestly.

"No," he said, "no, Bonnie. I can't do it."

When she urged her request he became very irritable. "If I let you," he said, "I'd have to let every other woman who's got a young baby do the same. And there are plenty of babies in this village, Bonnie."

"And plenty of them dies," Bonnie said to him. It was the first time she had said such a thing to anyone in a long time, and the first time she had spoken in that way to one of the higher-ups. She was frightened by her own words, and waited for days afterwards, watching for someone to come up, while she worked at the machines, lay his hand on her shoulder and say, "You can't work here any more."

Bonnie got a clothes basket from a store in town, and in this she left the baby on a chair by the side of Emma's bed. On the days when Emma could not get up Bonnie left the bottle on another chair.

A few weeks after Bonnie went to Mr. Burnett Jim got a place on the night shift, with a curtailed schedule of three nights a week. This was not much, but it helped, and they were confident that he would be taken on full time soon. With the work, Jim became more contented and Bonnie was happy in her baby and her husband.

In the mill one day Ora caught her at lunch time. "I've just heard," she said. "Everybody from Swain's Crossing is coming down to the mill."

"To work here? To stay?"

"Yes. To stay. Sally's coming with Jesse and their young ones. You tell Emma. The Martins and the McDonalds and the rest are coming. I don't know how many. Hit will do her good t' hear."

"I'll tell her," Bonnie promised.

Later Frank came over and told the news as he had heard it. The lumber mill had closed down at the Crossing, when the best trees were used up. A rich man had bought all the land from the lumber company, because he wanted Laurel Creek and its branch creeks as places where he could bring his friends to fish. All who couldn't pay their rent were given notice to get out of the houses by Hal Swain who had become the rich man's manager. Electricity was cut off, except in the large house which Hal and Sally kept open so it would be ready at any time for the owner and his friends.

Since most people had depended on the wages from the lumber company for paying rent, there was nothing for them to do but leave the mountains and go where they could find ready money.

On Sunday afternoon all the old neighbors from the Crossing visited Emma. Sally came with Ora, having left her three young ones at home with Esther for fear they might worry the invalid.

Jim Martin was there with Jennie, and they brought Zinie, who was grown up, and Lillie her younger sister, who was twelve.

They all gathered in the front room around Emma's bed, and Bonnie showed off her baby and was very proud that it did not cry. Granpap was in there with Frank. Presently they would take Jim Martin and Jesse McDonald out into the kitchen for further talk. Now it was Emma's turn to have all the company.

"Why, Zinie," Emma said, "you've grown real pretty. Who would have thought that little freckle faced, red haired Zinie would grow up so pretty!"

Zinie, trying to avoid all the eyes that were turned to her, looked into the doorway where John was standing. Emma saw the way her eyes had gone. "John," she said, "this is Zinie. You remember you used to play with her up in the mountains, don't ye?"

John did not answer. He vanished from the doorway, but Emma saw him before he went out of their sight turn and give a look at Zinie, and she saw that the girl returned his look.

"Hit's not the best time to come down," Frank said to Jim Martin. "Wages are getting low again, and never were very high."

"And they're making us work overtime in some departments, and curtailing in others," Bonnie added. She knew they might think it queer for her to work, when she had a husband. They did not realize the money it took to pay for a doctor for Emma. And Granpap made so little—and Jim was on half time only. The others would soon learn for themselves how hard it was to get on. When she got down to it, Sally would see that with three young ones it would be necessary for her to work as well as Jesse.

"Hit's a wonder we've stuck," Ora said to the others. "But Frank's a McClure and they will stick till the devil gets behind them with his tail. Others, here, when they get so behind with instalments and their books at the store pick up and leave."

"Hit's one way of paying the grocer," Frank said, quoting a saying that was popular among the people of the village.

"And if you move in the middle of the week, hit means two days of ceasing work in the mills. Hit's like having two Sundays right together."

"You can see people every day with furniture piled high on a wagon—a-paying the grocer," Frank said.

"Well, now," Jennie spoke up in her high little voice, "we've just come . . . we ain't a-thinking of moving. Not to-morrow, anyway."

"Please come back," Emma said to them all, after Bonnie had served black coffee to the women in the bedroom and the men in the kitchen. "Hit's done me lots of good to see you all. I feel as if I was right back in the hills, near old Thunderhead—by the fresh, cool spring."

When they had gone, Bonnie, who was looking after them out of the window, spoke to Emma. "Why, John was waiting outside all the time. And now he's walking off with Zinie."

"I saw him give her a look," Emma said. "And if Zinie's as good as Jennie, I'll be glad if he takes to her."

After that Sunday, for several weeks John and Zinie walked together on Sunday afternoons, or sat over the fire at the Martins. But during the week John did not go near the Martin's house. And there was a reason for this.

43

He was not sure that he wanted Zinie. At this time he was not very sure about anything.

He had envied those who went off to the war. But when the war was over and the men came back they spoke of it without much enthusiasm. Some of those who had been in France came back saying, "It was a rich man's war and a poor man's fight." John remembered that sentence, and pondered on it as he pondered on many things. Later he was to understand what it meant. Now he could only take it apart without having the knowledge with which to put it together again.

It was necessary for him to know, and after knowing he could do what was necessary without hesitation. But during the time of working out what he wished to understand, he was hesitant and upset. Drink gave him some temporary confidence, and he spent much time in the town. One evening as he was coming up a side street, a woman stopped him. She hesitated at first, looked up into his face, went on, then came back and looked into his face again.

"Are you John McClure?" she asked.

"Yes," he answered and looked at her closely. Her dress was of bright blue silk and around her neck was a string of bright beads that looked like diamonds. She was familiar to him, as she stood looking up smiling into his face. She put her little finger into her mouth, and with the gesture something old and familiar took hold of John. He was back in a cabin in the mountains, and Minnie was sitting before the fire, and she said, "John, will you get Minnie some water from the spring?" And he had gone with willingness to get it. Before she spoke again he knew she was Minnie Hawkins.

"I'm Minnie," she said. "Minnie Hawkins. Don't you remember me, John? But you were such a little fellow, then."

"I remember you."

"How's Emma?"

"Not very well."

"Oh, I'm sorry. And the others? Oh, John, I'd like to hear about them all. I've got a room down the street. Will you come up and tell me about everybody?"

He had nothing else to do.

"I knew you right away," Minnie said, as they walked down the side street and into another one. "I knew you because of your resemblance to Kirk. He was a fine boy."

Her room was in a two-story frame house on the edge of town. She opened the door with a latch key. In the hall she stopped a moment to turn on the light. A woman called out from the half open door, "Got a friend with you, Minnie?"

"Yes," she answered and looked at John apologetically, or he imagined that her look was apologetic.

They walked silently up the stairs. In the room which contained a bureau, a washstand and bed she spoke to him.

"Are you cold? If you are I'll build you a fire."

"No," he said. "I'm not cold."

"Well, I'll give you a drink, and that will warm you up, if you happen to get cold. You drink, don't you?"

"Yes," John said from the middle of the room where he was standing.

"Sit down," Minnie told him. "I haven't any chair. You'll have to sit on the bed." She rummaged in the bottom of the washstand. "I would guess that you like drink. All your folks do, and Kirk did. You're so much like Kirk," she repeated

She took a drink from the bottle she had found in the washstand. "Get that glass," she said, and he took it from the stand. "Now hold it while I pour you some."

The drink was warm in his throat. "Do you want some water?" she asked, and he shook his head.

"Now sit on the bed, John. You mustn't be bashful with Minnie."

She sat near him, and after another drink she saw that his eyes watered, and the little finger went up to her mouth. She was looking at him with big eyes.

"You're a fine looking boy," she said.

"Are you angry with me, John?" she asked when he did not speak. "Surely you don't hold it against me that I ran off with Sam McEachern. I've told you, haven't I, that I'm sorry about

Kirk. He was a man that was good to his woman. If he hadn't been jealous, I might have stayed. But I am punished enough with Sam McEachern. John, he's a man that goes after any girl that takes his fancy—then he comes back to me. He's a bad one, yet I can't get away from him. Maybe you think I'm bad, too: and maybe I am. I don't know. Basil says I'm bad. . . ."

"Basil?"

"Maybe I oughtn't t' have told you. He comes sometimes late at night. He thinks I'm bad, but he comes, sometimes."

Minnie was trying to make friends with him, and she was nervous in doing it. John could feel that she was interesting to him, because of her blue eyes, that looked at him innocently, and because of her body that was still shapely, though it bulged from her corset in places. There was a sweetness to her body that he felt. Perhaps it was too sweet and had an odor like molasses that has gone sour, but the sweetness was there.

Though she urged him to talk, she seemed to be glad of a chance to speak herself, as if there had been few people to listen.

"Basil came on a trip to the city," she said. "Hasn't he told you? Didn't you know I was here?"

"I don't see much of him."

Minnie leaned back against the pillow. "Hand me your glass," she told John, and without sitting up she filled the glass half full from her bottle, then with her head flung back she swallowed a drink and looked at John triumphantly over the bottle which she held next to her breasts.

"Basil says I still attract him. He said so that first time I saw him in the city. That's why I'm here, because he wanted me. He did not see me at Mrs. Phillips'. It was after she left. You know I was with Mrs. Phillips. I used to ask her about you all, and about you especially.

"Why don't you say something, John? You're mighty good-looking, you know. I believe you're better looking than any of the McClures. Turn your face around."

She raised herself and took his chin in her hand. "There now. . . . Now I can see you. You're very sweet, John. Did you know that?"

"Well," John said, and laughed into her face that was very near his. "Lots of girls have told me so." He did not pull his chin away from her hand.

"All along I've thought of you as a child, for that was what you were—then. Now—now I feel that you are a man."

He was startled when a knock came at the door. Minnie went there and whispered with the woman who had spoken downstairs. Then she said out loud, "Tell him to come back in ten minutes."

John stood up. "Had I better go?" he asked.

"No," she said. "Well, maybe you'd better." She lay back on the pillow.

"I want you to come back, John. Please tell me you'll come back."

"Yes," John said and went out of the door.

On the front steps of the house he met a man. Looking into his face he saw in the dim light from the corner street lamp that the man was Robert Phillips. They had not met since Robert had come back from the war.

"So you know Minnie?" Robert asked, and smiled at John with meaning.

"Yes, I know her," John answered.

"I'm busy right now," Robert told him. "But I'd like to see you again. Do you ever go to Carpenter's place?" It was a Blind Tiger that all of them knew, the restaurant on Lee Street in which John had sat with Granpap when he came back from the mountains long before.

"I go there sometimes," John said.

"Then I'll see you."

After that meeting John entered into a different life from that he had been leading. He became acquainted, if not at first hand then at second, with some of the men of the town. Sometimes he saw them in their hours of recreation, and talked with them at Carpenter's, and sometimes he only heard of them. There was Albert Burnett who had gone to college, and who now was a leading attorney. But it was Robert who held some interest for him, and they met several times.

They sat in the Blind Tiger one evening alone. Usually Young Frank or Statesrights Mulkey or some men from the town were with them. This evening they were alone.

Robert was persuading John to join a lodge that had a branch in the village and met over the Company store. Robert himself belonged to the town lodge, and in it were other young and old men. One of the members was Basil.

Through Robert, John learned that Basil was accomplishing what he had set out to do. The father-in-law had died and left each of his two daughters some money, and with his part Basil was starting a gasoline station and repairing garage. According to Robert, who had visited John's brother, the Basil McClures lived in a splendid house which they were buying, and in it was a piano, and much velvet furniture.

This was what Robert was planning to have for himself. He was engaged to marry the daughter of a rich grocer in the town. She was just a little bit off, as Statesrights had told John, and followed men around as if she wanted to eat them up, but her unfortunate characteristic made it easier for her father and others to forget that Robert's mother was living at the North on money made from an unmentionable source.

It was Statesrights who had told this to John. Yet Robert himself, when he had been drinking, was hardly less frank about his personal affairs. He was free, he told John that night as they sat alone at the table. His mother had given him the farm to sell when he could, and she would never come back again, but would stay in the North where she had put his crippled sister in an institution.

"You used to think a lot of your sister," John said across the table.

"I used to think a lot of things important that I don't think are important now."

"What is important?"

"Living, and getting what you want?"

"What do you want?"

"Ease and comfort, and the respect of my fellow citizens. I did without that long enough. Now I want it. When I get married I'll settle down, and if I want to kick up a row I'll go somewhere else, or hide it here like the others. And some day, John, you may wake up to find I'm in Congress."

"Maybe," John said. "Maybe I will."

"And I want you to vote for me. Will you do that for your old friend?"

"Well, hit's a long time yet."

"Not so long as you think. I'm going to hang out my shingle as a lawyer. Hellman wants to be Governor. Some day he will resign as Congressman, and that's when I'll step in."

"I've even joined the church," Robert said. "You can see I'm honest with you, John, because you know me, and you can be trusted. I can't fool you either, like I can some. I fooled Basil. He thinks I've been converted through him, and he thinks a lot of his religious protégé—the hypocrite!" Robert spat out.

"Look here," John leaned across the table. The several drinks he had put down made a warm rush of anger go to his head. "Basil may be just what you say. I'm not quarreling at the words, but the tone. He is my brother, and I don't like your tone."

He looked straight at Robert, angrily, and Robert answered his looks with one of anger. Then, very slowly, he smiled.

"I beg your pardon," he said. "Whatever Basil is, as you say, he is your brother. But I like you, John," he added tearfully. "I like you. And I'm honest with you, ain't I, John? I've been to college and I've been to France, and I've seen a hell of a lot of life: and still I have a feeling for you because you're honest. I've got no feeling for anything and anybody—usually. Religious people say God loves us all and guides us, and others say there is some kind of plan in the universe. I've read a lot, John—philosophers and others. And I tell you there is no plan and no guidance. There is no order, no law, no purpose, no progress for the human race. History repeats itself over and over, and here we are, the human race in all its ugliness, just the same as ever. It's for a man to get out and while there's a life to be lived, grab just as much as he can and to hell with everybody else."

"If a man feels as you do," John said, "then he might just as well go to hell as fast as he can."

"It's true. And I thought that for a time. But I've got too much energy. And I have a wish to lead men. I know I can do it. And men like to be led. They need a strong arm, and a strong head above them."

What Robert had said made its impression on John. It suited him to have someone take the lead, and the responsibility for his actions. And Robert was willing to do this for all those who would follow him. Yet there was a part of himself that John without knowing he was doing so kept away from Robert and the others. It was this almost hidden independence that Robert respected. And he had his own reasons for keeping John as a friend. He knew that the boy had the respect of the men in the village, and some day when he became a politician that influence might be of help in getting him votes.

With this in mind he persuaded John to join the lodge in the village. It stood for the protection of the flag, and the motto was "Keep out the foreigner and the nigger. Neither belongs." One night at twelve exactly, John was initiated into the lodge with many indignities—and became a very unsatisfactory member.

He saw the members dressed up in fancy costumes parading around the hall and speaking in loud unnatural voices. The strutting did not affect him in the way it was meant to do, for he could only laugh as he had laughed once when he saw Basil in a sort of nightgown at the cabin in the mountains.

So the meetings went on without him. He preferred to see his friends at Carpenter's—to sit at a table with drinks between them, when they could talk and have a real laugh together over a joke or some story that one of them told.

44

Zinie Martin and Bonnie sat in the front room where Emma lay in one of the beds asleep, with Bonnie's baby at the foot of the bed, asleep like Emma. It was Sunday afternoon.

"I came over to ask about Emma," Zinie said.

"She's about the same," Bonnie told her, looking toward the place where Emma's gray hair showed above the quilt.

"I've been washing," Bonnie said. "So everything is in a mess." She straightened her apron over her belly that showed plainly that she was to have another child in a few months. "I hate t' work on Sunday, but it's a thing that has t' be done."

"Everybody knows there's a-plenty to be done here," Zinie whispered. "Don't you worry over working on a Sunday.

"Is Granpap asleep, too?" she asked.

"Yes."

"How is he?"

"Well. But he tires easily, and sleeps most of the day."

"And—and John?"

"Why, Zinie, haven't you seen him?"

"Not lately."

"Why, he's been going to your house so steady, I thought . . ."

Bonnie saw Zinie's white face go whiter, and knew that she was saying the wrong thing.

"Maybe he's at your house right now, Zinie. I know he's been wild lately. But he's young. I think hit's just the same thing that Kirk was. I've always heard how good Kirk was to his woman. I expect John is at your house right now looking for ye."

"No, Bonnie. There's no use fooling myself. Bonnie, I saw him last night. I went to town. He was on the street with a woman."

"Are you sure it was John?"

"As sure as I'm sitting here."

"I knew he was drinking, but I didn't know there was any woman. Now, Zinie, maybe he couldn't help it. Maybe hit was just somebody he couldn't get away from.

"You see, I've heard him say such nice things about ye."

"Did he say nice things?"

"Yes, he did. He said you were his freckled girl."

Zinie put her hand to her face. She was really nice looking, Bonnie thought, at times pretty.

"Hit don't sound so nice," Zinie said.

"But if you could have heard how he said it. As if he loved every freckle on your face. And you have just a few, Zinie, across your nose. And he said another time that you were as sweet as you were pretty."

"Did he say that?"

"Yes, he did."

Zinie's fingers twisted together in her lap.

"You be patient, Zinie."

"I reckon hit's best," Zinie said.

She went out of the door into the barren front yard where the hard ground met her feet. She missed the soft ground of the mountains that was rich with growth. There was plenty of mud on the roads there, as in the streets of the village. But on the mountains the black soil sank under her feet, and in it grew small flowers and plants she had liked to pick in the spring. John had forgotten about the mountains. He was full of the town and of making something of himself. As if he ought not to know that there was just one life for them—to marry and be happy so long as they could, then take the burdens that life gave them. But he did not want burdens. He wanted to better himself. Zinie suspected that one reason he was so emphatic about all this was that he knew if he once took on burdens he would accept them completely. Perhaps, she thought, Bonnie was right; if she waited and was patient, he would come back and take things upon himself without any urging from her.

Soon after Zinie left, John came to the house. He had come to get Granpap's gun that always stood in a corner of his and Granpap's room. It gave him a peculiar pleasure to go about the streets on Sunday with a gun under his arm, for he knew that people looked at him and either thought sorrowfully of him as an unbeliever, or reproachfully as a wicked person.

He was to meet Statesrights Mulkey and Young Frank and drive out in the country somewhere to shoot at targets. After his mother's death Statesrights' father had married Alma, his mother's sister. Mr. Mulkey had reformed Alma, and made her into a religious, money-grabbing woman, who starved the young ones of the little they had, in order to save a penny. Statesrights felt himself free of the family when his mother was gone. He boarded with Mrs. Sevier, who lived off Company property, and was able to charge very little. Statesrights had bought a second hand car that he and John and the others used when they wished to go into town or out into the country.

Granpap was sleeping. John tiptoed to the corner of the room, but as he touched the gun it fell and the barrel struck the floor. The old man raised himself under the covers.

"That you, John?" he asked in a muffled voice.

"Yes," John spoke very low hoping that Granpap would go back to sleep.

"You taking the gun?" Granpap asked.

"Yes. You go to sleep."

"And hit the day of rest?"

"There's more to life than resting, Granpap." It did not concern him that he might hurt Granpap by what he said. If people were so easily hurt, then it was best they should be.

"What is there in life," Granpap sighed, "but to wait and hope for heaven?"

"I aim t' live a little, Granpap, before I reach the pearly gates."

"Yes," Granpap said, and huddled under the bed clothes again. "You're young."

"Is that you, John?" Bonnie put her head in the doorway between the two rooms.

"Yes," he slipped the gun under his arm.

"Can you stop a minute?"

"Not now."

"She wants you," Bonnie nodded back toward the room. John went in reluctantly. Emma was sitting in a chair. She had on her one dress, a dark brown calico. She sat as she always did when she was up, sideways, dejected and uncomfortable on the edge of the chair.

John glanced at her, and as it never failed to do the sight made him miserable. As always she was picking at her dress, looking down at her hands, rearranging the skirt with patient little gestures.

He put the gun on the bed where she had been lying not long

before, and went up to her. Though she had wanted to see him she seemed to have no words to say. She looked up once. He saw her gray hairs and the deep lines on her face. Bonnie came and stood by him. He looked into her eyes and saw on her face that had been so full of grace and fineness, a sickliness, a beginning of wearing out—the lines that in another ten years would make her like an old woman. It seemed for a moment that two old women were before him and that he was old and finished like Granpap. He touched Emma's hand and turned away, strained and impotent. There was an impulse in him to pick up the gun, kill them all, and then himself. The impulse passed, but he was trembling when Bonnie came and stood before him at the door leading on to the porch.

"I'd like to speak with you," she said. "Zinie was here . . ."

"I can't stop now."

He turned from her and ran down the steps, and Bonnie closed the door sorrowfully behind him.

45

Since John had joined the lodge in the village the authorities of the mill had been especially cordial to him, for some of them belonged to the same lodge, though, like John, they did not attend meetings very often. Then, one day, Superintendent Burnett called John into his office and made him a section boss.

This was an important event. It meant that John was beginning to rise in the world. Only one thing kept him from being contented. Frank and all those with whom he had lived and worked looked at him thoughtfully and questioningly. They wanted to know what he meant to do about this new work. Would he go on the side of those above or stand up for his kin and friends? He knew the answer to that question, but did not speak it to them, for he resented their silent questioning. He would show them that he could be fair, and yet climb higher than others had done.

He was working in the weave room, at the same looms that John Stevens had worked for so many years. John Stevens' bad leg had become worse, for rheumatism had set in, and he had been forced, some months before, to move to Sandersville where there was an opening for a night watchman. It gave John pleasure to stand at the looms where he had seen his friend in the past, and sometimes he thought of John Stevens with a keen pang of recollection.

Recently stories had circulated through the village of a strike in the Sandersville mills. John heard of it and wondered if his friend had taken part in the strike, and then he forgot; for there were other things which took up his attention.

One day word went around in the mill that a young lady had come to organize clubs for girls and women in the village. She was brought there by the mill management, which had one of its houses painted inside and out, sinks and other plumbing put in, and furniture installed. People were invited to a meeting at the school house where the young lady would speak to them. Men were invited, but the girls and women were especially urged to come.

That day John had an appointment with Mr. Burnett at lunch time. He had made the appointment, for there were several matters he wanted to take up with the Superintendent.

All those who had come down from the mountains were having an unhappy experience in the mill. They had been given five and eight dollars as a beginning and had been promised more wages later on when they knew the work better. They had become skillful at their work, but the higher wages were not forthcoming.

Others needed higher wages so that they might, for instance, put screens in their windows. No one ever seemed to have enough money ahead to buy the screens. If there were times when they spent money foolishly instead of on something that was necessary, then it was only natural. For people must have some pleasure. But Ora never spent a cent of money that was not absolutely necessary. Yet it was her baby that died of typhoid, and the doctor had said the disease could have been prevented if there had been screens at the windows.

John wished to present facts like these to Mr. Burnett so the Superintendent would agree to raise the wages of the other workers. So many things could happen to people who did not get enough pay. If they did not have enough food, and enough sleep, and were worn down, they could not do the best work for the mill.

In the office he spoke to Mr. Burnett quietly, referring to a paper in his hand where he had written down the requests he wished to make, and the reasons for making them.

"Well, John," Mr. Burnett said, "I didn't think, and Mr. Randolph didn't think, when we made you section boss that you would turn on us like this."

"According to my way of thinking," John told him, "hit's part of my work t' see what the people who are under me need in the way of things that are necessary to keep them working to the best of their ability."

"I'm afraid you are very much mistaken in your job, then. Your part is to get work out of those people in there. You get as much as you can—see? The management can take care of the rest. It's none of your business."

"It's like this, Mr. Burnett. You tell me to care for the machines, don't you?"

"Yes."

"If a machine gets out of order something must be done right away. And you've said to me, or Mr. Fellows has said every day. 'See that folks keep their machines in order.' Isn't that so?"

"Yes, and we expect you to do just that."

"So I figure that it's just as important t' keep a man or woman that's working at the machines in good order, and it's even more important, for they are people, and the machines, they aren't human, and can't feel misery."

"But you've got the wrong idea, John. You well know a machine costs the management lots of money to replace. We've been watching you, John, and want you to get along. But if you get any such ideas as you have been expounding here into your head, you can't be of use to us."

He looked at his watch. "Now I've got to get on to lunch. Good-by, John. I won't say anything to Mr. Randolph about this. We'll just forget it."

They walked together into the corridor that led from the offices into the mill. Mr. Burnett stopped at the doorway. "Now, John," he said, "those people you're talking about. They're satisfied. Why worry your head about them? You be sensible."

John's lunch hour was over and he hurried back to the weave room. Standing at his work he felt the emptiness in his belly and an emptiness and sadness in himself, whatever was himself, for he did not know.

At that moment, with the sense that kept alert to what was happening in the room while the rest of him concentrated on the machine, he knew that people's heads were turning toward the door. He saw that Mr. Randolph was standing there, and with him was a young woman. Mr. Randolph beckoned to John.

"This is Miss Gordon," he introduced them, shouting above the noise. "Show her over the room, then bring her back to the office."

The young woman smiled at him, but she did not try to speak above the noise.

He stood beside her when Mr. Randolph had gone, and when she looked up expectantly he led the way toward the looms. She stood close to him while he explained the mechanism and when she wished to ask a question raised her mouth to his ear. He felt her breath and once her lips touched his cheek.

As they went through the room some of the men smiled at him. The girls and women kept their eyes down as they always did when there were visitors.

After that on the days when Miss Gordon came to the mill to persuade the girls and women to join her clubs, John watched for her. When she came into the weave room, John Stevens' song that John had repeated under his breath at his looms turned into a song of praise for her. He always left his work to see if there was something he might do. The girls were very ugly about Miss Gordon. Many of them when they saw her coming ducked behind the looms until she passed. Their behavior made him feel a protective interest in Miss Gordon, for he could see that their indifference hurt her badly.

She had left college with the idea of working for the poor, and it was very hard that the people she was working for did not appreciate what she was ready to give. She was glad that John was interested, for if she could get a few or even one to lead she was sure the rest would follow. She had been taught that those who composed the lower elements of society were like sheep and would follow a leader. If John was loyal to her then perhaps his sister might become so, and his other relatives.

Miss Gordon invited John to visit the club rooms and after the first visit he found that there were many ways in which he could help her there. So he became a constant visitor on club nights, and stayed afterwards to straighten up the place, and lock the doors for Miss Gordon.

During the week John was happy with his new friend. Robert and the others were astonished at his desertion and tried vainly to make him return to his evenings with them. Minnie sent word that he must come back to see her. He had an interest that was greater than anything they could offer.

But Sundays were a torture to him. He was without companionship now, for Zlnie kept away from him, and Young Frank and the others at last left him alone. When he told Miss Gordon about the lonely Sundays she gave him books to read. With these he could stay at home on Sunday afternoons and write down the words that were unfamiliar, so that he would have an excuse to detain his friend in the club rooms after the few women who came to the meetings had left. They would sit before a fire in the dining-room and he would spell out the words, while she corrected his pronunciation and told him the meaning of the word he did not understand.

He was reading one of the books Miss Gordon had lent him one Sunday afternoon. Bonnie came into the kitchen with the baby in her arms and settled down in a chair opposite him. There was an uneasy silence, for he thought his sister had come in for a purpose. He was preparing to leave her there, when she spoke to him.

"Will you sit down again, John?"

"Have you got something t' say?"

"Yes. I would like to talk with you."

"Then say it." He did not sit down as she had asked.

"Is it true you're going with Miss Gordon?"

"I'm helping her at the club."

"You're hanging around just like Lessie Hampton that boot-licks all the higher-ups."

"I'm not bootlicking, and I'm sorry to hear ye say that of me."

"Well, hit looks like that, John."

"Is it any of your mind?"

"In a way. Because I don't think it right. I don't like the club. . . ."

"Why don't you go up and try it once?"

"I did try it at first," Bonnie said quietly. "But it seemed no use. She says, 'You must never have fried food,' as if hurrying home from the mill at dinner time a woman or little gal can do anything but throw together something in the frying pan, and at night with the men and the young ones so hungry and you tired, what can you do but the same?

"She tells us, 'You must feed your children milk every day and plenty of eggs, for otherwise young ones will get pellagra.' "

"That is true."

"Of course it's true. . . ." Bonnie stopped speaking. She took one hand from the baby. "Of course it's true," she repeated. There was a silence, and John knew his sister was crying.

"I'd like the best food," she said. "And everything for my young one . . . but how to get them. . . . I don't know."

46

Because he lived at home John could not keep away from Bonnie entirely. But he came in late every night and never gave her another opportunity to speak with him intimately.

Miss Gordon gave him a key to the club rooms, and he went there on Sunday afternoons to read. The room there was better than the kitchen at home. It was comfortable. He could build himself a fire and sit in one of the comfortable chairs to read. And if he grew tired of reading he could think of Ruth Gordon.

Like Kirk he had been accustomed to make love to girls and have them like it. With Miss Gordon he was not so sure of himself. He asked himself, "What are you afraid of? She can't kill ye."

This question was in his mind one evening after club hours when Ruth Gordon came into the living-room of the club house where he was sitting. The women had gone but it was still very early.

"Sit down," she said when he got up ready to help her close the house.

She sat in a chair near him. Together they looked in the fire. He raised his eyes and saw that she was deep in thought. Her fair skin was reddened by the fire toward which she was leaning. He thought how blue her eyes would be if she looked up. When her cheeks were flushed the red in them always accentuated the blueness of her eyes.

"There's something I want to ask you," she told him. "I have liked you so much, John, and I know and understand that you want better things than you are getting now."

He waited to hear what else she had to say.

"You know, don't you, there has been a strike in Sandersville?"

"Yes," John said, looking at her, and enjoying that more than her words.

"I know I can tell you a management secret, John. Mr. Randolph says you can be trusted. He receives a paper every month which tells what is happening in the mills everywhere, all over the country. It gives information about these unions."

"They didn't do much in Sandersville but run off with the people's money," John said.

"Is that true?"

"It's what people say."

"I'm glad if it is true. It will make the union unpopular. People only make misery for themselves by fighting against the owners. What did they get over at Sandersville? The leaders were expelled from the mills. And I happen to know that Mr. Randolph has a list of those expelled so that he won't take them in here. Think of the misery those men brought to their wives and children. Isn't it far better for workers and those who own the mills to live together in brotherly love?"

"Maybe," John said, for she seemed to expect an answer. At that moment love to him meant reaching out to get her head between his own head and shoulder. It meant getting his arms around her.

"I have been asked to see if you will do a favor for the management, John.

"They will pay you for it. You will get the salary of a foreman, with promise of advancement later. . . ."

Love to him meant kissing her mouth. . . .

"All you need to do is watch the other people and report any who speak in a dissatisfied way. We are afraid the union idea will spread. Watch the other workers and listen to them . . ."

. . . And touching her hair. . . .

"No one is to know. You will report to Mr. Randolph once a week. As you are section boss it will be natural for you to go to his office. Just say this person or that one spoke favorably of unions—or someone complained of low wages. But you must watch everybody. . . ."

"Watch everybody?" He repeated her words, for he had not fully understood before what she was saying. Now her words came to him more clearly.

"Yes, they will make it possible for you to go all over the mill and talk with people. And you must listen at lunch time and when you visit people in their homes. . . . Report everyone who is discontented. . . ."

Report? Report Frank, and Jim Martin, and Bonnie, Ora and Zinie—tell on them to the management? Watch neighbors and friends?

"What did you say?" he asked her again.

"I said report any dissatisfaction. And you will have the salary of a foreman. You can have nice things, books, a victrola, and a car even. You can buy things for your family, for your mother. Perhaps she will get well."

He looked at her. She talked on, nervously repeating herself.

"What is wrong? Have I said anything wrong? You look so queer and sad, John.

"Don't you see I want to help you? You're worthy of better things than—than other people here. I don't know. Either the women are stupid or else they are too lazy to learn anything. Many come once to the club, and never come again. The girls think of nothing except their beaus and a drink of ginger ale, or chewing gum in their mouths. I want you to have something better. I was so proud to give you the chance. . . ."

"You mean to be kind," John told her. He was standing before her and she was looking up into his face. He spoke to her softly, meaning to hold his voice steady. During the time she had spoken his strong wish for her had changed into anger. All the fire of wishing to hold her had turned into a fire of anger. But he wished to hold himself still and quiet.

"I thank you," he said, "for meaning to be kind. But that is not enough."

"What have I done, John?"

He did not answer directly, for there was nothing he could say that could be said to a woman. It took him only a few seconds to reach the lower floor, and then the street outside. He walked home covering the ground more swiftly than he had ever done before. In him there was a shame that he could not get away from, no matter how fast he walked. There was a shame for her and for himself. But the greatest part was for himself. He had thought he could rise up and had gone about doing so. His work as a section man had failed. To-morrow he would say to Mr. Burnett, "I cannot be a section boss any longer. I am not your man."

Even with this resolve the shame persisted. He reached the house, and stood irresolutely on the sidewalk in the dark. While he stood there the front door slammed and Jim Calhoun came out.

"Is anything wrong?" John asked, for Jim had hurried down the walk.

"Emma's sick. I'm going for the doctor," Jim answered and went past him up the street.

In the house John found Bonnie working over Emma. She had had some kind of sinking spell and called out for Bonnie.

Bonnie said, "Is that you, John?"

"Is she bad?" John asked, and stood by his sister at the side of the bed.

"My head is whirling," Emma moaned. "Give me another cloth, Bonnie."

Presently Jim returned and said the doctor would come in the morning. He thought there was no need to be alarmed.

"You go to bed," Bonnie whispered to Jim and her brother. "No use all of us losing sleep. You look terrible, John, as if you was sick yourself."

Jim went into the other room, but John stayed with Bonnie. They sat by the fire. Now Emma was quiet. The cloth covered her eyes, and the quilt with its squares and triangles lay across her body where it lay hunched up as if she was cold.

"She woke up thinking something terrible was going t' happen to you and me," Bonnie whispered to John. "She said, 'Hit's torture to think what will happen to Bonnie and John,' The doctor says people with pellagra sometimes get spells of thinking something bad will happen, so I reckon it don't mean anything."

"I hope not."

They waited, each thinking his own thoughts.

"Has she been the same to-day?" John asked, for he wanted to get away from himself.

"The same as usual."

"Bonnie," Emma called out.

"I'm here," Bonnie said, going straight to the bed. She leaned down to Emma and took the cloth from her eyes.

Emma straightened out in the bed. "Hit's good t' see ye, Bonnie. Will John come home soon? I'd like t' see him."

"He's right here," Bonnie told her and beckoned to John. He walked softly to the bed and leaned over Emma, ready to talk with her.

"I don't ache anywhere now," Emma said. "I do feel better." But her voice was thin.

"I'm s' glad."

"I'm anxious for ye both," Emma said. While they stood over her in silence she moved restlessly under the covers: then began speaking again.

John saw that her eyes were not focused, though they were open. "I tried s' hard t' make things fine for ye. I made plans. But hit seems there's no use making plans.

"You remember back in the mountains, Ora, they told us, 'Down there money grows on trees.' But the trees have produced none since we came down.

"I wanted so much, Ora, t' give my young ones a chance in life and see them have things that children should have. But I have made only misery and unhappiness for myself and them."

She spoke again during the night. It was hard to get her to answer anything about what was happening nearby. She seemed to forget that Granpap was on night work, and asked for him. But she remembered things that had happened some time before and spoke of them in a faltering voice.

In the morning when the doctor came she was in a stupor. Under the cover her body twitched continually. Her eyes were turned up toward the ceiling as if she was interested only in the gap between two of the wooden planks up there.

"She can't last out to-morrow," Doctor Foley said. John received the words and gave him the money for the visit.

On the second day early in the morning, when Ora had just left after staying up with her all night, Emma died.

47

THEY bought a ten-dollar grave for Emma. The funeral parlors had nothing in the way of coffins that were cheap. Bonnie and John went down, and Bonnie selected a gray one lined with satin, and a satin shroud. The undertakers seemed to expect that people would wish a fine funeral, and everyone usually did. It was the one time when they could, without thinking that the money should be spent on something else, use it without stint; for the insurance money would cover the costs.

John found this to be true. There was no cheap funeral. Looking at Emma, he thought, "Give me some pine boards, and I could put away what I loved without any of this." They dressed her up in satin, when she was dead. They laid her back on soft pillows, satin pillows, to rest—when she was dead, and could neither see nor feel any more. And they let what she was down into the ten-dollar grave, so that she was finally gone.

Mr. Turnipseed was there, and spoke soft words above the grave.

"Rich and poor, we come to it just the same," he said. "What does it matter, aristocrats, and those who live by the sweat of their brows—all must come to the same end. So we know that only righteousness counts. In my Father's house are many mansions. If it were not so I would have told you. I go to prepare a place for you."

"Jesus went before," he told them, "and he has prepared a place for Emma McClure. She has reached the Promised Land where we all hope to go."

"She was always looking for better things," Ora said to Bonnie after the funeral. "She thought once that down here money grew on trees. Maybe now she's found that place."

There were two bunches of flowers, and after they had been put on the grave, John saw Zinie go over to the mound and re-arrange them as if she wanted, herself, to touch something that was Emma's to show her affection and sorrow.

It was Saturday afternoon. They had hired carriages to take them to the cemetery, but except for the one that carried the preacher, they had hired none to take them back. John gave Mr. Turnipseed his fee for the prayers, and walked slowly to the village with Granpap who was almost prostrated by Emma's death. But he had insisted on going to the cemetery. It was the best he could do, and the last thing possible to show her honor.

On Sunday John got up early in the morning and went to stand out on the road, the one that led towards Sandersville. There was a need in him, and he was going to search out John Stevens, if he was still in that village. A farmer in an old car took him almost there, and he covered the rest of the way on foot. There he inquired about John Stevens, who was a watchman, as he told those whom he questioned. The third person showed him the way. The Stevens house was on the further side of the mill, near some woods. It was a little distance from the other houses.

John knocked at the door, and a woman came. Behind her stood three children, each one only a little taller than the others.

"Does John Stevens live here?" he asked.

She was about to answer when a voice from in the room called out, "Who is it, Nellie?"

"I'm John McClure, from the Wentworth Mills," John said to her.

She went back into the room and the young ones stood together, staring at John. The woman came back and smiled at him. "He's still in bed," she said, "but he'll get up in a minute. He'll be glad to see you."

"I don't wish to disturb him."

"It's about his usual time of getting up," she said comfortably. "Come in, now, and sit down in this room. When he's up we'll go in there and sit. This room is where the children sleep and play, and it looks like it." He could see that she was rather ashamed because the house was not cleaned up for a stranger.

He sat on a chair from which she took some jeans.

"Johnnie," she said to the oldest boy, "go put on these old jeans while I wash your good ones."

The boy took the jeans and went into the other room. John looked after him, for he walked with a peculiar hitching motion.

"He's got tuberculosis of the bone," Nellie Stevens said, "so I've got two that limp."

She did not say this with shame as someone else might have done, but very simply as if she had long ago accepted what was before her.

The door opened again and John Stevens himself limped into the room.

"I'm glad to see you," he said to John.

"I thought maybe you might have forgotten me."

"No," John Stevens said. "I'd never forget you."

"Hit's right kind of ye to say that," John told him. They were not at home with each other. Now he was there, John was not at all sure what he had come for, or whether he would find what he wanted. He had come and must wait to see what the day would bring forth.

He had remembered that John Stevens seemed a person who possessed a knowledge of events and people, and in himself kept something hid that he did not give out to everyone but kept it secret because it was precious; knowledge, that was not to be given lightly, or without preparation.

Mrs. Stevens had the dinner ready and they all sat down around the kitchen table. There was a feeling of understanding in the whole house that was something John had not often felt when among people. They seemed to take him for what he was, a young man they might like or might not like, but one who had with them some common interest that drew them to him, and held them all together; just as the food for the time being held them together around the table.

After dinner John Stevens said: "Would you like to walk out along the big road?"

"You don't wish to sleep again?"

"I've had enough for the day."

"Then I'd like t' go."

"Come back in time t' get a little supper before work time," Mrs. Stevens said to her husband.

He smiled at her from the door and she nodded to him.

The road led them down near a swamp. They did not turn to the left when the road forked, but took the outside road that skirted the swamp instead of that which went through. It was better in the sunshine.

"How are you getting along?" John Stevens asked, as a beginning. "And how are your people?"

John spoke of Emma's death, and repeated as far as he could remember what she had said the night before she died.

"A death seems worse," he said. "And hit seems to stay in you bitter and hard, when somebody dies wanting a thing like she wanted a good life."

"And, too," John Stevens said, "when you know she needn't have died."

"Needn't have died?"

"Didn't you say she had pellagra?"

"She had it."

"Do the rich have pellagra?"

"I never heard."

"It's a poor man's disease. Haven't you heard that?"

"Yes, I've heard that."

"If she had the right nourishment, she needn't have died. You see the mill owners killed her."

"I don't know that I'd go so far. Everybody thinks a lot of the Wentworths, and they are too kind to want anybody to die."

"I don't doubt that. There's plenty that are kind, and good. But during the time I was in the village, I saw grown people, young children, and babies die from lack of right food, and from lack of the right way of living, and I lay their deaths to the owners of the mill, and all those that get money from the mills."

John walked along in silence. He kicked a rock down the road, and saw it roll into the dry grass at the edge.

At last he spoke. "Those are hard words," he said.

"They are hard words. But they are true ones. You might say old Mr. Wentworth began the factory, but young Mr. Wentworth, what has he to do with the blame? He inherited it and must go on with the business. But I tell you, John, they are all to blame—from our side."

"You take a rattlesnake, or the copperheads. From their side, they shouldn't be blamed. They grew up on earth, but just because I know they can harm me or mine, I know I've got to kill one when I see it: and it isn't because I hate the snake as a snake, but because of the poison in his mouth.

"These owners have power, and their power is poison to our

young ones and to us. If you can take away the power, like you would cut the fangs from a snake, then you needn't have a grudge against the person. They're probably kind hearted (well, some of them), and full of good wishes to the world."

"Maybe," John spoke, "sometime they'll come to see they are doing us harm, and do better by us. I remember hearing a preacher who was a preacher to the rich say that some day the rich would get the love of God in their hearts and share everything half and half with the poor."

"As well expect a snake to come up and open its mouth gentle and humble for you t' take out the fangs."

They made a turn in the road. John Stevens looked back at the sun, as if he was trying to make out the time, but he did not suggest that they go back. John was glad, for he was not ready to go back.

"You know, John, I've traveled to the east and traveled to the west, as the ballad of John Hardy says. I have talked to many people, and with my eyes I've seen many things, curious, and some of them almost unbelievable. It's the same everywhere.

"Once in the West there was a strike of mining people. The owner of that mine was a God-fearing churchgoing man. He is one of the richest in the country. The miners struck for a better living, for they lived mighty poor—and this rich man that is good to his own children, and kind, and a builder of churches, had those people—who hadn't broken a law except the unwritten law that the poor must not speak for something better without crawling on their bellies before their owners—he had those people thrown out of their cabins. And when they put up tents to live in he sent soldiers down there and had two women and eleven children, I think it was, shot down. And not only were they shot, but those that were wounded were burned up with the tents. That man is what is called a good man."

"He must have been a hard man."

"No, he was just usual. And he didn't have t' use his own hands. There were paid servants to do this for him."

"You talked of a strike. There was one here, wasn't there? Hit's one of the things I wanted t' ask ye. I had almost expected t' find ye discharged, for there were some that came to our mill to get work that were discharged."

"I wasn't discharged," John Stevens said.

"Were you not in it?"

"I was in it, and in two before in the North, run by the same crowd. But my heart wasn't in it."

"Is it true they went off with the dues?"

"It's true. But that, to my mind, is a small thing compared to another thing I have against them."

"What was that?"

"Well—they want you to go up to a rattlesnake coiled in the middle of the road, and fondle him on the head, and say, 'Please, Mr. Rattlesnake, can I go by?'

"You see, they go on the supposition that I and the snake have got something in common. We have. We've got the road, and it's a public road, but unless I've got a gun or a big rock the snake has all the advantage.

"It's this they won't understand. They don't want you to fight. They simply ain't interested much in people that can't pay big dues. Sometimes they make a show of being interested, like here, but it peters out very soon. And then—they've got no further message. We have enough fear in us as it is. And they don't aim t' give us courage."

"Fear?" John asked.

"Yes, fear."

"I have not any fear," John said emphatically. It was something a man could not stand very well, to be told he was a coward. John himself was slow about getting up his anger but when he did, no man could walk over him.

He spoke again. "I'm not afraid of any man, not Mr. Wentworth or no one."

It was some time before John Stevens answered. "No," he said. "You are not afraid of Mr. Wentworth as a man. If he came down and tried to do harm to Bonnie, say, you would stand up to him. What you fear is his power, his poison. Don't you fear to lose your work? And if you were married with young ones, you'd fear that more. And don't Bonnie fear losing her work, and don't your Granpap fear his old age with no money? If it was demanded of him he would grovel in the dust at Mr. Wentworth's feet to keep the work he has. To get away from that fear, to show I was independent, I've traveled all over, and everywhere I've found my owner."

John Stevens looked back, squinting at the sun that shone almost straight in his face from the west. "We'd best turn back," he said.

They walked with their heads down, away from the sun, until some trees cut off the strongest rays.

"There are some," John said, "who seem to get on, by themselves."

"And there's less chance of that than there was. This country used to be open for those that wanted to get another chance. Now it's crowded with those struggling to make their way up. So if you want to get up you've got to push somebody down unless the start has been made before you, and then, ten to one, it was done in the same way."

John Stevens began to limp faster toward the house that was now where they could see it, through the trees that had no leaves on them. John was not ready to talk. There were things that had happened to him, and they had forced him to consider what was happening to himself and to others. He was trying to put events together, and make something of them. His trouble with Mr. Burnett, his friendship with Robert and the others—Robert's feelings about living—Emma's death.

Now he had received some words from John Stevens and those must be sorted out, so that he could try to fit them with the things which had happened. If he could do so, well and good. If he could not, he would perhaps try something else.

He ate supper with the others, then walked with John Stevens to the mill, which was not far off, and leaving him there found the road. He walked along it in the darkness that was getting blacker.

48

About four years after Emma's death Jim Calhoun had an accident in the mill that changed him and made his and Bonnie's life together more difficult. He was on night work, and because he was tired, or because he had been growing careless, no one could say, he broke his wrist in a frame machine. Doctor Foley, the same one who had come to Emma, set the wrist, but it did not heal, and the hand was cut off.

With a stump in place of a right hand Jim could not work in the mill. He got odd jobs around the village: but where he had been a man who took some pride in having his work done well, he became careless about everything, and uninterested. He had never been the best sort of husband, but Bonnie understood him, and had learned early not to expect too much. And she loved him. Loving was as natural to her as the breath she took into herself without thought, so she had a child every year. To them she gave every care she could, and was very proud of each one. The oldest, who had been born before Emma left them, was named Emma, the next was a boy, John, and there were two others, Laurel and Kirkland.

John was married to Zinie during the year that followed Emma's death. They had one child and another on the way; and lived in the same house with Bonnie. Together John and Bonnie managed to keep Granpap, who had lost his place as a watchman because he was too old and was caught asleep more than once.

At home, with nothing to do, Granpap lost all interest in life. He lay in bed most of the day, and at last stayed there. Until one evening, he called Bonnie and talked to her about his coming death, of which he was sure.

"I'm a-going t' my long home," he said.

"No," Bonnie told him. "You'll live t' be a hundred."

This was what she had told him so many times, but there was nothing else to say.

"No, Bonnie, I'll follow Emma soon. Maybe if the good Lord

had seen fit to let me stay in the country I might have lived. But hit was not t' be. . . . I want you and John t' give me a good funeral. And remember to turn my feet to the east, so I can meet my Lord face to face on Judgment Day. Now I want t' see John."

A few days afterward the old man died. He had asked for a tombstone, but this was something they could not afford. John cut out a headpiece from a slab of wood, and carved Granpap's name, John Kirkland, across the top. They set this up at the head of the grave.

With Granpap gone they all thought of moving to Bethune where a huge factory had been built by a northern manufacturer. They had seen word about it written in the papers for months before, and had heard many things—that new houses were being prepared for those who worked, with bath rooms and every sort of new device for making people comfortable.

The papers had great headlines across the top that were easy to read, saying that the people from the North who were building the factory were welcome. Everyone seemed happy about the new mill—especially those in the town. The stores and banks had signs of welcome in them, and even the preachers spoke of it, saying that at last the interests of North and South, which had been severed by the Civil War, were brought together again—the blue and the gray were one.

Zinie was rather cautious by nature, and she persuaded John to wait until others went to work in Bethune, so they might hear first how things went there. It was well they did wait. For, one by one, families came back, or those that stayed found they were no better off than they had seen before.

The bathrooms were there in the new houses. But the wages were lower, and no matter whether a man had one child or eight he must take in boarders; so people were forced to keep mattresses in the new bath tubs where a boarder of two of the youngest children could sleep. Sometimes when the boarder happened to be on the night shift the tub was used as a bed day and night. So John and Zinie remained at the Wentworth Mills.

One day, quite suddenly, in the twist room where he worked, big Jim Martin fell down on the floor. Doctor Foley said he died of heart trouble, for which he had been giving Jim medicine bought at his drug store.

Jim's death forced John and Zinie to break up the house with

Bonnie, for Jennie needed them to help with money, in order that all the Martin young might have enough food. Lillie was in the mill, and Jennie worked there, but this did not make enough for the rest to live on. They needed what John could bring in.

Bonnie could see that it was right for Zinie to go to her people, but she felt bereft when they were gone from her. She liked them both, and it had been more than good to have them in the house, especially since Jim Calhoun often stayed away for days together. Though the Company did not charge much for rent, she found it necessary to get a place that was cheaper.

In a field of broom straw, off Company land, she knew of a cabin that had been lived in by colored people. This would rent for a small sum. She moved in immediately; and one Saturday afternoon and Sunday cleaned the two rooms and kitchen leanto. She scrubbed the floors, and with a flour mixture pasted fresh newspapers over the walls.

During the day she left the children at home with five-year-old Emma. Each morning she rose at four, made her own breakfast, and left coffee and a pot of hominy with flour gravy on the stove where little Emma could reach them when the children woke. She left them regretfully, lying across the bed in which she had slept with them during the night. Thoughts of them stayed with her during the day while she walked before her looms. She was afraid a flame from the chimney might set fire to the house, and sometimes the fear that some accident had happened to one of them made her long to give up the work and rush back to see that they were well.

At night, being tired, she walked slowly home for part of the way. But as she neared the cabin, in spite of trying to be sensible, she would begin to walk fast and then to run. Only when she came just outside the cabin and heard their voices in the room, talking naturally, could her fears quiet down.

On Sundays she stayed away from church, partly because that was the only day on which she could be with the children. But she had lost interest in the church. Mr. Turnipseed had gone to Bethune, and a Mr. Simpkins had come to the Wentworth village. Even before she had moved to the cabin, Mr. Simpkins had made Bonnie angry, though she herself acknowledged at the time to Zinie that there was no good reason in her anger. The preacher was very much worked up over the way young people were behaving. He said they no longer had any reverence for parents: no longer any morals. The young girls went about painting their cheeks and lips and dancing unholy dances, learned from the moving pictures. They thought, not of God and heaven, but of the flesh and the devil.

Zinie said he was right, for recently Lillie, her younger sister, had gone away from the mill to work in the ten cent store in town. She still lived at home, but she painted herself, and danced, and even drank some while she was out late at night, with men who were not known in the village.

Bonnie felt that young people should enjoy themselves, and she sympathized too much with Lillie. Perhaps, she said to Zinie, the sort of time Lillie was having was not the best, but she could see that the girl was only feeling around to enjoy life so long as she could, while she was still young.

But the thing that really disturbed Bonnie was the preacher's insistence on the sacredness of the family, and his anger at those who did not keep their families together. Nothing would have pleased her more than to stay at home and raise her children in the best way she knew how. And there were many other women like her in the village. Mr. Simpkins seemed to think if they wished they could stay at home and have a life of comparative ease. Because his wife could stay at home, he thought that other men's wives could do the same. Bonnie could not go to church Sunday after Sunday and hear him scold them for letting the family and the home break up without getting too angry. So she stayed at home with her young ones.

She talked with John who came over sometimes—about the mill. At first she had been very glad to give the best she had to her work. Now she saved her strength wherever possible.

One day at the looms she was wondering where the money for cloth to cover the almost naked young ones would come from. And she thought, "Hit costs ten cents a yard. How much do I need?" She counted that up. Then another thought came. "I work at my looms and am paid fifty cents for making sixty yards of cloth. And to-day at the store I'm a-going t' pay ten cents a yard for the same cloth. The cloth I make for fifty cents is sold for six dollars."

She spoke of this to her brother and to John Stevens who had come for a visit, for John wanted Bonnie to get acquainted with his friend, and had brought him to her shack in the field, for she had a sick baby.

"Somewhere in between, hit seems that somebody makes five dollars and fifty cents," she said.

"Well, it seems so," John Stevens answered, looking at her and smiling a little. "But you see the owners, they figure that some money must be added to that cloth to pay for wear and tear on their machines and their buildings and such like."

"They pay themselves for wear and tear on the machines," Bonnie spoke. "But hit seems I don't get paid for wear and tear on myself."

She had spoken the words almost in fun, only trying to make a play with the words that John Stevens had spoken. But when she had said them she stopped short, for in those half playful words she felt that she had struck something that had been worrying her, some idea that had tugged at her while she worked, and at home.

She saw John and John Stevens give each other a look of understanding.

When they left after a short visit, for John Stevens must get back to his work since it was not his Sunday off, Bonnie held John back inside the door.

"He's nice," she said. "I liked him as soon as he set foot in the door. You bring him again."

The next day, about the middle of the morning, Bonnie came running into the twist room where John was working.

"John," she said, "John." He saw that she was pale and breathless. "Little Emma's come t' say the baby is very sick. You go for the doctor right away and send him."

"What's the matter with him?" John stopped his machines, but his sister was already gone, and the section boss was standing beside him.

Bonnie had sent her little girl back to the cabin. All the way over, stumbling on the road she wondered what the sickness might be. The cold he had been sick with for several days had been just like the colds all the children had at times. She cut across the field. The broomstraw, weak as it was, seemed to hold her back, and she pushed her way through as if it was a wall that she must break down.

Running toward the cabin she could hear no sound but her

own breathing, but at the place where the clearing began she could almost hear the stillness that surrounded the shack and filled it inside.

There in the room the other children were near the bed. The baby's head just showed above the bed clothes. Little Emma had one hand on the quilt as if she was hushing the baby to make it stop crying. Yet the child was not crying. The stillness she had felt outside continued in the room.

She hurried to the bed and pulled down the covers. The child was still. In her arms he lay without moving, but she had seen that his eyes were open. She shook him almost angrily, then held him close to her face. His lips touched her cheek, but there was no breath coming from his half open mouth. Then she had to accept what she had really known when she took him up. There was no life in him. She laid him down on the bed and turned to the other young ones.

The doctor was angry with her for not calling him before. The baby, he said, must have had pneumonia for two days at least. Bonnie was silent before him. There were words that came up in her, but with the child lying on the bed, she could not speak them.

When the funeral was over and Bonnie went back to the weave room, all who worked there were sympathetic and kind. Mary, the colored woman who swept on Bonnie's side of the room, came up and said:

"I heard about your baby, and I'm real sorry."

"Hit's kind of you t' say that," Bonnie told her as she had told the others. Now she could not speak of it. She reproached herself that she had not done something that might have prevented the child's death. If she had not thought of expense and called the doctor earlier. It was thinking of the money involved that had held her back.

Mary Allen came up to her again before the whistle blew for going home.

"My chile, Savannah," she said, "is a right smart gal. She's fifteen, and of cose can't work in the mill, so I'm trying to find her a place with some white folks in town. But I ain't yet found a thing. So if she could stay with your children for a few days until you get more peaceful in your mind, I'd be glad for her to do it."

Bonnie looked at Mary Allen, at her plump, good natured black face that was full of sympathy, and Mary Allen turned away. For a long time afterward Bonnie remembered with shame the thought that was behind the look she had given Mary. For she was thinking of what people said—that colored people were all shiftless and no account; and had believed what they said in face of the fact that Mary Allen did her work in the mill quietly and as if she was willing to do her best. There were days when she did not sweep so well. But there were also days when Bonnie felt that the threads might break and faults come into the cloth without her caring.

For Mary Allen sent her child to Bonnie that same evening. And after the first two days Bonnie left the children with her without any trouble in her mind. Savannah, skinny as her mother was fat, opened her eyes wide when Bonnie spoke to her of the things to be done for the children.

"Yes'm," she said. "We've got plenty of them at home. I knows what to do."

And she did know. Bonnie's terror about the other children left alone had been made so much greater by the death of one. And Savannah's presence during that week made her anxiety less. It was her need to have that anxiety lightened when the new grave had just been covered up that Mary Allen understood.

49

A LETTER sent by Bonnie reached Jim Calhoun, after following him from town to town. He came back and for a time he and Bonnie were reunited. With his one hand Jim helped around the cabin while Bonnie was at work. But he was very awkward with the young ones and irritable. One day he slapped little Emma, and though it was given with his left hand, the blow knocked her against the bed and cut a gash on her forehead.

That night Bonnie found Jim gone from the cabin, and Emma in bed with the rough bandage that Jim had put on her head lying on the pillow beside her.

She was almost glad something had made him leave her. It was not his fault that he had become worthless, not entirely, and she did not blame him after the first anger on Emma's account. But she gradually came to hope that he would find a life away from her. And she, loving her children, and the new one that was coming to take the place of the other baby, would find her joy in caring for them. She was still under thirty, yet she looked much older, and had no thought of another man.

Several months after Jim left, Ora came one night and helped to bring Bonnie's baby into the world. She was always regretting that she could not take Bonnie with her. That was impossible, for with her family and Sally's growing one their four-room house was full to overflowing.

While Bonnie was in pain she spoke to her of their life in the mountains. She told of the night when John was born and Granpap had to take her place at Emma's bedside. And though Bonnie knew the story, she told again about the storm and the frozen cattle.

When Bonnie could speak at all they talked of the members of the family. About Emma and Granpap who were gone, and Ora told how Young Frank had at last broken away from them and gone to live in a nearby town. He was, she thought, working as errand man for a grocer, though she was not sure, for the word had come through someone else. Young Frank could not write himself, and was probably too proud to get someone else to do it for him.

At least that was the explanation Ora gave, and Bonnie nodded agreement, and thought her own thoughts about Young Frank, and the others, until the time came when she thought only of herself.

She was back at work in ten days. And she found that during the ten days something had been happening. First, there was a tension that had not been there before. When she asked John about it, he spoke of a rumor that many were to be laid off, because new machinery was to be installed. Already they had the new device for tying threads. It was very interesting, and saved much work and trouble. It was held on the right hand like a pair of scissors, and when the thread broke a person simply had to press the ends of the thread together between a small device at the end, and there was the thread whole again. But no one, when they welcomed the new, had thought that a device or machine that would save work and trouble, meant that neighbors and friends would be put out of work. The tension in the mill was like the tension of people who know that a plague of small pox or some other disease has broken out, and no one knows who will be the next to go.

Almost everyone was laid off while the new machinery was being installed. It was almost a relief to get the word and know the worst at last. But when the machinery was in many were taken back, at less pay. But there were a thousand people who were turned out of the mill by the machines. For days after the thousands were put out there were processions of wagons piled with furniture going to the east and west, to the north and south, toward other villages. And neighbors spoke to neighbors with sorrow in their voices. They said, "It might be us next," as people speak of dying, when they look at a funeral.

Bonnie held on, and was glad of her place, for there were her four young ones to care for. She was in debt for the coming of her baby. The money she got each week was nine dollars, and sometimes not that much when there was a fault in the cloth. She made many figures at night on scraps of paper trying to work out a way to make the money go further than it seemed able to do. There were so many items:—rent, kerosene, life insurance, and in the winter one dollar and seventy-five cents a week for coal, and every other week, two dollars and twenty cents for wood—and in the summer wood was still needed for cooking. So, like all the rest, she had very little left for food and clothing.

And the children, dressed almost in rags, looked pale in spite of all she tried to do. Little Emma, who was almost ten, had the look of the mill on her though she had never stepped inside the factory but once. It was always that way. Those who had come down from the hills kept some of their healthiness, but the children of these and their grandchildren had the mark of the mill.

"The mark of the beast," John Stevens called it. They were sitting in his house one Sunday. John had come to Sandersville straight from the mill, for since the thousand had been dismissed he had been working until twelve Saturday night, beginning again at twelve on Sunday night.

John sat on the edge of his chair across the table from John Stevens. He wanted to ask something. There had been some words that his friend had repeated more than once. He had said "the message." "I'm looking for the message," something like that, but had never explained. The word ran in his head when he was at the frames, and could not reach any conclusion in his thoughts. He wanted to reason, yet always when he began, even when he went over things that John Stevens had said to him, his mind carried him back to hopelessness. He and Zinie would die without having really lived, and their young ones would do the same; and Bonnie growing old before his eyes would live and die, and her young ones would be mill hands like her. It went over and over in him, to the sound of the machinery.

Now he understood why Granpap and the others had said, "What is there to life, but to wait and hope for heaven." In his mind he would lie down as a hound does as it accepts a beating. Then the thought would come up in him that John Stevens had said there was a "message," and a little hope and life would rise up in him. Yet he found it was better to keep this down, for if he let any hope get in him then the realization that there was none became a sharp pain.

Yet he wanted to find out the furthest thing that John Stevens had to say, so that he could lie down and stay, knowing that there was nothing for them to look forward to but a life of going to the mill, coming home to rest for strength to work in the mill again. Over and over, forever and ever, Amen.

John Stevens fingered the Bible that was on the table before him. He was looking for a passage that he had promised to show John, a passage about the rich and the poor.

"I sometimes wonder," John said, watching the narrow, kindly face across the table, "why the preachers are always reminding us that death is the lot of all, rich and poor. They say, many times, death is not aristocratic. Hit's true, but I don't know why it is they talk so much that way. Hit seems they keep their eyes on death, and not on life."

"Do you know any preachers and their families?" John Stevens asked, and he let the pages of the Bible run through his hands: but he kept his kind eyes on John.

"Not well."

"I've been acquainted with some. They speak of death, but if you see and know them, you see they want to live. They have just as good food and clothing for themselves and their children as they can get, and every one of them tries his best to get the best education he can afford for his young ones. There are some who wish well to the poor, but there are mighty few that would fight to make their wishes come true. I mean fight for the coming of the message."

"Is it the gospel message you mean when you say that?"

"No, it's not the gospel message I mean."

He turned the pages of the book. "Here it is," he said and opened to a page toward the back. "If it's the gospel message they want, here's what they should preach." He read from the Bible. "Go to now, ye rich, weep and howl for your miseries that are coming upon you. Your riches are corrupted, and your garments are moth-eaten. Your gold and your silver are rusted: and their rust shall be for a testimony against you, and shall eat your flesh as fire. Ye have laid up your treasure in the last days. Behold the hire of the laborers who mowed your fields, which is of you kept back by fraud, crieth out: and the cries of them that reaped have entered into the ears of the Lord of Sabbaoth. Ye have lived delicately on the earth, and taken your pleasure: ye have nourished your hearts in a day of slaughter. Ye have condemned, ye have killed the righteous one: he doth not resist you."

"Are those words, right there, in the Bible?" John spoke in astonishment. John Stevens pushed the book across to him.

"Read for yourself," he said.

"I want t' show this to some others," John told him, and wrote down the chapter and name.

"Is that it, the message?" he asked hesitating, yet wanting to know clearly.

"No," John Stevens said. For a long time he was silent. When he spoke it was in his usual voice, but as he went on it became stronger and more full of meaning, as the machines when they first start up make little noise but soon their sound fills the whole room.

And John listened with all his attention, so that later he was able to repeat what he had heard. Not every word was the same, but the meaning and most of the words were just as John Stevens had spoken them.

"In that book," John Stevens said, "it tells you, 'The cries of them that reap have entered into the ears of the Lord of Sabbaoth.' Now, so far as I know, the sound of the sorrow of those that work has never been heard up yonder or wherever it might be they're expected to be heard.

"You speak of preachers who talk of death. I want to tell you now about people who speak of life: and who are killed for speaking so. No wonder the preachers speak of death to us poor, for if they spoke of life as these others have done, they would be punished by the rich.

"There were two men who were punished for speaking so. Both worked in a mill, though one of them later became a peddler of fish. They were people like you and me, though they were born in a country across the water, and could not speak our language very well. But they spoke in their own language, and part in our language to the poor. They spoke of life, and because they did the rich put them to death. The rich called them thieves and murderers. It was their excuse for murdering two innocent men. I would like to read you what these two 'thieves and murderers' said. I'll come back in a minute. A friend in the North sent me some of their sayings and letters. I'll come right back."

He returned with some papers and sat down again. The rustling of the papers sounded very loud in the still room.

"You remember," John Stevens said, "there in the Bible it says,

'Ye have condemned, ye have killed the righteous one: he doth not resist you.' These men didn't believe in resisting, but in just being good. And they were good. From these papers I'm going t' read you what these two 'thieves and murderers' said just before they were taken to the electric chair."

"They were killed in the electric chair?"

"Yes, and they walked in proud and strong, and one of them said, 'Good evening, Gentlemen,' for it was gentlemen that had done this thing to them. Not long before they went in for the gentlemen to watch them die, one of them wrote: 'This is our career and our triumph. Never in our full life could we hope to do such work for tolerance, for justice, for man's understanding of man as now we do by accident. Our words—our lives—our pains—nothing. The taking of our lives, lives of a good shoemaker and a poor fish-peddler—all. That last moment belongs to us—that agony is our triumph.'

"And they wanted to live, John. They wanted to enjoy life. And they thought of a world where all people would enjoy living. The day on which he was to die, one of them wrote a letter to his son. Here is part of the letter: 'So, Son, instead of crying' (he meant when they had killed him) 'be strong, so as to be able to comfort your mother, and when you want to distract your mother from the discouraging soulness, I will tell you what I used to do. To take her a long walking in the quiet country, gathering wild flowers here and there, resting under the shade of trees, between the harmony of the vivid stream and the gentle tranquillity of the mother nature, and I am sure that she will enjoy this very much, as you surely would be happy for it. But remember, always, Dante, in the play of happiness, don't use all for yourself only, but down yourself just one step, at your side, and help the weak ones that cry for help, help the persecuted and the victim, because they are your better friends: they are the comrades that fight and fall as your father and Bartol fought and fell yesterday for the conquest of the joy of freedom for all the poor workers.' "

There was the sound of a heavy sigh in the quiet room.

"I told you once," John Stevens said, "about workers being killed in the West. This happened in the North. I could tell you many more stories of people being killed by the rich because they wanted something better. I want you to feel that you are not the only one, that there are many others wanting what you and Bonnie and all those others in the village want, 'the joy of freedom for all the poor workers.'

"And the rich will never give it to us. We must take it for ourselves. You understand that? Take it for ourselves. They couldn't give it to us if they wanted to, even if they had that kindness your preacher once spoke about: for they have made something that is bigger than they are, bigger and stronger. But they like what they have. Don't you forget that, and they're going to keep it. And so we won't do anything about our misery, they keep us in the darkness of ignorance and talk about death, to keep our eyes on death and heaven, so we won't think too much about life. We are taught that to struggle is a sin.

"But it ain't a sin, John. People must learn that. We must work in a strike, but there is something else. We must go beyond the strike to the message . . . that we must join with all others like us and take what is ours. For it is our hands that have built, and our hands that run the machines and ours that dig the coal and keep the furnaces going; and our hands that bring in the wheat for flour. And because we have worked and suffered, we will understand that all should work and all should enjoy the good things of life. It is for us who know to make a world in which there will not be masters, and no slaves except the machines: but all will work together and all will enjoy the good things of life together."

"Can hit be done?"

"It has been done," John Stevens said, "though it isn't yet finished."

He spoke more words. They talked long into the night, so that John, reaching his work late the next morning, was told that he would lose a day's pay for his lateness. He did not hear everything the overseer said to him, and it was just as well, for the things said were not pleasant enough for a person to enjoy. He knew this dimly, yet there was something else in him greater than the overseer's words. He stood before his machines with a joyous feeling swelling in him.

50

THAT week something unusual happened in the mill. People at work at their looms or frames suddenly found themselves being watched by strange men. If one of them went for a drink of water, or something more important than a drink of water, the man stood looking at his watch, and put down something in a book when they came back. It was very distressing, for the watching kept up over several days. But it had to be endured, for everyone knew that more people were to be laid off very soon, and each was hoping against hope that he would not be one of these.

In the third week hank clocks were installed on the machines, and people were paid by the time the hank clock registered. Sam Carver who worked on the night shift in the card room, and knew something about electricity, tinkered with his clock, and made his wages very high. The others did not approve of his behavior. They spoke to Sam in no uncertain way, but he went right on. "For," he said, "they aim t' get as much out of me as they can, so I aim t' get the same from them."

For all except Sam the wages went down further. And there were other changes. The mill took off all helpers, which meant that boys and girls were left without work, and slubber hands had to drag in the creels, and there were no more doffers, but people must doff their own spools and mark them, which took up time from the frames and so cut down their pay. Card hands were forced to run forty cards instead of twenty-one and were given less for the double work.

Automatic spoolers were put in, and when this was done thirty-five people were used where one hundred and sixty had been used before. Weavers who had tended eight to twenty looms now had nearly one hundred each: but when it was found that people fainted too often the number was reduced a little. Most of the women had to give up weaving. Ora stayed on, for old as she was, she was still as strong as a horse, as she herself said. It was very different with Frank, because he had one lung gone from tuberculosis.

Ora said a thing that many others repeated after her. "I don't run the machines any more," she said. "They run me."

Everyone tried to take it all in the right way. They had been told how to take it. In each room Mr. Randolph, the manager, spoke to them. He said: "There is nothing that can disrupt the sincere spirit of brotherly love which for so long has been a bond between the management and the workers in our mills. Now when the management finds it necessary because of hard times to tighten up on time and wages, we hope that same spirit will continue so that we work together in harmony and peace."

For several weeks everyone tried to accept his words. For one thing they were naturally easy going, and for another they felt that behind Mr. Randolph's spoken words were others which said, "If you don't like this, there are plenty of others who will."

Then, like a cloud that comes without any warning over the top of a mountain, a feeling of misery came over the mill. Before there had been a feeling of deadness, which nothing perhaps could arouse, a feeling of stolid endurance. Now the feeling was different. It was one of acute, active misery. People fainted, others became sick because of the hard work, and lack of food, for in most of the homes, where there had been at least plenty of hominy and bacon, there was not even enough of these.

And always there was the thought of those who were waiting for a place if one of them should give up. There were so many who came to the village every day looking for work. They were lined up or in groups every morning outside the office.

Word went around in the mill that there were spies who listened for any word of complaint, so people became afraid to speak to their neighbors in the rooms, and so complaints were whispered from friend to friend, and even then there was suspicion.

Bonnie found Mary Allen crying at her work one day. Her tears were splashing on her hands that held the broom handle. Some of them she wiped away with her apron, but Bonnie could see them plainly. She went over and spoke to Mary, leaving the hated clocks to register that she was taking time off.

Mary was sweeping, and her eyes were looking at the floor. Bonnie, to get her attention, touched her on the shoulder.

"What's the matter?" she asked.

"I've got my time," Mary said. She looked up at Bonnie and then down again, and pushed the broom, as if she was afraid to stop working even for a moment. But she had really stopped.

"To-day is my last day," she said. "They're making two sweepers do the work of four. And I ain't one of them."

She looked up then and smiled at Bonnie, trying to make the best of it. "Many is called," she said, "but few is chosen."

"I've got fifty cents," Bonnie said to her. "You wait here till I go to the washroom."

"No," Mary insisted. "You better keep that. I got my pay to-day, my las' pay and right now it's enough. You keep your fifty cents, honey. But I thank you just the same."

"You're going t' take hit," Bonnie insisted stubbornly. And at last she did persuade her friend to accept what she had.

At closing time John was waiting for her outside the door of the mill. "Take the young ones to Ora's," he said, "and come to our house to-night with Frank and Ora."

Bonnie spoke out loud, "What is it?"

But she saw that his voice was very quiet and still when he spoke, and she lowered her own before she had finished.

"Don't tell anybody you're coming," he said. "Just come."

She saw that he was speaking of something very important. "I'll come then."

When he left her she saw that he went up to others and spoke the same words to them. He did it casually, as if he was talking with good friends, and that of course was what he was doing. Then he came back to her and they walked on together.

John spoke to her quietly, for there were people still around them. "A man came up to me the other night, and asked which way I was going. I told him. And he said, 'How would you like to come up to my boarding house. I'm boarding with Mrs. Sevier.' I looked at him, for I wasn't sure he was a friend. He spoke in a way that we don't speak. So I asked, 'What do you want?' And he said, 'John Stevens sent me.' Then I knew. I went up to the boarding house, and we sat there and listened to the victrola in the dining-room that was empty, for everybody had eaten. Then he said to me, 'What do you think of unions?' And I said. 'I think they're good.' So we talked. He's a-coming to-night. His name is Tom Moore, and he has worked in a mill the same as this one, only in the North."

The next day people who had been to the meeting the night before spoke to others, in the washroom, and at the frames, or between bites of food at lunch time. And that night Ora's house where they met was filled to the doors. They pulled down the curtains and had one light on, for the meetings were to be kept secret.

For a week they went on and had to be held in more than one house, since so many wanted to hear the words that Tom Moore had to speak. And they had words to speak for themselves, words that had been kept hidden. Everyone understood the importance of keeping what was going on a secret until it was time to carry out certain plans. And they were careful. But there must have been a spy among them.

Tom Moore went away on Saturday to another village which had sent for him, for there were many places where people were discontented.

On Monday, about the middle of the morning, something unexpected happened. In the room where John worked the section boss was summoned to the office. He came back, walked up to John and said, "Here's your time. You're to leave the mill right away."

He spoke softly, but John answered him in a loud voice, loud enough for the others to hear.

"What did you say?" he asked.

"You heard me," the section boss told him.

"I want you t' say hit for others t' hear."

"All right. You've got your time. Now get out."

Someone near by heard the loud talk and went up to the two men. Others, seeing that something was wrong, left their frames and gathered around.

"Will you tell me why?" John asked.

"No, I won't."

John looked around him. He recognized some of those who had come to the meetings. One of them was Jesse McDonald.

The section boss turned to Jesse. "And you, too," he said. "You're fired."

"Anybody else?" John asked.

"Not in this room."

He and Jesse were members of the committee that had been elected at one of the secret meetings.

"Get back to work, you," the section boss said to the other men.

Some of them slunk off to their frames, but others stood by John and Jesse. They spoke in low tones to each other.

"Get back to work," the section boss cried out, "all except those two."

"No," one of the men said slowly, "I reckon if they go I'm a-going too."

"And me," another one said.

"Well, John. It looks like we're in for it. Let's go," another neighbor spoke up.

The overseer came in the room and up to the group.

"Now, men," he said firmly, "get to work."

The men looked at him. In the short time that they had stood together they had felt something. They had felt a sense of standing up for each other. For so long each had been alone with his family striving after enough food to keep from starving, and enough clothes to keep from going naked. And they had been alone in that fight. Now they were going to stand together, side by side, and there came to them the feeling of strength.

They looked at each other with a new light in their eyes, as if they were seeing each other for the first time. And very slowly, almost imperceptibly, they smiled, before their faces turned to Dewey Fayon, the overseer.

One of them said. "We'll see you again, Dewey." And as John turned toward the door they walked with him.

In the hall they met others coming out. Almost the same thing had happened in the rooms where Bonnie, Ora, Frank and ten others had been given their time. Those who had attended the secret meetings, and some who had not, but were indignant over the dismissal of their friends, went out from the mill. In the middle of the morning they walked out into the sunshine. It was an amazing thing, that they felt the courage to leave their machines. There was excitement in this thought, yet they still felt the mill on them, and were quiet and thoughtful, for if this was a new thing they had done, it was also a serious thing.

They stood in the road near the gate, and did not look back at the mill which stood behind them, huge and quiet except for the low throb of the machines—until John called to them.

He had climbed up a little way on the thick wire fence.

"Come to this place to-morrow, at half past eleven," he said.

As they walked on the road people began talking, for they

had been as if they were dumb before. But the talking was not loud. They seemed to have a fear that the mill would hear them.

John spoke to Bonnie who was walking beside him.

"We've got to let Tom Moore know about this."

"I know hit," Bonnie said. She raised her face, and he saw that it was lit up with the warm fire that had not been there since she was first married.

"I'll find him." John said. "You leave your young ones with Ora, and all of you keep your eyes on the mill. I'll find him and get back to-night if I can."

51

BONNIE stood on Ora's porch with her baby in her arms, watching for John. It was the morning after they had walked out of the mill and John had not yet returned. Somewhere, she knew, he was looking for Tom Moore, or they together were hurrying to get back. When would they come?

She was anxious and disturbed, for something must be done very soon. She thought of John Stevens, but it was too late to get him a message. If they did not hear from John during the day, then someone must go for John Stevens that night.

She thought again of the words which John Stevens had spoken, when she had talked with him at different times. At first she had not believed in his words, for they seemed too fanciful to be true. Then she had been convinced that he had a message that was founded in the facts of her everyday life. It seemed reasonable and sure. For the present she was interested in the immediate need, the things that Tom Moore had suggested they might hope to win—a day in which they would work only eight hours, and pay that was not less than twenty dollars. To Bonnie, who had been receiving nine dollars a week, twenty seemed riches.

Ora came out of the house. "You don't see him yet?" she asked and stood beside Bonnie on the porch.

They sat on the steps and talked; Ora tall above Bonnie with her rawboned old face looking fine and earnest.

"We've got t' win," she said.

"Yes, and us women have got to fight hard, like the men," Bonnie added.

"There'll be some who'll say women should stay at home, and not mix in men's affairs. But they don't say hit when we go out t' work, and I can't see why they should say hit now."

"Yes, if we work out, we've got a right to speak."

"Is that Dewey Fayon's wife a-coming up the street?"

"I don't know. Is hit?"

"I believe so. I wonder what she wants."

Dewey Fayon lived on Strutt Street, and his wife did not often come down into the village, but stayed on her street or went into town where she had friends. She was a stout woman, but very pretty. She wore high heeled slippers and at every moment a person watching expected to see her topple over on one side; and often she did turn her ankle so that her heels were continually run down at the edges.

She came and stood right before Ora and Bonnie as if she had planned to speak with them.

"Good morning," she said.

"Good morning," Ora told her.

"Well, it looks as if you're not working to-day."

"Yes'm," Ora said. "Hit looks as if you're not a-working either."

"I was just walking around."

"And we're just setting here."

"Is John around?" Mrs. Fayon asked, looking at Bonnie.

"No'm."

"You know where he is?"

"Somewheres. I don' know."

Mrs. Fayon moved her heavy weight from one high heel to the other.

"Set down, if you want," Ora said. She could not keep a person who was visiting her standing for long.

"Well, I'll have to be going soon. So I won't sit down. Is it most twelve?"

"I'll see," Bonnie told her and went in to look at the alarm clock. She wanted to see for herself how much time there was. It was ten minutes of eleven. And everyone was to meet at the mill at half past.

She went out and told Mrs. Fayon the time.

"Well, I'll stay a few minutes," Mrs. Fayon said. "But I won't sit down."

"You know," she said, not looking at them. "I want to tell you something as a friend. People are talking about you two. It's getting around that you want t' be like men. And people say the Bible says let women look to their houses and let men tend to the world. It's what I do," she said, looking very righteous. "And I believe in it like Preacher Simpkins does."

"Well," Bonnie began, but Ora put her big hand out and laid it on Bonnie's arm.

"The Bible says women should be in subjection to their husbands."

Ora did not answer. She was silent as a mountain in an uninhabited country, and Bonnie sat like her, very still. Only the baby moved in her arms.

"It's well said," Mrs. Fayon told them. "I always let my husband decide everything. He wants to be master in his own house."

She looked up at Bonnie and Ora who sat looking out into the distance, which was bounded by the house across the road. Now Bonnie did not want John to come, not while Mrs. Fayon was there. She was hoping that he would not come—not at once.

"Well," Mrs. Fayon said to the silent faces above her. "I suppose I'll have to be going."

"Must ye?" Ora asked.

"Well, it seems people around here aren't used to polite conversation," Mrs. Fayon said and turned away from them. At the corner one of her heels stuck in the mud, and she had to lean over and pull the shoe out, while she balanced on the other.

Bonnie and Ora watched, then looked at each other.

"I don't like t' feel evil toward anybody," Bonnie said. "But I did enjoy seeing that."

"She just came snooping to find out what she could."

"Yes. I got t' know it, though, only after she asked us, 'Where is John?' "

Bonnie went inside to lay the sleeping child on the bed, and change her dress. That morning she and Ora had washed and ironed their extra dresses. For they felt a need to dress in a way that would point out to others the importance and splendor of the occasion when they went down to the mill.

"Hit's twenty after," Bonnie said to Ora. She looked at her anxiously. Perhaps they might be forced to take the responsibility of those whom John had told to meet at the gates of the mill at half past eleven. "You think . . ." she began but Ora interrupted.

"We'd better go along," she said firmly. "Maybe they'll come. Maybe they're there already."

In front of the mill, some distance back from the gate, but filling the road far down on each side, were those who had walked out the day before. Like Bonnie and Ora the women were dressed in the best they had, and the men looked as if they had prepared for church.

Bonnie and Ora joined the crowd of friends and neighbors. There was a feeling like that of an outdoor church meeting in the mountains, for people were talking as neighbors do who have not seen each other in a long while.

There were some who had not come out the day before, but who did not go to work that morning, and they were welcomed by the others, as if the open road was a house full of hospitable people. There was a great deal of talk, and some almost hysterical laughing from the women especially. From a distance it all sounded joyful, and in a way the crowd was joyful. But under the joy was a tense waiting, and perhaps some fear. For across the road, just outside the high wire fence of the mill, stood guards who carried sawed-off shot guns, and it was easy to see that in their pockets were pistols ready for use.

Bonnie saw that John and Tom Moore had not yet come. People came up to her and asked, "Where is John?" And she had to say, "Just wait, he'll be here soon," though she was not sure, and watched the road.

An automobile came from the east, the direction of the town. As it approached them Bonnie saw that it was the old car that Reskowitz had loaned to Tom Moore.

The car stopped right in front of the mill, cutting off the sight of the guards. John stepped out, and then Tom Moore. They reached into the back of the car and began taking out bundles of papers. Strikers crowded around and took bundles from them. Soon the papers were distributed, and those who could read the printing spoke it aloud to the others.

"To all spinners, loom fixers, weavers, twisters, carders, frame hands, inspectors, and all other workers of the day and night shifts:" it began.

And spoke of the reasons for a strike, and asked those who felt the need for one to come out to the railroad crossing where speakers would talk to them right after the twelve o'clock whistle that day.

Tom Moore drove off in the car to prepare a place for the speaking, and John remained to talk with those who had assembled.

"When the twelve o'clock whistle blows," he said, "we must give these papers to those who come from the gates. Each and everyone must receive one of these." He held up one of the papers.

"Did Zinie come?" John asked Bonnie who was standing by him.

"No," Bonnie said, and looked at John with sympathy.

"She's somewhat fearful."

"Yes, I know."

"There's the whistle."

The whistle blew loud and long. Bonnie saw that the guards lifted their guns, but during the whole time that day they did not move from their places. At that time when the mill was confident, the deputies had orders only to keep people out of the compound.

The two lines of workers came from the mills. Those outside crowded up to them in the road and gave out the pieces of paper on which were printed the important words. They also spoke to the ones who had just come out of the gates.

"We've got to stand together," they said.

"You won't go against your neighbors, will ye?" they asked.

And many said, "Come to the meeting, and see."

On the side toward the mill the railroad embankment sloped down into a wide grassy place. On the slope, near the track, and high up where all could see any speakers, Tom Moore had constructed a round platform made from two large packing cases.

When Bonnie with John and Ora reached the grassy place there were already many people there. John went up to Tom Moore who was standing beside the platform, for John was to speak when Tom Moore finished. They watched the crowds that came along the mill road and gathered with the others already there. Presently Tom Moore said, with excitement under the quiet of his voice, "It's time to begin."

He was not a tall man, but his voice was strong and confident.

"Fellow workers," he began.

"Yesterday some of your fellow workers were dismissed from the mill without any reason being given. We all know they were good workers. But they were suddenly given their time. Why? Because they wanted to start up a union here. But the mill owners did not realize that they were dealing with people and not machines. You can throw out a machine that doesn't work as you want it and the other machines will go right on working for the owners. But in this case the owners were dealing with people, people who have a sense of loyalty to their neighbors, to their fellow workers—people who possess something of pride in themselves, and a sense of justice to their own. Some of these people who knew why our fellow workers were dismissed followed them out of the mill. It was one of the finest things I have ever known.

"Now we want to share with the rest of you the reasons for this union. We have got to better our conditions. We are nothing but slaves. And who gets the benefit of our hard toil? Our families? No. Our children are forced to leave school at an early age to work long hours in the mill, in order that we and they may live. The owners are making good money, while through the use of the hank machines most of us do not know what our wages will be by the end of the week, except that we know they will not be enough.

"People have been laid off, and no one knows who will be next. What is left for us to do but make a fight for our own? How else can we improve our lives, raise our wages, shorten the working day, protect ourselves from insults, win for ourselves and our children the opportunities of education?

"The mill owners are against us, and naturally so—for the worse off we become, the better off they are. Our strength lies in standing together. The owners of the mills will call this treason and bad faith, but do not worry over those charges. You need only to be concerned with treason against your own people, against your neighbors and friends, those who work with you, and are now trying to get better lives for you and all that are dear to you. Be true to yourselves and your own, and you can't go far wrong.

"Some will wonder, 'How will we eat, if we go out of the mill?' Well, it can't be said that we eat very well as it is. But there are other workers in this country, and there are other people who will stand up for you, and send down money for food."

He went on speaking, and Bonnie, moving about in the crowd, heard words that gladdened her. For the words and the faces that were concentrated on Tom Moore, looking up to him where he stood on the boards, said to her that people were hearing something they had longed to hear, but had not known that it was on the face of the earth.

Toward the end of his talk Tom Moore said, "I want to know how many will stay out of the mill. All those who will . . ." Bonnie heard this much and then she could hear no more.

From the railroad siding near the station a freight train came up to the crossing and stopped just behind the platform. Tom Moore stopped speaking, thinking it would go on, for the noise it made prevented those further away from hearing him. But it did not go away. On the step below the engineer Dewey Fayon stood with his sawed-off shot gun in his hand and looked out over the crowd. Then he looked up and spoke to the engineer. From the bowels of the engine came clouds of steam. Tom tried to go on speaking, but the steam cut him off from the crowd. Added to this was another interruption. The engine began to whistle, long piercing whistles, so that those on the speaking stand were obliterated by the steam cloud and by the noise.

In the cloud Tom Moore spoke with his mouth close to John's ear. "We've got to let them know about the meeting to-night. They're breaking up. Quick. Take two or three others and go on the road across the track. I'll run down on the road to the mill. Say, 'Meet this evening at six in the vacant lot behind Mrs. Sevier's boarding house.' "

The crowd was leaving the meeting place. When he saw this Dewey Fayon gave a sign to the engineer, and with a last high derisive whistle the engine backed onto its siding.

52

On Railroad Avenue, a short avenue two blocks from the mill, there was about a block of stores that were empty. Tom Moore and John rented an old wooden one-story structure for the union office and two doors away the bottom floor of a two-story brick building for a place from which to give out food and other relief.

"Now," Tom Moore said when that was accomplished, "we must send a telegram—for help."

"They will send help from up there?"

"As much as they can. And some people will come down. We've got to work hard. In a week everybody here will have used up all the fatback and flour they have on hand."

Bonnie, Ora, Sally and some of the other women helped with the stores. Once Ora missed Bonnie, and found her out at the back of the store sitting on a keg. She was leaning over writing laboriously on an old brown paper bag she had found in the store.

"Why, I thought you had left us," Ora exclaimed.

"No," Bonnie said. "I was just writing something."

"What is it?" Ora bent over Bonnie's shoulder.

"You see, Ora, I was thinking about us, and I thought of a ballad we could sing. I thought of some words."

"Read hit to me."

"It's not very fine. I just thought of some words, and wrote them down."

"You read hit."

"I could sing better."

"Then sing."

"It's a mill mother's ballad," Bonnie explained. "I thought about us leaving our young ones . . ."

"You let me hear it," Ora said, knowing that Bonnie was trying to put her off.

So Bonnie sang, faltering at first, from the paper, on which words were scratched out and written over—until she had found the words she needed.

"We leave our homes in the morning.
We kiss our children good-by.
While we slave for the bosses
Our children scream and cry."

"It's all I've got so far," she said.

"It's real nice," Ora told her, really admiring. "I'm a-going t' tell Tom Moore and John so you can sing for all of us."

"Oh no. It's not good enough."

Bonnie slipped from the keg, and was going inside again to help, but Ora pressed her down again with one hand on her shoulder.

"You sit right there and finish, Bonnie. We've got enough t' help inside. You write that ballad. We've got t' reach people's hearts as well as their stomachs."

From the relief store that evening they went to the meeting behind Mrs. Sevier's boarding house. Bonnie had brought her covers over and her young ones were sleeping on the floor at Ora's, so she could leave them at night. The meeting was in a field, and soon after the time set the place was almost full. After the speaking the people did not leave at once and Bonnie moved among them. Lillie Martin who was married and was now Lillie Thatcher was there with her husband's father, old Ed Thatcher.

Lillie had married Tom Thatcher, one of the wild young men of the village. And it was a queer thing, but one that sometimes happened: after her marriage Lillie had settled down, but Tom kept up the sort of life he had led when he and Lillie ran around to the horror of all good churchgoing people.

"Where's Tom?" Bonnie asked her.

"In the mill," Lillie turned away, so that she might not have to answer again.

"We'll make him come out in the morning," Ed told her.

The people assembled had voted to picket the mills in the morning. This is what Tom Moore told them: "There are people like those who called a strike in Sandersville some years ago. These people would say to you, 'Now you go home and stay there and we'll talk with the owners and arrange everything for you.' Then they will go to the owners and say, 'You and me must come to an understanding.' And they will bargain over you like people bargain over the counter for a piece of goods. And you are the goods. They call it collective bargaining. And it is collective bargaining. For those strike leaders collect our dues, and the owners of the mills collect our blood and bone, and our children's lives.

"You all know how in the frame rooms the rove is drawn and twisted to make it stronger. First, six strands are put together to make a stronger thread. Well, we've got to stick together just like that rove. We've got to show fight. We've got to picket the mill and get all those still in there working for the owners to come out with us. And when we've shown that we can all stick together, then we will elect a committee from among us to talk with the owners. And the committee will come back and report, so we can vote on what we want to do. No one will decide what is best for us but ourselves."

It was this talk which had made Ed Thatcher say what he did. Many people felt after Tom Moore and the other speakers had finished that they could clean out the mill next morning.

Bonnie saw young Henry Sanders standing near the box from which the speakers had said their words. His mother, bent and scrawny, old in work, was at one side. Around her, varying in age, but not much in size, were the eight young children that her dead husband had left her. Henry was the oldest, and he was sixteen, with the burden of them all on him, for his mother was a sick woman. He had worked in the mill since he was ten and had to put newspapers in the heels of his shoes to make him taller. Now, at sixteen, nearing seventeen, he had grown no larger than he was at ten or eleven. But he did the work of a man.

"How are you?" Bonnie said to Henry's mother. She felt a loving care toward all the people, and a gratefulness to them for having come out, for seeing that this was the best thing to do.

Henry came up to them. "Hit looks as if there's going t' be a strike," he said, when Mrs. Sanders had answered Bonnie's question.

"I'm s' glad t' see you out," Bonnie said to him.

"Well," Henry told her. "I figured we was starving anyway, and might as well starve on our feet putting up a good fight."

"Hit's right," Bonnie turned to Mrs. Sanders, "I didn't have enough t' feed my young ones, let alone cover their backs."

Henry touched her arm. "Somebody's a-calling ye."

"Where?"

Then Bonnie heard Ora's voice. "Bonnie, Bonnie Calhoun,"

and Ora came pressing through the crowd. Behind her was Tom Moore.

"They want ye t' get up on the box and sing your ballad," Ora said.

A chill went through Bonnie. She had written the ballad because it had come to her, but she had not thought of getting up before neighbors and friends to sing. Her singing had all been done with other people.

"No," she drew back from Ora's hand that was pushing her toward the platform. "I can't, Ora." She was very frightened. Later she became accustomed to the singing. But for the first few times she dreaded getting up before the people as she did now.

Tom Moore said, "People don't seem to want to go home. We'd like for them to hear something, and have had enough speeches. If you'll sing it will help."

"Well, I can try."

They helped her on the stand. People turned to look and she felt their eyes on her. The faces were expecting something which she must give them.

"Friends," she said, "I am the mother of five children. One of them died because I had t' work in the mill and leave the baby only with my oldest child who was five and didn't know how to tend it very well. And with four left I have found it hard t' raise them on the pay I get. I couldn't do for my children any more than you women on the money we get. That's why I have come out for the union, and why we've all got t' stand for it. And it's why I have made up a ballad about a mill mother. So they have told me t' sing it for ye. And so I will."

She stood with her hands straight at her sides and sang in a high clear voice that reached to the edge of the crowd.

"We leave our homes in the morning.
We kiss our children good-by.
While we slave for the bosses
Our children scream and cry.

"How it grieves the heart of a mother
You every one must know.
But we can't buy for our children;
Our wages are too low.

"It is for our little children
That seem to us so dear.
But for us nor them, dear workers,
The bosses do not care.

"But listen to me, workers:
A union they do fear.
Let's stand together, workers,
And have a union here."

There was a silence when she had finished. She stood, rather uncertain what to do next, on the stand. Then someone in the middle of the crowd called out, "Sing it again." Others took up the words and from all sides came the demand, "Sing it again."

"Now I will," Bonnie agreed, "if you'll all join in when you can. You all know the tune, for hit's 'Little Mary Fagan,' so just listen to the words."

Some joined in. Then it had to be sung again, and before long many were singing together the Mill Mother's Ballad. When it began to grow dark the meeting broke up, and they went home to sleep or talk in preparation for the picket line next morning.

It was dark when they went home. And it was dark next morning when they gathered in the road outside the wooden store that had been rented for the union office.

Tom Moore met John at the door of the office. The light from the electric bulb in the store shone full on John.

"What's that in your hand, John?" Tom Moore asked.

"Why," John answered, "you can see. Hit's my gun."

"I thought," Tom Moore said straight out, "John Stevens had made you understand better than that."

"Hit's a fight," John insisted. "And this is the way I know how to fight."

"Are all the men armed?"

"Most."

"Come here," Tom Moore pulled him into a corner of the store, for other people had come in.

Presently John laid his gun on the counter and remained beside it, while Tom Moore went out to the others who were standing in the darkness up and down the street.

"Bring me a chair," he said to one of the boys.

He stood on the chair with the outside wall of the store behind him and spoke to the faces that he could not see.

"Some of our friends here," he called out and his voice sounded hollow in the early morning air. It seemed to be going nowhere, for there was no light yet. "They have taken down their shot guns or their pistols, and have said, 'Now I am ready to fight.' I want to say to you, we can't fight in that way now. We must use peaceful means to gain what we want. It isn't that I want to keep you from fighting in the way you are used. But I know from experience we must fight with numbers. We must overcome with numbers and with spirit and determination. John McClure came this morning with his shot gun. Now he understands that it is best for him to leave it here. He is in there standing by the counter. And I want to ask all you men to go there and leave your weapons with him."

Someone called out, "What about the Law? They're armed."

"They are, because they're afraid of us. They have got as many weapons as a porcupine has quills, and if they should drive us back, which they won't, they would speak of that as if it was a fine thing that they had subdued unarmed people. But we must go unarmed—first because we want the women and children along to help picket and don't wish for them to get hurt, and second because it's the best thing to do—and I'll have to ask you to take my word for that.

"I hope all those with weapons will go into the store. John McClure will care for them all, and give them back when you come from the mill."

He waited. One man stepped from the dark shadows of the crowd and went into the store. Others followed. They filed into the store and laid their weapons sorrowfully on the counter before John. He stood before them without a word. His head was bowed over, and he kept his eyes on the pile of guns and pistols and knives that were being heaped on the counter. When all had come he hid the weapons under the counter and left one of the boys on guard, for he had to help with the picket line.

As they neared the factory, marching two and two, John saw that the lights were on as if a whole force of workers was expected. Light had come, though it was only a pale glow from the east, and he could make out the forms of the deputies moving outside the wire fencing of the mill. He was watching them and did not see what was just before him. Something came across his belly and almost knocked the breath out, for he was walking fast. Frank said, "They've got a rope across the street." And it was so. A thick rope, doubled, was strung from one side of the street to the other.

The line behind them came pressing on and spread out over the whole street against the rope. Ora was at the end.

"We've got t' break it," she called out, and pushed against the rope, until she stood out from the rest pushing. They were soon with her, until they made a semi-circle in the road pushing against the rope, but held back at the ends where it was fastened. The rope snapped at one end, suddenly, so that some at that end fell to the ground. They were soon on their feet, and formed in twos again, to keep up the march toward the mill.

At the mill gates the armed deputies with the butts of their guns forced the line into the road. They stood there, the people in the line, and called out to the deputies, most of whom were the higher-ups in the mill—people they knew very well.

Soon the workers began coming and they concentrated on these, for it was necessary to get all to leave the mill and stay together outside. The more who were out, the better chance there was to win.

Tom Thatcher came down the walk and Lillie stepped forward.

"Come with us, Tom," she begged him. "Don't go against your own."

And Ed Thatcher who had lived in the mountains spoke to his son in a loud voice, "Be ye a coward, Son, that you can't stand up for your own?"

But Tom went sullenly into the mill, guarded by two of the police with their guns, one on each side of him.

Lillie called after him. "Ye needn't be so afraid, Tom. We ain't a-going t' hurt ye. We're just sorry for ye."

But there were many who turned right at the gate and joined the long line: and when they did, a shout went up, and they were welcomed by friends and acquaintances.

When the whistle for work blew the long line went back toward the office. There, with some words from John, they returned home. When the total was counted up they found that nearly all had come out. It was a great triumph. The Wentworth Mill was almost empty of workers. There were perhaps seventeen left in the mill.

53

For two days the mill did not try to bring in anyone to take the places of the strikers. Months before they had selected the best workers and laid off the others. Now they wished, if possible, to keep these since it would hold back production to take on new hands, or those who were not skillful with the machines.

So they waited for the workers to come back of their own accord, and when they did not, but picketed the mill, succeeding in getting almost everyone out, they did some positive things toward bringing the strike to an end.

First they sent for the leaders separately. Mr. Burnett, in the office, made certain promises to each one. To John he said: "You are a fine worker and we want you back. If you will come we will give you two months rent free, and forget that you have ever been out."

And John asked, "Can we keep the union?"

Mr. Burnett answered no. So John returned to his people. Each one who was called in was asked the same question, and asked the same one in return that John had asked, "Can we keep the union?" and was answered, "No."

The third morning a truck arrived at the relief store. It was piled high with boxes and bags of food, and toward the front there were clothes. All had been sent by workers and others who were interested in the struggle that was going on. In the front seat of the truck were two young women who had come down to help with the food. They brought a message from those who had sent the truck of supplies. The message said to the strikers: "What we send is not charity. Because your fight is ours, in sharing what we have with you we are only helping our own."

The news about the truck spread all over the village. Before it left people came to look at it as at a curiosity. Some even wanted to touch it, though it was empty of food and clothing, for all bundles had been taken into the store.

The two relief workers who had come with the truck, along

with Bonnie, Ora and Zinie, worked all morning getting the supplies put away on the shelves. When the friends from the North had gone to Mrs. Sevier's boarding house where they would have a room, the three others sat down on bags of corn meal to rest. Bonnie had a blank book before her. She had been given the work of keeping accounts and was very proud. They were to begin giving out food the next day, and she was to put down everything taken in and everything given out.

A handbill lay on the counter near her. Copies of it had been left at the doors of all the houses in the village that morning. It said:

"YOUR UNION DOES NOT BELIEVE IN WHITE SUPREMACY. THINK ABOUT THAT, WHITE PEOPLE."

They had read it over and over.

"It's just going t' get us in trouble," Zinie said fearfully. "I told John back yonder that he ought not to countenance that."

"The colored people work alongside of us," Bonnie spoke up. "And I can't see why they shouldn't fight alongside us, and we by them."

"It did worry me at first," Ora admitted, "when we spoke of it at the secret meetings. But I've come to see that if people let colored folks tend their babies and cook their food, they really don't think their color makes them dirty. A black hand can be as clean as my white one. And they've got souls the same as us."

"And they are just the same." Bonnie looked at Zinie. "The color don't seem to make any difference when you see that."

"Would you marry one of them?" Zinie asked spitefully.

"I'm not a-talking about marrying," Bonnie said. "I'm a-talking about working together and fighting together. The marrying can take care of itself. We are all working people and I can see without looking very far that what Tom Moore says is true. That if we don't work with them, then the owners can use them against us. Where would we be if they went over to Stumptown and got them in our places? It's plain common sense that we've got to work together."

"Are you going over to Stumptown like they want ye to?" Zinie asked.

"Yes, I'm a-going," Bonnie said stubbornly, and added, "I offered to go."

"I think it's a shameful thing for ye to be going and speaking with niggers."

"And it's a shameful thing for ye not t' know they're human beings the same as us," Ora said to her.

Jennie Martin came in looking for Zinie. She was trembling.

"I just came by the mill," she said. "They've got the militia there, guarding the whole mill."

"It's what the Governor threatened to do," Bonnie said.

"I didn't think he would," Jennie lamented. "I didn't think he would."

"Well, he's only protecting his own, for he's the same Hellman that owns stock in this mill. I know for when he was elected governor Granpap was so proud that he was the one that got him out of jail that time."

"It looks like Granpap's not the only one in the McClure family that will be a convict," Zinie said, and got up to go.

They looked at her, and did not speak. Because she was to have a baby in a few months, they were trying to be patient with her. She wanted rest and peace, that they knew from their own experience, but when did they ever get it while working at machinery? This was what they could understand and Zinie could not, for John had kept her out of the mills, working extra time so that she might not be forced to go in. And Jennie, small Jennie Martin and the younger children had worked. Zinie was a little spoiled.

That evening the picket line went down to the mills and faced the militia. And it was only then that Ora learned that Young Frank was among the soldiers dressed up in uniforms, with their guns to fight against the strikers. She called out to him from across the road.

"Young Frank," she said, "are you going t' fight against your own?

"Look," she said and walked toward him from out the ranks of the strikers. "Look, here I am. Why don't you kill me?"

Young Frank stood sullenly in the line of soldiers and looked straight in front. Ora spoke to them all. "Boys," she said. "Why don't you go home and stop fighting against women and children? Air we not your people? Don't you have mothers that have worked themselves to the bone for ye, and fathers that have slaved? And don't you slave in mills and other places for low wages? Go home, and don't fight your own people any more."

Others spoke to the boys. And during the rest of the week when the mill was bringing in truck loads of workers from other states and the strikers persuaded them not to go in, the soldiers did not advance once toward the strikers. If any came too near the gate they held out their bayonets, but did not advance a step.

Ora tried to see Young Frank but they would not allow her to go in, and he never came to the house. John saw him later under curious circumstances. But before that night something was done that made everyone feel the power of the mill.

Handbills were distributed through the village which spoke in no uncertain terms:

"TO THOSE OF OUR EMPLOYEES WHO HAVE PARTICIPATED IN THE LATE HAPPY HOLIDAYS—GREETINGS:

THOSE OF YOU WE CONSIDER RELIABLE MAY RETURN TO WORK BY WEDNESDAY NOON OR INDICATE YOUR DESIRE TO DO SO.

TO THOSE WHO DO NOT WISH TO REMAIN IN OUR EMPLOY: YOU MUST UNDERSTAND THAT YOU CANNOT CONTINUE TO OCCUPY OUR HOMES, NOR REMAIN ON THE PREMISES OF THE COMPANY."

THE WENTWORTH MILLS.

John spoke to the strikers. "If they force us out of our homes," he said, "we will put up tents. And there will be food. Do not go back."

He said much more. Yet on Wednesday at noon the picket line was noticeably smaller, and before the quarter of one whistle blew many of the strikers, with faces averted, went through the gates protected by the drawn bayonets of the militia. Some turned at the gate and came back to join the line, but most of them walked through and entered the door of the mill. They could not bear the thought of being put out on the streets with their young. Some of them had sick people at home, and there were others who were timid and frightened.

Their return to work was a great blow to the rest, for it had been a heartening thought that the mill could not go on without them: that the great building was closed and dark. For if it was kept so, sometime in the near future the owners would say to them, "Come back, and we will do as you wish." They were not asking for much. What they asked for was entirely reasonable. But they could see that the mill had power to hurt them and force them to their knees.

And the next day they felt the power more. For on that day men went to the houses of those who had not gone back into the mill, emptied them of furniture, and locked the doors of their own homes against them. They came to Ora's about eleven in the morning, and though it was raining they took everything she had and piled it out in the mud.

"You, Dewey Fayon," Ora said. "You'd better not do this. Hit's against the law. I'll get the law to you."

"Just try it," Dewey Fayon said. "I'm the Law," and he spat some tobacco juice on one of the mattresses.

When Bonnie came from Stumptown the furniture was still there in the rain, and Ora with her own, Sally's and Bonnie's young was standing on the porch of the house.

Next door they heard Sara Smith crying. Her husband was with her. He had been in the strike and would not go back, but he had been sorely tempted to do so, for his wife had a two days' old child. He had brought a mattress from the street back on the porch and laid his wife and baby there. Ora had helped to make her comfortable, then returned to the young ones on her porch.

Bonnie said, "John and Tom Moore and the rest are getting tents put up in the hollow north of Company land."

"Ain't it terrible?" Ora said.

"Yes. But we've got to work and not cry," Bonnie was almost downed to see that Ora had lost her grit for once. "I saw Sally Thomas' two young ones with small pox put right out on the street, in the wet and rain."

Fifty families were put out of their homes that day, and there were many sick among them. The furniture stayed on the streets in the mud. Fortunately the rain stopped about evening.

Some of those who had been evicted had oil stoves, and in the early evening the smell of kerosene mixed with the odor of food that was being cooked on these stoves for the families evicted. Many were still wet from the rain, and after supper fires were built in the streets, where people gathered to dry out, and to talk about what was to be done. All night they kept up the fires. The men who were striking made up watches, and walked the streets, watching the fires and those who were trying to sleep on the hastily made up beds. The fires flickered up and shone on the closed houses and the scraggly dark piles of furniture in front of them.

Toward midnight John and some of the other men went to the union hall, for that needed a guard. Yet they felt almost helpless without firearms. What could they do if the mill decided to make any sort of raid on the hall? Later in the night they found out what could be done when the mill decided to use all its forces to bring them to their knees.

Tom Moore was in Sandersville with John Stevens, for in that place as in several other mills people were wishing to strike. John took the first watch in the hall, and the others lay on the floor and on the counters to get some sleep. He sat on the one chair in front of the table where they took in the names of the strikers. He was not sleepy and could have taken the watch for the whole length of the night, but knew that later he must try to get some rest. That there was danger he knew, for the mill was now roused like a beast that has been disturbed in its pleasant slumbers, and comes lumbering forth to kill or maim what has disturbed it. Everything that could be done to break them would be done.

He had learned this, among other things: That so long as he was docile and humble the owners would be kind to him. But if he once began to think for himself and ask for a better life they wanted to crush him. There was a telephone in the union hall and many times a day it would ring and voices spoke to them threatening death if they did not give up the strike. And they received many letters, he and Bonnie and Tom Moore. They addressed Bonnie as "nigger lover" because she worked in Stumptown among the colored people. But Bonnie went right on, for she was strong in knowing that Mary Allen and the others there needed the message as much as her people did. She could not be so selfish as to keep it only for herself and hers. She was not made in that fashion.

Suddenly John became aware that people were walking in the street outside. He realized that for some time he had been hearing the noises some distance away, but they had come into his thoughts as noises come in a dream. He touched Jesse on the shoulder and woke him.

"I think there may be trouble," he said.

They listened. There were voices outside.

"Had I better call the militia to protect us?" Jesse asked. "They're not far away."

"Wait," John said. He woke the others. They sat sleepy-eyed, huddled together on the floor, and singly on the counters. John stood in the middle of the long room, facing the door. There was a heavy crash on the door, and then another. The butt of a gun came through the splintered boards, and then the head of an ax crashed through. The others were wide awake now. All were standing, waiting for what was coming through the door.

"If I had my gun!" Jesse cried out as if he was in pain.

"Get away from that door," John called out.

There was no answer, but a hand reached through the splintered part and unlocked the door. It was filled with men. They had on masks which hid the lower part of their faces. The first ones entered, and others followed them. There must have been a hundred altogether, crowding into the room and filling the street outside. They had guns and axes in their hands.

"Get out," the leader said to the strikers. "Get out of here. If you don't want to be carried out."

John looked at the faces of his friends. "Comrades," he said, using a word that he had not thought of using, "I reckon since they're armed and we not, hit's best for us t' go."

The men turned slowly without speaking. Together they walked through the back entrance, down the alley between stores, and came out on the other side of the street. There in the dark they watched the mob at its work.

Everything was smashed. The whole wooden structure was made into a heap of wood. As each wall went down a hate like fire came up in John. It was not a hate against the men who were tearing down the building, but against those he knew had sent them, against the Power that was behind the lawlessness. He and the others in the strike had not broken one law since it had begun. And the Power could break every law.

Standing in the dark with the others he saw the masked men go to the relief store. They knocked in the glass windows. The splintering of the glass fell on him as if it was the splintering of his hopes for the union. They knocked in the door and came out carrying the precious bags and boxes of food. These they scattered on the sidewalk and in the mud of the road and stamped on them. Then they went back for more. When everything was finished one of the leaders stood outside the door and fired his revolver three times into the air. As he raised his face the mask fell off and John saw that it was the night superintendent of the mills, Jim Strothers.

The mob moved off to the east, and before they were out of sight the militia came running from the other direction.

John and the others crossed the street to see the wreck that had been made. The militia halted before them with bayonets outstretched. Their commander came up and spoke to John. He did not look at the mob that was still near enough for him to reach.

"What is this?" he asked sternly. John pointed to the smashed union hall.

"You might see," he said. "That mob you see going up the street did it. A mob from the mill. Jim Strothers, the night Super, was one of them."

"You can tell that when you come up in court," the commander told him. He called up some of his men and they surrounded the strikers.

"Where are we going?" John asked.

"To jail," the commander said.

"What for?"

"For disturbing the peace."

They marched along the road, surrounded by the militia. John saw Young Frank two rows ahead. Without seeming to hurry he moved forward faster than the others and pulled the militiaman who was holding his arm forward until he was just behind Young Frank.

Young Frank was holding the arm of Henry Sanders.

"How long, Young Frank," John said to him in a low voice as they walked along, "how long you going t' fight us?"

"Here," Young Frank said to the militiaman who had John's arm. "You take this man and give me yours." The young militiaman sleepily reached ahead and took Henry's arm. Young Frank came to John's side.

"Look here," he whispered, "we don't like this kind of work. We want to go home, and told them so. We hope to get away by the end of the week. It's dirty work. I may be mean . . . but I don't like dirty work."

When John was bailed out of jail two days later, he found the militia gone. But something had come in its place. Over a hundred of the worst men in the town and county had been sworn in as deputy sheriffs. They were stationed day and night on every street leading to the mills. And leading them was Sam McEachern, who had lived in the mountains, the one that Minnie had spoken about. Ora picked him out the first day. She remembered him well, though years had passed since he had left the hills with Minnie behind him on his horse.

54

AT the north of the Company property there was a high piece of ground with two new houses on it, at some distance from each other. Behind the houses was a large open piece of ground sloping down to a grove of trees. The trees filled a hollow or small valley, which had a spring at one end and a small stream running through the center. It was in this hollow that John had been taken by some of his school mates during his first year in school, when he had knocked down Albert Burnett and run away to the mountains to find Granpap.

The union rented this hollow for the tents, along with a piece of land on the high part of the ground just between the two new houses. There they built, with the help of Mrs. Sevier's husband who was an excellent carpenter, a small building that was the new union office.

Down in the hollow they put up the tents, and people who had been evicted—and many more had been put out since the first day—moved in all the furniture they could. They put up a rough shelter for a kitchen, and ate in the open, or if it was raining took the food into their tents. During the day one of the relief workers and some of the women took the old car and drove into the country where they asked farmers for what they were able to give. It was amazing the numbers of poor who were farmers. Yet they were willing, most of them, to share what they had, potatoes, and other vegetables, with those who were striking.

Each day some of the women took charge of the children in the tents while the others worked at various things, going into the country, working in the office, and picketing. Bonnie had brought her furniture and young ones to the tent colony, for she could not pay rent any more, and the children stayed there while she was out working for the union.

Bonnie learned that the word scab has two meanings. She had known it to mean an ugly piece of mattered growth over a wound. But she learned that a scab was also a person who would take the place of another who was fighting in a union. She felt a sympathy for them, since, like her, they were poor and only wanted to make their bread, but she knew they must learn that if they scabbed then they were really cheating themselves in the end, and were also being traitors to their own people.

She had explained this some days before to Mary Allen in her tumble down cabin in Stumptown. And Mary, who had been asked by the mill to go to work as a weaver, because she had swept the floor in the weave room and knew the process somewhat, spoke with her reasonably about it.

"Well, it's mighty hard for us not to give in, honey," she said. "For they have never given us a chance before to do nothing but sweep and work in the opening room, or something like that."

"But you'll see," Bonnie explained anxiously. "They won't keep you long when they can get somebody else. And if we get a strong union hit means they'll take back workers, and the union will get better wages for you, too."

She went further and spoke of the message to Mary. And Mary's brown eyes stared out of the white eyeballs at her.

"Oh my Lord," she said. "Could it be? Oh Sweet Jesus.

"I'll try," she said. "I'll try to get the others here around the house, and you can speak to them what you've told me."

So Bonnie spoke one morning while Dewey Fayon waited with a truck from the mills to take the colored people. She stood on Mary Allen's steps and spoke to the black faces that were looking up at her.

"We used t' live way back in the hills," she said. "And up there they told us, 'Come down to the mills and work. Down there money grows on trees.' Well, I have seen that those trees have produced nothing except what the bosses have gathered for themselves."

She saw Dewey Fayon leave the truck. He came forward and spoke in a loud, heavy voice that seemed to strike them. Some even winced as if a blow had been struck across their shoulders.

"Hurry up now," he said. "Whoever's going has got to hurry. I can't wait all day."

He pushed into the crowd and called out again, then he pointed at Bonnie. "Shame yourself, Bonnie Calhoun," he called out, "for keeping people from making good wages."

She looked down from the steps on his white face raised up among the black ones. She felt anger at him and a sorrow that pulled her heart down. But her anger was greater.

"Shame yourself, Dewey Fayon," she called back to him, "for going against your own people. Not so long ago, you was a mill hand yourself. And now you've reached a higher place you've gone back on your own."

Then she remembered something John Stevens had said and taking her gaze away from the white face of Dewey Fayon she turned to the black faces.

"Can't you see," she spoke to them anxiously, "they look on us as owned cattle? If we die, or our children, hit don't matter to them, for they know there's plenty more of us to get. What we must do is show them we're people that have got pride in ourselves, and won't be used. If we scab on each other then we're no better than driven cattle that don't know any better. Please, good friends, don't let him take you to the mill."

It was the best she could do, and not nearly good enough. In the seconds that followed while she waited to see how many would follow Dewey Fayon and his shot gun she held to Mary Allen's arm, to keep her knees from giving way.

"All right," Dewey Fayon called out. "This is your last chance." He turned toward the truck. About ten followed him. When he saw that only a few came he turned back for a moment.

"We'll get you for this, Bonnie Calhoun," he said. And many of that company remembered his words afterwards, when people in Stumptown and those in the village were mourning.

When Bonnie reached the union hall the others had just returned from picketing the mill. And she heard with joy that they had persuaded the ten who had gone with Dewey Fayon to go back to their homes. But many had suffered from the deputies. Mrs. Sanders was lying on the plank floor of the hall, and Ora was trying to revive her. Two of the other women bathed her bruised head, for one of the deputies had knocked her in the eyes with his fist. Her dress was torn to shreds by the bayonets.

"Henry was near by," Ora told Bonnie. "And when they had knocked her on the ground and began twisting her arms he rushed through the crowd. Small as Henry is he would have gone at those men. We had t' hold him back by main force."

The union lawyer was in the room sitting at the table. Some had been arrested and carried to jail, and he was getting their names in order to bail them out with money sent by workers and those sympathetic with workers. When Mrs. Sanders was well enough to sit up he went over to her.

"Mrs. Sanders," he said. "I want you to put that dress away." He pointed to her clothes that had been torn by the bayonets. "We should have that for evidence."

"I couldn't put it away," Mrs. Sanders told him, but she would not give the reason and was too weak for him to urge her. Later she told Ora, "Hit's the only dress I've got. I couldn't give it up."

When Ora came back from helping Mrs. Sanders down to the tents she spoke to Bonnie.

"They chased us like rats. Hit was good you were not there, for you always get mad, like Henry, and want to light into them."

Bonnie had been in jail several times already.

"Hit's something I can't help," Bonnie said. "When I see them stomping down people . . ."

"Do ye know who's living in the house to the right?" Ora asked her.

"The Coxeys."

"And who else?"

"No."

"Minnie Hawkins. She's got a room there. I saw her to-day at noon talking with Sam McEachern, right out in broad daylight on the porch."

"I reckon she's got a right there, if the Coxeys will have her."

"Yes. But hit looks funny. For on the same day she comes t' stay on one side of us, Lessie Hampton takes a room on the other. Lessie has got a job now working in the office of the mill at a big wage."

"Listen to this," John said to them. He was reading a newspaper the lawyer had left in the office.

"The Governor has written something about us. He says Tom Moore and the others from the North have gone about 'bedeviling the issue'—and that we all have got in the way of a 'dis-passion-ate approach to the problem.' "

"Maybe he means a dis-passionate approach is them approaching our union hall on Railroad Avenue and throwing our food into the streets," Jesse McDonald said. "Only we didn't seem to prevent hit."

Frank spoke up from his place in the corner where the sun could come in on him, as it could not come down in the shady hollow. "Maybe he means that the deputy sheriffs twisting women's arms and tearing their dresses, and beating us in the faces, and sticking us with bayonets and stomping us on the ground—is a dis-passionate approach. We have certainly got in the way of those things—though we didn't mean to."

"Once," Ed Thatcher told them, "up in the hills a man stole my hog. I recognized my hog in his pen by a crotch in the right ear. So I told him. 'Give me back my hog!' And he said, 'Now look. Here's fifty cents. If you'll go on your way and leave the hog, there won't be any trouble.' I reckon that might be what the Governor means by a dis-passionate approach."

They spoke lightly, but thoughts were beneath their words. John was thinking, "There is a spy among us," and he searched the faces before him. His eyes dwelt longest on one of the younger strikers. Fred Tate was a weakly young man who had never been much good at working. It was a wonder the mill kept him on when they had dismissed so many. He had seemed well disposed toward the union, and had come to live in the tent colony. His wife and baby were staying with an aunt in the country, but Carrie Tate had written that there was not a dry place in the house when it rained, and Fred had asked if he might bring them to the tents. Tom Moore said, yes, though he and John suspected Fred of being a spy.

As John looked Fred Tate turned his eyes away. Then John heard some words spoken that drew his attention from Fred.

Someone said, "It's time we used our guns!" and there was no joking in the voice.

Everyone in the room, men and women, looked at John intently, questioningly. And he had no answer for them. He knew as they did that hate surrounded them. It was in the air, in the gaze of people from the town. The newspapers were full of hate in the day, and at night while they slept or tried to sleep down in the hollow they heard men walking in the brush around the tents, and hushed voices. One night some shots were fired.

Robert Phillips, John's old friend, who was Captain Phillips now, from having been in the war, and was a lawyer for the mill, would not speak to John on the street: and Albert Burnett who had never known him well, but who had spoken to him pleasantly before, passed him on the street and spoke a name that was hard to leave unchallenged. "And him a government lawyer," John said to himself, and spat on the ground to take the bitter taste from himself, that he could not, since they were all together, think of personal revenge.

John knew all this. Yet he had to keep silent before the eyes that looked at him questioningly asking him how long they could go without defending themselves.

While they all sat in the room, quiet, thinking about what had been said, a young girl walked into the office.

"Is Tom Moore here?" she asked.

"No, Helen," John answered, for he recognized Mrs. Sevier's daughter.

"You are John McClure?" She spoke to him, as if she had recognized him, too.

"Yes."

She held out a letter to him. "One of our boarders, the one named Jackson, sent a suit to Reskowitz to be pressed," she said. "Mr. Reskowitz found this in the pocket. He said, give it to you or Tom Moore."

"Was there anything else," John asked.

"I was to say they are watching our house."

"Thank ye." John said to her.

He opened the letter. It was addressed to no name but to a number, V-500. At the top was the name of a detective agency in the North. The person who wrote the letter said that V-500—who was Jackson of course—must always report to the clients, the mill management. Jackson had been trying to sell washing machines in the village. The letter went on:

"The cover you have arranged—selling washing machines—may be all right, except that I do not think you can sell many washing machines at their current prices to a lot of people making eight and ten dollars a week. It is all right to associate with the employees of the clients, but I repeat the people for you to become acquainted with and cultivate their friendship are the leaders of the union and in the strike. These are the people you want to buddy around with and get real inside advance information from. And, remember, your client wants to hear from you daily."

John looked up from the letter. "Fred, was it you that wanted t' bring a man named Jackson up here?"

Fred did not answer. He looked at John with his sad, weak eyes, and looked away. Just then John was interrupted, and this was a pity, for the opportunity was lost then to bring Fred and perhaps others into the open. And in the stressful days that followed there was no time to search for spies again.

Jim Allen looked in at the window. "There's a preacher outside to see you, John," he said.

"A preacher!" Ed Thatcher exclaimed.

"Well, he might be well-intentioned," John told Ed. "For there's one at Sandersville that has taken up for the union so he's been run out of his church by the mill."

"Maybe it's Mr. Simpkins," Bonnie said.

"Not him," Ora told her. "Didn't you hear? He's sick in bed of a sour stomach, from preaching hate at us."

"I knew he was a-saying Tom Moore was preaching the breaking up of the home, but I . . ."

"And he don't yet seem t' know that we and our families and goods have been put on the streets. If that isn't breaking up the home, I don't know what is."

55

Mr. Warmsley was waiting for John.

"Are you John McClure?" he asked.

"Yes," John answered and took the hand that was stretched out to him.

"Can we walk down the slope a little way?" Mr. Warmsley asked. "I would like to speak with you privately."

They walked as far as the trees that began the woods filling the hollow.

"You have been helping to lead this strike," Mr. Warmsley began. He hesitated when John did not answer. For John there was nothing to say. He wished to hear what the preacher had come for, and waited to know if it was in friendliness. Preacher Warren in town was speaking terrible things of them, and the others were after them like a pack of hounds. Perhaps this man of God, too, was an enemy.

"I have come as a friend," Mr. Warmsley said.

"I'm mighty glad t' hear that."

"You see, Mr. Wentworth, young Mr. Wentworth, belongs to my congregation, and Mr. Randolph the manager, and others . . . so I—I know them rather well."

"I see you must."

"I went to them," Mr. Warmsley said, "to the mill and begged them to end this terrible war—for it is a war. I went there prepared to blame them—but I came away satisfied that all the blame is not on their side.

"They told me this. For a long time they have not made much money on the mill. And many times during the past four or five years they might have stopped the mill altogether and would have done so, had it not been that you people must be looked after. They felt a responsibility for you."

"They did lay off more than a thousand, not long ago," John said.

"But they kept some of you. And only hard times made them dismiss those others."

"Hit was the machines, not hard times."

"They had to spend large sums of money on the machines. And it made them get behind."

"You mean they were hard up?"

"Yes, hard up."

"How hard up were they?" John asked.

"Why . . . hard up as anyone could be," Mr. Warmsley used John's phrase, and smiled at him, as if he said, "We understand each other's language, you and I."

"The reason I ask," John said slowly, "is this. Maybe they were hard up, but they went on living in big houses. Maybe they were hard up, but their children never died for want of food, or a doctor's care—maybe of other things, but not of that. For the last five years—and that is as far as I'll go, for it's as far as I remember well, I know from the testimony of my own eyes, that Mr. Wentworth has had his cars, and his big house, and others have, too. Hit don't seem t' fit, Mr. Warmsley, t' say they have kept the mill going at a loss."

"They paid bigger wages during the war."

"Yes, sir, they did. And why? Because other mills paid bigger wages t' get the best hands. They did hit for that reason and no other—because most of the best young men had gone t' the war."

"They are sincere, honest men, John."

"Yes, sir, maybe they are. But sincere and honest to their own kind, and not t' me and mine."

"And they think so much of you," Mr. Warmsley said, very sadly. "They tell me that you and the other strike leaders are some of their best workers. And because you are they will take you back, on certain conditions."

"Is that what they said?"

Mr. Warmsley reached into his inner pocket. "I have it here in writing," he said.

John took the paper and held it where he could read. He heard Mr. Warmsley speaking. "I have felt for so long that you were people after my own heart. And I have praised you to everyone —your dignity and fineness in poverty. And now you have disappointed me so keenly. I hear that some of the women even hurl unmentionable words at the deputies. The day will come, John, when the rich will give up everything they own, and each will share in the wealth. But we must be brothers first, living in harmony, before there can be any equal and just distribution of wealth.

"And these wealthy people really admire you. In the past I have pointed you out to them, you and your people, and they have agreed with me about your goodness, and your spiritual dignity. They have said to me, 'Our villages are the bright spots in this torn country. In other places there are unions and strikes. Here we are peaceful communities living together in brotherly love.' And they have known it is because of you. Will you not come back and live in peace again?"

"You mean, and give up the union?" John asked.

"That is one of the conditions. You read it on the agreement, didn't you?"

"I might think you're right, Mr. Warmsley. If hit was for me only, I might give hit up and go back. But there are many others, and there are children that cry for food. You say you want peace and harmony. While my people cry for a better life and the young are held down to slavery and nothing ahead but that, there can't be any peace."

"And you're making a hopeless fight, John. I wish to warn you. Do you realize how strong they are?"

"Yes, Mr. Warmsley. But I know a place where the rich were even stronger, and the poor got the best of the fight."

"Do you mean that country? Don't let them fool you with lies about it, John. They tell you that it is a paradise, but I know better. There is no freedom there."

"Hit may be there is no freedom for people like you, Mr. Warmsley. But to us, hit means freedom and joy."

"Then you would make of people like me outcasts, and starve our children?"

Mr. Warmsley's face was red. His generous mouth twisted into a smile that had no amusement in it.

"No, sir," John said. "For just as soon as you got ready to work alongside us in understanding, we'd give you a living. Hit would be according to how much you understood."

"You won't need that paper," Mr. Warmsley spoke sharply and reached out his hand.

"If you don't mind, I'd like to hold it, and show it to the others. I can't decide for them."

It was almost dark. Mr. Warmsley walked away from John. A few feet up the slope he turned and came slowly back. John could not see his face, but he could hear his voice, and it was no longer irritated.

"I almost went away in anger," Mr. Warmsley said. "And I don't want to do that." He held out his hand.

"I have no hard feelings," John told him and shook hands.

The union hall was lit up. Everyone had gone inside or wandered down to the tents. A woman came from the house on the left. John saw her white dress waving back as she walked. She was like a ghost coming so quietly over the grass toward him.

"John," the woman whispered." It's Minnie, Minnie Hawkins,"

"What are you doing round here, Minnie?"

"Never mind. I want to tell you something. I'm your friend, John. And I tell you you'd better give up this union. Or something bad will happen."

"What could happen, Minnie?" He spoke evenly, but her frightened voice in the dark communicated fear to him.

"Nothing, I reckon. Only I beg of you before it's too late—to give in."

"Can't you tell me something?"

"No. Only I ask you, for Kirk's sake, and Emma's, who are dead, to give in."

She went swiftly across the grass and entered the house without a sound that he could hear. It was as if a ghost had spoken to him words of warning. He was glad to go into the union hall where the lights were on. Yet he did not feel afraid. For he had spoken to Tom Moore and they had decided that the time had come for them to use guns in their defense. With a gun in his hand he was afraid of nothing.

That night a fiery cross was burned on the slope above the tents. The next day John returned the paper to Mr. Warmsley saying that the strikers had voted not to give up the union. If they might keep the union, they were ready to talk with the mill.

At the same meeting everyone had voted to place guards around the tent colony, guards who were armed. The guns were not to be used on the picket line, only at the tent colony, and in defense.

At the same time they drafted a letter and sent it by special delivery to the Governor, telling him that they had not broken a single law, but that the law had been broken constantly by the other side. And they warned him that they were preparing to defend their homes with guns.

56

From that time the men who were striking guarded the union hall which was on the slope, and the tents which were at the bottom of the hollow under the trees.

For several days nothing unusual happened. It had become a usual thing for people to be beaten on the daily picket line and arrested.

Then the tent colony began to have visitors from the village at night. These were those strikers who had gone back to work when they were threatened with eviction. They had been timid. Now they were dissatisfied, for they were getting no more money than before, and were forced to work long hours overtime to make up for the absent ones. They visited the tent colony in the night and laid their complaints before John and Tom Moore.

At Tom Moore's suggestion they sounded out the others in the mill and found that they, too, were ready to come out, if something was done so that they could all leave the mill together.

Friday evening was the time appointed for this to happen. All had voted to have a picket line on Friday after the evening meeting, but the fact that some in the mill had been appointed to lead the others out was kept a secret.

There was a general feeling that something decisive was to be done, and people in the tents began to whisper to each other, "We're going t' bring the others out. Then the strike will be won."

The mill had its own ears that listened to the whispers. Mrs. Sevier had sent the young man, Jackson, away from her home. But there were others who were listening.

On one side of the union hall Minnie Hawkins was living with the Coxeys and on the other side Lessie Hampton was boarding. She was not backward about mixing with those who often stood outside the hall waiting for the evening meeting to begin. Fred Tate had brought his wife and child to live in the tents. They were suspected of being in the pay of the mill, but it was almost impossible to refuse them food and shelter when they asked for it.

On Friday morning word came that John Stevens was arrested and jailed in Sandersville. Tom Moore sent John over in the car and remained himself to carry out the plans they had made.

That morning Jesse McDonald and two others were building a rough platform against the back wall of the unpainted union office in preparation for the large meeting that evening. They saw Sam McEachern talking to Minnie Hawkins at the back of the Coxeys' house. Sam McEachern was head of the deputy sheriffs, and led the raids on the picket lines. He had become a very important person, for the town papers had made him a sort of hero. His election had come about through Minnie, really. For when he renewed his friendship with her, he had met others in the town who possessed the influence necessary to make him important.

Occasionally Sam McEachern, standing beside Minnie Hawkins, would look up at Jesse and the other two. Then Jesse would stop hammering and look back at him.

"Hit bodes no good to us," he said to the others, "that they're over there talking together."

"I wish John was here," one of them said.

Statesrights Mulkey came around the corner of the Coxeys' house and spoke to Sam McEachern. They went away together, and Minnie walked up the steps, with her head down, into the Coxeys' back door.

That day Lessie Hampton stayed away from the mill. She came to the union hall and talked in a friendly way with all who came in. At dinner time she walked down the slope with Sally McDonald, and whispered that it was her monthly that had kept her at home. She was not sick enough to stay in bed.

"Did she ask ye anything?" Ora spoke to Sally when she came down to the tents.

"She asked, did we expect to bring out a crowd to-night from the mill? And I told her, we always expect."

"And nothing more?"

"Nothing more. Not to her."

As night came on all except the children and two women who were left to care for them, and the three guards appointed for that night to protect the tents, came up the slope to the open ground back of the union hall for the meeting.

From the village came those strikers who were secretly living with friends there. And with them came several who had been working in the mill. They had left the mill of their own accord to join the strike again.

They gathered with the others on the open space. With their coming an excitement went through the crowd. Men and women came forward to greet them and once again there was an upsurge of gayety and hope—a sense of power—because they were together again.

The two guards who had been appointed for the union hall that night were standing by the platform, one on each side. Their guns were visible, held upright at their sides.

One of the women relief workers climbed to the platform. The people listened silently, and with eager attention. This was the message they welcomed: that other people were thinking of them; that the fight was not theirs only, but for all like them. They had been drawn and twisted in the struggle as Tom Moore had said they would be. But had not others gone through the same experience? And because they had were now sending help and words of sympathy.

The relief worker finished, and Tom Moore took her place on the platform. He looked out over the people, and into their faces. Now he knew them all, not casually as a person knows those he has seen in the same town for many years. He knew them through sharing an experience that had been full of danger to all of them. It was still full of danger. He knew that he was leading them into danger that night. How could he help but understand this? It was useless to believe that the owners did not know of their plans. There would be some sort of reprisal, some attempt to check them. For it was certain that if they could bring out the rest of the workers that night, the strike would be won.

He had meant to explain the significance of the picket line they were to go on in a little while. But he had not spoken many sentences when he saw that two cars had come from the road into the open space on the other side of the Coxeys' house. The sun had gone down, and the daylight was getting very dim, so he could not see who occupied the cars. But as he talked, he thought that one of the guards must be sent over to investigate.

If he spoke of the picket line too soon, then those in the cars could drive away and warn the sheriffs that they were coming. So he put this off, and he could tell by the restlessness and the murmuring when he stopped that people were disappointed that he had not spoken of it.

As soon as the meeting was over he would suddenly call out to them, "Form in twos," and they would go toward the mill. One thing was certain. They must reach the factory before the last whistle blew. Those inside the mill would be ready at ten minutes before closing hour to say, "The picket line is outside, fellow workers. Let us go and join them." Or words something like these.

Tom Moore looked anxiously at his watch. Then he spoke to Henry Sanders, who left him to go towards the cars which had stayed like large vague shadows on the edge of the gathering of men and women.

Bonnie was on the platform speaking. He thought, "I will give her ten minutes more," and kept his watch in his hand. He heard Bonnie's voice. It seemed clearer than usual. That was perhaps because he was standing close to her near the platform. The evening was quiet and except for Bonnie's high voice there was no sound. He thought he heard the pines in the grove across the open ground moaning a little as they did when a breeze came up. But there was very little breeze. The summer evening was as quiet as the people who were listening to Bonnie's words. He thought, "If it was all accomplished and we could enjoy, just enjoy what is before us—the quiet evening, and songs, and the people who are our friends."

At that moment a shot broke up the stillness. Another followed it. He heard a sound as if rocks had been thrown against the plank wall behind Bonnie.

She had stopped speaking. He looked up and saw her standing there with an astonished look on her face. She turned a little to one side as if she was ashamed and hurt, then fell to the floor of the platform.

He heard the sound of cars starting up and moving away. He was already on the platform when Henry Sanders ran up. "They got away," he panted. "But I saw. It was Doctor Foley and Statesrights and others. I saw them."

Ora was leaning over Bonnie. Tom Moore spoke. "This is war, and it must go on. This is war." He stood in front of Ora and

Bonnie and spoke with authority to the others, who were standing in bewilderment.

"We're going to picket the mills," he cried. "And bring everybody out to-night. Form in twos. Jesse McDonald and Sally, are you ready?"

For Jesse and Sally had been chosen to lead the pickets that evening. They responded to his words at once

He saw Sally walking very proudly beside Jesse out into the road. Behind them the two women relief workers fell in and then the others. Jesse and Sally began the march. Soon, two by two, the people were marching along the road toward the mill, in the quiet darkness.

Tom Moore turned and knelt down by Ora. Bonnie lay on her side, for Ora had not dared to touch her. Very tenderly they turned her body.

"I'm afeard," Ora said, "I'm afeard she's done for."

"Henry," Tom Moore called out, "go for a doctor." He and Tom Bachley lifted Bonnie into the union hall and laid her on the long table.

"I don't see how I can stand it," Ora said.

"You go on," she said to Tom Moore.

He knew that he was needed with the others. He ran to overtake the line. He was proud of their fine discipline, of the way they walked together. Soon, after they had passed the railroad, they would begin singing to let those in the mill know they were coming. They would sing one of Bonnie's songs, and others they had been taught. There was one they had not been taught. It went through him as he stumbled over the rough ground beside the people who were marching. "Arise, ye prisoners of starvation," it said, "ye wretched of the earth. . . . A better world's in birth. . . ." That sounded under the circumstances almost sardonic. "But pain," he thought, "accompanies birth—pain and sometimes death."

He was nearly to the front of the line. The leaders were going up the slope of the railroad crossing. "Faster," he called out to Jesse McDonald. Then he saw Jesse and Sally and the others turn. Men with guns came up from the other side of the embankment. The lights from the poles near the station made them black shadows. The shadows were thick like an army, and they came over the track and charged the line of strikers.

"Run-n-n," a woman's long wail came and another shrieked, "The Law's coming!"

Then there were no more words. The strikers scattered before the deputies who were running them down. There was the sound of blackjacks smacking bare flesh; cries of horror, and groans of pain, came from those lying on the ground.

Some escaped to the union hall unhurt. The others, when the deputies had finished with them, made their way slowly along the road.

Between Tom Moore and another striker, with his arms across their shoulders, stumbled Jesse McDonald. He had tried to protect Sally from the gun butt of one of the sheriffs and had been struck in the belly. At every step blood came from his mouth and stained the shirt that Sally had ironed for him that morning in preparation for the triumph they had expected that night.

57

ORA came up through the woods from the tents. A light breeze was blowing and the pine needles far above her were beating the air softly, making their usual whispered moan.

Down in the tents she knew people were whispering together, "Bonnie is dead." She had quieted them as much as she knew how to do, for it had been decided that everyone must go to bed except the guards, and that the lights must be put out. Those who had been wounded in the picket line were tended. She had seen that Bonnie's four young ones were put to bed and had left Sally with them. They were so accustomed to having Bonnie away, at the mill, and then in the strike work, they were satisfied to sleep without her.

She was going back to stay with Bonnie. The doctor had already come and said he could do nothing except send the people who were necessary.

In the office the two boys, Henry Sanders and Tom Bachley, were standing near the table on which Bonnie lay. The blood was on her dress, a heavy black stain now, a blotting of ink like that she had sometimes made and worried over on the pages of her account book, only much larger than those. The hair lay back from her high forehead, and spread over the end of the table. The mouth that had opened to speak not long before was closed in a sort of smile. Her brown eyes that Ora remembered well because they were like Emma's, were closed.

"Where's Tom?" Ora asked.

"Gone up the road."

"He wanted to meet John if he happened to come now."

They spoke in whispers, as if they were afraid of waking Bonnie.

"You boys go on out. I'll stay now."

They filed out of the door. She heard them moving on the ground outside and talking in low tones. There was the clear sound of a match being struck out there. In the office there was no sound. Ora sat in the chair near the table and rested her head on the back. Thoughts of Emma came into her mind, and of Bonnie as a child in the mountains, and then a young woman when she was so bashful at the Christmas party—the time when the preacher had spoken of brotherly love, and the spirit of good will toward men. There was Bonnie's marriage and her happiness at that time, and Emma's death. She saw Bonnie taking part in the union, speaking, singing to her people who were heartened by her speeches and songs. Now she lay on the table, without life. And she had not wanted to die. There was no one who had wished more for life. And she had wanted enjoyment not only for herself but for others. For that she had been killed. But what she had begun was not ended with her: and never would be until what she had dreamed about had become a fact.

Tom Moore came into the hall. "I don't see anything of John," he whispered.

"Pore John," Ora said. "I left Zinie down there a-crying. This may make a woman of her."

Outside the hall the two boys stood near the wall of the building. They saw that Ora and Tom Moore had put something over the light inside to make it dim. The murmurings that had been going on in the tents below died out. Then the windows in the house next door became dark. The darkness pressed on them.

"Did you hear that?" Henry asked Tom, standing close by him against the side of the hall.

"It sounded like a car coming up the road."

"I reckon it's John."

"Or maybe the undertaker coming."

They peered into the dark.

"It hasn't got any lights," Henry said and took a step forward.

The car stopped just at the place where the Coxeys' driveway met the road. A man stepped out of the car, and after him came three others. They stood together for a moment, then one of them came toward the union hall.

"Who's there?" Henry called out.

The man in front was Sam McEachern. "It's the Law," he said.

"Where's your warrant?" Henry asked.

"We don't need no warrant," Sam called out, and spoke to the men behind him. "Come on, men," he said.

One of them ran past him and went up to Henry. "Put down that gun," he ordered. But Henry was not ready to give up. They struggled, each one trying to get possession of the gun.

"Let that man go," Tom Bachley called out and went to the two who were struggling. Two guards from the tents came running out from the trees, and the two men from the car ran toward them a little way and stopped.

A shot sounded, then another and another. They came again. The bright powder spurted from the guns in flame, but no one saw them. And no one saw where the bullets came from nor where they went. Tom Bachley dropped his gun and held his arm, into which one of the bullets had gone. And Sam McEachern fell to the ground. When he fell, the shots stopped as if a command had been given. The men who were with him carried his limp body to the car and drove away.

It had taken perhaps five minutes for this to happen. The houses on each side of the union hall remained dark and quiet, but men and women came up from the tents and surrounded the hall, asking questions, speaking excitedly. They were there when the men the doctor had sent came for Bonnie: and stood quietly and sorrowfully in the dark while her body was carried out to the waiting hearse.

And they were still there when men with white arm bands came. Tom Moore, Ora, and about a hundred others were arrested and taken away in cars to the jail. But some of the white banded men stayed. They went down to the tents and drove the children and women out, so that they ran about under the trees, until they got into the open where they wandered all night hunting for a place to stay.

The tents were torn down and left flat on the ground, and the food was scattered everywhere so that it dammed up the spring and the stream that had given water to the strikers.

Coming back very late that night from Sandersville, John McClure walked into the unlighted hall, and found it deserted and wrecked. The table was still in the center of the room, but it lay on its side and one of the legs was broken.

He went down to the hollow and found the tents as they had been left, and no one there. In the union office he turned the table in the hall right side up, propped its leg on a bench, and slept there the rest of the night.

The next morning, waking early, he went down to the hollow again. The place looked as if a storm without human knowledge had passed across it. But he knew that the storm which had come had full knowledge of what it was doing.

58

SAM McEACHERN was dead. And fifteen strikers, including Tom Moore and the two relief workers from the North, were held accused of murdering him. The rest of those who had been arrested were let out on bail furnished again by those workers and sympathizers who had in the first place sent money for relief.

When the women came out of jail they went about the country looking for their children, who had been driven from the tents that night. Jennie Martin found two of hers twenty miles away with a farmer who had picked them up on the road the next morning.

John broke in the door of the cabin in which Bonnie had lived, and some of the furniture that had not been broken too badly was moved there. Ora, Sally, their families, Jennie and her families, and three other families lived in the three rooms of the cabin. There was only one bed. This they gave up to the children at night. And all the young who could not be crowded into the bed slept on the floor between the older people.

The morning after his return from Sandersville John had gone straight to the lawyer, then on to the place where they were keeping Bonnie. Now he was preparing for her funeral.

A sign was written and put on the door of the union hall. Jennie Martin and Sally placed it there with some sprigs of honeysuckle, and a small piece of black cloth above the sign. On the paper was printed in black ink, "Come to the Burying of Bonnie Calhoun at the cemetery." And it told the day and hour.

They did not expect many people to see the sign, but it was right to put it there, along with the flowers and the black cloth. For they were mourning for Bonnie, as well as for those who were in jail accused of murder.

When the funeral procession that carried Bonnie's body to the cemetery passed by the Wentworth mill, those who were working there left their looms and frames and crowded to the windows.

They spoke to each other softly, while the hank clocks behind them ticked off the money they were losing each minute. "It's Bonnie Calhoun," they whispered, seeing the hearse and the long line of mourners walking behind it. "She was killed for . . . the union," this they whispered fearfully, for the mill had ears.

In the weave room one girl said, "That's John, the tall one just behind the hearse."

"Yes, it's John."

"Why, he's got a red band on his arm," another one said.

"A red band?"

"He ought t' have a black crape."

"I wonder now . . ."

"There's Mary Allen that used t' sweep in here."

"Is she there?"

"Just behind Ora."

They watched until the procession went out of sight, toward the cemetery.

In some of the rooms the section bosses called them back to their frames before the hearse had gone past the mill.

It had rained all night. The road out to the mill cemetery was deep in red mud, in which the wheels of the hearse sank to the axels. Twice some of the men who were marching in the back had to put their shoulders to the wheel of the hearse to help it move forward again.

As they reached the grave the rain began again. It came down in slow fine drops as it does in summer. It was not a heavy rain, but it prevented them from opening the casket so that those who wanted to might go by and see Bonnie's face for the last time, as the custom was in that part of the country.

People crowded around the grave, standing in the deep red mud, while the casket rested beside the open red hole in the earth.

Someone who had come from the North to take Tom Moore's place spoke a few words. In the silence that followed them the faces of the people gathered around the grave—faces drawn down with grief and thin with lack of food—looked into John's face. And he knew looking at them, that he must speak what was in him. When he stood forward he saw Ora and Jennie standing together, and knew, though he could not see, that they were crying. He saw Bonnie's young ones by the grave in front of Ora, and saw that little Emma, holding the youngest child, the baby, was like a little old woman who has gone through much pain.

"Friends," he said. "We have not invited a preacher here to-day. But if one was here, he would say in the presence of death we should not have any bitterness in our hearts. It is true that bitterness in the heart wears it down, like too much acid in the dye eats at a piece of cloth. Yet there are times when not t' have bitterness is the worst sin a man can commit. And I consider this is one of those times.

"A preacher would tell us that the people who killed Bonnie are fine, honest men.

"Maybe they are, but they killed Bonnie.

"I don't mean those misguided ones that fired the shot, but the ones who are behind the killing.

"The ones with Power, they killed her."

"Maybe they are fine, honest men. But they tore up our union hall and had our food thrown out, good food for our children. They had it thrown on the ground.

"They call themselves dis-passionate men.

"Yet they have had their paid men beat our women and force us to the ground when we were unarmed.

"They say what they want is peace and harmony.

"But they have leveled our tents and driven us out to live in the wilderness.

"They call themselves just men. Yet they have jailed our people and not one of their law breakers has been brought to justice.

"They will say we have killed. But if one of us did that it was done in a fair and open fight, while we were defending our homes against a lawless attack. And we had given fair warning that we would.

"They call us murderers, and the preacher will tell you they are fair, honest men who call us that. And maybe they are.

"Yet they shot and killed Bonnie in cold blood.

"I can't forget that as I can't forget the other things they have done. And I'm going t' remember—in bitterness. I will remember these fine, honest men. But I will remember more what they rep-resent. For what they rep-resent is an evil thing that must be put off the face of the earth."

He stepped back with the rest, and with his head bent looked down into the open red grave.

"Sally," Ora whispered, and Sally stood forward. She had been chosen to sing one of Bonnie's ballads at the grave.

Her head lifted and the song came from her mouth.

"How it grieves the heart of a mother," she sang and went on to the end.

As she finished, there was some disturbance in the crowd of mourners. A man pushed his way through, and as he came to the grave they saw it was Preacher Simpkins. They had not expected this. He held his Bible in front of him—open—and as they lowered the coffin into the ground he read from the pages.

"In my father's house are many mansions," he read. "I go to prepare a place for you."

When he had finished reading he looked up at those who were around him. While the clods of red mud were shoveled on to the coffin he spoke. "Death is not an aristocratic event," he said. "It comes to poor and rich alike, in the mansion and in the hovel. This mill woman is not different from the man who owns the mill, for he, too, must come to the same end. All are the same before Jesus. And the rich may be as fine and honest as the poor, just as the poor may be as fine and honest as the rich. And rich or poor we must humble ourselves before the Lord, for the Lord giveth, and the Lord taketh away. Blessed be the name of the Lord."

He stood until the last clod had been put on the mound that sloped down the hill, for it had been hard to fit Bonnie's grave into the space which they had been able to buy.

Ora and Zinie put the few flowers on the mound. Then they all walked down the slope to the road. Ora held Bonnie's youngest child in her arms and little Emma and John helped the two others through the mud. At the gate Preacher Simpkins got into a car that was waiting there for him. But the car did not drive away. From it stepped State Attorney Albert Burnett, with a long white paper in his hand.

He walked up to Ora and John. "You are to give those children into my care," he said to them.

"We aim t' care for them," John told him.

"The law demands that those who wish to adopt orphans be able to swear that they have a certain income," Attorney Burnett said. "Have you that income?"

"I have nothing," John said. "But with hit I will care for my own young, and together we can care for hers."

"This is a court order," Attorney Burnett said, and held out the paper. "It says you must give up the children to be put in an orphanage."

"We're ready t' care for them." Ora spoke out and held tightly to little Emma's hand.

"I'm afraid we must take the children." With a possessive gesture Attorney Burnett laid his hand on the child's shoulder. "All of them," he added firmly and reached out his hands to take Bonnie's youngest from Ora's arms.

The other mourners gathered around John and Ora. They watched while Albert Burnett and Preacher Simpkins lifted Bonnie's children into the car.

"It couldn't be helped," John said. "Not now." Red flamed up under his skin as if the red mud below his feet was reflected in his face.

"What I hate," Ora told him, and he heard in her voice that she was crying, "what I hate most is her young ones will be taught that Bonnie was evil, when she was s' good. . . ."

The newspaper that afternoon had a story about Bonnie's funeral. John read it in the parlor of Mrs. Sevier's boarding house where he had gone to meet John Stevens.

The story began:

"To-day in a little mud-hole to the northeast of the Wentworth Mill Village, the first revolutionary movement in this state was buried. Ostensibly it was the funeral of Mrs. Bonnie Calhoun, mill-worker. . . ."

John Stevens coming into the room some time later could not see John's face. It was hidden between his arms on the table. The paper was spread out before him.

"I have read that, too," John Stevens said. He put a hand on John's shoulder. "I cried when I heard about Bonnie . . . cried from anger and shame."

"This on your arm," he touched the red band on John's sleeve, "stands for blood that has been shed, and that will be shed before we reach that which we are fighting for."

"It seems a long way," John said.

"It is a long way. Stand up, John."

John slowly got up from the chair. He stood looking at John Stevens, and in his face he saw just what he had seen when he first knew him, hope and belief.

"To-night," John Stevens said, "there will be a secret meeting in the woods north of Bonnie's shack. You and I will go to all we can trust and tell them to come. We must let everyone know."

"I was feeling," John said, "as if everything was finished."

"No," John Stevens said. "This is just the beginning."